PLEASURE OF BELIEVING

PLEASURE OF BELIEVING

A NOVEL BY
ANASTASIA HOBBET

This novel is a work of fiction. Any references to historical events; to real people, living or dead; or to real locales are intended only to give the fiction a setting in historic reality. Other names, characters, places, and incidents either are the product of the author's imagination or are used fictitiously, and their resemblances, if any, to real-life counterparts are entirely coincidental.

"Hurt Hawks" from *Selected Poems* by Robinson Jeffers, Copyright © 1928 and renewed 1956 by Robinson Jeffers. Reprinted by permission of Random House, Inc.

Published by
Soho Press, Inc.
853 Broadway
New York, NY 10003

Library of Congress Cataloging-in-Publication Data

Hobbet, Anastasia, 1954-
Pleasure of believing : a novel / Anastasia Hobbet.
p. cm.
ISBN 1-56947-085-5 (alk. paper)
I. Title.
PS3558.033638P58 1997
813' .54--dc21   96-37223
                                                     CIP
10   9   8   7   6   5   4   3   2   1

To Randall

And to Ma

And in memory of my father, who told me many stories

I love all waste
And solitary places; where we taste
The pleasure of believing what we see
Is boundless, as we wish our souls to be...

—Percy Bysshe Shelley

PLEASURE OF BELIEVING

Chapter One

The wind dropped during the night. Roberta woke suddenly, as if the silence had snapped its fingers, bringing her out of a trance. Glen slept beside her, placid, the blanket tucked up under his chin. He never noticed the wind, not even a five-day Chinook that made the house moan. He had told her once, many years before, when she complained about the wind, about its damn, awful, endless noise, that you had to make your own silence. At least the air would be calm for a few days now, and she would be able to hear the faint sounds of earliest spring: the creak of ice as the sun hit the roof of the big barn, the stir of sparrows in the loft, the soft, sliding murmur of sound when the raptors shook out their feathers in the morning, like silks; and the eagles calling along the river.

She closed her eyes, concentrating, to lure her dream back.

What was it? There had been wind in the dream, too. The Chinook had blown into her sleep, becoming warmer, grassy, moist, rolling over the windowsill of a speeding truck, pummeling her face—

Glen stirred, mumbling. He had stayed up working in his office long after she was asleep.

—a summer wind rolling over the windowsill like surf, sun-soaked, gravel spraying up. It rushed back whole into her mind, brilliant, burnished by wakeful memory. The black truck, new after the war, flashing through deep green prairie under wide blue sky. Her father at the wheel, taking up the whole road, swerving from ditch to ditch around all obstacles, careening past cattle stopped dead and staring, around potholes and washboard and rockfall and ruts and other old ranchers driving as if it were Sunday. She's beside him, grabbing at the dashboard, the armrest, the edge of the seat, because her feet don't touch the floor. Her red braid whips out the window. Jeremiah clings to the steering wheel fiercely, knuckles knobby with the grip, elbows sticking out like chicken wings, conversing with her at a yell. He flattens his foot on the accelerator and goes fishtailing fast around a turn. A bow wave of larks rises in front of the truck. Jeremiah hollers at them, waving an arm out the window. "Here he comes, boys! Fly, boys, fly!"

She sat up, throwing the bedspread back, tossing the dream away.

Glen lifted his head. "Bertie? You okay?" His face was asymmetrical with sleep.

"I'm going for a drive."

"Eagles?"

She pushed her hair from her eyes. "Mm."

"Anything wrong?"

"Bad dream," she said in a whisper.

The pain was worst in the morning, first thing, when Carl tried to sit up in bed—low in the back, a bite at the spine that chewed all day if he wasn't careful. The doctor, for a hundred-fifty bucks, said arthritis. The chiropractor, for a hundred-thirty more, said bad alignment. He'd spent two hundred and eighty dollars to find out he had the same problem as his pickup, a diagnosis he could have made himself if he'd just opened his eyes. While some men came to look like their wives or their dogs over the years, ranchers got so they looked like their trucks, bouncing along the dirt roads every day on sprung frames and balding tires. Alignment, Carl thought, was a thing of the past.

He swallowed a groan, pulling his T-shirt down over his belly, and hauled his legs over the edge of the bed. The cold seeping up through the rag rug told him all he needed to know about the temperature outside: heavy, cold air from the north had stomped the energy out of the Chinook. Twenty degrees, maybe twenty-five. He stared toward the window, a square of purple-black, gauging the slow rhythm of Flo's breathing. She didn't wake up easily. She slept flat on her back the whole night through—had for all the forty-five years of their marriage. He didn't like it; she looked too dead. He'd complained about it in the past, and she'd shot back that she was too tired to turn over, which seemed close enough to dead that it still worried him, although he'd learned to keep quiet. She hadn't had a day's pain from her back, and her posture showed a benefit, too, erect as a piano teacher's, while he had a hunch in his spine that sucking in his stomach didn't hide anymore.

She'd chide him for getting up so early but he was wide awake; he wouldn't fall back asleep again. And it might be a good day to watch the sunrise. After a wind like that, with so much dust in the air, dawn sometimes took on a particular look, one he liked to witness.

He dressed quickly, zipping up his jeans on the way downstairs. The snap pressed against his skin like a chip of ice caught in the waistband. The best place to watch was from the gate of the front corral. He walked down the packed-dirt path toward the barn and climbed slowly atop the wide gatepost. He sat with his boot heels hooked over the middle rail, facing east, and tilted his hat back. It wouldn't be long now, if it was going to happen at all. Sometimes clouds hid just over the horizon, screening the rays of the sun. But this looked hopeful.

A thread of sunlight flared at the horizon and spilled across the prairie, pushing a breeze before it that smelled of cold sage and gritty soil. He licked his lips. It had a taste to it, the aftertaste of a big wind, tired out and gone. Then the light went pale and shallow, spreading out like a river in flood, like the Platte back before it was put to work with dams and diversions, when it could spill over its banks and fill the valley as far as the eye could see. The light washed against the line of frozen sage in the near distance, just over the rise of the pasture, firing it into the halo he looked for. This was it. Once a year, twice if he was lucky, a bright and haloed head rose in the east over his land. For the moment it lasted, he sat without breathing, without blinking, his creased face lit in the flare. He didn't go to church much anymore, only when Flo dragged him along. Church couldn't compare with this.

The halo dimmed. He'd seen all he wanted to see. A bald and dirty yellow sun peeked above the horizon. Its light edged across the prairie, sketching in the details of the sage and the alkali, the coarse blades of knapweed, and the rigid clumps of prickly pear crouched against the earth, and he saw what he didn't want to see: the ragged line of the fence, the dry scarcity of the pasture, the peeling paint of the old white barn. He saw his own worn boots, his belly in thin flannel, and an ivory-colored button straining against his sigh.

CHAPTER TWO

Flo's house rule stated that whoever got up first cooked breakfast. Carl didn't mind. Lunch and dinner were another matter but breakfast was always the same: eggs, toast with jelly, black coffee. Figuring out what to make was the mysterious part of cooking, the genius of a good, every-day cook like Flo. She could throw together suppers with the same ease as breakfast. She never stopped to frown over recipes or to tap her chin with indecision. She just began cooking. Yet, if he asked her what she was making, she always looked a little bewildered. "We'll just have to see what happens," and it was thick lamb stew with new potatoes, or buttery bean soup with ham hock, set next to a steaming basket of corn bread and a jar of honey. Or antelope steaks broiled to rose pink with creamy bakers and a pile of fresh snap beans on the side. When Hank was little, there had always been a crowd for supper. If it wasn't some of the Drummond crew up from Evanston, it was a bunch of ranch kids that Hank had dragged home. Flo was happy to see anybody, and she never told a visitor they weren't welcome to stay for supper. She simply added more ingredients, threw in another handful of seasonings, set out a higher stack of plates on the counter, and there was enough for everyone. It was a kind of miracle she worked, like the loaves and the fishes.

"I'm putting the eggs in the pan," he hollered.

He waited until he heard her slippered feet on the floorboards above, then cracked the eggs into the skillet. She paused at the top of the stairs, scratching her head and looking into the studio they'd made of the smallest bedroom. She did this every morning of the world, as if she still couldn't believe it was there.

"Are you coming or not?"

"I'm coming," she said, stumping down the stairs.

He flipped the eggs and punched at the toaster whose thermostat didn't work, rescuing the slices before they burned. He slid the eggs onto the plates. "You want jelly?"

Flo sat at the kitchen table. "I'll do it."

"I can jelly your toast, Flo."

"Just a smear, then."

She unrolled the newspaper. "You got up at dawn, didn't you?"

He slathered jelly on the toast, shrugging.

She studied him benevolently over the newspaper as he brought the food to the table. He sat down, frowning at the print, patting at his empty breast pocket. He'd left his glasses upstairs again, next to the bed. He needed an upstairs pair and a downstairs pair, or he needed a house all on a level. He felt too old to always be climbing steps.

Flo's paper drooped. "You need to wear them on a necklace, Carl."

"I'm not wearing a necklace."

"You want me to go get them?"

"No," he said wearily. "I can make out the headlines. I don't need to know any more than that." He glanced toward the radio, thinking of the morning livestock report.

"I'll turn it on," she said.

He shook his head as she started to get up. "I don't give a damn about it, Flo."

"They've been worse."

"It ain't the daily thing. It's the trend."

"The whole world's trending down," she said. "Why should sheep be any different?"

"Our goddamn expenses aren't trending down."

She watched him again, solemn now.

"What?" he said.

"I'm going to the gallery this morning. You know my show opens a week from Friday."

"I heard it a hundred times. I hope I know it."

"And you're coming?"

"I thought I'd get that old horse out this morning, ride on up to the valley."

"I'm talking about a week from now, you know darn well."

He scratched at his jaw. He dreaded going. He didn't like her paintings, particularly one of him that was going to be hanging up for everyone to see. Portraits were supposed to favor a person, but Flo had made him look every bit as pudgy and old as he really was. "What do I have to do?"

"Put on some clean clothes, your good boots that don't smell like sheep shit, and be your own charming self."

"I've seen all those pictures before, you know."

The paper drooped to her plate. "Carl, this is my first painting exhibit ever in my long, long life. Skip my funeral if you want to but come to this."

He hated this sort of talk and she knew it. Pouting, he cleared his dishes from the table and folded his napkin neatly onto his placemat, a plasticized color photograph of the Tetons. Flo's showed the Bighorns. There were four others in the set: the Absarokas taken from Meeteetse; a herd of sheep crossing a high plateau in the Snowies, Devils Tower rising out of the lush Belle Fourche Valley, and the high wall of the Wind Rivers, lime green in early summer. Flo rotated them from time to time, although they both knew she didn't like them. Carl had bought them for her years before, when Hank was small, and Flo had always honored the gift. None showed anything near Casper, which had always irritated Flo. The area around here was plenty beautiful enough to warrant big color pictures but some of the sights were hard to photograph, like sunrise on a dusty horizon.

"I'll be there," he said.

He walked to the barn for the second time that morning. It sat in the lee of a low rise, like a ship in the trough of a wave, large and airy and fine. As a boy, he had liked to sit in the doors of the loft, his legs dangling, to look out over the scoured prairie and pretend he was a sailor in the crow's nest of a ship, seeing the world. There was no real ocean for thousands of miles but the pioneers had called the high prairie a sea of grass and that had been enough for him. They tramped westward here, across this very land, close down along the Platte, which flowed in the opposite direction, swiftly, toward the Missouri and the Mississippi, back toward the homes they had left behind.

Pan came to the door of his stall through a carpet of straw, his gray-flecked muzzle shivering in anticipation of breakfast. Carl dumped the feed in his tray and watched the horse eat. It was the most peaceful thing in the world, that slow, sure crunch of the oats, Pan's even breath, and the calm brown depth of his eyes.

Carl didn't wonder much about oceans anymore, or about traveling. Now he wondered only if there could be an existence other than his own that would fill up a life so completely. Other people had lives made up of parts: of work and recreation, of family activities and household chores; they lived their days in sections. But his own life had made a seamless circle around him from his earliest teenage years, as it had for his grandfather before him: the livestock and the land and the family. That was all. One made no sense without the others.

Pan snuffled at the bottom of his tray. Carl drew him from the stall, letting the halter rope fall to the floor, and curried the horse rapidly, with vigorous strokes. Pan's skin rippled and he dropped his head, grunting softly. Carl switched hands, letting his right arm rest. This was calming, too, the routine and the rhythmic strokes, the sharp-smelling warmth of the horse, the solid feel of the coat under his palm.

He saddled up and pulled his rifle from the locked cabinet across from the tack room. He slid it into the scabbard on the saddle muzzle-down and patted the butt as he straightened the stirrup leather. Chances were he wouldn't see anything that needed shooting but he wanted to go prepared. He led Pan outside, closing the barn doors behind him, and mounted, glancing toward the house. He didn't expect to see Flo—she'd still be reading her newspaper—but neither did he want to miss waving to her if she happened to be there watching him from the kitchen window.

CHAPTER THREE

Roberta roared down the gravel drive, raising a wall of sunstruck dust behind the truck, and turned west along the state road paralleling Uncle John creek. The eagles were heading to their breeding grounds in Canada, and she wouldn't have many more chances to see them until they returned next fall. Wyoming's winters were only marginally less brittle than Saskatchewan's, but bald eagles found the difference significant. They spent the cold months in the shelter of Jackson Canyon, hunting in and around the open waters of the Platte.

She watched the trees, driving one-handed with her window down, leaving her left hand free to hold the battered military field glasses slung around her neck. The balds could be anywhere along the river, sitting hunched in the cottonwoods on the banks, waiting for breakfast to come by.

Her hair blew across her face. It was graying and fine and cut straight at her jaw. She tucked it behind her ears, impatiently. She wore no hat, although the morning was cold. Hats altered the purity of sound or muffled it completely, like near deafness. She wanted to hear everything, even if it was nothing more than the grumble of the engine or the tires

chewing gravel on the side of the road. And she wanted to hear the
eagles if they had anything to say.

A truck passed, going fast in the opposite direction. She read the
image as a whole, as she might a bird winging by in precipitous flight:
blue truck, bill cap, narrow shoulders, a forefinger raised over the steering wheel in a casual hello—Samuel Oakes, a neighbor to the west, heading toward town. She put a hand out the window to return the greeting
in his rearview mirror. Samuel had a smile on his face. She knew without seeing it—a wry smile, decidedly tolerant. The Uncle John Ranch
included some of the best land in the region, river-bottom grassland. But
Roberta ran a hospital for injured birds here, not cattle. Two quarter
horses that Glen had insisted on keeping were all that was left of the livestock. Carl Drummond, her immediate neighbor to the west, joshed with
her about it sometimes but the others didn't dare. They gossiped instead,
though the hospital was nine years old. *You should see that place—birds
everywhere. She's even got those stalls made into cages, birds sitting in
there with all kinds of stuff, casts and bandages and what-have-you, like
a bunch of goddamn war wounded. You know that old equipment barn
of Jeremiah's? Well, sir, she took the walls out and turned it into one
huge bird cage....*

Though they didn't pretend to understand her passion, she knew they
guessed at its origins, wrongly. Their theory ran that in the years since
Glen had become a successful oil man and state senator, he hadn't had
much time for her or for the Uncle John. And a woman's mind was apt
to bend a little under those circumstances, you know, especially if she
didn't have any children to steady her. Nevertheless, they treated her
with respect. As Jeremiah Shea's daughter, she deserved no less. But that
didn't stop them from smiling when they saw her grinding along the
road in her faded red Ford, only half on the pavement, staring out across
the prairie at a black speck in a tree with those old monster binoculars
of her father's.

At a long curve in the highway, she gunned the pickup straight ahead
and bumped onto the unofficial extension of the state road, a bad-tem-
pered dirt one-lane that traced Uncle John creek to its meeting with the
Platte a mile to the north. The eagles often perched there. A stand of leafless cottonwoods grew along the drainages, and barren willows choked
the banks where the creek spread out and joined the river. She slowed

down, peering over the steering wheel at the tallest trees along the river. A red-tail screamed. She stuck her head out the window. A pair of hawks circled above her, the brick red of their tails visible as they banked. Another scream, hoarse and irritable, verging on outrage. They spiraled, rising higher. She had disturbed them, probably, with the fast approach of her truck. She studied them through the binoculars: the flare of their wings in the sunlight, the rusty buff of their breasts. Her morning's dream flitted to life again in her mind.

"Aw, quit complaining," she muttered to the birds, "I'm not going to do you one damn bit of harm."

She turned eastward just below a wide curve of the Platte, toward town. During a recent thaw a passing truck or two had churned the road into deep ruts. Now they were frozen in place, foot-high ridges of obdurate bentonite clay. The truck bounced violently, suspension screeching, popping her up and down on the bench seat. In five minutes she was close enough to scan the trees along the banks. She slowed, spotting one eagle, then two. These were juvenile birds, feathered in an unremarkable brown, lacking the brilliant white head and tail of adulthood. They sat in a lone tree along the river a mile away, an Impressionist's stab at birds in the distance: single long strokes of paint, ragged at the edges, indistinct in form. But she had no doubt they were eagles. She raised the binoculars and switched off the ignition.

She could not recognize individual birds. These might be females, judging from their size. Males tended to be smaller. She could see the fine shape of their heads against the muck of the river. They sat low over their feet, like gold-panners crouched at creekside, and stared out in different directions. One faced north, the other west, sleepily. They were not hunting. Perhaps they had already eaten breakfast, she thought, and they were drowsy with their digestion. She wouldn't hear them call today.

She started the engine and moved closer, lifting the binoculars again to scan the length of the river. Ducks on the water—mergansers—and the wind-drifted cry of a killdeer, somewhere off to her right. Then a horse and rider. She fingered the focus wheel of the glasses. A half-mile off to the west, coming along the river and edging south. A fat horse in a gentle lope, a man slumped in the saddle. She cut the engine.

Carl Drummond, you old fat-ass. Sit up.

She would cross onto his land soon unless she headed back to the highway, but no one minded the trespass as long as gates were closed and livestock left alone.

The horse's direction changed subtly toward her. He had spotted the pickup and intended to say hello. He pushed the horse hard but the gait was still liquid. Pan, of course.

Roberta waved. A few more lopes and Carl raised a hand. He hauled the horse up at the front bumper of the truck. Although he was not far from home, lather striped Pan's neck beneath the reins and highlighted a rifle on his flanks. His nostrils flared.

"Little Bertie," Carl said, swinging from the saddle. "Out on feather patrol, are you?"

Little Bertie. Her childhood name. Only Carl still used it.

She stepped from the pickup. "Carl, where are you taking that fat old horse in such a hurry?"

He patted Pan's neck. "He is fat, huh? We both are." He said it regretfully. "I thought I'd give us some exercise instead of driving around all the time."

"Then you should do some of the loping."

Carl looked toward Hartsong mountain, pulling his hat from his head. He was almost bald on top now. He was at least sixty-five, perhaps more.

"I'm going to walk him the rest of the way. That won't hurt him. He was itching to go a little. You know how it is."

She did. She rubbed Pan's nose. The rush of his breath was hot and sweet with hay.

Carl scanned the horizon. "So where are the birds?"

"Balds," she said. "In the cottonwoods. Just a couple. They're leaving for the season. You don't mind if I wander on along, do you?"

"Hell, no. You go on far as you want."

"Thanks. How's Flo?"

"Fine. You should stop and see her. She'd love it. You and Glen never get around anymore. I know he's busy counting his oil wells and running the state and all that, but you aren't a politician, Bertie; you haven't got to calling your neighbors constituents yet." He grinned at her.

She adjusted Pan's bridle behind the ear. The horse scrubbed his sweaty head against her arm and rib cage.

Carl nodded at Hartsong. He leased grazing land from the government along the mountain's western end and into the valley behind. "Well, I'm heading on up back of the mountain. Take a look at things, get this old horse out."

"Many lambs yet?"

"Things are stepping up," he said, examining the sky.

"We're due for some moisture."

He narrowed one eye at her, comically, his teasing expression for children. She knew what would come next: he would say that he was surprised she'd venture a guess on the weather, things being what they were. She wasn't ranching, so the weather could hardly be important to her anymore. But his expression faded, as if he suddenly saw her gray hair and her angular, lined face. She wasn't Little Bertie anymore.

"Don't you miss it at all, Bertie? Having some beasts around? My God, but your old dad would sure be surprised at you."

"I doubt it."

He smiled slowly. "You're right. He wouldn't be one ounce surprised. But he might be damned mad." He rested an arm on the pommel of the saddle. "I never saw a girl ride like you could. We all used to sit around on the fence and watch you cut calves. You never looked up, you were that keen. You never even knew anybody was looking on."

"Of course I did, Carl."

He shook his head, refusing to doubt his memories. "You worked like there wasn't nothing in the world but that horse and that calf and you."

He knocked his hat back a notch. "I hear your niece is coming out for a visit. How long's it been—four, five years?"

"Eight. Since she was fifteen."

"My God, she'll be grown up. She must have some kind of job by now."

"She quit."

"Quit?"

The word had no good connotations for him. Roberta could see the neurons firing in Carl's brain, making the link between Roberta quitting ranching and Muirie quitting her job.

"What kind of thing was it she did?"

"Advertising," said Roberta.

Muirie had spent the summers of her childhood on the ranch, and Roberta had hoped that Wyoming might beckon to her after college despite the fact that it offered little in the way of upscale jobs. Advertising was a quintessentially urban occupation, a California-style career that came close to denying a childhood spent partly on a ranch. Muirie's phone call hadn't informed Roberta much of the whys and wherefores of her decision. She had found herself wondering if she'd still know her niece. Eight years was a long time, especially the formative years between fifteen and twenty-three.

"Well I'll be damned," Carl said, still digesting the thought. "There ain't a whole hell of a lot to sell out here, is there?"

"You couldn't sell me anything in California either."

"Amen to that."

Carl climbed back into the saddle and scowled toward the river. "Eagles, huh?"

She nodded. "You been seeing them up in the valley?"

"Now and again. I can't spot them like you do, you know, but I see them now and again."

She eyed the rifle.

"Come on, Bertie, I don't aim at nothing on the wing. Couldn't hit it with this thing anyway. You got people around here so sensitive about these eagles I don't think boys shoot starlings anymore."

"I got a gunshot Harlan's hawk last week."

His face went sour.

"Somebody's target practice," she said. "Took the upper part of the beak off. The vet couldn't do anything for it."

"I'm sorry to hear that," Carl said. But he was ready to go. He gathered his reins. "Stop by and see Flo if you have time. She's going to have some of her pictures in town next week. Did you know about that?"

"I heard. It's about time."

He touched the brim of his hat to her, and Pan eased forward into a lope toward the mountain, easy as the roll of a rocking horse.

CHAPTER FOUR

Carl squinted at the north face of the mountain, figuring the time to the valley beyond. In the settling dust of the vanished Chinook, Hartsong looked faded and farther away than usual. But it wasn't far, and there was no need to push the old horse; Roberta was right about that. He let Pan fall into a plodding walk. They could both enjoy the sunshine. He slipped his feet from the stirrups, stretching his legs, and let them hang over the barrel belly of the horse. He expected a twinge from his back but it felt fine.

"Look at the gut on you, old boy."

The horse's ears flickered backward. Carl relaxed in the saddle, patting his own round belly with dismay. As his sheep outfit had shrunk in the last years, his own girth had expanded. Less work meant more time to sit around and eat Flo's cooking. He flexed a bicep, tucking the arm against his chest. He still had muscle and plenty of endurance, enough to do the same work he'd always done—if there was any point to it. More and more these days it meant working almost for free, paying out in order to stay in business, borrowing money you couldn't afford in order to make money you couldn't keep. It was a crazy game, one that would have horrified his grandfather. Fresh from Scotland, Colin Hoyt Drummond had been his own boss, able to determine his own fate. He had founded the C. H. Ranch by staking out the acreage and calling it his own.

Carl worked the horse along the toe of the slope, avoiding the cold shade of the mountain as long as he could, then crossed into it grudgingly. A breeze fell like a blade along the north face. He saw Roberta's face again in his mind's eye. If he'd had trouble adjusting to the size of his belly, she must have come close to a stroke looking in the mirror one day and seeing how old and gray she was. She was in her late forties somewhere, but the only thing that didn't look old about her now were those eyes he'd always had a little trouble looking straight into. She was too sharp-tongued for her own good, he thought, although she'd come by it honestly, by way of her father. Still, a quick tongue seemed different in a man.

He hunched forward and the horse lifted into a cautious jog, head down like a scholar, studying the rocky ground. It rose in broken angles toward the west end of the mountain. Carl contoured across the slope below the mouth of Jackson Canyon and its drainage, toothy with boulders and gravel, and paralleled the highway past the gray, squat buildings at Goose Egg. The lonely little café there had a few morning customers, it looked like.

Growing a paunch was the least of things. Some men he knew had heart trouble, ulcers, arthritis, and were hardly any use to themselves anymore. How they could put up with being so pitiful was hard to understand. It wasn't getting old in itself that was shameful, of course, it was being useless.

Intercepting a gravel access road, he kept the horse just to the side, off the hardpan of its center, following it around the west end until it entered the valley between Hartsong and its twin to the south, Sacajawea. Here, he came into the sun again, expecting to see the sheep scattered across the valley, a view he loved, whatever the season. Now, between storms, the snow had melted out in the belly of the valley leaving the mellow golden grasslands fully open to the sheep.

But something was wrong. He drew the horse to a standstill. The sheep were bunched, streaming away from him, edgy. He read them quickly, their numbers, condition, the vigor of their movements. He didn't puzzle over it, wondering consciously what he should see. This was another kind of consciousness, hidden and instinctive, a thing he hadn't learned by rote, that couldn't be taught in books. He squinted, head up, tilted his hat back on his crown. Pan stirred, took a waltzing step sideways, ears funneled back. Carl jerked the reins, gaze raking the valley.

There: what in the hell was that?

On a low rise on the valley floor, straight east. Two white splashes, inert as tombstones.

Dead sheep.

"Yaahhh!"

Pan leapt forward, a grunt of surprise, pebbles flying. Carl kept his eyes on the sheep. Coyotes, sure as hell. Hit and run, and they'd seen him coming like as not. If there was this much left to see, the kills were fresh. Any more than a day old and there'd be buzzards flapping around, but the sky was empty, he could see that without looking away from the sheep. Buzzards were big as airplanes, you couldn't miss them.

The flock divided, bleating wild alarm, woolly footstools on spindly legs, and crowded the edge of the valley at the foot of the mountain's southern slope. They watched him, pressed close together in drifts like last year's mangy snow.

"Goddamn it to hell."

He wheeled Pan around on the rise and was on the ground before the horse came to a halt. He pitched the reins to the side, Pan snorting at the snaking reins or the ferrous stench.

Carl stood, hands on hips. The sheep were mangled. A ewe and her spring lamb. They'd gotten the lamb first, tore out its throat. The mother, defending, more or less eaten alive. They'd played with her, ripping at her udder, probably after the lamb was dead. She'd been chewed on, tasted for the hell of it. This was a sport for them, a bloodlust, killing for the thrill. You could say anything you wanted about coyotes, anything at all—people did—but here was the real evidence, smeared around on the grass: the still-warm stink of guts and wrenched flesh. He looked away, grimacing. This was what coyotes did.

He didn't need to prove it. Nothing else did this kind of damage. Splattered blood like from a cup. And there were tracks, scrapes in the hardscrabble on the top of the rise where they'd snarled around the ewe.

They were probably still close by, watching, panting grins on their faces, yawning at their own cleverness. He studied the foot of Sacajawea, the aspen, the beds of white limestone like a highway turned on edge, the layer-caked red rock, the pine. He couldn't see them, but they were close. This was fresh, warm. He'd scared them off. He should have been quieter coming in, snuck up on them, suspected their presence. He had his rifle, he could have gotten a shot off.

He kicked at the ground as if at the coyotes, spraying the dead animals with scabs of the earth. He should have been able to get a shot off, if he'd been careful. But they were sharp-eyed as eagles, those dogs, they had a second soul floating up in the sky, or an Indian lookout of a soul that told them when to run.

He pushed Pan home at a jog, urgent, wishing for an accelerator and a stick shift. At the door of the barn he uncinched the saddle, then yanked it off, letting it fall to the ground. Pan stood hangdog, raspy with phlegm, saline heat rising from the lathered swamp of his coat.

"Goddamn it, boy." He pulled the bridle off, rubbing behind the ears.

Flo had gone into town. He'd have to walk Pan out himself despite his sense of hurry. He couldn't just stick him back in his stall; he'd chill as sure as anything.

He commanded himself: *Settle down, concentrate on the horse.* He got a towel from the tack room and rubbed Pan's coat down, doubling and tripling the towel, then slipped a halter on the horse and led him, weary hooves scoring the dirt, in wide, slow circles in the front corral. It gave him more time to think, to cool down himself, to be logical, to pace himself. The ride home had been a torment; he couldn't let that frame of mind guide him. There was no certainty it would continue; sometimes there were isolated hits and the coyotes moved on, or they just went back to whatever else they ate—mice, grasshoppers, jacks, birds if they could get them. But he'd bet fifty-fifty it would go on. They'd make a hit every day, like a few years back, running flesh off the stock, the ewes aborting left and right. He'd lost a sheep a night for a month until the government men coptered in for an air hunt. Men conducted the war but the enemy knew the country better. Even from the air you missed them; they dodged, they were smart as hell and fast as the devil. The *thwop-*

thwop-thwop of the blades; the coyotes heard it coming, they saw you coming. You could try anything, and they saw you coming. Poisons, you name it, arsenic, cyanide; and traps—traps with teeth as mean as their own—lures that shot poison into their open mouths; shotguns, rifles, practically cannons; bulbous poison collars you put on the sheep, gushing liquid centers like candy, and collars that flashed lights, hell, sirens. What could you do; they knew. Helicopter gunships, for God's sake, and yet there were more of them every year, slanting around looking for an easy kill. Pink fleece. Cold meat.

Pan was deadweight, like pulling a boulder through water, but his breath was slowing, evening out. He had good lungs, a good heart; his broad chest showed it. Carl patted the withers, tacky with sweat.

"Come on, fella. You can have a drink now."

The horse sucked a gallon and shuddered with the pleasure of it, shook himself, ears flapping, and went for more. Carl wrestled his head up from the tank. "Take it easy, there. Not so fast."

The laws were too specific. As if you could get the one coyote that did the killing, as if you could tell, as if he'd bark words at you, *Here I am, it was me, shoot me down if you can, nyah-nyah-nyah.* Half the time you couldn't even find prints, couldn't tell which direction they came from, like they dropped out of the sky. Before, it was easier; you may have gotten more than just the one that was responsible, but you damn well got the right one. And even that hadn't stopped them, even when anything was legal, they survived. They stuck around, thick as ticks, waiting for the laws to change. And now, as if they needed help to survive, the law disarmed a rancher of everything including his peashooter. It wasn't only coyotes after the stock, either. There were mountain lions and rustlers— and eagles. No matter what Roberta Shea Thompkins had to say about it, there were plenty of witnesses. Eagles preyed on lambs. Maybe not her precious balds, but those other eagles, those goldens, that lived here all year long, they lined their nests with fleeces. Plenty of people had seen it. How could you argue with that evidence?

He should call the government trappers, register his request and let the wheels start turning. They could take their time unless you had influence, unless you were somebody, while your stock was decimated. They were getting flak about the control program from people who didn't know one damn thing about ranching, and that was slowing things down, too. There was confusion about what was being slaughtered and by who. Some of the trappers weren't sure anymore what to think, things were that screwed up. And if there was something in danger of extinction, it was trappers and ranchers and livestock and adequate methods of predator damage control. Sure as hell not coyotes. What coyotes were being saved from and at what cost no one would say. Just vague things like "balance of nature," even though eating meat had nothing to do with true nature, since no coyote depended on sheep or cattle. It was fast food for them; they considered it entertainment. They liked the taste of easy blood, it was a drug. They weren't after the meat as much as the lazy chase and the sure kill, the smell of the flesh, that fat feeling of power, of delivering death.

He picked up the phone and slammed it down again. He knew what he'd hear if he called. *Hold, please.* A monotone voice, blank eternity, then a click and he'd have to answer a bunch of form-filling questions, giving locations and dates and numbers, estimates of damage, the method of attack. He'd dutifully take down notes on a scratch pad, names and numbers, dates, possibilities, legalities. His throat knotted up with the thought of it: he needed to do something now, something useful, not just create official paperwork. There were no livelihoods at stake for the form fillers; no one in a government job had to worry. They were transferred to other departments if their jobs gave out, because there were other departments to go to, endlessly; they didn't have to count sheep.

"I'd say this warrants keeping an eye on it, Carl," the government trapper had said.

Carl. He'd been Carl to that guy, though they'd just met—one of the men in the copter, shooting at coyotes like he was at a carnival, with a sneer of pleasure, a coyote on two legs. That wasn't what he wanted. He'd find no pleasure in it himself. Only relief, and justice. But his investment in the sheep, a hundred and thirty years of stewardship of the land, it didn't mean much to anyone else. Forms and duties and quotas. Allowances. Political pressure from all over the map. People were going to give up eating meat, maybe, give up wearing wool. Or they just wanted livestock raised somewhere else, so they didn't have to look at it, or smell it, or know about it. So their world could be pure.

He shoveled out Pan's stall, filling a wheelbarrow, threw in fresh straw knee-deep. Pan waited, edging closer to the door of the stall, nosing

Carl's shoulder. He wanted in, wanted peace and a Folger's can full of rolled oats, sweetened with molasses. His life was simple.

In the house, he grabbed the keys to the pickup and wrote a note to Flo: *Coyotes in the draw. Got two sheep. Back later.*

The truck started with a grudge of smoke and vibration. He nursed the accelerator, the door open, one foot on the ground, looking toward the barn.

Why not? Just one of the carcasses. They'd come back for it and he'd get them easy and clean.

He revved the engine, then eased off the accelerator, waiting for the motor to find an idle it could maintain. It chunked and whirred, steadying.

He got out, left the door open, and went to the barn, into the smell of hay and Pan's contentment, freshly lopped onto the straw, steaming. In the tack room he rummaged through the dusty drawers of a cabinet beneath a narrow counter and sink, fumbling jars of liniment, cans of saddle soap and tonic, stomach tubes, forceps, a thermometer, a pair of ear-tag pliers. He dumped them onto the counter and turned to a small wall-mounted cabinet over the door. The latch was gone, hinges loose. He stuck in a hand, pulled out an ancient slab of soap, hard and porous as dried bone, grabbed an open box of horseshoe nails. They sprayed to the floor, down his boots, into his pockets, metal splinters.

"Goddamn it."

He nudged the counter, pulling off his boots, shaking them over the floor, tested his waistband with a finger. He needed a flashlight to empty the cabinet. He scratched his head, too many thoughts at once. It was in the broom closet, on the shelf above.

He pulled the door open to a scuttling at his feet as a mouse dashed across the top of his boots. He jiggled the flashlight, batteries clunking, and shot a feeble beam into the cabinet. There it was, in the back. He shook the flashlight, snorting. It was no better than a candle, not as good. He reached, felt a cobweb, something else vaguely greasy, then the metal of a lid, the glass of a jar. He pulled it out. The lid was gripped with rust. It ground open with a screech, the white powder inside clotted like humid sugar. He didn't sniff it; wasn't about to taste it. He found an old jam jar, discarded from Flo's kitchen, relegated to the litter of the tack room for some other project long ago, yanked on an old pair of gloves, tied his kerchief over his nose and mouth, and edged some pow-der from one jar into the other with the handle of a teaspoon, a few small clumps at a time, hardly breathing. It was old, so he would use more to compensate: a couple more lumps, like lazily made snowballs. And a little more, in case he decided to use both carcasses. He added water slowly, swirling it into the powder. The stuff dissolved well. He pulled the kerchief from his neck, then screwed the lid on the jam jar and shook it vigorously. He held the jar up to the light for inspection. It would do all right.

He grabbed for the bone-hard bar and scrubbed his arms to the elbows, rinsing under the spigot turned on full. He'd wash the kerchief and gloves later after the whole job was done.

One more thing. He knew where that was, in the drawer next to the sink, within easy reach. He pulled it out carefully. A glimmer of metal. He freed the tip from its block of cork and slid a forefinger down the long, slim reed of the needle.

This time it wouldn't take long to get there. He took his rifle. Ten min-utes of bumping. He held the jar between his legs to warm the mixture, the syringe tucked into the seat. At the entrance to Gotheberg Draw he left the truck, taking his rifle, and walked up to the first view of the val-ley. They weren't back; it was too soon, or they'd heard him coming again, probably the latter. He drove the rest of the way in. The herd scat-tered nonchalantly, less wary now.

On the low rise, he inspected the carcasses again. Yes, he'd dose both, what the hell, and move one down to the other end of the valley, in case the coyotes came in that way. He had to be sure.

The lamb was slit open at the neck but he cut the skin again, loosen-ing it, making it easier for the coyotes to get at the flesh. He worked with his pocketknife, under the belly, pulled the skin up from the sinewy haunches, and slashed into the young flesh, tenderizing. Here, on both sides, on the shoulders, so that anywhere they nibbled, if they were only curious and not really hungry, they'd be likely to get a lethal dose. He didn't want to make them just sick. Aversion programs didn't work, just like the other nonlethal methods didn't work. The only thing that worked was this: certainty.

He pulled the liquid into the syringe, injected it into the flesh of the lamb, anointing it gently—here, and here. The same for the ewe. This was all; he wouldn't do more. This would solve the immediate problem. He'd waited in the past, mostly gone by the rules. He couldn't afford it anymore. These were his animals, his risk, his investment, his income, retirement, security, annuity, his heritage, the heritage of his grandchildren. There had to be something left to give them.

CHAPTER FIVE

The sweet stink of overripe bananas lingered beneath the aroma of coffee in the kitchen. Roberta went for the coffee, sloshing herself a cupful. One-handed, she worked a slice of bread loose from a loaf left open on the counter and jammed it into the toaster. She took a plastic tub of margarine from the refrigerator, the contents peppered with toast crumbs from other mornings, and swirled a generous portion onto a knife. With the toe of her boot, she edged open a scuffed cupboard next to the dishwasher. No Cheerios. Or she'd put them elsewhere. The toast popped up, smoking along the crust.

Glen ambled in from the hallway, wrapped in his terry-cloth robe, a coffee cup in hand. He seemed to be growing shorter as he aged. Being a politician sped up the process, she thought; it shrank him down, dried him up. Or perhaps she was growing straighter and taller. Glen bent; she didn't.

"Where are the Cheerios?"

He still looked sleepy. A gray cowlick spiked over one ear. "No idea, Bertie." She buttered her toast. "Did you look in the linen closet?"

She eyed him blandly, tore the toast in two.

He sighed, thoughtful. "I found a half-gallon of melting ice cream in there once. And there was that roadkill skunk in the freezer."

"It was for the raptors. The freezer in the big barn broke down. I did not serve it up to you."

He looked doubtful. She let a smile creep onto her face.

"Split a banana with me," he said.

"No. They're mushy."

He reached for one atop the refrigerator. "Then I won't have to share." He peeled it and took a large bite of the deliquescing flesh.

"Anyone who can eat rotten bananas shouldn't mind a little panfried skunk, it seems to me."

"You *did* feed it to me."

"I'm merely speculating on your character."

He took another bite of the banana. "So what's up today?"

He was jockeying for a ride to the airport. He commuted to and from the capital during the legislative session, flying to Cheyenne on either Sunday night or Monday morning, and returning to Casper Friday evening. He had his own truck and the airport had a long-term parking area where he could leave it during the week, but he liked Roberta to chauffeur him. As with everything else, he was politic in his request, asking indirectly and with a proper outward respect for her schedule.

"Sherman's coming out to check over the balds in the flight barn," she said. "I assume he'll give the okay, and we'll release them. That means a cleanup of the flight barn so I can put a couple of hawks in there, and a cleanup of the hawks' cages so I can shift some other birds into them— and so on down the line. I'll be busy."

He scrutinized a blackened elbow of crust. "So how's Sherman doing at that clinic of his, anyway?"

Roberta wiped her mouth with a paper towel. "He'll be flat broke in a year."

"I never did understand why he quit the Game and Fish. A vet there makes fair money."

She refilled her cup. "But you have to work for the state to get it."

He squinted at her, scratching absently at his scalp. He discovered the cowlick and patted it experimentally, as if measuring its tensile strength.

"You'll have to wet it down," she said. "What time do you need to go?"

He considered. "I figure I'd better be there by late tonight sometime. I've got an early committee meeting in the morning so I might as well get the traveling over with. Could you spare the time?"

"The birds come first."

"That's nothing new," he said peacefully, sipping his coffee.

"With evening feedings, it'll be seven at least."

"That'll be fine. What about getting ready for Muirie? I'm leaving you with all the work."

Roberta shrugged. "She asked for the pine closet. I'll just throw some sheets on the bed."

"Why the pine closet?"

"God knows."

Glen ruminated. "It's going to be something to see her after so long."

Roberta set her cup on the counter. "I have a feeling she's grown up and turned into Ellen."

He looked horrified for a moment. "Naw. Can't be true. If she's turned into your sister, she wouldn't be coming here."

He was right. Ellen had left Wyoming for Berkeley thirty years ago and had returned only rarely, for brief visits.

Glen, watching her, held his coffee cup up as if in a toast. "See, Bertie? There's always hope."

The frozen weeds of the empty pasture crunched beneath Roberta's boots as she lugged a pet carrier, two blankets, a pair of leather gauntlets, her platform scales, and a bucket of chunked beef hearts to the bald eagles in the flight barn. She wore her binoculars slung across her torso, out of the way.

These eagles had come to her within a week of one another. Both were immatures, and young birds tended to get into trouble. One had been shot out near Red Butte. Luckily, the bullet had passed through the wrist without shattering it. The second bird had been hit by a garbage truck near a Dumpster in Mills. A witness had rescued the bird, and reported to Roberta that it had tried to fly away as the garbage truck approached, but had eaten too much Kentucky Fried and couldn't get off the ground. A messier break, also a wing, but Sherman had said that the permanent damage was limited to one primary feather, which would always grow in slightly crooked.

The flight barn stood across the back corral, close down to Uncle John creek, out of sight of the house. Although it was superior to most facilities she had seen for recovering raptors, the sight of its ghostly chain-link walls rising amongst the cottonwoods wearied her. If the birds were to have a good chance of survival once she returned them to the wild, they needed a large, quiet, private place in which to strengthen their wings after their injuries had healed. The flight barn gave them two stories of empty air, twenty-five yards long, furnished at either end with perches made from full-grown pines. To Roberta's tour groups, the barn looked generous and well-designed. The teachers of the elementary school classes and the ladies of the garden clubs complimented her on her selflessness and nobility in providing for the birds. She bit her tongue in response. The barn could not hint at the open sky any more than a Chinook could be mimicked with a paper fan. It was nothing more than torturous imprisonment to an eagle. The raptors covered the space in a hop, two wing beats, and a brief drop to the ground, where Roberta fed them like caged dogs from rubber bowls.

This would be their last meal in captivity. But a rough morning lay in store for them. She and the eagles had reached an understanding in the weeks since they'd earned their way out of the big barn. She came at a regular time once a day, six days a week, with plenty of food, varying the menu. She poured it into the bowls, freshened their water, raked up the birds' debris, and left. She did not jabber at them or spy on them unnecessarily. They, in turn, remained calm, ate well, and gained strength. This morning, though, she would betray their trust. She would capture them, then she and Sherman would give them a final physical, which meant they would be subjected to more handling. She didn't like the job. The birds' outrage disturbed her. But it served a useful purpose too. As they flew away from her, free for the first time in months, they would have learned one lesson well, one that could save their lives in the wild: People couldn't be trusted. They'd hurt you every chance they got.

She went through the small chain-link doorway of the flight barn and divided the beef hearts between the two bowls on the ground. The eagles sat on their perches at opposite ends of the building, watching her closely. She'd let them eat in peace; the extra weight in their bellies would make them easier to catch.

One eagle swept to the ground the moment she stepped outside the door again. The other bobbed its head in immediate paranoia: the first eagle might claim all the food. It dropped to the ground soon after, but neither bird approached the bowls. They stalked around gravely, full of suspicion.

She retreated to the pasture to watch from a distance. Her presence, coupled with the unusual appearance of the pet carrier, made the birds anxious. Glancing behind her at the sound of the gate, she saw Sherman swinging along through the frozen expanse of the pasture. He touched the brim of his hat to her, almost a salute, and came quietly to her side, arms folded, his eyes on the birds.

"You'd think they were looking at used cars," he said softly.

"They won't last long. I fasted them yesterday."

As if on cue, one of the birds decided to take the risk. It edged toward the bowls watchfully, intent on the meat, rushing the last few steps, and snatched greedily at the food.

Sherman sighed. "I always kind of expect them to be more dignified somehow."

"Rule one of eagledom," Roberta said. "Fill the belly."

The second eagle, pressured by the other's sudden courage, flapped heavily into the air but landed again at the far end of the barn, where it stood craning its neck for a view of the now-distant meal.

"Scaredy-cat," said Roberta. "Just come over here and eat."

"Maybe he doesn't like the menu today."

"They know something's up."

The second eagle hiked toward his bowl via an elaborate, circuitous route that used up most of the floor space of the flight barn. A few feet from the bowl, it paused, glaring with dark distrust in every direction before making a headlong dash for the food.

"I wonder if it relaxes them to eat," Sherman speculated.

Roberta gave him a skeptical glance. "Well, it does fill a certain void."

They waited until the birds had emptied the bowls, then approached the barn with the blanket. Both eagles flapped away from them but only one succeeded in becoming airborne. The other landed with a jolt and lumbered away on foot, still flapping.

"Him first," Roberta said, unfolding the blanket.

They herded the eagle into a corner and made short work of the capture. Roberta tossed the blanket low, like a matador's cape. Sherman secured it around the bird.

Carrying the eagle, he followed Roberta back outside. She pulled on leather gauntlets and took the bird from him, gripping it at the ankles. The eagle struggled but was soon calmed by its blindness.

"Do your stuff," she said. "Fast."

Sherman took a dog-eared spiral pad from the pocket of his jacket and flipped back through a dozen pages covered with his scrawl. He delicately rolled back the blanket to free the eagle's head. The bird blinked in the sudden light and wrestled vigorously against Roberta's grip. The curve of its beak looked savage but the bird's three-inch talons were its most dangerous weapons. Roberta held tight.

"They've been flying pretty regularly?" he asked. "They're not just sitting on their duffs in the barn?"

"They sit on their duffs most of the time. Eagles do. But they cruised around some."

Sherman had developed a slight paunch, Roberta noticed, a narrow roll of flesh above his belt. He was in his late twenties, and lean otherwise. He'd mentioned, once, obliquely, a divorce in Laramie. No children. And now he had a new, halfhearted career as a small-animal vet. Perhaps he was the one who ate for solace.

Sherman worked quickly, weighing the bird, checking its wings, feathers, legs, beak, eyes. He fingered the broad aluminum-alloy U.S. Fish and Wildlife band around the eagle's leg, double-checking its number against his records, though he had banded both eagles himself when the birds entered the hospital following Roberta's standard operating procedure. Roberta liked this efficiency, this insistence on following through. Sherman didn't chatter like volunteers she'd had in the past, and she'd never before had a vet so generous with his time. In all the years before this last one, when he had moved back to Casper from Laramie, she had called on a vet only rarely, for advice, amputations, and compound fractures. Most everything else she had managed by herself or with volunteers from the local Audubon club. Sherman had his faults. He was still too inexperienced to recognize the difference between saving the life of a bird and merely keeping it alive. Against her advice he'd refused to euthanize a horribly injured ferruginous hawk a few months before. With admirable skill he'd kept it from dying but it was totally blind. It had no life and no prospects. To his credit, he had respected her dis-agreement with him enough to take total charge of the bird, giving it a home at his clinic. And unless she asked him about it, he never mentioned the hawk at all.

Sherman finished his exam, touching the bird's breast to check its store of fat. "He looks good."

Roberta eased the bird gently into the pet carrier, covering the door with the blanket. In the darkness the eagle made a short, obligatory fuss.

The second bird had the worse temper of the two. It could not avoid capture, but as Sherman gently palpated the bone that had been broken, the bird fought hard, freeing the wing, and flapping with such force that Roberta grunted in her effort to hang on.

"I'd say they're raring to go, Bert."

He always muddied the *t* sound slightly when he said her name.

They rewrapped the bird and Sherman took it from her.

"Okay," Roberta said, picking up the pet carrier. "I'll just let this one walk out of the carrier. You can launch yours."

They walked up to the drive in front of the house, Roberta's preferred spot for releasing her patients. No power lines loomed close, and the view of the high prairie stretched unimpeded south to Hartsong mountain and Jackson Canyon in the mountain's west end.

She set the carrier down in the driveway. "You go first. It'll give mine some inspiration."

Sherman hesitated. "You did all the work, Bert. You should get to release both."

"I'm not so sentimental," she said. "Let's get him going."

She twirled the blanket away a final time and stepped aside as Sherman repositioned the bird on his fist. The eagle glared at the sky, hunching, as if shocked again by its expanse. It had grown accustomed to the raftered ceiling of the flight barn.

The bird flapped wildly, its wings brushing Sherman's head.

"Get it done," Roberta told him. She could see his lips moving: he was murmuring to the bird, offering up his best wishes for the journey.

He swept his arm forward and upward, suddenly, pitching the bird into the air. Its wings came out fully, six feet of feathered surprise, and the eagle flew in a straight line away from them, pumping deeply. It lost altitude, passing over the fence along the drive, its wing tips grazing the upper rail.

"Get up," muttered Roberta.

The eagle began a wide, slow turn, tail ruddering wildly, low to the ground.

Sherman had come to her side. "Give him a minute," he said, as if they had a choice. "He's a little shaky."

The bird gained altitude on the turn, despite its raggedness, and began another, heading northeast.

"My turn," Roberta said, squatting. She whisked the blanket from the pet carrier. Standing again behind it, she opened its gate. Some birds bolted from the carrier. This one cowered inside.

"Come on," she said to Sherman. "Let's give him some room."

They retreated to the front porch, where their dull clothes might blend with the wood of the house. "What's he waiting for?" Sherman said, worrying, just as they saw the back of a chocolate head.

Roberta liked this moment, that first recognition of freedom. They saw the whole of the dark and slender bird. It flourished its wings but did not fly.

"A pedestrian bird after all," Sherman said.

"He just can't believe it yet."

They waited. Roberta urged the eagle so softly that the sound of her voice could not have reached the bird. Even so, it seemed to. The eagle strolled out, purposeful now, looking around with a critical eye, spotting them immediately. Perturbed, it walked with a stiff and determined gait across the grass to the driveway, where it stopped dead.

"That's the one that got hit," Sherman said. "You bet he's going to look for traffic this time."

"Get going, get going," Roberta whispered.

The bird gazed intently at the sky.

"Gauging his flight coordinates now," said Sherman.

The first eagle had come full circle and was heading back across the river toward the mountain beyond. The second lifted its wings without extending them. Then, in a burst of gravel and dust from the driveway, it rose above them, setting off in a direct line for the path of the first, flapping so deeply that its wings seemed to meet beneath its belly.

Sherman gave a whoop. Roberta could feel him grinning at her. She watched the birds silently through her binoculars. A fragment of her dream returned, her father yelling at the larks. He waved his arm out the window wildly, as though brandishing a weapon. The birds flushed up before him in waves. *Fly, boys, fly!*

CHAPTER SIX

Florentina Drummond knew the sounds of Carl by heart. Even with the door to her studio shut she could tell exactly what he was doing and why. He was a man of loud habits and big feet, and the timbers of the old ranch house carried his vibrations to her through the soles of her shoes. He stomped around the kitchen, trying this drawer and that with too much violence. He wasn't fixing himself something to eat; he was looking for a utensil he could put to a purpose it wasn't designed for. It happened all the time. He called it making do. She'd say, *Carl, you're just too lazy to find the right tool, now go on, get out*. Like shooing chickens.

She tested a color on the small pad of paper at her side. Too thin and bright, too yellow. She added a little umber and tried again, rolling the tip of the brush on her tongue. She wanted an exact color, the winter gold of grass beaten down by the wind. Still too much yellow, it gave the color a summery look, changing the mood of the painting. She intended it as a winter landscape, mostly sky, with dry pasture in the foreground and a storm looming on one edge.

She paused, looking at the ceiling. Carl was coming toward the stairs. It took three strides from the kitchen. He wouldn't come up at first but would plant one foot on the bottom step and holler up at her. If she didn't answer, he would take them two at a time, seven resounding booms, and hit the door like a bull at a flimsy gate.

"Flo!"

He hadn't wiped his feet when he came in. She could hear the grit on his boot when he set it on the step. She didn't want to leave her painting.

"Hang on," she called, setting down her brush. She went to the door. "What, for heaven's sake?"

"Where the hell is my needle-nose pliers, anyway? I can't find a damn thing anymore."

"Your pliers never were in my kitchen, Carl. Don't you take one single piece of silverware."

He shifted irritably.

"It's probably stuck up on a shelf in the barn right where you left it," she said, "or you put it in a drawer somewhere."

"I didn't put it in any drawer."

"Then why were you going through my silverware, may I ask?"

Silence. A smile fluttered on her face. He hadn't stopped to think she could hear him slamming around in the kitchen.

"I got an outlet in the old lambing shed tore out," he said, as if that justified everything.

She lifted the gold watch on a chain around her neck. "Well, whatever you're doing, you'd better get it done. Hank will be here with the children in an hour or so."

He frowned. "An hour?"

"Well, for heaven's sake. I thought you'd be glad."

He mumbled, moving away. The kitchen door slammed behind him. She turned back into her studio. He could hardly string two words together in the grandkids' presence. They stared at him and he stared back, scratching at his chin a little, that was about the extent of it. But he looked forward to their visits like Christmas. Usually. The coyote attack had upset him. It was a constant war, always had been, always would be. She admired the animals for surviving it but Carl took everything personally, right down to the weather, like it was conscious of him and turned against him on purpose.

She sat again at her easel but didn't pick up the brush. Every time she came back to this painting she realized her heart wasn't in it. She could become absorbed by the action of painting itself, but when she stepped away or let her thoughts wander and then looked back at the canvas, she was always disappointed. She was forcing it, she decided, which never resulted in anything good.

She cleaned her brushes resignedly. There was no point in continuing to work on a painting she didn't care to look at. Better to spend the time until the children came doing a chore she'd put off too long.

She pulled a lined pad from the small desk under the windows. A blank sheet of paper was a worse enemy by far than a bad painting. But this was one of those hurdles she'd decided she would leap come hell or high water. If the gallery was willing to invest the money to publish a brochure about her, an old lady who only just started painting in time to die, she would give them whatever they asked for.

She fiddled with her bifocals, which were new. They made her head ache dully when she wore them for long.

A few paragraphs, Frances had said, with a nonchalance that didn't fool Flo at all. Frances never wrote anything. If she did, she'd have done this herself long ago. She'd have interviewed Flo, then written up the quotes in the scholarly style of art museum catalogs. Instead, she'd dumped it onto Flo, and Flo had delayed until the last minute. The brochures were at the printer's, waiting for her contribution before they could be printed for the opening next week.

She tapped her pencil on the first line. She shouldn't blame Frances. The Durbin Street Gallery was not a fancy place and Frances was the owner, not a curator. Besides, the town didn't expect scholarship of its artists. She'd just write something down, anything at all, and see what came of it. That's what she did with paintings, let her brush guide her. Writing couldn't be all that different, she thought. If you imagined each word as a brush stroke, maybe it would be easier.

Instead, she stared at the paintings around her, the few Frances had not yet collected for the show. Flo had chosen to display them because they were the ones she wanted most to keep, proof that they were her best. None depicted anything farther than fifty feet from her front door. The first showed the path from the side door to the barn. The packed-dirt path, scraggly with weeds bleached blond in the sun, led the eye through the open door. Nothing was visible in the barn but sunlight and dust and empty space and the red hood of the parked tractor gleaming like a dusty carnation.

The second was a self-portrait of sorts. It looked at the porch from in front of the house, up the gentle slope from the road. The roof had a ragged look to it, a gutter gaped at a corner, a screen curled on the door. A yellow stretch of high prairie behind the barn showed to the side. Her grandchildren played on the wooden steps with miniature sports cars. Luke launched them like rockets from the highest step. The painting caught one flashing in midair and Luke's mouth fallen open in fascination. Charlotte squatted beside him, her hands out as if to catch the car, but she didn't dare. In the deep shade of the porch, behind the mesh of the screen door, stood her own bulky form, dim and unreadable, watching.

The last, her favorite, looked from her kitchen door into the dining room. The remains of breakfast lay on the table, a half-jar of jelly, a crust of toast. The newspaper draped over an edge. On the far wall hung faded school portraits of Hank, looking stiff and slicked down as a cadaver. At the window, one arm resting over his head and against the frame, stood Carl. Beyond him was a stretch of fence, a smudge of winter pasture and the dim line of Hartsong mountain in the distance. His face did not show but the details of Carl were there: the long sleeves of a work shirt, the rounded heels of his boots, and the tired hunch along his spine.

She didn't know what to write about the paintings. She didn't even write letters anymore, except at Christmas, and they were limp and stale, obviously tortured out of her by duty. She had never written anything philosophical or about art. She didn't know if she even thought about art in words. She didn't know where the ideas for her paintings came from, they just came, she lived them. They all depicted real events but she couldn't tell if the truth had universality or a deep poetic meaning she should talk about. It seemed pretentious to do so. The one of Carl grew from watching him for the instant he struck that pose. That's all it had lasted, an instant. He got up from breakfast and stood at the window while she read her paper. She watched him from the kitchen and was so struck by the mood of it that when she went to her studio she shoved her current painting aside and began a sketch of Carl. She did not want to think about it too deeply. There would be something like sentimentality at the bottom of it, a trivial longing for something she couldn't have and didn't want to admit to.

She put the eraser lightly to her lips. You could reduce everything in life to trivialities if you didn't make the linkage between the trivial and the important. She was intimidated by the language of art criticism, intimidated by the thought that people who led larger lives might consider her work ordinary. She had led a small life, a narrow life, but if she felt disappointment sometimes, it was reflective, not bitter, which gave it some grace, she thought.

She turned to the paintings, allowing herself to love them again. Repositioning her pencil, she began to write.

"I was born here and I have lived here all my life. I like to paint what's around me. Maybe I'm staying too close to home, but it seems like I need to stare at something familiar before I see how strange it is."

She paused, smiling, a memory coming to her, long-lost; then wrote again with more confidence: "When I was a girl we used to play a game where we said our names over and over again until they lost their sense. Nobody's name sounded as strange as 'Flo' once you'd said it a hundred times."

When Hank pulled into the driveway with the kids, Carl was washing up in the bathroom upstairs. By the time he came down, Luke and Charlotte were already sitting cross-legged on the floor two feet from the television, their faces changing from one comic-book color to another as Luke zapped through the channels. Hank sat in the kitchen with his mother drinking coffee.

"I poured you some," Flo said as Carl came in.

He picked up the cup from the counter, glancing in Hank's direction without meeting his eyes. Hank restirred his coffee.

"You'd think they didn't have one of them damn things at home," Carl said.

Flo looked at him, befuddled.

Carl nodded his head toward the living room. "Fanning the channels like that. Their eyes'll fall back into their skulls."

Hank edged his coffee cup toward the center of the table and moved to get up, but slowly, as if he were weary. "They know better than that."

"No, no," said Flo. "I'll go tell them. You stay and drink your coffee."

Hank sat again, drawing his cup back toward him.

Carl sniffed, took a noisy sip of his coffee. "So you and Annie off again somewhere, huh?"

"Skiing down in the Snowies," Hank said. "A friend at the college has a cabin there."

That was the thing about Hank: he liked his five-day weeks. He talked about how much work he did after hours, grading essays and such up at the college, but he could put it all aside if something more inviting came along.

Hank shifted his chair around so he faced Carl. He looked skinnier than ever. Annie probably had him on another one of those feather-headed health food diets. He was pale as a toadstool too, from working under fluorescent light all the time.

"Mom told me about the coyotes," Hank said.

Carl nodded, uninterested.

"I'd help more around here, Dad, you know, if you'd just ask."

Carl swallowed another slug of coffee, hoping his anger would go down with it. As if he would beg a favor of his own son. If Hank couldn't see what needed to be done without being told, then he wasn't competent to do the work. It was that simple. And there he sat, tapping his coffee cup with a finger, like he had a tune in his head he was listening to, like he was as free of responsibility for the place as any stranger pulled in off the highway.

"What's keeping Flo?" Carl muttered, turning to the door.

CHAPTER SEVEN

Glen rolled a pair of wool socks into a ball and tucked them in the corner of his suitcase atop a stack of undershirts. By leaving on Sunday evening, he'd have to spend five nights away from home, in Cheyenne. He counted, to make sure: five pairs of boxers and socks, five dress shirts, five undershirts, five ties. He'd have to wear everything in the suitcase, one set a day, before he could come home again. Friday looked a long way off.

He zippered the suitcase and glanced at his watch. Roberta would be about done with the birds. His plane would leave in forty minutes. He picked up the phone and punched a single digit, the number for the big barn. It gave a double-tone ring, signaling an in-house call.

"You're ready?" she answered, her tone vaguely peremptory.

"About. How soon can you go?"

"Now."

"Okay. I'll come on out."

Years before, he had looked forward to each week of the annual legislative session. There'd even been a time when he'd considered running for governor, back before he realized that you could get more done behind the scenes. But now he simply felt tired. This final week, with its rounds of parties and receptions, lunch socials and dinner meetings, offered him little more than the challenge of staying awake and keeping away from the hors d'oeuvres. While it was true that most political work was done outside of the legislative chambers, between allies and over a drink, the ratio of mindless badinage to useful discussion was over-whelmingly on the side of mindlessness, and he was weary of it. He had considered retiring after his last term but had allowed himself to be pres-sured into running again by appeals to his sense of duty from colleagues and constituents alike.

There were other solid legislators, of course, but they were outnum-bered by the wastrels, some of whom had considerable seniority. The idea of relinquishing influence to them rankled. Roberta didn't see why it should matter to him. She said quit. But she put all politicians in one pot. *Demagogue* and *statesman* were synonyms to her. She wouldn't admit the critical differences: A statesman had to remember what he said, and the only way to do so was to tell the simple truth, which held a man to his principles, which, in turn, meant he had to have principles. He also had to remember what everyone else said in order to tie up the loose ends, a much more difficult task. Invert all that for the demagogue. The conviction that a political career could be powered on gassy charm alone seemed to be the only conviction such a man held.

Glen scolded himself for his cynicism. He hated cynicism. It was just a reflexive and hateful method of diversion used to conceal a dying spir-it. Some politicians employed it brilliantly, combining it with charisma. His role had been to listen to them as if they meant to make sense. They rewarded him with a bountiful supply of inadvertent solecisms and sophistries, fallacies and contradictions, tautologies and non sequiturs, the loose ends that he then tied up with statesmanlike diplomacy, some-times around their necks. But constant close association had sent him devolving in their direction. He found it more and more difficult to treat them with respect, and he dreaded their society. Every time he left the ranch, he left with more reluctance.

He slipped on his coat, leaving it unbuttoned, and took the suitcase from the bed. Another part of his unwillingness to leave was Roberta's readiness to have him gone, a readiness that verged sometimes, it seemed, on impatience. It wasn't his imagination. They had been married too many years for him to expect sentimental farewells from her or heartfelt confessions of how much she would miss him while he was gone. She'd never had much impulse toward sentimentality, and less toward confession. Even when they were first married and made love every time they had more than three minutes alone together, she had treated his departures on business trips with a coolness that had made him feel that he was the one being left behind. Her restraint went as deep as her passion and she had control of both even back then. Jeremiah had caught them once easing their way out of the pine closet when they were supposed to have been working on the accounts. As ranch manager, Glen had cultivated and valued the old man's respect. Spending part of a workday afternoon bending Jeremiah's daughter over Jeremiah's chair in Jeremiah's office didn't seem calculated to preserve it. But Roberta was unfazed. She looked Jeremiah in the eye with faint derision, as if she suspected he had been watching through the keyhole, then walked past him, out the front door, and let the screen smack shut behind her. Jeremiah, pulling at his long jaw, gave Glen a frank stare and said, "I see you opened the month with a profit."

Her readiness to have him gone had its roots in the years just before Jeremiah's death. She had begun to lose interest in the Uncle John then, and after her father died she began to make changes. It had been her idea to trim the operation, to scale back the ranch, to sell down the herd. He fought the trend, though he agreed with her overt rationale. Ranching was a difficult, risky business. It made little sense to work so hard and risk so much in ranching when the mineral investments they'd made in recent years had paid off so well. Oil and gas exploration was risky, too, but someone else did the work once you put your money down. You chose your play, paid your share, and waited for the royalty checks to come in. When you ranched, you ranched twenty-four hours a day, every day of the year. You gave everything up to it. Physically and mentally, you handed yourself over. You gave up your body, and you gave up your mind on all levels, conscious and unconscious, right down through every Greek-lettered level of sleep. You didn't just live on a ranch; ranching inhabited you.

But her real reasons for closing down the place as a cattle ranch hadn't been economic. Nor had she grown suddenly fearful of the physical toll a lifetime of hard work would exact; she still spent long hours on short sleep doing hard physical work for her hospital. Simply put, she had shut the place down for the birds.

He doubted that even Roberta had understood the full portent of her actions then. He could place her attitude change exactly. They had gone to California together once, years before, when Muirie was a child. He had come home again in a few days, but she had stayed a month. The length of the visit was out of character for her. She and Ellen had never been close, so it wasn't that Roberta had stayed for the sake of visiting with her sister. Nor had she stayed to help around the house. Ellen and Hugh had money; Ellen headed a family counseling center, and Hugh was a founding partner in a large law firm. They had a nanny for Muirie, a housekeeper who cooked, and a gardener who took care of their small, lush hillside estate. Roberta had spent her time dragging Muirie up and down the northern California beaches to look at birds. That's when this fixation had started.

Over the years since, she had come to reject almost everything about their old life together. The welfare of wild birds became more important than the welfare of the cattle had ever been. He had adjusted as well as he could by pursuing his interest in politics, something he'd never had time for previously. Roberta disapproved from the start, but his energies needed a consuming purpose just as hers did. She had done more than put a hawk in the stall where his cutting horse used to be; she had gradually ended their partnership in the operation of the Uncle John. It had been a partnership based on a joint love of the place, a partnership that had permeated their lives, and when she had fallen out of love with the ranch, some of her love for him had gone with it.

He heard the pickup. She had pulled up in front of the house to save him the walk over to the big barn or to get him out of the way all that much quicker, depending on how he chose to interpret things. He walked slowly through the house, relishing its comfortable familiarity, and hesitated on the front porch to judge the weather for his flight to Cheyenne. High overcast, no wind. But he was also studying the ranch itself, fixing it in his mind, mourning it consciously. Outside, the place still looked genuine enough: the buildings, the setting, the low-slung, rambling house, the willow furniture on the porch, the odd piece of machinery sitting around in the pastures. But that was superficial. Beneath it was a look of tidy abandonment, of things too much in order, like a diorama of a ranch in a museum. THIS IS THE WAY THINGS USED TO BE. That's what the plaque would read. But it was a lie. This wasn't the way things used to be. They used to be hectic to the point of bone-weariness—and haphazard, unpredictable. Life used to be tangible; it used to get under his fingernails, grind into his skin, sting his eyes, dull his hair, stain his clothes. It used to smell of afterbirth and fresh shit, of sweaty leather, of salt and ammonia and alkali, of gravel dust, of bag balm. Life used to hurt, physically; muscles twitched from exhaustion, were wrenched and bruised and torn and toughened. Life used to hurt, and it used to smell. It used to stink something wonderful.

Roberta threw the passenger-side door open. *Come on, Glen.*

He stepped off the porch.

CHAPTER EIGHT

Locked in its fifth month of deep freeze, the landscape of the Uncle John looked no different than it had in early November and would continue to look for weeks to come: cold and spare and empty. And yet great horned owls were nesting in the groves of leafless cottonwoods down along the Platte. In the marshy areas where the creek joined the river, brash male redwings staked out provinces among the wind-beaten cattails, a month in advance of their females, and killdeer raced in headlong flight over the deserted pastures of the ranch, crying out their own names in penetrating voices: Kill-*deer*! Kill-*deer*! However wintry the weather, it was spring and Roberta had no time to waste.

She sat at the small, built-in desk in the workroom of the big barn working up a schedule of priorities for the coming weeks. Events, as always, would render it useless but she made one anyway as a method of girding herself mentally for spring, as if for war. The analogy was apt, she thought. By the peak of spring migration in mid-May, the hospital would resemble a M.A.S.H. unit, short on staff and supplies, long on patients. She never said no, never closed her doors. Although she called the place a raptor rehabilitation center, when it came to migration a one-eighth-ounce hummingbird was as welcome as a fifteen-pound goose. She took them all in, victims of every evil fate that could befall them, natural and man-made, from diseases to blizzards to deadly collisions with plate glass windows, parceling out her care to those that had the best chance of a full recovery.

She thumbed her appointment calendar. The local elementary schools rediscovered the hospital each spring. She could plan on more than a dozen classes, from kindergarten up. The first group of the season came next week. Also a few garden and bridge clubs, several Scout troops, and an ornithology class from the college. She took her show on the road too, if requested, to school assemblies, Scouting jamborees, anything where kids were involved. The one purely positive aspect of the hospital was its role as a teaching facility for children. If she got to kids young enough, there was a chance that they would accept what she said as truth. Between six and eight was the prime age, when her counterindoc- trination had a chance of convincing them that the perpetual war ranch- ers waged against wildlife wasn't right or necessary. Older than that, they began to wonder about the scheme of things and to see humans at the center. Birds became expendable, or exploitable things of value. *Make him do something.* She heard it all the time from ten-year-olds, mostly boys, greedy for entertainment and impatient with mere beauty. They wanted action from her tour birds, a small group of permanently injured, unreleasable raptors she kept in the big barn as educational visual aids. During these tours she put her birds on freestanding perches, keeping the children behind a line she drew with her foot in the gravel of the barn floor; otherwise they would wave their arms, lunge at the birds, throw wads of paper, anything to get the birds to move, preferably to startle. These were the same kids who went away unimpressed, who later, in an extension of the same desire but with imperfect skill, loaded a shotgun and took potshots at hawks on telephone poles. Death was bad enough but more often they maimed the birds, which was worse. They blew away wings, feet, legs, tails, beaks, feathers, freedom.

She put the calendar in the drawer by the phone. She would have help this spring with the preparation for the incoming wounded. A crew from the local Audubon group had offered to spring-clean the big barn for her. The plans for that had to be finalized and carried out within the week. That meant one day given over to supervising volunteers while they swept out stalls, repaired netting, rehung hinges, doors, and shelving, built new perches, rearranged the contents of drawers and cabinets, washed windows, defrosted the big freezer, and any number of other, critical, miscellaneous chores. Muirie might help with some of the work, depending on how long she stayed. She had been good with the birds before—had been a natural with them, in fact—but the hospital had been tiny then. There was no guarantee Muirie would wish to be involved at all.

In the first year or so after her last visit, Muirie had written regularly, long, adolescent letters enthusiastically detailing all the expanding plans for her life. The flow had petered out to a trickle of postcards by the end of high school, each card affording only enough space, given Muirie's loose handwriting, to explain why she hadn't written a "real" letter: exams, a new boyfriend, a job. When she graduated from college, she had sent an eight-by-ten photograph of herself, a tony portrait with colors so bright they seemed to throb. Roberta had thought of her as a flattering amalgam of both parents when she was younger, with the shadow of the Sheas falling more strongly on her face. She had Hugh's ivory skin and the same straight dark brow, which gave her a look of contemplation that was, except for her smile, almost solemn. Her smiles had been quick and uncalculated. Roberta had watched closely over their summers together, waiting for Ellen's impact to hit. The second summer after Jeremiah's death, when Muirie was fifteen, she had still seemed wholly herself, a child of good judgment and warm spirit, unaffected by her mother's icy authority. But the photograph showed that Ellen had gotten to her in the years since. Pulling it from the envelope, Roberta had seen only her sister. There was the same smug and smoothly sculpted face, the smile carved out of stone, the same square set of the shoulders, a posture Ellen assumed with conscious design to intimidate, and the same stubborn, veiled cast to the eyes. Muirie had sent only one or two postcards in the last year and a newsy Christmas card that Roberta had thrown straight into the fireplace rather than set on the mantel. For a long time after Muirie had stopped coming, the thought of her had filled Roberta with disappointment and regret. She'd tamped the feelings down over the years but they were resurfacing now, only a little less strong than before.

She consulted her patient list. Two great horned owls, two red-tails, and one golden eagle that had spent the winter at the hospital would be ready for release soon, freeing up their cages for spring arrivals. A third red-tail that had flown into a barbed-wire fence, breaking one wing tip, would need a foster home. Although the injury had not been serious and had healed completely, the hawk would not fly. Roberta had tried every method she knew to renew the bird's confidence, even putting it into a large flight cage adjacent to Jasper, Roberta's resident Swainson's hawk, in the hopes the red-tail would regain its nerve by watching another bird fly. Jasper had been tame-raised and then abandoned, and so was unreleasable, having never learned the critical basics: fear of humans and how to hunt. But he was a spirited and healthy hawk, a good teacher by vigorous example for younger or less confident birds. The red-tail, however, proved itself perverse. It had crouched stubbornly on the floor of the flight cage, the healed wing drooping slightly at its side, as earthbound as Roberta herself. In time it might learn to fly again, but she had neither room for it here nor the time to coach it into the air. It would have to go elsewhere, to a nature center or a larger rehab facility. That meant making multiple phone calls and writing conciliatory, pleading letters, neither of which she enjoyed, with no guarantee of success. Placing a large bird, especially a common bird like a red-tail, took patience and diplomacy, two character traits she had in short supply. That was Glen's specialty. But he wouldn't use his talents on behalf of her birds.

He'd been melancholy on the way to the airport. She often found his moods oppressive now. The sharp edge of energy and impulse he'd had as a young man, the virtue that had driven him to apply for a job at the Uncle John in the first place, had withered away. He existed now in the safe little world of good-old-boy politics, where he was one of the best of the boys, respected by his peers, consulted on all matters of import, guaranteed to give a thoughtful, considered, conservative opinion. But at twenty-five, knowing nothing about cattle, having never worked on a ranch, he had applied directly to Jeremiah one afternoon for a job as ranch manager. He had walked onto the ranch with all the confidence of a proprietor, a bushy-haired young sucker who didn't know one end of a cow from the other. He'd come toward the end of the day, when several of the cowhands were hanging around the house waiting for supper,

Roberta among them. They fell silent as he passed, and listened in open-mouthed surprise as he told Jeremiah in a firm voice why he had marched onto his property uninvited.

"I'd like to apply for a job with you, Mr. Shea."

One of Jeremiah's cheeks twitched. "A job? Now what job would that be?"

Glen spoke right up. "As ranch manager. I've heard you'd like to make some changes at the Uncle John."

It was true, vaguely. Roberta's mother had died in a car wreck on an icy highway five months before. Jeremiah's grief had expressed itself in restless commotion and irritability, and he had told some of his friends over numerous beers that he was sick of ranching and needed a change. This ambiguous news had gotten out, and Glen Thompkins saw in it, somehow, his opportunity.

The hands, dressed in their chewed-up boots and grimy old jeans, glanced at each other, insolent grins flickering to life. Everyone knew the Thompkins family. Glen had grown up in town in one of the big old houses on Grant Street. He'd gone to some hoity-toity West Coast college, Stanford or somewhere like that, funded by his oilman father, who spent most of his time out-of-state, too, in Denver. The son was proving himself to be an outsider of the worst sort: one who pretended to belong. He apparently gave no weight to the fact that the Uncle John had never had a manager other than Jeremiah and his father before him or that any human being on the place, including the part-time cook, who was sixty-two and minus three fingers and four toes, or even one of the dogs, take your pick, was better qualified for such a position than he was. The only thing you could say in his favor was that he'd come bareheaded, wearing regular street shoes. Applying for a nonexistent job he didn't qualify for was bold enough. Laying claim to hat and boots would have gone beyond toleration.

The men made themselves comfortable, leaning on the fence, slouching against the wall of the bunkhouse. Roberta coiled a lead rope slowly in her hands. This would be delicious. The old man didn't put up with nonsense from anyone. They knew exactly what he'd do: He'd listen awhile, letting Glen think he had a foot in the door, when Jeremiah was actually just waiting for the ridiculousness of the situation to ripen like a piece of fruit. Then he'd pluck it with a single swipe of a sentence, a masterfully articulated piece of squelch-work that would make Glen Thompkins wish he could dissipate like a cloud into the thin, dry air of the evening.

They waited.

Jeremiah fingered his mustache, eyeing Glen from head to toe. "Well," he said. "Why don't you come on inside for a bit?"

Jeremiah held the screen door open. Glen passed through and closed it behind him, shooting a glance at his audience that hesitated on Roberta, not a cocky glance at all, but one that wondered, amused, at their surprise.

No one said a word. On the highway a quarter-mile south, a big rig geared down for the rise toward Red Butte. The hands looked to Roberta, stunned. She stared back, the lead rope unrolling into the dust. "Well I'll be damned," she said.

By evening, Glen had nailed down the job. He got it by listening intently as Jeremiah raged about unfair markets, interest rates, bovine diseases, government interference, and the cussedness of the weather. Then he responded, with bold intelligence, about the future of ranching. He left all Jeremiah's day-to-day concerns behind and talked about diversification and change. He told Jeremiah that the future of Wyoming was in its mineral wealth; that the Uncle John should become a mineral company as well as a livestock enterprise, expanding its interests into the oil and gas and coal-rich regions of the Powder River basin to the north. He had earned degrees in both business and law, and had even worked in the oil patch for a year. He convinced Jeremiah that he knew how to proceed, how to judge the value of oil plays, contracts, land deals, and how to mold a business into its most efficient shape—any business, ranching included. He was young and tireless. If Jeremiah would create the job, he was the man to fill it.

It was the right moment precisely to give Jeremiah such a vision. Suddenly, he wanted the future as much as he wanted his next breath; he wanted lungfuls of it. He struck a deal with Glen: a one-year trial, an hourly wage, rather low, and a spot in the bunkhouse, no more. He would start on Monday.

Roberta had never seen anyone do so much work with so little fuss as Glen; Jeremiah doing nothing raised a cloud of dust you could see in the next county. Glen was a machine. It didn't matter that he knew nothing about cattle; he found out. He read voluminously, everything from the newsletter of the Cow Belles to *Scientific American*. He learned to ride and rope passably; he pulled a calf the first week on the job; he was an inventive mechanic and diagnosed problems by listening to engines with his eyes shut. The hands began, grudgingly, to reassess the worthiness of higher education, at least as far as it applied to mechanical devices. Jeremiah let Glen have his head. He talked to anyone, asked endless questions, and remained indifferent to his cool reception in the ranching community. The coolness didn't last. It was replaced by frank admiration of his energy. He had a deep-down assurance in him; he never forgot anything, and he never failed to weave new information into the whole. Within months, the surprise became disgruntled respect. Glen could see the big picture. The Big Picture. He went beyond them all, rose above their little world of ranching and saw its context. They were behind the times. Diversification meant revolution. You needed more than better bloodlines. You wanted quick methods of marketing. You needed to push your roots outward; times were changing. There were vegetarians out there, if you could believe it, gaining proponents. There was talk of saturated fat and there was cheap beef south of the border. You wanted to look deeper; this was a rich state. Oil, gas, and coal to fuel the entire country for a thousand years. Literally. Imagine it. The grass was just the frosting. Beneath it was the cake of good fortune.

The first year came and went, the trial period all but forgotten in a headlong metamorphosis of the Uncle John into a modern land and live-stock company. Glen never hesitated. He had a passion for taking action that seemed to derive not from any usual personal goal of wealth or importance but from an unalloyed fascination with the mental and physical challenges of the business. It was contagious. The improvement of the ranch became Roberta's cause, too. The Uncle John could not be the biggest, but it could be the best, the most diverse. They needed capital. They got it, slowly at first, from mineral investments throughout the state and in Montana and Colorado. Glen did most of the prospect evaluation himself, poring over reservoir maps and electric logs, picking tops, reviewing production records. Then he presented his findings to Jeremiah with deference and tranquil self-control. Roberta, home from her freshman year at Laramie two weekends a month, set up files and kept production records for each well and field. She kept track of royalty payments and rental fees, learned to review scout reports and make sense of drilling jargon, fielded phone calls from potential partners. Only Ellen remained uninvolved, irritated from the first that Jeremiah had hired a non–family member to run the ranch and outraged that Glen had turned out to be competent. She was working on her master's in clinical psychology at Berkeley and came home occasionally, she told Roberta, to see some textbook personality disorders firsthand. She studied the family as if she were no longer a member of it herself. Roberta's response was a squinched smile. Jeremiah bore her presence pacifically. Glen, with the best strategy of all, stayed completely out of her way. It was another of his talents, one he had honed in recent years: knowing when and how to say absolutely nothing.

Roberta studied the dull tip of her pencil. Glen had chosen to be silent on the way to the airport the other day too, a brand of silence she knew exactly how to interpret. He meant it to illustrate how seriously he took his governmental responsibilities in the final days of the annual session. She didn't believe that the gutless issues the Wyoming legislature considered were so weighty, but perhaps he had to believe they were. As long as he let himself be seduced into doing the job, he had to convince himself of its value. Between themselves, they rarely discussed politics. But he always voiced his opinions to anyone who asked. And everyone asked, except Roberta.

She tapped the pencil on the desktop. She had seen no balds on the way home from the airport. But many had left for Canada by this time. She wondered if she had waited too long to release the two immatures. Young birds were inexperienced, even stupid, and months spent in captivity, despite her care to keep them as wild as possible, would have left them a little dazzled with their freedom.

CHAPTER NINE

The lamb carcass was gone.

Carl trudged to the top of the rise where it had been. Not a scrap of it left. The rib of prairie had become anonymous again, marked only by a tuft of fleece snagged in the twiggy remains of a weed, and a fudge-colored stain on the ground. He should have staked them, he knew, but he had been in a hurry, too much of a hurry.

He studied the edges of the valley. Chances were the coyotes would have gone a good long ways before they felt the poison. The pains would have begun in the belly, perhaps with a cramp of violent indigestion. They would have started loping, trying to outrun it. Maybe miles. The chances of finding one were almost nil, but he'd cruise the valley anyway, just to make sure, and to check out the ewe as well.

He returned to his truck and headed west along the road, a faint set of ruts worn into the hummocky sage. It was a job for sharp eyes, and his own watered these days whenever he tried to concentrate on something in the distance. The sheep drifted south, away from the path of his truck. He made a slow, wide turn beyond them and curved back east toward Hartsong. Its warmer southern face was delineated with dark pine, bare aspen, and the gray and dun rockfall of the draws. The aspen wouldn't green up until May on the other side of the blizzard season. The most dangerous weather of the year still lay ahead.

He stiffened at the sudden scent of musk. His eyes smarted, moistening. Fox, he guessed. He slowed the truck to a halt. The open meadows on Hartsong and Sacajawea were full of them. You saw them often on the road, dead and alive, and heard their yappy, squally voices lifting in the air. He let the truck idle, searching along the front of the mountain, then decided to get out, to walk a bit. He killed the ignition, left the door open, strode toward the rocks of a narrow draw. He knew he was close, but there was no telling which direction he should go by the smell; it was everywhere at once.

He paced diligently, eyes searching the ground, hands jammed in his jacket pockets. Just as his nose had adjusted to the stink so that he could no longer smell it, he saw the fox's brush. The animal lay, torn limb from limb, at the bottom of the draw, its tail and narrow head the only untouched part of its body. He squatted beside it. A fresh kill, certainly, but it didn't look like a coyote's. The meat looked snipped, gouged, the fur torn away in strips. He glanced up at the pines on the ridge. A raven sat back from clear view, in the screen of branches, waiting. He was surprised it didn't scold him, caw at him in its gravelly voice. He studied the soil closely. It was damp from the recent snowmelt but hard-packed. He couldn't see much. Scratches.

"Damn," he said softly, pulling on his gloves. If coyotes hadn't killed it, the poison probably had. A collateral kill. It happened. There were other possibilities: the fox could have been injured somehow, by a trap or someone's bad shot, or it could have been sick and it died here where the ravens had found it. He fingered each of the legs quickly, ran a thumb across the thick-furred paws. No chew marks, no breaks; it hadn't been a trap. And he could find no evidence of a bullet wound, though he couldn't be sure. He cursed again softly. The conservative conclusion was that fox had gotten to the lamb. And whatever had eaten the fox had gotten a good dose of poison, too.

He glanced up at the vigilant raven. "Git!" he yelled, waving his arms. He lurched to his feet. "Git!"

It didn't move. And it sat, he noticed, at a tipsy angle against the trunk of the tree. He scrubbed at the moisture in his eyes. It was hard to focus.

He blinked fiercely, chin thrust forward in concentration. It was a big bird. Too damn big. And not so black as he had thought. Browner, broader at the shoulder.

He crashed forward to the lip of the draw, studying the short slope above him. The climb wasn't far, just across the tumble of rock debris. Wary of his back, he began climbing, walking his hands over the rocks, feeling his way. Limestone talus cascaded over his hands and forearms, clinked under his boots. He halted, breathing too fast, sucking air, and felt the gravel shift beneath his soles, the sharp crack of rock against rock, then silence. A few more yards of careful steps. He looked above him, calculating his hand- and footholds, and stepped carefully, edging the toe of his boot into the rock, giving it his weight slowly. He tested a root at the top, hugging tight to the thin soil, wedged into the rock.

Sweating in the cold air, he eased over the top and straightened up cautiously, fearing the ache in his spine. He would pay for this later. The bird hadn't moved. He trudged to the base of the pine. From thirty feet below, in the dimness of the trees, it was less recognizable, its configuration lost in the branches. He hit the trunk with the heel of his hand, a gentle vibration in the four-inch diameter of wood, and circled the trunk, searching for a better view. Grabbing a lower branch, he tugged at it vigorously, rocking the tree slightly. The lower branches swayed, teetering the bird like a bowling pin. It fell forward slowly, as if through glycerin, into the cold swish of needles, and landed in a skeleton of sage.

Carl let go of the branch. It whipped into the air, fanning his face with the sharp scent of pitch. He took a breath, wincing. His shoulder hurt; his knee was skinned through his jeans. He took a step forward. The bird's mouth was half-open, described by the savage curve of the beak. An eagle. He set his teeth, hissing. He peered around, fearful of witnesses, though he knew there were none—there was no one around for miles—and saw another dark shape suspended high in a densely interlocking net of branches, farther back in the cover of trees. Another one. Now he knew what they meant by spread-eagled: this one had died in convulsions, it looked like—wings out, neck arced far forward. The branches had broken its fall.

Two of them. Two he could see straight off. A bunch more spent the winter in the canyon, just over the ridge and west, only a minute away by air.

The second bird was closer to the ground, but it was going to take some work to get it to fall, to tease it loose. He sure as hell couldn't shimmy up there after it.

He stepped closer to the bird on the ground, crouched over it, touched its brown flecked plumage with a forefinger, pressed into the flesh. Cold. There were hardly any white feathers on this one. Perhaps it wasn't one of Roberta Shea's balds. The differences were confusing. Until balds were several years old they didn't have a white head and tail and looked identical to goldens, at least to his eye. The balds were considered scarce but there were plenty of goldens around, thousands. Roberta herself called them common. This could even be a plain old hawk, he thought, although it was too much to hope for. It was too big, too bulky, and if he considered the proximity to the canyon, it had to be an eagle. Two dead eagles.

His gaze shifted toward Jackson Canyon. There might be more in there. This one wore a band around one ankle, engraved with an identification number. He fingered the cold metal. You were supposed to notify the Fish and Wildlife when you found one, so they could trace the bird's movements and piece together a picture of how it lived—and died.

He found a downed pine branch that had torn loose at the trunk, leaving a heavy curl of bark at the end. He hooked it around the tallest branches he could reach, pulling down like a bell ringer. It rained dead needles and bark, a scattering of granular snow. He closed his eyes, flexing his knees, putting his weight into the task. The eagle plummeted, crashing through the branches in its final stoop, and thumped softly into the needle-cushioned rock of the slope.

It had been a long time since he'd picked up a dead eagle. He had shot buzzards in the old days—like everybody else—hawks, eagles, vultures. But not much lately; Flo didn't like it. These felt incredibly light for their size, almost weightless, as if they were dried out. But they were freshly dead. The tissues of the mouth, around the sunken eyes, were still bright, the colors clean.

The frozen, outstretched wings of the second bird would not fold down flat against the body. Carl tucked the eagles under his arms awkwardly, like firewood. Where the slope fell to the valley, he halted, measuring the distance to the truck, plotting his descent. But the eagles were dead; why should he carry them down? Exasperated, he hurled them one at a time, in a sweeping, underhand toss, out into the sunlit valley.

He stumped back down into the draw, his back tweaking hard with every step. He pressed a palm to his lower spine. He'd overdone the poison, gotten impatient, hadn't thought the thing through. It was a stupid mistake but one anyone could understand. Any rancher, that is. But ranchers didn't go into the canyon much, so if there were dead birds to be found there, it wasn't likely to be a rancher who would find them. The canyon was state land, set aside partly because the eagles hid out there in the winter. Grazing wasn't allowed, as it had been years before on the narrow canyon floor, and no one likely to be wandering around in there would be the type to understand: skiers, hikers, Girl Scouts from the camp on the mountain. He'd have to check the place out himself. Prosecution for killing eagles could mean big fines and the cancellation of his lease on the land. Maybe even prison. Convictions were rare but most ranchers didn't live next door to an ex-rancher bird maniac. And there was nothing worse than a convert.

He cursed at the thought of going into the canyon, wanting to talk himself out of feeling it was necessary. Those big birds, though, they ate carrion when they could; he'd seen them plenty of times, and they'd fly back to wherever they felt safe afterward, to rest. Which meant the canyon. They could have got to the carcasses, the fox, a coyote, or anything else that had eaten of that poison.

He retrieved the dead eagles and put both in an empty feed sack, the remains of the fox in another, rolled them tightly shut, then tucked them into the floor space of the passenger side of the cab and drove, charged with adrenaline, to the site where he'd placed the ewe. She'd been hit, too. He swung her body into the bed of the truck, turning it over so that the wounds didn't show. He had nothing left to cover her with. Now for the canyon.

But the hopelessness of it began to dawn on him as he turned onto the road up to the mouth. The canyon plunged deep into the mountain, and he didn't know where inside it the eagles might be. In the trees in a clump? Or scattered out over the whole distance? And the road stopped short of the mouth: he couldn't drive in, he'd have to slog on foot through the snow, which would be deep, since the sun wouldn't have penetrated far this early in the year. He'd sink up to his hips, giving himself a heart attack probably, maybe to find nothing.

The mouth lay above him, narrow and dark in the northern shadow of the mountain. His luck didn't tend to be good. If it was bad this time, there were dead eagles in there. Some would fall to the ground and be buried until late spring by the next snows. If there were some in the trees, they'd decay fast come warmer weather. The chances they'd be found were small. But even if someone did happen to find them, there'd be no evidence to link him to their deaths. The lamb carcass was gone, he had the fox, the two eagles, and the ewe in his possession, and most of the land around the mountain was government land, leased to several ranchers for grazing. There was no reason to suspect Carl Drummond more than anyone else.

Dusk had soaked the sky with underwater gray by the time he turned into the drive at home. The lights were on in the kitchen. Forty minutes to supper. It wasn't much time to chip out a grave in the frozen ground, but he didn't have time to burn them. That would draw Flo's attention anyway.

Another possibility occurred to him. He pulled to the far end of the barn, away from the house, and parked next to the muck pile in the pasture. Flo might wonder why he hadn't parked in his normal spot, but let her wonder; she didn't have to know every little thing. The top layers of the pile froze, but lower down the ammonia and rot kept it soft. The ground beneath it would be warmer, too. He could bury them there.

Even so, the digging was hard. The ground sloped away from the barn so that melting snow drained quickly and left the soil dry. A few inches below the muck pile, the richer topsoil gave way to ash-colored bentonite, a clayey hard pack he chunked away with the shovel. He stopped to take off his jacket, to wipe his forehead with a handkerchief. A shallow indentation would have to do. He threw down the shovel and opened the door of the truck.

He pushed the ewe in first, then the fox, bag and all. The bag containing the eagles he opened, gingerly, hating the sight. The leg band on the one would have to come off. If the birds, by some fluke, were ever found, they would be evidence enough against him; he didn't want the band as additional proof of his decision to ignore the law.

He hesitated, thinking. There was a market in eagle parts. Down in New Mexico or somewhere. Feathers, claws, good prices, he'd heard.

You had to be careful who you asked but he knew some men who might be able to point him in the right direction. But no: he couldn't risk it. And he had to do something with these birds right now.

With a twist of his needle-nose pliers, the band warped open and fell from the reptilian leg into his palm. He closed his fist over it and dropped it in his jacket pocket, reclosed the bag, and fitted it next to the other in the ground. It would take only a few more minutes to cover it all up again. He would make it in time for supper.

He turned to look at the mountain, at the long stretch of pine at the ridge line. It had to be a first, he thought: he was actually wishing for a big storm, for a blizzard that would fill up Jackson Canyon and keep it filled until late into spring.

CHAPTER TEN

As the plane climbed eastward over the ramp of the high Sierra, Muirie kept her eye on the land below, watching as blasts of mirrored sunlight exploded up from a succession of tiny, alpine lakes.

The day had started with a niggling sense of the ominous. She'd stumbled to the front door and flapped the paper open to the weather map to check developments over the Rockies, and found, to her surprise, a menacing gray mass of snowflakes obscuring southern Wyoming and northern Colorado. The day before, the graphics had shown the sky there to be clear. The sight had waked her up so thoroughly she hadn't needed a second cup of coffee. How could a storm like that develop in twenty-four hours? She hated flying in storms.

Then the phone had rung. Her mother, of course, calling to say good-bye ostensibly, the real reason being to display again her deeper understanding of Muirie's motivations for leaving. She always had deeper understandings to display.

It smacks of escape, you know.

Smacks: a warhead of a word with the impact of a slap and wide connotations of bad character, weak will, and overall failure. Its deployment triggered all the weapons in Muirie's own armory.

But that's just what her mother wanted, to seek and destroy; she had a faultless aim. This time, Muirie deflected the attack. By agreeing. Ellen was right, Muirie was escaping. Escape was the whole point of going, to find an empty place and start over again, clean. She had come of age once, searching, in her adolescence, as everybody did, for separation and identity. She'd achieved separation in spades, at least by conventional measures: she had a good education, a promising talent, an independent lifestyle, all those obituary-style phrases people passed around. But now she quibbled with the standards. In reality, the claim of total indepen-dence merely camouflaged isolation, and a claim of strong identity sig-naled the absolute lack of one. These things seemed clear.

"It's about time I escaped," she had said to her mother.

Now that she was airborne, even the thought of the storm ahead failed to unnerve her. A snowstorm was fine news. She liked everything about it, including the sudden thump of her heart at the thought of the final leg of the trip to Casper, a one-hour, low-level flight along the Front Range north from Denver in a commuter plane half the size of a city bus—in a snowstorm. Ha. Nothing was going to spoil her departure, least of all a little bossy weather. She downright welcomed this storm.

She pulled her focus inside the plane, studying the layer of dust that adhered to her window, a corona of pink in the sunshine. It was the dust of civilization, a linty, greasy dust from pillowcases and upholstery and winter coats, the dust of skin desiccated in tanning booths and hair brushed and blown and glued into place, of nails shaped and filed and varnished into claws. She looked beyond it again to the summit of the Sierra, and Mono Lake beyond, watching California fall away from her. She could feel it fall away from her, like an anchor axed from a chain. It felt good, a weight off, an expectation rising, and she was floating into Nevada, emptying out where there was plenty of empty room. There was nothing to be greedy about down there, nothing to make her think of column inches and ad lines and who got where first at what profit. Nothing. Not a thing of any kind—only a gray limitless sky and camel-colored grasslands veined with snow, only endless bare mountains and the flat desolation of the plains between.

She hadn't brought much with her: a light suitcase, a few shirts and a couple of pairs of jeans, her old boots, a single dress, and a teeth-gritting determination to reclaim the tough mental heritage of the Sheas. Her mother had rejected it completely, opting instead to go pro with her angst, and she hadn't had a single non-Ellen-centered thought in twenty years. Muirie's goal was to learn to aim her mind out the window and keep it there, on something besides herself. Her grandfather had lived that way, straight-ahead, his thoughts traveling outward, his actions following right behind. Roberta was like that, too, and so was she, at heart. Growing up in California had stunted her—growing up as Ellen's daughter had delayed her development—but she recognized her strong points. She made no excuses for herself. She fought doubt and defeatism—all those miserable little whisperings of *I can't*—with a single, deadly phrase, snarled like a gangster: *Oh yeah? Who says?* It was elemental. It got right to the point. It didn't fool around with justifications and excuses and analyses. She was her own hired gun, taking aim.

She had a second phrase she hauled out of the holster when caution threatened, when there was no reason not to go forward but she wasn't going forward anyway, when the craven little voices whined, *You shouldn't-shouldn't-shouldn't*. She replied, in a tone that was reasonable at first, *Why not?*—accompanied by a shrug and a look of mild bafflement and pity—because there was rarely any good reason why not. It was the kind of question that rendered any answer trivial; you incriminated yourself no matter what you said. Sometimes she had to jab the phrase a little, punch it up to a threat. After all, she wasn't talking about insignificant decisions, like whether to have the chocolate torte. Not anymore. She was talking about *Why not quit? Why not leave? Why not change everything?*

It was, at bottom, the most hopeful of questions. She felt determination, and the question crackled with it. It sparked and zapped and sizzled. She liked it, liked its impetuosity. She was impatient with cowardice and had dispatched her own. She had the potential, she thought, to make a damn good Shea.

Thirty thousand feet over central Utah, the sonorous voice of the jet engines interwove with her own internal hum, allowing her to relax. Here it was easier to float free of her usual judgments, curling around the earth, held in orbit by thoughts of its beauty. She could see how the world worked from up here, she could understand it: earth and air and water, in simple opposition. Wind chafed at stone, water dissolved it. A mountain sifted away in an eon of breezes, washing away in an ocean of streams. In a single glance she could see whole ranges of mountains and the broad dendritic watersheds that drained them. She could comprehend river courses, see them whole in their maze of meanders, imagine the tilt of the land, the tug of the sea. She could see, in one instant, as far as the overland pioneers had traveled in a month. They went on foot, step by step by step, and got where they were going without the benefit of a view from the sky.

She looked at the other passengers, rumpled vacationers and business clones, strapped into their sardine-seats. They had their mantras, too. They chanted below their breath, hoping repetition would convince them: *It's not so bad, it's not so bad, it's not so bad.* She telepathed in passionate counterpoint: *Yes it is, yes it is, yes it is.* She told them to look out the window. She willed it. Everyone's head would turn at the same moment, a moment choreographed by the power of her thought. They'd lean their heads against the tiny plastic portholes and would see and feel the same thing in the same tick of time: uninterrupted emptiness, their souls expanding out into open space of the western lands. For at least one tick out of the reach of eternity, they'd escape their own minds into a moment of purity, unaware of themselves, set off like fireworks for one split-second spectacle of release.

Storm clouds lay over western Colorado like a vast, lumpy mattress. In Denver, she transferred to a commuter plane piloted by the same guy who checked her in. He weighed her luggage by tossing it onto a cart. "What's the weather look like from here to Casper?" she asked him casually. She got a casual answer. "Weather," he said.

She remembered Denver as a beautiful place, but in the wintry light, bare of all greenery, it cluttered the foothills of the Front Range like debris blown onto a drift fence. North of Fort Collins the litter of civilization petered out, giving way to blown prairie and stark, snow-sealed mountains, trending northwest. The air grew rougher, warning of the wilderness, and the little plane rose and fell like a sailboat crashing the waves. There was no heat. The plane was a freezer with wings, a flying icebox. Muirie ground her teeth to keep them from chattering and zipped her parka up to her neck. This was good for her; her blood had thinned, and she needed this shock to her system. Heat wouldn't do it. She was a sometimes-runner and she knew: you got hot, you cooled down. The atmosphere worked in your behalf, drawing your warmth into space. It was cold like this that tested you.

She kept her eye trained on the ground. Casper was an hour north and Hartsong mountain was visible over a fair part of that distance. She looked for a long reach of curving spine, a humpback coming up for air, an unspectacular sight to strangers but for her the landmark signaling home. She wanted to spot it the moment it came into sight. The family had a summer cabin there, a two-story log box built by Jeremiah in the thirties. Roberta and Glen had gotten married just beyond it, at a point on the southern slope that looked out over the valley to Sacajawea. Muirie hadn't been born yet, but she tended to reminisce about the wedding as if she'd attended, something that had irritated her mother. She was merely grafting her later memories onto Jeremiah's "interminable" stories, said her mother, further removing them from the truth. It seemed a petty objection to Muirie.

Another second of release stretched out behind her—Jeremiah so close she could smell his tobacco. Then, another: Hartsong on the horizon.

The plane leapt suddenly, punched in the belly by a fist of rising air. Muirie *ooffed*, on the verge of a screech. The other passengers, nineteen businessmen who no doubt flew this route often, made not a sound. Muirie loosened her grip on the armrests with effort. She contained a smile. What a heroic impulse, to grab for the seat, which was flying, too.

When she looked out the window again, she'd lost the mountain. Nothing looked familiar. She saw no spiny line, bowed and breathtaking as it bent the crust, just a gray moonscape, its corrugations lit with snow. In summer, she would have reoriented quickly but this time of year she was lost. She summoned her patience, telling herself to look carefully. She'd see something familiar from a different angle; she'd recognize it if she turned it in her mind like a pebble in her palm. She'd find a spot she'd seen before—look for it—a sparkling splinter of quartz, and she'd remember. *You're here, at this point.*

Then—a white brow of land, a flexed muscle of stone, snowbound. Closer, and the vision sharpened, defined by black pine and bare cliff faces scrubbed by the wind. She saw a gaping valley, wider and shallower than she remembered, gray with low light and blowing snow. No roads, no cabins, no color. In her mind, the place had existed in perpetual early summer, the valley Ireland-green, the single-track dirt road as red as a coral snake from the air.

She saw a sprinkle of sheep in the valley, gray on gray, as the plane roared over the Hartsong mountain road. She could make the road out, barely, in the dim light, as a plowed passageway between walls of pine. The cabin would be east of the road a mile or so, through the trees and along a southerly ridge. She searched for the aspen she knew to be near there, a whole hillside of them, but bare of leaves, they were skeletons piercing the snow.

The mountain dropped away, steep and dark on its north face. Just beyond lay the Platte, the beige jumble of the town along its banks, and the wide bowl of the high prairie stretching empty and frozen up to the Bighorns. She had envisioned a drive to the ranch through huge drifts but it looked as though the town and roads were largely blown free of snow. She could make out the highway leading west from town, a dark, thin line cutting across the land like a crack in the surface of an icebound lake. Somewhere out there was the Uncle John, tucked up close to the river on the west end of the mountain, but the details of the land, the landmarks she had known throughout all her summers, were rubbed out by the cold.

The plane bounced to a landing and taxied toward the terminal, rocking side to side in a horizontal rush of snow. The attendant wrestled with the door. It was a storm from her grandfather's legion of stories in the category of Wyoming Winters.

I'll tell you what, little girl, I knew a man got lost in the snow trying to get from his barn to the house. Wife found him next spring practically on the doorstep, been frozen solid for three months. She takes one look at him, thawing out like an icicle, and she says, You wipe them boots before you come in, Thomas.

She stared out her window toward the terminal. The plane vibrated like a tuning fork. Gritty dust blew with the snow, dulling the horizon, pitting the older snow plowed into piles along the runway, scouring away her hours-old memories of a gentle spring on the coast. In California the roses had been blooming—hadn't they?

The wind hit her at the door of the plane as though it had been aimed.

Someone steadied her from behind, a hand on her shoulder. She took a step down, pulling her parka closer, folding her purse in her arms, and stumbled toward the tiny terminal. The sudden absence of wind inside almost knocked her down. She looked up, rubbing the grit and snow from her eyes. Roberta had already spotted her; Muirie saw her face flinch in recognition. She stared back, uncertain. Maybe the flinch had come before the recognition. That was it: for an instant, shocked, Roberta had seen Muirie's mother in the crowd. Muirie knew that if all you did was glance, she looked like her mother. Ellen in real life looked like a snapshot of herself, static. Muirie had the same face, but in motion. You had to look deeper, longer. In two dimensions, they were alike. In three, they were unrelated.

Roberta came striding across the tiles, arms open wide. "Hello, kiddo."

Muirie blinked away the tears. "My God," she said. "The wind."

CHAPTER ELEVEN

There it was, at the curb, that old bulldog of a red-weathered-down-to-pink Ford, broad-shouldered and bulky, with its underbite of peeling chrome bumper. One change other than the expected advance of age: it now carried a camper shell that was none too young itself. The passenger-side door shrieked like an old arthritic when Roberta hauled it open, its joints of cold metal in agony. Muirie got in, grinning. The worn bench seat stretched for miles. Rigid red imitation leather, curling at the tears, yellow batting peeking through. At its far end, just within shouting distance, were the most basic landmarks of transportation: a monstrous steering wheel, a bare metal stick shift, a choke, a couple of gauges, and a wiper control knob marked LOW-MED-HI. She shivered convulsively. Her body seemed to suck cold from the vinyl like a milk shake up a straw. And she thought she had been cold before.

Roberta fired up the engine. The truck shimmied to life, roaring, holding the ice age at bay, Muirie thought, with the power of a few cylinders. The windshield wipers exhumed themselves from three inches of down, and Roberta wheeled away from the curb, casting a look back over her shoulder. She had not changed much. A little slackness around the mouth, and her face had sharpened some at her cheeks and along her brow, giving her aquiline beauty a stronger touch of severity than in the old days. All the Sheas had the same angular jawline. Any more length in the chin and they would have looked like horses.

Aunt Bert did not look like a horse. She looked rangy, sinewy, ramrod straight. She looked worn smooth and rock-hard. Her eyes were gray, the color of a storm coming or going. She could look mean if you didn't know her. Her hair had been redder before. Now it was ashen, as if the color of her eyes had seeped up through her scalp. She seemed immune to the cold. Her denim jacket hung open. She wore no hat, no gloves. Her long, withy fingers had not turned blue.

She glanced at Muirie, smiling, as she swung onto the highway. All the harshness in her face vanished. "So. You remember the way?"

Muirie peered through the pitted windshield at the black mass of the mountain. Along the riverbank to the south the giant cottonwoods were black, too. She was colder than she'd ever been before and dizzied by the horizontal blast of the snow. The wind made it worse, jabbering all around the truck, relentless as a madman, wanting in. This looked like another planet, this place. And yet if she let her eye follow the line of the land, slowly, there was something familiar in the way it draped in gentle folds from Hartsong down to the plain. It lay in her mind quietly, beneath all this guise of winter.

"With my eyes closed," she said.

You could pick out the ranch house a good distance away. Muirie leaned into the windshield, waiting to see it. The house had expanded little by little over the years, changing with each generation of Sheas. She was of the fourth.

"Glen will be back Friday night," Roberta said. "There's one more week of the session, then he's home for good." There was a note of weariness in her voice.

Muirie kept her eyes on the sloping prairie. "I can't believe he's not governor yet."

"He'd laugh to hear you say that."

"He hasn't considered it seriously?"

"He likes his power quiet," Roberta said. She lifted her chin. "Look. We're almost there."

Muirie saw a certain bend in the river, a long sweep as familiar to her as the curving strokes of her own handwriting. Then the house, long and low, crouched against the shelter of the red sandstone hogback, facing the mountain. Roberta turned into the drive.

"You took down the land and livestock sign!"

The truck rattled across a cattle guard. "It blew away years ago," Roberta said. "Just as we were selling off the biggest lots of cattle, appropriately enough."

The Thompkins name, painted in black on the mailbox, had almost flaked away. "Then how many head are left?"

"None."

"None?"

"Glen kept a couple of the horses. He never rides them. They're wild and woolly as bears."

Muirie sat back in her seat. She had known that Roberta and Glen had stopped ranching on a large scale, but it had not occurred to her that the place would be empty of livestock.

"But none?" she said again, unable to keep the disappointment from her voice.

"That's right," Roberta said. She pulled up in front of the house and switched off the engine. "I've expanded the hospital, though." She sighed, leaning her forearms on the wheel. "The place looks a little weary, doesn't it?"

Up close the house looked squatter than Muirie remembered it, as if it were hunkering down to get out of the wind.

"All these months of wind and weather," Roberta said. "It wears everything out. And as if the house wasn't enough of a warren, Glen added an office three years ago to give me more room in the big barn. You can't see it from here. It's at the west end, set back a bit. It faces the mountain so he gets the southern sun." She popped her door open to the storm.

"These blizzards," Muirie said, raising her voice over the blast. "Does the snow ever land, or does it blow all the way to Nebraska?"

Roberta cocked her head. "This is no blizzard."

In the living room, Muirie was happy to see, nothing had changed at all. Every piece of furniture was where it had always been and the room smelled of the old leather of the chairs, of the red dust sifted in through closed windows, strong coffee brewed that morning and left to steep, of old books and stale wood smoke. It smelled dry and rough-textured, a little scratchy. It smelled like home.

Muirie's smile felt indelible. "Moose is still here."

Roberta, scowling, put the suitcase down and walked to the mounted head over the cold fireplace. "Look at that, will you." She brushed away cataracts of dust on the marble eyes of the moose. Its goatee was shorn up close to the chin in a square cut that made it look like a Roman-nosed Chinese.

"I thought I was doing you a favor. People sheared sheep, so I figured you should shear Moose too. How old was I, six?" She patted the jowl, big as a platter. "I thought you might have taken him down."

Roberta swept the suitcase from the floor as though it were empty. "I never would. He reminds me of you." She nodded toward the fireplace. "I don't know why you'd want to sleep in this old cubbyhole, but it's ready."

She tripped a small iron clasp in the wall. A door, camouflaged by the pine paneling, opened outward. Roberta put the suitcase in the doorway. "Settle in. I've got some birds to attend to. Come on out whenever you want. I'll be in the big barn."

Muirie did not hurry. She went into the room, Jeremiah's ranch office in the old days; a room so historic it even had a name, the pine closet. Jeremiah's father, Patrick Aloysius Shea, had built it behind the main fireplace in the living room. It was just twelve feet long and six feet wide, more a large coffin than a closet, with tiny windows up under the eaves along the full length of the outside wall. She sat on the narrow bed, the only thing in the room that had been updated since Jeremiah's time. He had catnapped on an old metal camp bed like the ones in the bunkhouse. A desk and bookshelves were built into the wall at the head of the bed. The shelves contained dime novels and classics, biographies and chronicles of world history, veterinary manuals, histories of water law, account books, the family Bible brought from Ireland by Jeremiah's Uncle John, and volumes and volumes of the ranch's daily log dating from its founding, back when it was called the Red Ridge Ranch, the Triple R. The walls were bare save for an original Thomas Moran sketch of his eponymous Teton, marred, in one corner, by a coffee ring—Moran's own, Jeremiah had insisted—and a rectangular mirror, desilvered with age, hung so high that Muirie, standing before it, saw her face from the eyebrows up.

The story, as Jeremiah told it, was that the room was a fortress, the high windows meant to keep Indian arrows from coming in at anything less than ceiling height. When the Sioux got restless and poured down out of the Powder River basin with scalps on their shopping lists, Patrick Shea herded his brood into the closet, knocked out one of the windows with the barrel of his rifle, and defended the family. This antique still hung on the wall behind the door, and under it Jeremiah's shotgun, a battered Winchester, dim with dust. She had believed the story well into adolescence, when it hit her that the native American history she was learning at school did not mesh with Jeremiah's version. The pine closet had been built around the turn of the century, after the Indians had been massacred into near extinction. If Patrick Shea had fended off any savages, they were his own children, Jeremiah and his sprite of a younger sister, Moira. When Patrick disappeared into the closet to catch a nap or work on the ranch accounts, he locked the door behind him. The kids weren't tall enough to peer through the windows, so he was as good as hidden. It was his only vacation.

Her strongest memories of the room were of Jeremiah at the desk, elbow-deep in paperwork he never seemed to finish but stirred around a good deal. The desktop was empty now except for a tiny reading lamp, its base covered in faded, green leather, and a small, stand-up, metal-framed calendar, printed in black and red, from the year her grandmother had died. Family photographs showed Aura Shea to be sturdy and unsmiling, but Jeremiah always told stories of her in an admiring voice. When he'd asked her to marry him, she'd looked him in the eye and said no straightaway. *We was at some sort of big picnic down along the river. She said to me, "Jeremiah Shea, I don't like a scratchy beard." So I rode home, raked those whiskers off with a straight razor, along with a piece of my chin, galloped back to the picnic, and said to her, "You got any other objections?"' and she said, "You looked better before."*

Muirie strolled through the rest of the house, peeking into the rooms. The dining room sat in dusty darkness, the draperies closed. Aura had apparently exerted such total control over the household that neither Roberta nor Ellen had learned to cook or clean as girls. Ellen had learned some basics as an adult, but Muirie could see that cooking and housekeeping still remained at the bottom of Roberta's priorities. The kitchen provided further proof: a peanut butter jar stood open on the countertop in a wide scattering of toast crumbs, and in the sink, a nest of dishes from the night before.

At the end of the hallway, where there had been a linen closet, she saw distance and light. Glen's new office. She stepped inside. It was a huge room, lined with south-facing windows that brought the mountain close, and furnished with a deep comfort the rest of the house lacked. A broad, paper-strewn desk. Behind it, a credenza piled high with folders. A couch against one wall, and two generous, slouchy reading chairs facing the windows. On the north wall hung one of Glen's treasures, an heirloom of his family, and a landmark of her own childhood: an oil by Frederic Remington of a cavalry charge across the plains.

As she stepped outdoors, the story of the rancher in the blizzard came to her again, a little too vividly. It was nonsense, of course. The big barn loomed in the snowy dusk fifty yards away, and she could still see Roberta's footprints leading there. She followed in them, finding the strides too long, like walking from tie to tie along a railroad track.

The wide double doors stood open a few inches. She slipped inside, expecting the old, familiar smells of sweet hay, linseed oil on leather, the tangy shit of horses, but a dank stinkiness filled her nostrils instead. She stared around her, shocked by the strangeness of the place. What had been beautiful roomy box stalls for the ranch's fine quarter horses had been converted with nylon mesh into cages. Inside each, she saw in the low light, were the silent forms of large birds perched on whole logs, which were suspended from wall to wall or anchored in wooden frames to the floor. Along the wall closest to the door were cages stacked in tiers, like beach condos, containing smaller birds, unidentifiable to her. Some cages were covered by towels, as if the birds demanded privacy. For Roberta to say that she had expanded the hospital "a bit" was the understatement of a lifetime. She'd had five or six birds before, housed in the old equipment barn down by the creek, a thoroughly modest operation.

Roberta was at the far end, her back turned, inside what had been the tack room and adjoining ranch office. She worked at something Muirie could not see. The room was brightly lit. Roberta glanced over her shoulder. "Come on in. I'm almost done."

The wall between the tack room and the office was gone. Muirie's eyes took in the transformation in a single sweep: cabinets and countertops on the two longest walls; a freezer, a large double sink, a microwave oven, open shelving cluttered with books, pamphlets, magazines, and medicine bottles; white-painted drawers yawning open, spilling tools, shears, scissors, bandaging, gloves, gauntlets, old towels, syringes, brushes, and stacks of yellowed newspapers. On the wall, a series of large nets like butterfly nets. The room smelled of bird poop and slightly rotten meat.

"There," said Roberta, turning toward her. A large owl stood on a freestanding perch behind her. "Meet my resident great horned owl. I call him Oscar."

The owl, seeing Muirie, gave an openmouthed gasp of horror, flushing its feathers to full upright position. Muirie froze. She was three feet from the bird, closer than she'd been to a bird since her last visit to the ranch, if you didn't count cockatoos. And this one looked mean.

"Don't stare," said Roberta. "Great horned owls are the paranoids of the bird world."

Muirie ducked her head. "Tell *him* not to stare."

"He's spooked. You raised the hair on his neck, so to speak."

"Same here."

"I'll take him off the perch. It'll calm him."

Roberta reached for a strap attached to the soft leather bracelets around the bird's ankles. Securing it in her gloved left hand, she disconnected a clasp that linked it to a ring on the perch. The owl stepped up onto her wrist like a pompous dignitary onto a dais, then cast another malevolent stare Muirie's way. Roberta spoke to him softly, directing her gaze over his shoulder, at his feet, toward the walls. The bird's girth shrank slowly, a balloon losing air.

"I was giving him a pedicure," Roberta said. "Coping him. Beak and talons."

Muirie peeked. "He's beautiful."

"Don't say it. He's vain as hell."

Muirie came slowly closer, drawn by the beauty of the bird. She was staring again but Oscar had become fascinated with the edge of Roberta's gauntlet and paid no mind. He inspected a seam with near-sighted concentration, nibbling at it with his newly coped beak.

"What could be wrong with him?" she asked. "He looks perfectly healthy."

"Look at his eyes. Study them a little."

"You told me not to stare."

"From a distance. He may hiss. Let him have his fuss." She turned toward Muirie, putting her-face-to face with Oscar. Gasping, he swelled into an enormous globe of feathers.

"Lean forward a little," said Roberta. "He won't bite anything but raw meat."

"I'm raw meat."

Roberta laughed. "In smaller servings."

Muirie took a step closer and brought her head on a level with Oscar's. He hissed a persuasive threat and leaned away as if she smelled disgusting. One eye was darker, the pupil fully dilated. The pupil of the right eye was smaller, the size of a pea, and expanded and contracted as the bird blinked in offense at her scrutiny.

"The left pupil's bigger. Is that it?"

"A detached retina."

Muirie's sense of danger drained away as she looked into the vivid depths of the eye, a gold sun eclipsed by the wide black moon of the pupil. "How did it happen?"

Roberta reversed her procedure, returning the owl to the perch. "He fell out of the nest when he was a baby. Clunked down on the ground and knocked the retina loose. A woman who lives down on the river out near Edness Kimball Wilkins Park found him under the nest tree. I use him for my tours."

When Muirie looked at her, mystified, she nodded to the opposite wall. It was covered with letters and drawings in brilliant crayon and scrawly pencil. Muirie went to look closer. The drawings showed a vivid variety of spindly birds, unsteady barns, and a large stick woman with a bird bigger than she was perched on her arm.

"I give tours of the place to different groups around town. Kids most often, from the grade schools, Scout troops, that kind of thing. Oscar's a star, of sorts. Out of sorts, mostly."

Muirie scanned the letters. Many were written from the point of view of a bird.

My name is Susy. I am a owl. I ranned into a fents. I don't have a mother excep Mrs. Tomkins. The only thing I don't like is the kids. They are lowd. I wake up from my naps.

Thank you for the tore of your birds hospital. I will never shoot one. If there is a sic bird I will bring it to your birds hospital.

I am a Egal, in a hors stall. I have one wig broke because I got runned over. I like to think about flying.

"You have an eagle that was run over?"

"Hit. By a truck. I released it last week."

"What was it doing, hitchhiking?"

Roberta settled atop the counter. "Trying to survive." She offered her forefinger to Oscar, who nibbled on it primly as though it were an ear of corn.

The children's drawings looked typical enough, with a dozen smiling yellow suns beaming down upon flowers and spiky green grass and multitudinous roundheaded little kids—until you looked carefully, at the details. Then you saw scrawls of red gushing from a broken wings and shattered legs; an eagle wearing a huge splint, bawling blue tears; another huge bird, far bigger than the Roberta that held it, looking up with human eyes at a sky filled with Vs of geese.

"What about all those other birds out there?" Muirie asked. "The ones in the stalls and the cages."

Roberta was matter-of-fact. "Well, one of the red-tails got caught in an illegal trap and lost a couple of toes. The rough-legged at the end made a crash landing into the side of a barn. He was lucky, just one bone broken. The other red-tails, the kestrel, the Swainson's, all somebody's target practice. And the passerines in the little cages, well, you can imagine. Storm windows, cats, shotguns. Oh, and there's a Canada goose with lead poisoning."

"Lead poisoning?"

"Lead shot left behind by hunters. It's illegal but some people use it anyway. Waterfowl pick it up when they forage for food."

Muirie stared at her.

"You've seen injured birds before, Muirie."

"I know, but never on this scale. This is an infirmary."

One of Roberta's eyebrows rose. "You make it sound like my expansion somehow caused the injuries."

Muirie slumped against the table in the center of the room. "I still expected to see horses in here, remember."

"You're disappointed."

Muirie did not want to admit this. She smiled. "How can it be a ranch without any livestock?"

At the windows behind Roberta, the snow sped by like the bright debris of a comet. "It's not," she said simply. "It's not a ranch at all anymore."

CHAPTER TWELVE

So this was the grown girl.

Muirie stood before Roberta, laughing, dressed in a startlingly short black dress and a pair of Roberta's work boots. She had yanked her gray wool socks halfway up her slender calves and slung a too-big, beat-up old cowboy belt with a silver buckle around her waist. A ridiculous out-fit—and she knew it—yet she looked wonderful, her slim liveliness accentuated by the graceless bulk of the boots and the belt.

"It's jeans or this. What do you think?" She twirled on a lug-soled toe. A sock wilted onto a boot.

"I think if you wear that, no one will look at Flo's paintings."

Muirie dropped onto the couch. As a young girl, she had worn her black hair in a long ponytail. Now it was cropped elegantly close to her head. "It just wasn't something I thought of when I packed, you know? I didn't say to myself, 'Oh, and of course there will be all those gallery openings to attend.' I brought jeans, shirts. I closed my closet door, I thought, 'Whew! I can leave all that other crap behind.'" She unlaced a boot. "Who would have thought it, a gallery opening, here? It's almost disappointing."

"You did bring the dress."

"Reflex. You don't go anywhere without an LBD It's the universal dress code of the West Coast. You never know when it might come in handy. And it takes up this much room." She showed an inch between thumb and forefinger.

Roberta could well believe it. "An LBD?"

"Little black dress." Muirie whipped off the belt. "But this is not the time for it."

Glen would be back tonight, making his own way home from the airport while they were at Flo's opening. The thought touched Roberta with something near resentment: ruefulness, perhaps. She wasn't ready to share Muirie, not yet, though Muirie clearly looked forward to seeing him. She had asked about him several times, quizzing Roberta on his health, his political interests and loyalties, his recent reelection campaign, the part he had played in quitting ranching at the Uncle John. She asked earnestly, expecting a depth of response Roberta couldn't quite manage. Her answers came out truncated. *He's fine. No, he doesn't miss the cattle.* She found herself mildly impatient with the questions, wanting less to talk than to listen, to simply be with Muirie, to observe the woman she had become.

Best was seeing her with the birds. She had not handled the large raptors before, only a diminutive kestrel, and perhaps an injured duck or two. But on the morning of her first full day on the ranch, she had made it clear that a tour of the hospital wasn't enough; she wanted to learn how to handle the birds as Roberta did. Setting aside her doubts, Roberta had given her an orientation session with Oscar, who, once he got over his fit of pique, was the easiest of the tour birds to handle.

Within an hour, Muirie had graduated to Jasper, taking him onto her fist and walking with him slowly around the big barn. More than one volunteer at the ranch over the years had gotten no further than that first moment of close approach to a raptor. It was not so much the proximity of the beak and talons that panicked them as it was the sudden, transfixing nearness of the raptor's alien eye. If you had a shred of cowardice in you, that gaze would light it up like a filament and the rest of you would go black. Roberta watched closely for signs of panic in the hawk and in Muirie. The Swainson's looked alert but at ease, she decided, and Muirie looked the same. With a bare minimum of coaching, she was applying all the rules of bird etiquette. She did not crowd Jasper with a stare, and yet she kept a close eye on him, peripherally, understanding that her size and gaze would threaten the bird if she did not work to make herself invisible. She knew, intuitively, it seemed, how to read the bird's movement on her fist, its shift in weight, adjustments in posture. Subtleties of health and appetite and mood would soon follow, intuitive as well, if she was interested in learning them.

"You show a lot of confidence with him, kiddo."

Muirie continued walking, slowly, like a bridesmaid down the aisle, her escort literally on her arm. "Hmm. I wonder now, is that a compliment or a critique?"

"It's a state of grace."

Muirie looked up then, eyes keen. "Thanks."

They had flown Jasper, too, that day, using a technique Roberta had not yet learned at the time of Muirie's last visit. It had stopped snowing during the night, leaving low drifts against the buildings and fences, but the open areas were clear. Roberta fitted the hawk with a fifty-foot leather strap, a creance, and took him outside, anchoring the line to a heavy bolt screwed into the cold ground. She had Muirie take Jasper on her fist, then stood opposite at a short distance, fifteen feet, and called the hawk to her using a small chunk of raw chicken as bait. Jasper did not hesitate once he saw the meat. Bobbing once or twice to sharpen his aim, he swooped from Muirie's gauntleted fist, flying in a straight line to Roberta's outstretched arm, his creance sailing behind him like an endless tail. He ate hungrily, tearing the chicken into smaller pieces with his beak.

"We fly all the tour birds that can fly," she explained to Muirie. "My vet helps me. It keeps them active; they remember their wings. And I bring them outside on their perches as often as I can, to weather awhile. They get some sun, I spray them down with the hose, and they get a taste of the old days when they didn't have a roof over their heads."

Muirie's concentration ticced only slightly when Roberta suggested that she call Jasper herself with a second course of chicken.

"Don't worry. He's hungry. He'll go straight for the food. He knows the drill. And believe me, hawks have a good aim."

"And there's no chance he'll get loose?"

"You can't guarantee the gear won't break but I keep it in good condition. That's one of the rules: you always double-check everything before you come outside. Then, if something's worn, or you don't get the hook snapped securely, you've just got a bird in the rafters. Outside, you've got a unreleasable bird released, one with a bunch of dangling gear attached. Not a good situation."

Jasper fluttered his wings, restless with hunger. Roberta slipped Muirie a piece of chicken out of his sight. "Here. Give it a try."

They separated by thirty feet with the anchoring bolt midway between them. Muirie secured the chicken between the thumb and forefinger of her gloved hand. As she lifted her arm and called Jasper's name, the hawk hunched, taking fast and faultless aim. Then he was in the air, wings at full length, sweeping silently through the short space between them. One deep flap, two; an economy of energy only creatures in the ocean could match. He braked onto Muirie's fist, landing with precision, one foot on either side of the meat. Muirie's mouth hung open. She had not flinched. She watched the bird with complete absorption—as if it had appeared on her fist by magic.

Roberta had been wrong about Ellen's influence on Muirie. Ellen had become as much a stranger to Roberta as any other urban San Franciscan, sophisticated to the point of provincialism: *If you don't live here, you're nobody.* But she hadn't ruined Muirie yet. That's what Roberta had been searching for, she realized, as she watched Muirie: fragments of her mother in the way she moved, talked, touched the leather lead of the hawk. But Muirie's state of grace extended to her body. She flowed, her balance on the balls of the feet, with the fluid motion of a dancer.

Jasper, having finished eating, touched up a shingled feather on his breast with perfect after-dinner fastidiousness. A smile splashed onto Muirie's face. She looked up at Roberta, amazed, delighted, hoping she had seen.

Roberta nodded, all her fears of disappointment in Muirie dissolving. The regret, though, grew keener. They had lost so many years. Irretrievable years. The thought tugged at her, though she tried to banish it, from throat to heart, from heart to throat, as physical as bone.

CHAPTER THIRTEEN

Flo gave a gentle pat to the bun at the nape of her neck. It felt firm. The hair fraying at her temples she could do nothing about except trap it with bobby pins, and she didn't want to do that tonight. She smiled, remorseful, into the bathroom mirror. God knows a few visible bobby pins didn't normally bother her. And the absence of them wasn't going to add color to her hair or smooth out the wrinkles in her face. She thought she'd stopped worrying about such things long ago, in her late thirties, when she realized that a regular inventory of her face only made her regretful of inevitable changes. Instead, she had begun concentrating on other people's faces, studying the lines and shapes, the expressions, trying to understand why she found them so beautiful, regardless of their age, while her own face seemed so plain and empty. She had figured it out, eventually. She could not look at her own reflection candidly, but she could easily observe others when they did not know they were being observed or, at least, being observed with such purpose. And that was the beauty of the faces: the uncensored expressions that ran there like a river.

Understanding this had not automatically led to better paintings, though. She had done a score of full-face portraits, thinking she could capture what she saw, but they were never successful. They lacked life, the only thing she wished to convey, and it was obvious that she was trying to paint Character, which drew attention away from her subject and focused it on her technique. The portraits became, despite her intentions, reflections of herself. The answer was to capture the range of facial expression by not showing the face at all, or showing only an impression of it, from an angle, from a distance. It was the context that told the story: the posture of the body, the light, the surroundings, the color. She'd figured this out in the slowest, most painful way, by doing it wrong again and again, by painting for years without displaying a single piece of work. But now she felt certain that when people looked at her paintings, especially the one of Carl standing at the window—even though only the back of his head was visible—they looked directly into his eyes.

"Flo? Where's that boot polish?"

He was in the living room, stumping around in his stocking feet. She leaned into the hallway. "Upper left-hand drawer of the buffet."

"I looked there."

"Look again. Don't tell me you're even going to polish your boots?" She heard the drawer open. "It ain't here." Silence. "Oh."

Flo considered her reflection in the mirror once more. He was even going to polish his boots. She picked up the comb and pulled it firmly through the hair at her temples. She'd do without the bobby pins.

It didn't take much of a crowd to fill the Durbin Street Gallery. The place consisted of two rooms, front and back, and a small foyer. Sixty art-lovers and it was shoulder to shoulder. Several people hailed Roberta as soon as she and Muirie stepped inside. She touched Muirie's elbow. "I see Flo over in the corner. Come find me when you're ready and I'll reintroduce you. Carl's here, too, believe it or not."

"Okay," Muirie said, making her way toward a portable table in the foyer that offered self-serve white wine in clear plastic cups. She grabbed one, wishing it were a tall mug of steaming coffee she could wrap both hands around, or get into, up to her neck. The pink truck, for all its charm, let in cold air as if its windows were wide open, and the heater at full roar could not compete. If she had worn the dress, she'd have gone into hypothermia by now. She'd put on long johns and jeans instead, which seemed, at the moment, to be keeping the warmth of the room out.

She cast her eye across the rooms, more interested in the people than the paintings, which was just as well, since she could get glimpses of the paintings only through the throng. Most people were dressed with as much practicality as herself, for warmth. An older crowd, forty-plus on average, she judged, except for two younger women whom she took to be gallery employees, both dressed in conservative dark, skirted suits. Lots of couples, ranch couples she judged, neighbors and friends of the Drummonds; the men dressed in their too-tight brown wool Western-cut trousers and suit coats, dragged out once a year when the wives insisted, bola and polyester ties knotted at the Adam's apple so that they rode up and down with every swallow; the wives in roomy slacks or freshly pressed pleated wool skirts that flared out at the hips, just where they shouldn't, squared off jackets, a modest string of pearls, boxy shoes, a little rouge high on their cheeks. They talked and laughed easily with one another.

She wandered, eavesdropping happily. Their conversation was as much of recipes and grandchildren as it was of the paintings. She saw no eligible men, at least not obviously eligible—not that she was looking, particularly. She had not come here for romance. On the other hand she wasn't running away from it, either. Keeping an eye out was reflex, like packing the little black dress. She made her observations not in a specific way but in the hopeful spirit of the general cause.

A couple of younger men were there, one of them staring at her in shy surprise from a few feet away. He had two heads, one above the other. The upper was a baby boy's, blond, four-toothed, and gaping wide at Muirie, drooling on the head below. Nope. The other man, farther away, tall and black-haired with a beard and mustache. Married too. A severe-looking woman stood at his elbow, sipping wine as if she were sentenced to drain the glass. Muirie peered into her own plastic cup in sympathy. Jug-stuff, sour as lemons, tasting of metal.

She worked her way toward the wall. Everyone seemed to be taller than she and planted where they stood as firmly as trees. She slipped sideways between two women discussing a failing fund drive for the symphony orchestra and found herself looking straight into the warm yellow light of a sunny kitchen. She stepped closer, as if to a hearth. A woman's hands, old but capable—surely this was Flo herself—assisted a child's in rinsing a dinner plate under a silvery column of tap water in a worn porcelain sink. On the countertop were two china cups and saucers of a delicate blue-flowered design, a child's plate, bordered with kittens chasing one another's tails, a bowl lined with soggy cornflakes above a puddle of milk. On the bright windowsill sat a spiky cactus in a tiny china wheelbarrow pushed by a cherub. And in the pane, ghostly, was the merest suggestion of the people reflected there: the tiny young girl, blonde and rapt, and Flo, her face tilted forward slightly and turned to the side, as if peering through the window at something outside the frame. In the window, gray-green prairie stretched beyond a line of flat asphalt road as empty of detail as the kitchen was crowded with it.

She studied the painting, fighting the jostling crowd to stay put. The few prints and posters on the walls of her apartment were nothing like this. Her taste leaned toward the trendy abstract, and yet this painting held her.

She gazed into the soapy sink, feeling the warmth of the water on her hands, the chill of it as it dripped from her elbows to the floor—her own memory, tapped, gushed like the faucet in the painting. Perhaps it was a cheap effect after all: what woman had not stood on a chair at a sink as a child and helped do dishes? But she continued to stare, a sense of alienation creeping over her. This was no Rockwell. A sentimental painting would invite her into the scene and allow her to stay, smiling sweetly— or gagging. She scrutinized the dim reflection of Flo's face in the glass, uneasy. This painting pushed her back to the doorway of the kitchen and held her there, setting her apart, as if she had wandered into the house unannounced, unwanted, undiscovered, to witness a moment she was not meant to see.

Carl sneaked another glance at his watch when he was sure Flo wasn't looking his way. More than an hour to go. He'd hoped the cold would keep some people at home but they were all here, ready to stay put until somebody threw them out. He'd never had to smile so much in his life. But Flo was enjoying herself. He didn't know how she could feel so at home in a crowd of any sort, given her experience, but particularly this crowd with so many strangers in it. Hank and Annie had come early but had already left, unable to get a baby-sitter for the whole evening.

Hank with that damn black beard too; he looked like a Communist. There were other familiar faces in the room, true enough: Roberta Thompkins and three or four other sets of neighbors, husbands and wives. They looked like they were having fun but they didn't seem to have much to say to him, which he blamed on the pictures.

He glanced quickly at the painting of himself standing by the window. If Flo thought she was disguising him by turning his face away, she was dead wrong. Anybody who had ever seen the house could tell it was him. And if they hadn't, they could guess, given that he was standing right beside Flo in the gallery. There wasn't much mystery to it. But he couldn't challenge her. She could be touchy about her pictures, and he'd learned that the best thing to do was just let her go about it and stay out of the way. She was going to go on with it whatever he said anyhow, so it was only common sense to keep the peace with her. It hadn't been easy. Her paintings had soaked up a lot of time over the last years, and now she was getting too old to work out. She was still strong, but she was slower and her balance wasn't as good as it used to be. He didn't want her standing in the back of the pickup anymore. She was lucky in some ways, though: doing something she wanted to do, something she could do sitting down, and she could look forward to it the rest of her life. She'd never get too old to paint.

He sighed, feeling fretful. That last snow had fallen short of his hopes. He needed a bigger one, a solid, spring snowstorm to sock the canyon away. And yet such a storm could threaten his animals. The coyotes hadn't come back but a mean blizzard could do far worse damage. It was always something, he thought, always something beyond his control.

He tried again to study the paintings without appearing to. It was amazing that what looked so plain and familiar to his eye would strike other people as interesting. Flo had painted in things he hadn't gotten around to fixing at the house, and some of these people were pointing to them and talking about how much they were affected by it. His own reaction was embarrassment that Flo would paint those things like they were when it would have been so easy to paint them fixed. But he wasn't going to say anything about that either. They'd worked their fingers nearly to the bone all those years, until they were stooped and old, and they were still strapped for cash. Now she was making money by sitting in one place, in one little room, daubing paint onto a piece of canvas.

There wasn't a thing he could say anymore.

Muirie went from painting to painting, intent on each. She had known the Drummonds in her childhood only as fixtures of summer in Wyoming, old neighbors on a ranch nearby called the C.H. Carl had teased her; Flo had plied her with sweets and told her how pretty she was. She had been to their house but she could not have recalled, until she saw Flo's paintings, any details of what she had seen. Yet now each stroke of each painting seemed inevitable.

She stopped in front of another canvas. Here was the kitchen again, the same cups and saucers on a well-used wooden table but the painter's eye was aimed into the dining room where a man—it was Carl—stood hump-shouldered and tired at another window, looking out onto brown grass and a bare fence line. His wrist hung limp from a forearm cocked above his head, resting on the frame of the window. In the far distance was the purplish bulk of Hartsong, its west end marked by the shallow incision of the canyon. The scene struck her into silence as if in fear that the Carl of the painting might discover her there straining to look past his shoulder.

She scanned the room for Roberta and spotted her in the opposite corner in what looked like a heated conversation with a short, stout man in a starched white shirt and string tie. She made her way across the room.

"It's your choice," Roberta was saying. "But if you're looking for me to whisper approving comments in Glen's ear in the hopes that he'll be swayed by them, forget it. It went down in defeat once and I hope it'll stay there."

The man's puffy face was bright with irritation. "You're telling me Glen's unalterably opposed to it?"

Roberta sighed. "I don't know of anything that Glen is unalterably opposed to. But you're talking to me at the moment and I'm not his stand-in."

She turned to Muirie, breaking up the conversation.

"What was all that about?"

"He wants to build the world's largest garbage dump near Hanna so Colorado has a convenient place to haul its trash." Her mouth twitched. "He thinks it would diversify Wyoming industry."

"And he wants you to bend Glen's ear."

Roberta guided Muirie toward the Drummonds. "Glen supported the proposal in an earlier incarnation. Scaled down, of course, a nice little *compromise.*"

Flo was talking with a circle of people but saw them coming and smiled at them generously—gratefully, Muirie thought. Carl's hands were clasped under his belly. He studied the floor, glancing up uncomfortably.

Flo's eyes went straight to Muirie's face. As Roberta reintroduced them, she took Muirie's hand, not in a shake, but at her side in a warm clasp. Carl nodded, courtly, meeting Muirie's gaze for an instant, but he turned his head away sharply, sawing at his upper lip with a forefinger.

"I love your stuff," Muirie said to Flo. "I can't believe this is your first show."

Flo threw her head back with a sudden laugh, her hand at her throat. "First show! I can't believe I'm having any show at all. But here I am. Here I am."

"Those two," Muirie said, turning. "*Doing Dishes* and the other one there, *Looking toward Hartsong.* I could stare at them for hours."

Carl put a fist to his lips, as if covering a belch. Flo couldn't smile any wider. "That is just about the nicest thing I've ever heard."

"I'd buy them both if I hadn't just quit my job. I'm living off relatives now, you know," Muirie said, knocking her temple gently into Roberta's.

Flo's mouth gaped open. Roberta, laughing, put an arm around her shoulders as if to keep her from sinking to her knees. "I've been telling her for years she could sell her paintings. What do you think of that, Carl?"

He nodded. "That's what they're here for you know, Bertie." But he did not want to talk about it. He eyed Muirie again. "You're Ellen's girl?"

Flo scolded happily. "Well, Carl, who else would she be? It hasn't been that long."

"So she didn't come with you?"

"My mother has a lot of clients. They don't like her to take vacations."

"Clients?" he said.

"She's a psychotherapist."

He frowned deeply.

"A counselor," Muirie said. "A psychologist."

"Lord," he said. "Who would of thought that?"

"Carl, for heaven's sake, Bertie told us that years ago." Flo shook her head at Muirie. "He never remembers a thing."

Other people pressed in from behind, extending their hands to Flo and Carl. Muirie and Roberta fell back into the crowd

"You said you liked the one of Carl at the window?" Roberta asked.

"Yes. Maybe the better of the two."

Roberta nodded, sober. "Good. Me too. I'm going to buy it for Glen's office."

"You're kidding! Why didn't you tell Flo?"

Roberta hesitated. "Maybe because Carl was there. The idea of me having a painting of him on my wall, looking at him . . . I don't know. It's such a private vision, really. I don't think he likes it."

CHAPTER FOURTEEN

As soon as the pink truck's headlights flashed across the front of the house, the front door flew open. There was Glen, backlit by a huge fire on the hearth, waving with both arms and hallooing like a cowboy into the night. "Huh," said Roberta, cutting the engine. "He's only been gone five days."

He wrapped Muirie in a bear hug at the threshold. "My God, look at her! A hundred years go by but she finally comes back."

Inside, he put her at arm's length in front of the fire, peering at her over his glasses. His gaze had a pinpoint focus, something that had unnerved her as a young girl. Now she saw in it good-humored amazement. Rather than the work clothes she always pictured him in, he wore soft wool slacks, a pale blue cotton dress shirt, and leather slip-ons, and he was a little thicker through the middle, she thought. He squinted at her as if she were a line of fine print.

"You know, you look more like Bertie than your own mother." He turned to Roberta. "Don't you think so, Bertie?"

"I was never so pretty."

Glen's glasses dropped to the end of his nose. "You were too." He looked at Muirie, aghast. "She was too."

"Watch that past tense," Roberta said dryly.

He sat them down in the leather chairs near the fireplace and disappeared into the kitchen, returning with a bottle of iced champagne to applause from Muirie. While he poured, she pulled off her shoes and thrust her feet as close to the fire as she could get them. Roberta didn't build fires. Muirie's toes hadn't thawed since Denver.

"Now," Glen said, settling on the couch and fixing her with a look of affable outrage. The evidence he saw before him, of a young woman fully grown, was not enough. "What have you been doing all these years?"

A general answer would not do. He tugged on his earlobe, shaking his head, flummoxed, able to approach comprehension only by examining all the details that had occupied those years, of Hugh, Ellen, their careers, the divorce, everyone's reaction to the divorce, Muirie's college years, her job, what her boss was like, what she did for fun. He asked dozens of questions across a range of topics, full of astonishment at each of her answers, for they seemed to add up to one mind-boggling, inescapable conclusion in his mind: she had become an adult.

He ranged farther backward, into their histories together, setting her into the old context in order to draw her forward into the new.

"I wonder if you remember that trip Bertie and I made to California when you were, oh, you must've been seven or eight," he said, bemused, still seeing the little girl more clearly than the grown one. "We took a drive up there north of San Francisco somewhere and saw cattle grazing out by the ocean. I never saw anything like it before or since—cattle wandering along a beach in the fog, the sound of surf crashing beyond. I feel like I dreamed it."

"That was sixteen years ago," Roberta murmured. She had slid from her chair and sat on the floor with her back propped against it, her long legs stretched out before her, mostly silent, staring into the flames.

"Was it?" Glen said, still looking at Muirie. His gaze turned slowly and deeply regretful. "How can you be that old?"

The fire reached perfection at midnight: a few flames devouring a single log atop six inches of glowing coals. Muirie did not want to leave it. Roberta and Glen, headed for bed, embraced her with such tenderness that she fought back tears. She turned off the floor lamp after they had gone, and stood in front of the hearth, hugging herself in their absence.

Glen had read her with gracious goodwill, skirting the questions she wanted least to answer in detail: how long she would stay and exactly why she had come. Nor had Roberta asked during the days they'd spent alone. They thought it was a difficult subject, probably, that she had gotten fired from her job, or had ended a nasty love affair and wanted to go into hiding for a while, to put it all behind her. They had topics, too, upon which their conversational tread was light. They answered Muirie's questions about the changes at the ranch with brief, passive sentences, stripped of specificity, as if the decline of the Uncle John had been inevitable, a matter of fate. They were quiet as well on the topic of each other.

Muirie wandered to the doorway of the pine closet and gazed in by the mild yellow light of the lamp on Jeremiah's desk, her mood shifting to a sad uneasiness she didn't understand. She still missed her grandfather, even after all this time, missed the lively disorder of this room in the old days. The neatness of his desk was painful, a neatness that could only have followed a death, a putting in order of a life that had passed, and the room was less his because of it.

She ran her finger along the dusty spines of the ranch journals ranged over the desk. Jeremiah had passed away, and so had the life of the Uncle John. The place seemed barren now, unfitted to its purpose. She missed the animals, but it was the energy of the old ranch that she had looked forward to in returning here, a life that absorbed you completely, leaving no time for badgering self-examination. She loved working with the birds but somehow they added to the loneliness of the place.

She squinted at the dim lettering on the spines of the journals. The first volumes were tally books kept by Patrick Aloysius Shea after his elder brother died of tetanus at age thirty-four. John had founded the Triple R and pulled it through those first backbreaking years.

People were all the time saying to us wasn't it peculiar that Dad renamed this place the Uncle John when John was his brother, not his uncle.

It was another of Jeremiah's stories.

But Moira and me knew what to make of it. Uncle John, he died for this place, you know. So every time we heard that name, or saw it on a deed or a brand or wherever, it spoke right up to us. It said: This ain't just land, child. This is your Uncle John.

As a child she had sometimes studied the volumes, laying them on the thin pillow of Jeremiah's camp bed and propping herself up on her elbows. She had found them dry. Patrick had started jotting longer notes alongside his tallies in later years, but his newfound reflection limited itself to the weather and the health of his cows. Jeremiah had kept a journal for its own sake, but he showed no flare for the written word, either. The journals were practical. Plain, terse, straightforward, the history of her family laid out in the chores they had accomplished day by day.

She reached for a journal midway along the shelf and blew softly at the dust, wondering if she had been the last one to touch it years before. The first page was dated January 1, when Jeremiah Shea was a thirty-six-year-old bachelor, looking for a wife. She read aloud to herself, softly, hearing his voice instead of her own. "Cold. Clear. Danced with Aura Connelly at Starkey's last night. Cow froze in creek. Broke pelvis."

That was all, scrawled in a grudging hand with a blunt pencil. It read to her as though there were a connection between the dance with her future grandmother and the frozen cow. She knew enough to guess at the fuller facts of the cow's death. Approaching the creek for a drink she had slipped and fallen on the crystallizing mud of the bank, breaking her pelvis. Unable to rise, she had frozen to death. Jeremiah had not connected the events of the dance and the cow, of course. These were quick notes, the framework of the day, a code to remind himself of the details. He would not have read his words so bare.

Leaving the door open so that the warmth of the fire would reach her, she pulled out Jeremiah's chair and sat in it carefully, monitoring its stability. The thing had a hair trigger. If you leaned back too far, it dumped you on the floor. She relaxed her weight by degrees and laid the journal on the desk, turning the pages forward in time.

Glen and Roberta were being patient, waiting for her to tell them why she had come and wondering just how disastrous the problems could be that had driven her to quit her job and leave California. Would a couple of weeks in isolation at the ranch solve them? Would it take the whole summer? Or was she here for good, a refugee from civilization who needed the custodial care of foster parents?

She twiddled with a loose knob on the desk drawer. What were her reasons? They seemed fuzzy to her suddenly, the fault of the champagne on top of the rotten gallery wine, she thought. Alcohol poisoned more than your body; it poisoned your determination too, infecting you with confusion. When she tried to think of how she could reduce her reasons into words that she could actually speak aloud to Glen and Roberta, they sounded like whiny excuses for failure. Other people coped. Other people managed to stay in the real world and still find happiness. Enough to prove that it was possible, and if it was possible for someone else, it was possible, for her. She was as talented and capable as anyone she knew, as likely to recognize happiness if it came within her grasp— which was also a talent, she thought. Perhaps the rarest of all.

It was odd how you could get so caught up in the pace of something you didn't truly love, how you could talk yourself into believing that this route was the right one and how everyone around you encouraged that delusion, partly out of a blind adherence to the eleventh commandment: *thou shalt be supportive*, and partly because almost everyone she knew back home had the same delusion and needed the same support. She had begun opting out of the system when she declined to go straight into graduate school from college. She'd told herself then that she needed some time out of school, that she wanted some experience under her belt. Lacking an advanced degree, she got a grunt-level job at an ad agency but was soon writing copy. She had a good ear, a practiced materialistic eye, and a quick-witted willingness, at first, to mine her life for catchy phrases, including all her relationships and every conscious thought of her own: a prescription for success. In her second year on the job her boss offered to help pay her way through graduate school. He thought she should get an M.B.A. He recommended "formal training."

Formal training. What exactly did it mean? Did it train your eye and ear to creativity or only prejudice you toward conformity? It could be "the opportunity of a lifetime." Another phrase, repeated ad nauseam by friends and family, notably her mother. It made it sound as if life stingily offered one opportunity, and this was it. Passing it up might mean a future of mean little regrets but she'd rather have some regrets, she thought, than a mean little future, circumscribed by formal training and "professional" expectations.

She paged forward through the ranch journal, scanning the entries. By early spring there was marginally more writing per page, notations of the numbers of sheep and calves born. April 14 read, "Blizzard come up fast. Might be losses." On April 15, Jeremiah had written, "Still snowing. Figure loss high."

One of his stories told about a time he had gone out after a storm to find half of his stock safe in the lee of the low hills and in the shallow gullies and tucked into the crevices of the red hogback to the east. But the other half, exhausted by the onslaught, had given up their volition to the storm, letting the wind push them. They'd stumbled before it until they collapsed against distant fences and were quickly buried by the snow. She could not tell, from the sparsity of the journal, whether this was the storm of the story, but Jeremiah's entry for April 16 read, "Animals in piles."

Such simple words. Wyoming haiku. Nothing more need be said. And life was so damn talky nowadays. You had to talk to yourself constantly in order to bear up in the modern world. Not like an old lady mumbling to herself but to keep yourself convinced of who you were and that you were sane and moral and absolved of all guilt for your nasty little victimized past. That's how her mother set her hooks so deep into her clients. People couldn't talk fast enough to beat away the fears, and no one had close friends to help them. Who had time to nurture friendships? So they hired her mother by the hour, a surrogate pal who would quietly bear witness to all degrees of existential effluvia without expecting so much as a Christmas card. And no matter what course the patient's therapy took, more therapy was always indicated according to one simple, circular assumption: although every sane person had doubts, doubts also implied underlying illness. Illness implied health; health implied disease.

She flipped a page of the journal, a wave of confidence rising up within her. Her mother placed such superior value on her own powers of analysis that no matter how clearly and with what insight you talked about your problems, she always saw through to a more fundamental source, invariably something ancient and undiscovered, a deep, dark shape gliding around in the vast pool of the unconscious, a Loch Ness monster of the mind. And once you netted the monster, there remained the fertile muck at the bottom of the lake where the thing had laid her eggs. Ah, it was wonderful: a never-ending, self-perpetuating biosystem of chronic sickness and transient health, so perfectly accepted that no one thought to ask: Why is it I'm not chronically happy? How come I'm not transiently ill?

The handwriting in the journal changed. On July 16 of that year, it became that of a neat schoolgirl, Aura, written in dark, earnest ink, and each page was filled to the last line as if the journal were a writing assignment to be judged primarily by its length. The energy of the writing suggested prim disapproval of all the nearly empty pages before, as if Aura equated empty pages with lazy days.

I told J. that the fences are in a disgraceful state and must be fixed immediately if we are not to lose stock. We will hire a fencing crew, as that is most efficient.

J. demands that each calf have a name as well as a brand and a number. It loses us much time thinking of names for so many, and there are inappropriate ones, such as the one that trod on J's foot, which became S.O.B. He yelled it aloud, so I wrote it down. I am as stubborn as he is profane.

Muirie had gotten stubborn, too, in those last months before she decided to leave. She'd gone through a phase of such hard-bitten intransigence that she had driven all her friends away, including one man she thought she might possibly, potentially, conceivably, regret having lost. She'd set up rules for her behavior. Total honesty in the fewest number of words possible was one. Tact took a backseat. Tactfulness was akin to supportiveness, and supportiveness was a euphemism for *mealymouthedness*, a word she liked better because it sounded like what it meant. Looking back, she saw it as a necessary process, a gathering of momentum, a buildup of steam for the blastoff of her departure.

But she'd sacrificed Paul in the process. She'd given a small dinner party, intending it to be friendly, even consonant with digestion, and then proceeded to assault everyone present with sarcasm so uncontrolled that it made her head ache to remember it. The conversation zeroed in on psychoanalysis, and everyone salaamed to Freud as if he'd been God. She was the only holdout.

Although she remembered her rule to be tactless, she'd forgotten, by this time, her rule of telling the truth in as few words as possible. Paul grew quiet. He stopped eating. It didn't faze her.

Freud, a genius? Listen: Freud made the world unfit to live in. He trapped us all inside our heads. He did more to undercut individuality than science would if it cloned people by the thousands. He made us a world of judgmental assholes.

The candles guttered on the table. Paul's raspy voice said, *Like you, for instance.*

The pine closet felt airless suddenly. Muirie escaped into the living room, throwing herself onto the couch. She sat up slowly, cross-legged, and folded her hands into her lap. The fire played over the coals, blue at the edges.

You had to forgive yourself for being young, for going too far one way and then too far the other. How could you evaluate the extremes unless you'd tried them—or test your limits or know what you really believed?

She'd tell Roberta and Glen she'd like to stay for a while. She didn't know how long yet, and that would be good enough for them. There were practical things to consider. Her apartment was subleasable if need be, but her father could handle it for her. She'd work for her keep; she wasn't on vacation or welfare. She'd run tours for Roberta, help Glen with his legislative correspondence, anything. She'd cook, gladly, since what Roberta did in the kitchen could be described only as subsistence-level hunting-and-gathering.

As for the whys, they would come to understand them. Perhaps they already did.

Feeling sleepy finally, she dressed for bed, and crossed the living room, heading for the main bathroom in the hall. A light shone under the door of Glen's office. Surprised, she approached, listening, and heard the rustle of a newspaper. The door was not quite latched. She knocked softly, pushing it open.

Glen hadn't heard the knock. He sat in one of the big armchairs, reading, his legs stretched onto the spacious ottoman. He wore a pair of slippers, but otherwise was still dressed as he had been earlier: dark trousers and a cotton dress shirt open at the neck.

"Hi," she said.

He turned his head, his glasses slipping to the end of his nose. "You're still up, are you?"

She came into the room. "So are you. I thought you'd gone to bed long ago."

He rattled the newspaper. "Homework assignment. Gives me nightmares. I don't know why I do it." He set it aside, watching her over the rim of his glasses. "You're not having trouble sleeping, are you, someone your age?"

She sat on the arm of the other chair. "I've been sitting in there reading some of the ranch journals. It makes me miss the old days so much." She sighed, studying the bright image of the room mirrored in the picture window. "Don't you miss them?"

Pondering, he pulled off his glasses. He inspected them for a moment, reminding her of Oscar, then folded them and patted them into his shirt pocket, done with reading for the day.

"What do you say we take a ride tomorrow," he said. "Saddle up those two old nags out there and see what we can see?"

She grinned. "I'd love it."

CHAPTER FIFTEEN

In the morning, they dumped the tack in the bed of Glen's three-quarter ton, and he drove to a small pasture a half-mile from the house. The horses, as hunched and wary as musk ox, took immediate refuge in the farthest corner, behind a small wooden shelter, tempted but not tamed by Glen's bucket of oats. Spotting the halters on his arm, they whirled away every time he got close.

"I thought so," he said, and retrieved a rope from the bed of the truck. He had Muirie block their escape from behind the shed and snagged them in three throws, missing his first by the flick of an ear. The horses gave up when the rope gripped their necks as though it drew their wildness from them in a current.

Muirie exulted. "Now this is more like it."

He gave her a wistful smile. "I wouldn't have missed in the old days."

They followed along the Uncle John creek upstream as it trended from the mountain. The creek tumbled toward the Platte through snow crusted along its steeper, shaded banks. The prairie itself was mostly barren, the snow melted out or blown away. Its scent in the cold air was of moist sage and damp, alkaline soil. Glen reined to a halt on a small promontory overlooking the creek and gazed out over the land.

Muirie watched him, wondering about his thoughts. She never would have imagined him a nonrancher, a full-time politician who wore camel-hair coats and regimental ties. Here, sitting on a horse, he looked right again.

He glanced at her suddenly, caught her staring.

"I know what you're thinking," he said, winking at her. 'What in the world has happened to the Uncle John?'"

Her horse shifted a hind leg, resting. "It did come as a shock," she said, wondering if he might be persuaded to say more in Roberta's absence. "What made you and Aunt Bert decide to shut it down completely?"

Glen's expression grew cautious. "Is that what Bertie told you, that 'we' shut it down?"

She hadn't, not exactly, but she had seemed to imply a joint decision. "She hasn't talked about it much."

This did not seem to surprise Glen. "She doesn't believe in ranching anymore. That's the long and the short of it." He smiled, his caution dissipating. "I was only half the team, you know, the half that married in."

"She doesn't believe in it?"

"I don't mean like Santa Claus. I mean she doesn't think it's the right thing for her anymore." He paused. "For us, I mean. It's not right for the land, if you listen to Bertie."

"You don't listen to her?"

"Hoo. I listen all the time. You haven't been around long enough yet." He tugged on his earlobe. "It all depends on what you believe, like everything else in the world. If you take the long view, there's not much future in ranching. And, of course, Bertie's got points. She's always got lots of good points."

Muirie had her doubts. "Like what?"

He considered. "Well, when the land's this dry and rocky, you need a lot of it to raise stock. The government's a big landlord out here, so people lease public land and add it to their own. It's a tempting deal. The government has helped to shoulder a part of the cost of ranching on public land all the way back to the first days of the industry in the late eighteen-hundreds. It keeps the fees low on the land, even builds and maintains facilities—dams, pipelines, stock tanks, roads, fences, corrals.

During droughts, when there's not enough grass to go around, and that's common in the West, it pays half the cost of supplemental feed. It pays for predator control too. You know that's a thorn in Bertie's side, that taxpayers would end up paying to have wildlife killed in favor of live-stock."

They moved along, up the creek. The breath of the horses blew white in the still air.

"It's all in how you see it," Glen said, "what you choose to throw into the equation. The way she sees things, the economics should tell us something. If ranchers need tax breaks and price supports and predator control to make a profit, then they really aren't making their own way."

"And I know how she'd solve that." Muirie swiped an arm through the air. "'Off with their heads!'"

A frown. He didn't like her to criticize Roberta. "Well, you do have to ask why things are this way. Is it because our methods are outdated and sloppy or because the land can't support this kind of use?"

"What do you think?"

"I think that even if you believe the latter, you have to remember that the government has long-standing commitments here and you can't just ax them overnight. Not because of all the jobs at stake; ranching's not a big employer. But because you need mutual respect between the parties if you're going to make real progress—at anything. If you force change down someone's throat, they're going to change in a way you don't like."

He gave his mare a gentle swat on the neck. "I thought for a long while that Bertie and I might work out a sort of middle-of-the-road approach here. Bertie could do her birds, I could do a little politicking, and we both could do a little ranching—maybe make this more of an experimental ranch, try new methods. I've always thought that the land is pretty robust, capable of recovering from bad methods. But she wouldn't have it."

"What could be wrong with trying?"

He gave his head a shake. "A 'model' ranch—it's a contradiction of terms to her. There aren't any good ranches, just degrees of bad. She thinks the industry is an anachronism."

"Then she must see all the support as a kind of welfare," Muirie said.

"Absolutely. Forget the 'kind of.' But it's a loaded word, a word that attacks people's integrity to no purpose. I could give you a list as long as my arm of industries set up in a similar way. Not that anyone around here is going to defend the government very hard, but it's been a partner for a long time."

"That's the approved word, then: *partnership*," she said, mocking him a little.

"Bertie would call it *complicity*." He gave her a smile. "But she likes loaded words."

They wandered farther up the creek. It narrowed, its banks steeper and rockier. Muirie began to feel cold, despite the loft of her ski parka. It was good for her, though, part of her training.

"Do you think we could we ride up to the canyon?"

"It's farther than it looks," he said. "And the north side of the mountain doesn't get much sun. The snow's probably six feet deep there. You thinking about Bertie's eagles?"

She nodded. "Do you know where the roost is?"

"It's been years since I was up there, but it's a ways in, in a steep part, pretty protected, a good place for them." He inspected the sky. "They stuff themselves with fish and anything else they can find, then they sit out the storms up there, cozy as kittens."

Muirie halted her mare to scan the bulk of the mountain. "I can't quite spot the mouth."

He pointed. "Follow along the top of the ridge there. You can see it there as it falls off toward the west. A little notch at the top."

The ridge was jagged and dark against the graying sky. She wasn't sure she was seeing the notch. It was something Glen's eyes picked out from habit, knew from a lifetime of looking, as he knew every nuance of Roberta's face.

They rode along a line of fenceposts stripped of their barbed wire. Muirie found herself searching beyond them for the familiar shapes of the cattle. "They look so lonely to me," she said. "Sentinels with nothing to guard."

"We took down a lot of fencing," Glen said. "Antelope come through here. With no cattle, there's no reason to maintain it unless it adjoins someone else's land."

"All my family history went with the herd," she said, unable to rid the words of petulance.

He considered for a moment. He always hesitated before he spoke, a careful habit that politics had taught him, she thought.

"Bertie followed her conscience," he said, pausing again. "She can't see this place through her father's eyes."

"But what about you?" she asked, defensive of him, of them both.

Again, a pause. "I miss the old days; I can't pretend I don't. But that life's behind us. I see that as clearly as she does."

Muirie's horse slowed to pick its way across a patch of low and broken ground that Glen's horse cleared with a hop. *That life's behind us.* What life did he mean? Ranching, or something else: his life with Roberta? She couldn't tell, and she knew from his careful phrasing that he would not make it clear.

CHAPTER SIXTEEN

The place, thank God, was noisy again. From dawn to dusk, it bumped and hummed with the comings and goings of footsteps and voices, the rich music of women talking, a sound so welcome to Glen's ears that he found himself sitting stock-still at his desk, eyes closed, as though it were a symphony.

It smelled good, too, after Muirie's invasion of the grocery store and her subsequent assault on the kitchen. She had emptied the cobwebby cabinets onto the countertops of everything right down to the dead bugs at the back. He'd come to watch, along with Roberta. They stood in the hallway, on the other side of the open bar, out of harm's way. Muirie tossed a blackish jar of what had been cherry preserves onto a box of pancake mix, spilling powder over the edge and sending a *poof* of mix into the air like a smoke signal. Next came a rock-hard half-bag of brown sugar, an empty plastic bottle labeled BLACK PEPPERCORNS, a dented can of artichokes, a little brown jar of baker's yeast, a greasy-looking toothbrush, three containers of Christmas sprinkles, and two cans of black olives. She dug through the pile as though it were an archeological dig.

"Look!" she said, shaking the jar of yeast at them. "This yeast has been dead for six years!"

Dinner that night had been a garlicky roasted chicken so fragrant that his mouth had watered half the afternoon. While it cooked, Muirie had rediscovered the dining room, forced the creaky doors, advanced on the furniture with a dust rag, and transformed the place by dinnertime with candles, a tablecloth, and Aura Shea's china, so long out of use that it looked new to Glen.

"I'm not dressed up enough," he'd told her when he saw the room. "I need my medals. My sash." And she laughed, taking his hand.

He wondered now, after only a few days in her presence, how the silence of the place without her had not driven him crazy. It had descended slowly, over the years, like a windless snow, falling straight out of the sky to bury Roberta and him inch by inch.

He could hear Roberta and Muirie now, cleaning up the kitchen together, talking. Muirie's voice ran all over the scale, from screechy mock outrage to deep-in-the-diaphragm laughter. Roberta's came to him less often, and struck a lower chord, resonant and fine.

He snagged a moment in the past, the morning before he and Roberta got married. She was in the kitchen then too, spatula in hand, a stack of pancakes on a plate. It was a split-second glimpse of their life together, unimportant in itself, yet everything shone clear in his mind: the jeans she wore, the red flannel shirt with see-through elbows, her hair pulled back with a rubber band, showing off her small ears. He could see the griddle, black metal, one of the oldest things in the house, never washed but wiped with a damp cloth and stored like a family heirloom by itself on a shelf. And the stack of pancakes, all sizes, all levels of doneness from gloppy to burnt. She was turning her head toward him. That was the moment: he was standing next to her; she turned her head, smiling, and bumped him with her hip.

It made him smile to think of it. They had set no specific date for the wedding. Early on, she had gotten the idea into her head that they would get married on the first sunny Saturday or Sunday in September while the aspen were at their peak. She wanted a beautiful wedding day, she said, and she was going to get it. But none of the churches in town could accommodate such an impromptu arrangement.

"They need specifics," he told her. "They want it down to the minute and we've only got it down to the month."

They were in bed at his house in town. Although the other ranch employees lived at the Uncle John, Jeremiah had shipped Glen into town a couple of years before, when his interest in Roberta had grown past his ability to hide it. The idea was to keep him off the ranch at night, a symbolic gesture that he and Roberta had not honored for long.

Roberta scowled. Her hair had pulled loose and hung over her temples. She had on a faded shirt, unbuttoned, and her socks. Her jeans and boots were on the floor.

"Let's just get married," he said. "Let's just go down to the courthouse and get it over with."

She turned those gray eyes on him. "Get it over with?"

He pushed an arm around her waist. "Whatever we have to do so that you don't have to go home at night."

She forgave him and fell silent. He drowsed, breathing her in, his nose against the soft flannel at her breast. She sat up suddenly, rolling him to the side. "We'll get married on the mountain."

He grunted. "On the mountain?"

"At the cabin. It's perfect. We'll make it more of a picnic, put some supplies that will keep aside now and grab them when it's time. Beer, champagne, all that, can store."

Glen raised himself on his elbows. "That's a one-holer up there, you know, Bertie. You give a couple of hundred people all the beer they want and there's going to be a lot of dancing around in line."

She smiled, that full, happy, mischievous smile she'd had then. "That's one way to get them to dance."

"What about that wedding dress you were looking at, that kind of chiffon one? You're going to haul around in the woods with that on?"

She crossed her bare legs, regarding the cotton socks that bagged around her ankles. "I want to dress like this."

His eyebrows flew up.

"I mean socks. To hell with nylons and chiffon."

"What about the invitations? We can't just have them say to come up some pretty September day."

"Simple. We'll call everyone the day before."

"Two hundred people?"

"Sure." It was typical of her to be casual when she caught the least hint of concern in him.

"You mean just pick up the phone and say, 'Hey! We're getting married, come on up!'"

"Why not?" She hopped off the bed and paced across the room. It was wide enough for about five and a half of her long-legged strides. "Everyone knows we're getting married anyhow, so all they need is a date. And if the date depends on the weather, then invitations are pointless. We'll just call everyone. It's so simple, it's elegant."

"That's because there's nothing to it. It's a planless plan."

She came back to the bed, planting both knees between his. "Is that so terrible?"

To his amazement, the wedding took care of itself. It was the Shea luck. Word got around town quickly that there would be no written invitations, so everyone who knew the Sheas or knew of the Sheas considered themselves invited. Jeremiah invited everyone and anyone he saw from mid-July on, including a number of ranchers from Colorado, Nebraska, and Montana, the telephone man who installed an extension in the big barn, and a woman whose car he rear-ended at a railroad crossing as he was watching the train instead of her bumper. "When is it?" they asked him. Jeremiah's customary voice was a near bellow. "Watch the paper!"

"Jeremiah," Glen said, "the paper's not going to write stories about our wedding."

But it did, first a feature, then a regular update in the society section, which included a report on the aspen and the probable influence of the coming weather on their change in color.

The involvement of the newspaper convinced Glen that the wedding would be crashed by every subscriber. He also felt certain that the moment they settled on a particular day, a blizzard would rise up out from nowhere, or a sudden wind would sweep all the aspen leaves away overnight, or the most spectacular day of the fall would be a Monday.

But one thing after another fell into place. The food was organized as a wedding gift from an old friend of Jeremiah's who ran a restaurant in town. He stocked his freezers with steaks, prepattied hamburgers, hot dogs, and buns, then solicited other friends to supply relishes, potato chips and Fritos, cheese curls and pretzels, which he stored at the restaurant. Another family friend delivered five kegs of beer to the cabin early in the month, placing them under a tarp in the trees where they would stay cool and undisturbed. The champagne Jeremiah bought himself and stored in the big barn, ready to be shifted to the bed of his truck the morning of the wedding.

By mid-September, the only thing that hadn't been offered was bridal flowers, and Glen realized Roberta had never mentioned them to him. "Glen," she said when he asked, "I have a whole mountain."

On the fourteenth of September, it snowed six inches on the mountain. The aspen were still green, with a few flares of yellow here and there. Roberta studied the slopes from the flatland of the ranch and said, "It'll be okay. A little moisture will make the colors more intense."

On the twentieth, the temperature dropped to fifteen for two nights in a row. In town, gardens froze solid and the residents harvested tons of green tomatoes the size of Ping-Pong balls, gas stations announced winterizing specials, and the department store downtown sold its entire supply of woolen gloves. At the ranch, the horses stamped and muttered in the cold, the cattle huddled against the south sides of the outbuildings and along the lines of cottonwoods. The Uncle John creek grew ridges of delicate ice along its banks.

"Winter's here to stay this time," Glen said to Jeremiah. They were out in front of the big barn, inspecting the mountain. "It's going to be the first wedding ever on skis."

Glen was a native, but he'd grown up in town, which Jeremiah considered to have a different, softer climate than the ranch. He snorted at the prediction. "There hasn't been a spring or a fall here in the whole history of the world where it hasn't snowed and then got nice again."

On the last Friday of September, Glen woke up just after a cold and cloudy dawn and headed out to the ranch early. He drove it fast, irritated by the weather and by Jeremiah's and Roberta's refusal to express the least concern about it. The wedding couldn't take place the next day, it seemed clear. The air felt testy, ill at ease, and the mountain was obscured down to the plains by clouds. It looked as if it had been scraped away, leaving a view of endless flat gray distance. If they waited another week, until the first weekend in October, the aspen were sure to be gone, it was sure to be cold, even snowy, and he did not like the omen of a snowy day.

He stopped at the ranch gate and pulled the paper from the mailbox, unrolled it behind the wheel of his truck. Clearing and warmer, said the weather report; highs in the mid-fifties by Friday afternoon, warming to the mid-sixties on Saturday. An accompanying short column announced tomorrow as his wedding day. He kicked the door open and stared straight up at the sky. Directly above him the clouds were thinning. He saw a wash of blue.

Roberta was alone when he walked into the kitchen, making pancakes. He saw her backside, her fine tight bottom in those eternal jeans. She turned as the screen door slammed. He went to her side. "Have you seen the sky?"

That was the moment. She smiled, bumping him away with her hip. "I smelled it coming."

He reached for her. "The hell you did. All you can smell in here is hot grease." But he could smell her too: clean skin, warmth.

She whispered to him, grave. "You sure you're ready for this?"

Before he could answer, Jeremiah clumped in. He had on a battered pair of short work boots, and one orange sock came up over a trouser leg. He wrapped one of his leather gloves around the handle of the percolator and poured himself a cup of coffee.

"I'm glad tomorrow's the day," he said. "You two can stop sneaking around."

Roberta flipped a smoking pancake. "We haven't been sneaking around."

"No," Jeremiah said thoughtfully. "I guess it ain't sneaking if everybody knows about it."

Glen laid the *Star-Tribune* on the table. "Paper says mid-sixties tomorrow."

Jeremiah looked like he might spit. "Paper, my eye."

The phone began ringing before they'd finished breakfast. The whole town, it seemed, had waked up early with the certainty that tomorrow would be the day. Roberta, on an inspiration, began asking each caller to phone five or so others. Before ten she'd gone through the entire list of guests. At ten, the newspaper called to confirm the time of the ceremony, then the news editors from both radio stations. When they turned on the radio at lunch, the noon news included a piece on the Shea wedding.

Roberta smiled at Glen across the table, kicking at the soles of his boots. He motioned with his eyes for the door. She followed him out as Jeremiah and the hands went for seconds.

"What were you talking about earlier?" he said. "Are you having doubts?"

She put her arms around his waist, pulling him to her at the hips. "I always have doubts. If I waited for all my doubts to go away, I'd never do a damn thing."

"Doubts about us?"

"Sure."

"What are they?"

"Glen, don't you have any? Not one?"

"Not one."

She kissed him. "Well, I doubt that."

He woke up the next morning to the smell of dry pungent soil and knew the sky was clear. He'd left his window open, determined to smell the weather, and he had. There had been no frost, no dew, and the horizon was the red-orange of poppies.

More than four hundred people came to their wedding and stood with them out on the point as they said their vows in steady voices against a backdrop of brilliant aspen and a valley flooded with sunlight. It puzzled him, but one of the finest memories he carried away with him from that day was the warmth of the sun on his shoulders and the feel of his flannel shirt on his skin.

CHAPTER SEVENTEEN

"There he is," said Roberta.

Muirie scanned the highway. A pickup sped along from the east, slowing as it approached the driveway of the Uncle John. Sherman had called half an hour before to tell Roberta he had a golden eagle at his veterinary clinic, brought in the day before by a local rancher. It had been shot through the wing.

"Bring it out," Roberta had said abruptly into the phone, and hung up without saying good-bye.

A hand came out the driver's side window in greeting as the truck bumped over the last cattle guard and turned to park in front of the big barn. Roberta waited, hands on hips. The truck was a well-kept GMC in its middle age, powder blue. A door opened. A compact man got out and came toward them through a light breeze, holding on to his hat at the brim. He was your basic model of average-looking guy, Muirie thought, somewhere near thirty, less worn than his pickup. She saw him study her, too, as he approached, but he spoke first to Roberta.

"Hello, Bert."

"Sherman," Roberta said, flatly.

He reached out a hand to Muirie, head bowed. "Sherman Lloyd. You're Bert's niece, by the look of you."

It had sounded as though he'd said "Bird" instead of "Bert." He had a quiet, steady voice.

"Muirie," she said, shaking his hand.

Sherman pulled off his hat, turning toward Roberta. "You're not going to like this one. He's a youngster, big as a bomber and strong, a kicker. My assistant helped me tube-feed him, so his belly's full and he's pretty well rehydrated."

Roberta was already moving toward the truck. Sherman took a breath, ready to follow, then cocked his head at Muirie. "Mary? Is that it? I didn't quite catch it."

A perennial misunderstanding. "Muirie," she said. And, smiling: "Rhymes with *fury*."

A large cardboard box sat in the bed of his truck, lashed tight with bungee cords. Airholes had been punched in its sides near the bottom. Sherman opened the gate, unhooked the cords, and drew the box forward carefully into his arms. "Just guide me through the doors."

Roberta had him set it on the table in the center of her workroom. She pulled the flaps of the box open slowly. A young golden eagle, blinded with a hood and wrapped in a light blanket, hunched inside, unmoving.

"Holy shit," Muirie said. The bird was huge.

"You want to tell me about it?" Roberta said.

"Jim Casey found it directly beneath a cottonwood next to the river," Sherman said.

"On his own land?"

"Yeah. That's why he brought it to me instead of you. He thought you'd figure he'd shot it."

"Jim Casey couldn't shoot a picture."

"The bullet went right between the radius and the ulna. Broke the ulna but didn't shatter it. He was a damn lucky bird. Only problem was that he thrashed around a lot before Jim got to him. He displaced the bone a bit."

Roberta handed him a pair of heavy leather gauntlets and took a lighter single glove from a drawer for herself. "Let's take a look at him."

Muirie stood back. Sherman pulled on the gloves. "He's strong, which is good," he said, "but he's no picnic to handle. I think I'll keep him wrapped up, keep that wing bound close to his body."

The bird was quiet, calmed by the hood.

"Okay, fella," Sherman said softly, reaching for the eagle. Only when he touched it did it move, flailing against the wall of the box.

"Do it quick," said Roberta.

Sherman struggled to grab the bird at its ankles and yet stay clear of the talons. Muirie watched, eyes wide. None of Roberta's resident birds were eagles. They were too large to handle routinely, and she had warned Muirie that it would take months for her to gather the strength and experience needed for the job of managing a wild one. Muirie doubted if she ever would. Each taloned foot looked as large as one of her hands.

"You ready to lift him?" Roberta said. "You'd better have a grip on those feet."

"He'd have a grip on me if I didn't."

Sherman glanced at Muirie, then heaved the bird from the box and set it on a waist-level standing perch, maintaining his grip. The eagle's talons locked tight on the wood. Roberta reached cautiously for the hood and lifted it free. The bird gasped, blinking wildly in the sudden light. Though young, it was fully adult in size. The burned-toast feathers of the crown stood straight up, like hackles on a dog.

"Damn," Muirie whispered, taking a step farther back.

"I thought I might give him another dose of antibiotic," Sherman said, drawing a dropper bottle from his pocket.

"Muirie's in training; let's let her do it," Roberta said. "I'll open the beak. You shoot the medicine in."

"No way," Muirie said distinctly.

"Don't worry," Sherman said. "I've got him. He's not going anywhere."

Roberta brought one hand up behind the eagle's head and grabbed the upper mandible. The eagle tossed its head, but the mouth came open, revealing razor-sharp edges behind the savage hook of the beak. The mouth looked cavernous, half as big as the head, a guillotine with an angry bird attached.

"Go," Roberta said. "Just get as much into the dropper as you can. I'm right here."

Muirie stared. Despite the size of the mouth, there seemed to be nowhere to put the dropper without risking violent contact with the beak.

"Here," Roberta said. "You take my place, I'll take yours. I'll show you how."

That sounded more reasonable. She came to stand at Roberta's shoulder.

"Okay, put your arm around behind him," Roberta said. "Just grasp the mandible where my fingers are. When you've got a grip, I'll let go. It's not hard to hold open."

Muirie pinched her thumb and forefinger just behind Roberta's. The beak felt like a thickened toenail.

"Ready?" Roberta said.

"I hope so," Muirie said, glancing at Sherman.

He was already watching her. He smiled.

Muirie held her breath. Roberta stepped away, her eye on the eagle. It didn't struggle, didn't move.

"Good," she said.

She wasted no time in preliminaries, just angled the dropper into the mouth and emptied it by half.

"Now you try." She slipped the beak from Muirie's fingers by lifting it up and to the side. "Go on. It's easy."

Muirie took the dropper, shaking its contents to the tip. Her stomach fluttered.

"The trick is speed," Roberta said.

"So I won't have a chance to think about it."

"Better not to."

Muirie watched the bird's brown eyes. Unlike Oscar, the eagle did not stare back but seemed to be looking beyond her, through her, behind her, out the door.

"I wonder what he's thinking."

"You wouldn't want to know," said Roberta. "Give it a try."

Muirie held the dropper delicately between thumb and forefinger. "Okay, here goes."

She put the dropper in at the side, not neatly and cleanly as Roberta had done, but as though poking at a bit of stuffing protruding from an upholstered chair. The bird tossed its head, the beak slicing upward, and the dropper fell to the floor. Muirie reached for it.

"No," Roberta said. "Can't risk contamination. I got most of it down him the first time anyway."

The bird struggled in Sherman's arms, throwing its head upward as if it could will itself into the air. Sherman tightened his grip. "Whoa, boy," he said.

The eagle, thwarted completely, screamed—a single, cold note of fierce and desperate anger that froze them all to the floor.

The shriek rang in Muirie's ears, the rebuke of an Olympian god. How dare she force anything down his throat?

They eyed each other, uneasy.

"I guess he told us," Sherman whispered into the silence.

Roberta recovered quickly and wiped a drop of the medicine from the bird's beak with a moistened rag as though he were a messy toddler. She tossed the rag into the sink. "Okay. He's had enough handling for one day."

"Where do you want him?" Sherman asked.

"One of the wooden cages at the end."

Roberta slid a corner of the blanket over the bird's head to blind it, then led Sherman to a smooth-slatted wooden cage in the main part of the barn. It was hardly bigger than the eagle.

"We don't want him to move around much right now," Roberta explained.

Sherman maneuvered the bird inside, then pulled the blanket free. Muirie started as the eagle exploded into the narrow confinement, splint thumping once dully against the confining wood. Roberta fastened the door quickly behind it and draped a thin blanket over the cage.

"It looks bad," Sherman said to Muirie, "like a fat guy in a phone booth. But he won't hurt himself in there."

"He'll calm down," Roberta said. She nodded toward the door of the barn. "Come on. There's coffee."

"You guys go on," Muirie said.

Sherman glanced back as he closed the door behind them. A hopeful look, as if he wanted her to join them, but coffee was the last thing she needed. The eagle's scream still echoed in her head. She felt a little deaf, as if she'd been too close to a lightning strike.

She walked slowly to the far end of the barn, keeping a polite distance from the tour birds in their larger cages. She studied them, glad to set her eyes on birds that were not trapped by blankets or splints or Sherman's arms, or jammed into immobilizing boxes. Only Oscar was alarmed by her proximity. He watched her, head low, as though he expected her to pounce. They all looked perfect. Unharmed, untouched, unmaimed. Their lean lines made streamlined sculptures in the dim light.

"Hello, Beetle," she whispered to one of the birds, a diminutive kestrel, the feathers at her chest a tender, checkered brown.

The bird regarded her with calm brown eyes, then flourished one wing as if stretching in preparation for sleep. Muirie's heart caught, although she knew the history of this bird. She had handled Beetle several times and fed her minute portions of chicken from her hand, which the bird ate as delicately as a fairy. Still, the sight shocked her. Where the second wing ought to have been was a tiny upright flag of feathers attached to a smooth stump at the shoulder. The bird had lost a wing to a gun. She was an amputee.

Sherman and Roberta were sitting at the kitchen table when Muirie walked in. The coffee left over from breakfast boiled on the stove. She flicked off the burner and pulled the pot onto the tiled countertop. How Roberta could serve it was beyond her. How long could fresh coffee take?

"There's nothing else to tell you, Bert," Sherman said.

Clearly, Roberta didn't believe him. "Okay, then, how did he find the bird?"

Sherman nodded. "All right, but it's not going to clear up a thing. His cows were looking at something. He saw his cows standing in a circle staring at something and he went to find out what it was. That's how he found the bird."

Roberta let her cheek fall into her palm. "His cows."

"Bird cows. They stayed right on point."

She blinked slowly at him, but a smile was coming on.

He raised his hands. "Honest to God. Call him up."

Muirie lifted the coffeepot. "You guys actually want a cup of this stuff?"

"Sure," Roberta said, as if it were an odd question. Sherman held his cup out, watching Muirie with a diplomatic smile. Sneering a little, she filled their cups.

"You don't like my coffee?" Roberta said.

Muirie's voice rose turbulently in her chest. "Isn't shooting raptors against the law here?"

Roberta took a sip of coffee. "Of course."

"It's kids, most likely," said Sherman, levelly. "Close to the highway, and only a couple of weeks after that hawk."

"You talk so casually about it," Muirie said.

"Casually?" said Roberta. "Routinely, maybe."

"Where were these kids' parents? Do they usually let children loose with weapons around here?"

Sherman ducked his head, grinning, but Roberta's patience thinned. "Look, some people shoot anything that moves, Muirie. And if they don't shoot it, they poison, cudgel, burn, or trap it. It's not different in the rangelands of California, believe me. If it's big and dark and on the wing, it's fair game."

Muirie sat down with a bump, glowering. "They ought to have a hunting season on people, damn it."

"That's an idea," said Roberta. "I'd like to wing a few myself."

Muirie struggled for calm.

Sherman had his eye on her. "I need to hit the road," he said, as if to her. Then he drank his coffee down like a tonic, his face crimping with the last swallow. "I'll check back in a couple of days, Bert."

"You don't have to come running out here," Roberta said, brusque. "I'll call you if I need you."

He glanced into Muirie's face as he stood up, studious. He had pale green eyes, muddied a little with brown. "You two look a lot alike," he said. He regarded them both seriously, one hand wavering around his jawline as if trying to trace the similarities of their faces in his own.

Muirie studied him in turn. He wasn't so average-looking at this distance, she thought, surprised at her own misjudgment. His expression had an interesting mobility, as if all his thoughts surfaced on his face.

She got to her feet, restless. "I'll walk out with you."

He held the door open for her as he gave his little salute to Roberta, then closed it solidly behind them, settling his hat on his brow. The breeze had felt almost springlike earlier in the day. Now it knifed through Muirie's heavy sweater. She hugged it closer, buttoning it to her neck.

"You were good with that eagle."

"Thanks," he said. "I've still got a lot to learn."

"How long have you been working for Aunt Bert?"

"A year or so. Not long. I'd handled birds some before, for the state. But I've learned most of what I know from her."

She settled lightly against the fender of his truck. "She told me about your clinic."

Although he had an air of diffidence about him, he returned her gaze directly. "I'll be bankrupt next year. Was that about the size of it?"

"I don't think she gave you a whole year."

He laughed. He hadn't had a haircut in a while, which she found oddly refreshing. His hair grew in pale stubbles down the back of his neck. "I'm surprised she let me stay for coffee. She usually tells me I've got a business to run and punts me off the place."

"How do you drink that stuff?"

"You're Californian, though," he said, as though he considered her alien.

"Maybe I could see your clinic sometime," she said.

He smiled so spontaneously that he embarrassed himself. "There's not much to see."

"Only pets," she said, imitating Roberta's grinding disapproval of domestic dogs and cats.

"I've got a bird there. She didn't tell you about that, I suppose."

"You mean a raptor?"

"A ferruginous hawk. It's blind."

She thought of Oscar. "Completely?"

"Yeah. His eyes are gone."

"Christ," she whispered.

He leaned an elbow on the cab, lessening the distance between them. "A lady on the outskirts of town found him late last summer. I call it a 'him', but I don't know. He's young, just now adult, but he's small so I think he's male. He was probably in a stoop, heading for something juicy on the ground, and he hit a thick power line dead center, like a dive-bomber. When the lady found him he'd been sitting there on the ground for a couple of days, keeping all the varmints away somehow. Everybody around here knows your aunt, so this lady called her, and Bert went and picked him up and then called me. By the time I got to see him, she had

him here and his head was about the size of a soccer ball. One eye was
burst, the other lacerated, his skull broke open, and he was dehydrated
and half-starved, but proud as the devil and as alive as anything you ever
saw."

He zipped his jacket against the breeze.

"Bert wanted to put him down, but I talked her out of it, which I know
she regrets. I thought I could save that other eye. It took about two
months before the swelling in his head went down. Every morning we
thought we'd find him dead, and every morning he was sitting there stubborn and hungry as a goat." He sighed. "But the second eye atrophied,
despite everything. Bert said it was going to be hard to find a permanent
home for him, and she was right. It upsets people to see a raptor without eyes and he's more work than your regular unreleasable bird. I've
done some checking around. Nature centers, zoos, and she hates zoos, so
that's a last resort. The people I'd be comfortable sending him to won't
take him, and the people who'd take him I won't send him to."

Muirie struggled against her own repulsion, the thought of shriveled
eyeballs. "Couldn't she use him in her tours? Oscar's half-blind."

"But he's got eyes. This bird's sockets are as empty as your palm."

He stubbed at the gravel with the toe of his boot. "She wasn't happy
having him here so I took him to the clinic. Not that she wouldn't have
kept him if I hadn't been able to, but he's extra work and her space is at
a premium, all for a bird that'll never recover, according to her defini-
tion of the word. And I'd started thinking about manning him down,
taming him enough to handle him."

"Did you?"

"Yeah, but to what end I don't know. He can't fly, of course, being
blind. But he's gentle as a baby and he listens to you like I've never seen
any other bird do. Being blind calms him, I guess, like a hood does."

"Or your patience," Muirie said softly.

"Bert thinks I'm nuts."

Roberta walked out onto the porch of the house, slamming the door
behind her. Seeing them, she stopped and planted her hands on her hips.

"I'm supposed to be gone," Sherman said.

"Does she own shares in your clinic, or what?"

He slid onto the seat of his truck. "She's trying to keep me in line. I'm
lazy."

"I've noticed that about you already," she said, shutting his door for him.

He rolled the window down and glanced with a smile toward Roberta as she walked toward the barn, ignoring them.

"You call her 'Bird'," Muirie said.

"What?" His eyes locked with hers. "How do you mean?"

"Bird. You say 'Bird' instead of 'Bert'. Admit it."

"No I don't." He grinned, crookedly. The Jimmy rumbled to life.

"You do."

"No."

"Lazy tongue," she said.

He hesitated, lifting an eyebrow. "Wrong again." He said it slowly, holding her gaze. She'd figured him much shyer. "When can you visit?"

She couldn't help her smile. "Well," she said, regrouping, "I help with the birds in the morning and evening."

"After hours on a Saturday is good. I'm open nine to two."

"I need an appointment?"

He put the truck in gear. "Nope."

Muirie watched him go down the drive and turn back onto the highway toward town, raising a spray of gravel and dust as he accelerated past the mailbox. He turned east, and the dust drifted west in the chilly air, over the fence line and into the pasture, empty of everything but scrubby, weather-beaten grass.

Sherman. A funny name, she thought. A little stodgy and old-fashioned. A name that had seemed to suit him until that last exchange. She snorted out a laugh, wondering if she should have felt offended. She didn't.

She let her eye roam across the land. To the south was the long ridge of Hartsong; to the east, the spine of the hogback that had inspired the ranch's first name—Red Ridge Ranch—rare-meat pink in the dying light. North of the house, the land sloped gently toward the Platte, intersected by the muddy little creek also called Uncle John, unforested except for the cottonwoods along the drainages and the pines eking out a stingy existence in the crevices of the rock.

It wasn't a name you could shorten to Sherm and still maintain any self-respect. Not like Muir, or Bert, which had some spirit. She tried it out, whispering it a couple of times—"Sherm"—wondering if any lover had ever called him that. Doubtful, highly doubtful. Some names couldn't be shortened. Sherman was one of those.

She turned to see a car coming down the driveway, a big, bronze Chevrolet or Buick, a boat. It rounded the bend, bouncing its way slowly over the bumps, springs wheezing. A dark silhouette behind the wheel waved, a woman's handkerchief-wave, not the solemn, no-speakum-English raised palm that Sherman had shown.

The woman maneuvered the car slowly, its power steering whining, to a parking place in front of the big barn. It was Flo Drummond. She waved again at Muirie, killed the ignition, and set the emergency brake with a tremendous heave-ho, as if she were on a precipitous slope.

Muirie folded her arms, smiling. What would she do in San Francisco, where you had insinuate yourself into a space six inches longer than your car on a thirty-degree incline?

Flo took Muirie's hand as she got out of the car. "Good grief, you're frozen," she said, eyeing Muirie with instant, motherly indignation. "What in the world are you doing out here with no gloves on? And no jacket. Just a thin little sweater."

The sweater was a two-pound alpaca of Roberta's. "I refuse to wear gloves in the spring," Muirie said. "Long underwear, a parka, wool socks, okay. But not gloves. I'd feel mummified. It's too much."

"You sound just like Bertie, rebelling against the weather. Where can that lead?"

"I'm trying to harden myself."

This pained Flo. "Why in the world do you want to be hard?"

Muirie saw a rolled-up shopping bag on the front seat of the car. "Come in the house," she said. "There's even a fire. We can both warm up."

Flo glanced toward the door of the big barn. "Oh, I can't stay. I just brought something for Bertie." She put a hand to her lips, perplexed. "It's a dead bird. A raven, I think. I found it when I was out walking."

She looked at Muirie in dismay. "God knows how many dead creatures I've seen in my life. I even lost my second child, a little girl, when she was born. You can't think about it, you just go on. But Bertie has got me to noticing birds over the years. I never used to see them, and now I even know the names of some."

A sudden look of distraction chased away her smile. She touched Muirie's arm "Maybe I won't bother her with it."

"Come on," Muirie said, linking arms with her. "She's in the barn."

Roberta stood before the open freezer in the workroom, clipboard in hand, inventorying the supply of frozen food for the birds.

Flo held up the bag like a huge sack lunch. "You're going to think I've lost my mind, Bertie. I brought you a dead bird."

Roberta, surprised, took the bag without a word. She unrolled it on the countertop. "A raven," she said, reaching inside.

Flo put a hand to her heart. "Oh, what would Carl say if he knew I was bringing you a dead bird? He'd think I was turning into a crazy bird lady like you."

"God forbid," said Roberta, smiling.

Roberta laid the bird out on the counter. Its size surprised Muirie. It was as large as some of the hawks in the hospital, and black from the tip of its heavy, lancelike bill to its curling toes, the glossy, gloomy, black of an elegant hearse. Roberta touched the joints of its wings, moving them gently against their rigor mortis. Muirie saw no obvious injury. The bird's head was turned to the side. The bill gaped a little above an ascot of ruffled feathers at the chin.

"Where did you find it?" Roberta asked.

Flo pulled a tissue from under the belt of her dress and glanced up, abashed. "This seems so silly suddenly, doesn't it? It's a dead bird."

"Then a fair chunk of my work is silly," Roberta said, wry.

"Oh, I don't mean that. I only mean, what can you do for it now? Not a thing in the world."

Roberta ran her thumb and forefinger along the scaly legs of the bird, checking for breaks. "Where did you find it?"

"Well, you know how I like to get out for a walk sometimes," she said hesitantly. She gave Muirie a smile. "A long winter here, you start to lose your mind shut up in the house."

She put the tissue back without using it, tucking it away carefully as if it had to be stowed just so. "It was mild out this morning, so I just threw on my coat and took off. Didn't even change my shoes. And I ended up down there where the Eberson road swings close to the high-way. I was just about to turn back and head home when I saw something black on a patch of snow next to some sagebrush."

She smiled again, her hesitation leaving her. "I think it caught my eye because there's not much that's so pure black as this on the land. Everything's brown, the color of a sparrow, or else snow white. But this gleamed at me, and I walked over to see what it was, and it looked so perfect, like it might get up and fly in my face."

She might have been describing one of her paintings, Muirie thought.

Roberta was still studying the bird. "How close to the road? Could it have been hit?"

Flo's hand went to her heart again. "Oh. A ways. More than the length of this room. It would have had to fly there after it was hit, but there's hardly any traffic on that road. It's just a rutted dirt path."

"Was there anything on the road? Any roadkill? A prairie dog the raven might have been feeding on?"

The rapid-fire questions confused Flo. "I'm not sure. I didn't look close enough to say."

Watching her, Roberta stepped back from the bird. "Well, it's hard to tell. It could have been hit. Internal injuries don't always kill immediately. It might have flown a ways. If it had been dead long, scavengers would have found it before you did."

"Does it look healthy otherwise?" Muirie asked.

Roberta smiled grimly. "Other than that it's dead?" She touched the breastbone, the beak, fingered the glossy feathers of the tail. "It's got a good fat store. No signs of disease that I can see." She aimed a thoughtful gaze at Flo. "Carl's not purging his pastures, is he? For prairie dogs or anything?"

"No," Flo said firmly, defiant. "Not us. We got rid of all our poison years ago. I told Carl I wouldn't have that stuff around with the grandchildren." She turned to Muirie. "I read that a child could die from just touching a can of one of those poisons we used to use—if he put his fingers in his mouth—and you know a child always will. I won't have it around."

Roberta's lips tightened. "I'll store this in the freezer for now," she said, slipping the raven inside a plastic garbage bag. She twisted it shut as if it were somebody's neck.

Muirie walked with Flo back through the barn, linking arms with her again. They strolled, looking at every patient as they went. Flo stopped to peer in at Chugwater, a red-tail, who peered calmly back.

"They give me the willies a little," she said. "The way they stare. They remind me of cats."

"You don't like cats?"

They moved on to Beetle's cage.

"Oh, we have some barn cats, of course. It's not a matter of liking them. But you never know what a cat's thinking, do you?"

"I kind of like that about them. The mystery."

"It seems like they're always after something, though. Slinking around, figuring their chances."

"Keeping themselves fed," Muirie said equably.

"That's true," said Flo, smiling again. "Just like the rest of us."

Roberta was standing motionless by the window when Muirie returned to the workroom.

"You think it might have been poisoned?"

Roberta answered flatly. "Yes."

"But why would anyone poison ravens?"

"For the most part they wouldn't. Not directly. But it's spring. Ranchers want to defend their stock. They're after coyotes, prairie dogs, foxes, but the poisons they use can kill anything."

"Do they put out some kind of poisoned meat?"

"There are a dozen methods. One is to mix poison with hot fat or lard and then pour it in ice-cube trays. Then you disperse the congealed cubes by hand or from the air. They're impossible for people to spot, but hungry animals find them fast enough."

Muirie slumped against the counter. "That can't be legal."

"Legal," mocked Roberta, turning from the window. "When does legality ever matter?"

"Then it isn't legal?"

"The deadliest poisons were banned by the feds before you were born. All the supplies in every state were supposed to be destroyed but some were relabeled, hidden, sometimes by the state officials themselves. It's been available on the black market since. You hear rumors about illegal manufacturing. You just have to know who to ask."

"The one Flo was talking about, the one that could kill a kid. *It* must be illegal."

"She probably means sodium fluoroacetate. They call it Compound

1080. Its only legal use is in sheep collars. They fill bladders in the collar with poison, and then if a coyote happens to attack a sheep wearing a collar and it also happens to go for the neck, it gets a dose in the mouth. It's an almost perfect poison: hard to detect, easy to mix, stable, so it won't biodegrade fast. And it works slow, so the coyote or fox or bear or mountain lion or eagle will eat its fill before it starts to get sick. That way it gets a lethal dose. And since coyotes are always on the move, it's easy for a rancher to avoid detection. A poisoned coyote might travel miles before it dies. Who would ever find them? Who would ever know?"

Muirie stared at her.

Roberta sat on the table, her feet on the straight-backed wooden chair. "Every wild animal out there costs a rancher money. Prairie dogs not only eat the grass that the stock needs, they also fill the pastures with burrows that the stupid cattle blunder into, breaking their legs. And coyotes prey on sheep; they say eagles do, too."

"They 'say' eagles do," Muirie repeated.

"You hear stories about eagles carrying off lambs. It's been documented in some places but it doesn't happen often. I've never seen it myself. You'd have to have a small lamb and a large eagle. What happens is that lots of ranchers leave their bands unattended out in the middle of nowhere, and the lambs die of exposure, illness, snakebite, a thousand things, and the eagles clean up the carcasses. But when ranchers see an eagle on a carcass, that makes the case for saying it killed the lamb."

"So what's next, then?" Muirie asked. "How do we find out if the raven was poisoned?"

Her earnestness amused Roberta. "One dead raven doesn't mean much. I could send it off for a toxicology test, but they're expensive. I have my own method. It doesn't identify the poison but it shows if one's there."

"Then let's do it."

Roberta pursed her lips. "You won't like it."

Muirie fell silent for a moment. "This is why, isn't it? The reason you quit ranching? It sounds like a war with no holds barred. They're using chemical weapons against the wildlife."

Roberta studied her, kindly. "I know you'd rather have things the way they used to be. Like when my dad was alive."

"That's not what I'm talking about," Muirie said, irritated.

"We didn't worry about these things then."

"That's not what I mean." But she wasn't sure. She shrugged. "I'll admit that I'd like a few cattle around. Just a few, maybe, here and there. Would that be so bad?"

"For atmosphere, you mean?" And Roberta smiled. "Lawn ornaments, Western style."

CHAPTER EIGHTEEN

It seemed to Carl that he and Flo had the grandkids almost every weekend lately. He'd mentioned this to Flo earlier in the day before Annie dropped the children off. "The ski season's just about over," she said. "They want to take advantage of it."

"Of us, you mean," he'd said, grumpily.

He didn't mind the kids so much, especially Luke, but they were a couple of tornadoes when the weather was bad. He could escape, Hank and Annie could escape, but Flo had to stay cooped up with them.

"Carl?"

Flo was staring at him fixedly from across the table. "Yoo-hoo. Luke is trying to talk to you."

Carl's distraction evaporated. Whatever irritation he felt with Hank and Annie, he did not want to communicate it to the boy.

"Can we go for a ride now, Grandpa?" Luke had already spooned up the last of his stew.

Carl looked into his own bowl. A couple of big spoonfuls and a little juice left over to sop up with his bread. He could do without it. "Well, you can't ride sitting in that chair."

Luke stood up as if the chair had scorched him. He tucked in his shirt, wiped his milk mustache neatly on his sleeve. Charlotte blinked, her spoon held upright in midair like a lollipop.

"You can come, too, Lottie," Carl said, gruff.

Pan came to the door of his stall when they walked into the barn. Luke went directly to him, reaching out his hand, and the horse lowered his head, ears cocked forward, to breathe him in, nuzzling the crown of Luke's head, nostrils flaring with interest at the strange little-boy odors of soap and ingrained soil, of sweat and mutton stew. The boy didn't flinch at the investigation. He patted Pan's neck seriously, his nose just inches from the gleaming coat. Charlotte held Carl's hand and watched the horse warily, her tiny body tensed to flee. Carl picked her up and carried her to the tack room. He would use Flo's saddle, he decided. It fit Pan but the seat was smaller and would be more comfortable for the boy. He slung a bridle over his shoulder and one-handed the saddle by the horn.

"You're going to have to get down while I saddle up that horse, Lottie," he said, walking back to the stall.

She clutched at him like a monkey.

"I can saddle him," Luke said. "I'm tall enough now."

Carl doubted it. He threw the saddle over the half-door of the adjacent stall and hung the bridle over the horn.

"Got to groom him first," he said.

"I can do it," Luke said, reaching for the lead rope hung on the wall. He clipped it to Pan's halter and opened the latch on the stall door.

Pan walked peacefully from his stall, head low and steady, trusting this boy to know what he was doing. Luke walked close to his shoulder, not shying away from the massiveness of the horse or the thud of his hooves on the barn floor. He talked to Pan gently.

"Good boy, good horse."

It was amazing, really, given that Luke hadn't spent much time around horses. Lots of ranch kids seven years old already knew horses inside out, had their own. But Hank didn't encourage his children to think of themselves as ranch kids. The clothes he and Annie dressed them in were testimony to that. Charlotte looked like a picture in a magazine, always matched from head to toe, even her socks and a little bow in her curling hair. Luke wore new denims, faded at the factory, bright-colored shirts with wide stripes, and sixty-dollar sneakers. He had a fire-engine red parka and wore a woolen ski cap with a little fluffy ball on top that looked like something Charlotte should wear. When Carl and Flo had given cowboy boots to Luke for Christmas two years ago, Annie said they were "inappropriate for growing feet."

Luke fumbled with the lead. His head dropped. "I forgot how to tie it," he said clearly, owning up.

Carl tied it for him, slowly, and without a word. The boy was observant; he didn't need someone telling him over and over. And sometimes you learned a thing faster if you thought you were already expected to know it.

Luke gave the knot a tug and threw a satisfied glance at Carl. Carl smiled inwardly. A boy who could appreciate a knot at so young an age was a boy he could love.

Pan bobbed his head; looking around his eyes met Carl's briefly. Those old brown dog eyes, always sad. It made you want to apologize to him.

"Hey, old boy," Carl said.

Luke slapped Pan's neck. "Hey, old boy."

Luke went at the job of grooming confidently, brushing with a swift downward stroke. Pan's eyes fluttered with pleasure; he shook himself gently and the boy startled, then realized what had happened, all in a second or less. He didn't look up, didn't move away, didn't miss a stroke.

"Should I clean out his hoofs?" he asked.

Carl wanted to appear to consider the offer seriously. Pan had been on clean straw all winter, and Carl brushed him down twice a week whether he'd been ridden or not. "Skip it this time. You'll need a saddle pad."

The boy took the brushes back to the tack room and brought out a lamb's-wool pad, the wrong one, too large for the saddle, but it didn't matter. He let Pan see the pad, touched the horse's shoulder, then swung the pad onto his back. The saddle, though, was too heavy for him. Carl lifted it for him, letting the boy bear some of the weight, and they swung it together over the horse's back. It landed crooked, one stirrup caught beneath the skirt but Luke's motion had been smooth.

The boy threaded the cinch, then hesitated. Carl could see him wondering whether he could get it tight enough by himself.

"I'd better cinch that thing up," Carl said. "Pan sometimes, he can blow up a bit on you."

Luke stood back, watching keenly. He hadn't been sure about this either, Carl realized, and he was going to memorize it this time.

Carl gave Pan's withers a pat. "You take care of Lottie here and I'll slip that bridle on."

He lowered Lottie to the ground. She sniffled, grasping at him. Luke ignored her and stood at Carl's side as he slipped the bit into Pan's mouth.

"Take the halter off his neck?" Luke asked, his hand already on the clasp.

Carl nodded.

"Can I be first?"

"Don't you think we ought to let girls go first?"

Luke grimaced, shoving his hands in his pockets. Lottie shook her head vigorously.

"I'll go with you, Lottie," Carl said. "Just like last time."

As he picked her up, she struggled, whining. He swung quickly into the saddle, securing her against his belly with an arm around her waist. If you let children think about things like this, they'd think all the wrong things. You had to fill them with sensations and show them some confidence. The last thing a kid needed was a hesitant adult. Despite the noise of Lottie's fuss, Pan walked to the barn door, so smooth he might have had wheels. Luke swung the door open and stood aside proudly as if he owned the place.

"Should I get that corral gate now, Grandpa?"

That corral gate. As if he knew its peculiarities. Carl nodded. Charlotte braced against him like her spine had fused. She gripped the arm of his jacket with both hands forsaking the sucked finger.

Luke closed the gate behind them and climbed up onto the top rail to watch, hunching forward like an old cowhand. He'd gotten it off TV, that slouchy look of nonchalance. But he looked painfully suburban perched there in his red parka and sneakers, like a kid at his first rodeo imitating the cowboys.

Carl guided Pan to the fence line. Charlotte was relaxing, he thought. Her grip on his jacket sleeves wasn't so steely. It surprised him. Last fall, she'd been a crybaby about the riding the whole time, panicking when he'd urged Pan into a slow trot. But now she let loose of his sleeve with one hand and took hold of the horn. A definite move of independence.

He pressed Pan gently with his knees and the horse lifted into a trot. Lottie grabbed for his sleeve again but she didn't cry.

Luke gave a shrill whoop from the sidelines. "Make him gallop, Grandpa!"

Carl shifted his weight so minutely he didn't think Pan would read the message, but the horse lengthened his gait into a slow canter without a single hop of indecision. It was smoother than the trot and only a little faster, a gait Carl loved. But it was too soon for Lottie. She screeched, fighting to release herself from Carl's grip. It was crazy; she'd fall off. Carl whirled the horse to a standstill, a fancier move than necessary, and one that only scared Lottie more, but he wanted her to see that a horse could move fast without hurting her. As long as she was scared anyway, he might as well broaden the lesson.

She flailed like a wet cat, screaming. Luke leapt from the fence and grabbed Pan's bridle as Carl dismounted, wrestling the girl.

"All right, Lottie. You can stop the god-awful racket now."

He set her down purposefully next to the fence and held her arms against her sides to calm her.

"You're all right. That didn't hurt you at all."

He released her. She bounced away from him in her panic and sat down solidly in the dirt, her mouth dropping open in a bawl.

"All right, all right," he said, grabbing her again by the armpits. She kicked. "I'll take you to Grandma." He turned to Luke. "You just hold on there."

Flo was already coming down the path from the kitchen door. "She fell off, didn't she?"

He handed the child over. "She didn't have a chance to fall off. She's scared of horses. She's scared of everything."

Lottie clung to Flo's neck. "For heaven's sake, Carl, she's four years old."

"You were riding a horse at four."

"I was riding a pony at four." She looked past him to the corral. "And now you've gone and let that boy ride alone."

Luke was astride Pan, circling slowly along the fence, his posture relaxed, head up, and he hadn't been on a horse in a couple of months.

Carl yelled at him, trying to sound fierce. "Git down off that horse! Hold him over there next to the fence like you were told!"

Luke slid from the saddle, reins in hand, and stood at the horse's shoulders, looking calmly at Carl across the width of the corral and the yard. There was a fine looseness to him, a confidence and grace that made Carl's face twitch with the need to smile. He turned back to Flo, chewing on his lip.

"I didn't tell him to get on that horse, Flo. He did it himself."

Lottie hiccoughed, her finger in her mouth. Flo's lips were pursed into a silence he didn't like.

"I want to find one of those old pairs of boots Hank had when he was a boy," he said lightly. "I know you kept them around somewhere, up in the attic or somewhere."

"Annie won't have it."

"I can't have him riding in sneakers. His foot slips through the stirrup and he falls off, he'll be drug around for sure. It's dangerous and you know it. He needs heels."

Flo's eyes narrowed. "For that old lunk of a horse?"

"It's possible."

She swept Lottie's damp bangs to the side. "I don't even know where that stuff is anymore."

"It's all in boxes upstairs. You never throw anything out."

Flo sighed. "All right. I'll go up and look around."

"No, I'll go. You stay with Lottie. Just tell me where."

She knew exactly where. She hollered instructions from the bottom of the attic steps, directing him to a far corner, behind a rack of old clothes swathed in dry-cleaner's plastic wrap. There they were. It looked like every single pair of Hank's boots from age two to eighteen, tucked into their original boxes and piled in two stacks, the smaller boxes from the younger ages on top, grading down to the boots he'd worn just twenty years before. *Just* twenty years. You had to be old to have a thought like that. It seemed like a blink of time, and two blinks to the tiny boxes at the top of the stack.

He pulled the uppermost box open, snorting at the dust from the lid. Miniature red boots, scuffed through to dingy dry leather. Hank's head was always a little in advance of his feet back in those days and the boy had been utterly indifferent to collisions. His head, more often than not, had looked like these boots, scuffed and beat-up, bonked around. He rarely cried, however hard he fell. He simply got up, stubborn and a little angry, and charged off again headlong.

"What's keeping you?" Flo called.

He ran his finger down the sides of the boxes. "I'm coming, I'm coming," he said. But he opened another box, one of the biggest sizes. This was a pair he'd picked out for Hank himself for his sixteenth birthday. Fine, soft leather, hand-tooled, two-toned, camel and brown, rich colors, and Hank had hardly worn them. The bottoms were just scratched. He drew in a lungful of the smell of them, unsullied by socks and mud and shit. They were good as new. Or as bad as new, seeing as how they'd been bought to be worn. It was another of Hank's insults, an early one, a refusal to appreciate anything his father did for him, especially in a matter as personal as boots. He'd worn his old boots until they'd cramped his toes rather than wear these. It had been the kind of situation where words would have made things worse, and the silence was bad enough.

He shifted another of the small boxes at the top. These were plain boots, about the right size, dark brown, with good, sturdy heels, and pretty well beat up with use, something to tone down Luke's imagination about being a hotshot rodeo cowboy. They'd do fine.

"Carl!"

He grunted, straightening up.

"What in God's name is taking you so long?"

"Where's some hats?" he yelled.

"What?"

"Hats!"

He heard the attic ladder creak, a whimper from Lottie as Flo put her down, then the sound of Flo coming slowly up the ladder. Her head appeared.

"Honestly, Carl."

He scratched at a temple, looking down at her. "Annie can't have objections to a hat."

"I don't know about that."

He sniffed, intransigent. She sighed. "There aren't many. Up on that shelf over the stairs here, to your left. There's a few boxes. One of those ones clear to the end."

Lottie said something, whining, and Flo's head disappeared. Carl took out a straw hat, size small. It was battered on the top, bent up on the sides, sweat-stained along the inside. Hank must have slept in this one, or sat on it. Carl smoothed the band and bent down the brim, trying to straighten it out, but it made no change in the looks of the thing at all. It was thoroughly used-up—a nasty, mean-looking little cowboy hat. Luke would love it.

"Just sit right back in your seat," he told the boy. "You got to relax a little more for the trot. Sit too stiff and you bounce all around, lose control."

Luke slouched forward like a humpback, watching Carl.

"No, I don't mean sit like your spine's gone soft either. I mean just relax."

The boy straightened again, adjusting his shoulders.

"That's better. Now take him around again. Go ahead and trot."

Luke had put the hat on proudly, self-consciously, smiling. Now the smile disappeared, giving way to intense solemnity, like a crown prince attending to royal duties. He kept Pan on the fence, circling the corral at a gentle jog.

"Looks good," Carl said. "You're not bouncing around like an old woman now, see?"

After several revolutions, Luke reined Pan to a halt in front of Carl. "Could I lope him, Grandpa? Just once around?"

Carl considered, then winked at the boy. Luke turned Pan on the fence once more, and the horse leaned into a lope as though the command from Luke had been mental.

Carl stepped back. It was a beautiful thing to see, a young boy in the saddle, riding like he was part of the horse, in charge, in full control, master of an animal so much larger than himself. And he did it naturally. It looked like no effort at all.

CHAPTER NINETEEN

Glen slathered margarine on a second piece of toast, swirling it liberally to every edge. He studied his handiwork with satisfaction before taking a bite, then washed it down with a gulp of coffee, and poured everyone another cupful. "So what are you two up to today?"

Roberta glanced up, amused, from the newspaper. "Just the usual stuff for us. We don't lead the exciting life you do."

Glen gave a laugh. "Yessiree. Kiwanis one day, Junior League the next. Nothing but excitement for me."

"I want to deal with that raven, and the flight barn needs some work," Roberta said to Muirie. "I was thinking of running the hose out there and washing down the whole damn thing. You up for helping?"

Muirie hesitated. "Can we do it this morning?"

"Sure."

"I was thinking of driving into town this afternoon to see Sherman's clinic."

Glen set his cup down. "Really? He's still running the place, is he? Bertie always makes it sound like he'll be on the dole next week."

"He's got a hawk there I'd like to see. A ferruginous that he and Aunt

Bert saved."

Glen considered jelly, deciding against it. "He keeps a hawk in that little place?"

"The blind one," Roberta said flatly, scanning the newspaper again.

"You don't mean the one that lost both eyes?" Glen touched the nosepiece of his glasses. "I thought you put it down."

"We should have," Roberta said.

Muirie watched her for a moment. "You haven't seen it lately, though, Aunt Bert."

Roberta turned a page. "I don't need to."

Glen turned to Muirie. "So what's Sherman doing with it?"

"Not a thing," Roberta answered. "It sits around in the darkness surrounded by barking dogs."

"Sherman's been training it," Muirie said.

Roberta pushed her chair back, rubbing at her mouth with her napkin. She touched Muirie's shoulder as she passed into the hall. "I know, I know. He's doing his penance."

"Penance?" Muirie echoed.

But Roberta was already striding toward the living room. They heard the front door boom shut behind her.

Glen topped off his coffee, meditative. "So that's why Sherman keeps the hawk at his clinic. Bertie won't have it here."

Muirie couldn't shake her surprise. "He said she was a little touchy about it."

"Touchy?" Glen said. "Bertie?"

Muirie sipped her coffee, smiling. They had taken to sitting together at breakfast almost every morning for a few minutes, minus Roberta, and sometimes again in the evening, in the quiet of his office after Roberta had gone to bed. During Muirie's childhood, Glen had stayed in the background, an eternally busy presence: kind, soft-spoken, quick to smile, but unsure how to engage the mind of a child, and therefore a little intimidating. She found a peacefulness now in his company that she could not have imagined then.

"I expect Sherman's over there polishing the place up for you," he said.

"I hope not. I want to see it in its natural state."

"You like him?"

"I just met him, Uncle Glen."

"I don't expect he meets many girls. I'd judge him a little shy."

"He didn't seem all that shy to me."

Glen's glasses dropped to the end of his nose. "Oh? That's significant. You must have made him feel comfortable."

"I doubt it," she said. "That's not exactly my history with men."

"Your history with men?" He waved a hand at her. "You're not old enough to have a history with men. You only think you do." He gave a sigh. "Sherman, though—I think he might have been married before."

"Was he?"

"I don't know any details."

"You wouldn't," she said. "You're too decent to listen to gossip."

"Oh, I listen to gossip all the time. It's ninety percent of politics. Ask Bertie."

"You're warning me away?"

"From Sherman?" Another wave of the hand. "Not a bit. I like him. So does Bertie, whatever she says, and you know she doesn't like just anybody."

Kneeling on the dank dirt floor of the big barn, Roberta reached for the live trap behind the row of cages nearest the workroom. The metal door was shut: she had a catch. As she touched the trap, something scuttled wildly inside. She peeked through the mesh, tilting the trap so that its occupant slid forward into the light, scrambling like a rock climber losing its grip. A deer mouse, *Peromyscus*. It would do fine.

She had defrosted the raven and laid it out on newspapers on the workroom table, along with the necessary tools: latex gloves, a scalpel, some disposable Styrofoam bowls, a plastic eyedropper. Muirie came in as she teased opened the skin of the raven's abdomen from cloaca to esophagus with a series of quick, clean cuts. She heard Muirie's intake of breath—this might be a little much right after breakfast—but didn't look up. "Don't touch anything. Poisons can go through any little break in the skin."

Muirie pulled a stool from beneath the counter and sat at a distance, leaning forward; scooted closer and leaned again. She gave Roberta a weak smile. She hadn't noticed the trap; the mouse, terrified, had frozen into immobility. "What about breathing it? You're not wearing a mask."

"I would if it were in powder form."

With the tip of her scalpel, Roberta moved aside a neat loop of intestine, exposing a solid, bean-shaped organ. "A testis," she said. "A sign of spring: it's swollen."

"What are you going to do?"

Roberta probed the crop, just above the stomach, finding it fuller than she'd expected. Ten-eighty was the poison of choice around here. It acted more slowly than some, often allowing time for a meal to be partially digested. If the crop was full, the bird had died with relative dispatch. That didn't eliminate 1080. It could indicate a big overdose.

"We're going to see about secondary poisoning," she said.

"How?"

Roberta sliced open the crop and the narrow stomach below, scraping the brownish contents into a Styrofoam bowl. She nodded at the trap. "I caught a mouse last night."

Muirie's eyes shot to the trap, then to the smear of muck in the bowl. She cupped a hand on her belly. "You're going to feed that to the mouse?"

"I said you wouldn't like it."

A note of desperation. "There's no other way?"

"If there's no poison here, all the mouse suffers is a free meal. Force-fed, true enough, but that's not so bad."

"But couldn't there be any other reason why the raven died? Something other than poison?"

Roberta sighed, staring again into the graying mass of the bird's innards. "I'm not a physiologist. I don't see internal bleeding from an impact, but I don't see the organ abnormalities poisons can cause either. I don't know enough to differentiate them from disease with confidence anyway."

The mouse shifted, scratching at a corner. Muirie closed her eyes.

"We feed mice and rats to the birds all the time, Muirie."

"I know that. You don't have to tell me that."

"What should I tell you, then?"

"Why this kind of thing happens at all."

Roberta snorted softly. "Welcome to adulthood."

"That's very helpful. Thanks."

Roberta laid her scalpel aside. "I'm sorry, kiddo. I don't mean to sound heartless." Muirie lifted doubtful eyes. "I don't want you to think that. You have to be a little tough to do this job."

Muirie nodded. "I know."

She helped with the force-feeding, but could barely watch its aftermath. The mouse died.

"Fast and ugly," said Roberta, with something close to satisfaction. "If it's 1080, it may mean a heavy concentration."

"So what do we do now? Call somebody? Make a report to the state or something?"

This suggestion seemed to amuse Roberta, grimly. "Let me tell you something. Up until it was caught a few years ago, the state published a little brochure on the use of predacides that included specific instructions on how to calculate lethal doses of 1080, a recipe for dosing carcass baits using poison that had been made strictly illegal almost twenty years before."

Muirie sat back, almost afraid to ask. "And the federal people?"

"Same breed, one level removed."

"Then what else is there to do?"

"How about banning ranchers?"

Sherman's clinic was part of a row of flat-roofed cinder-block shops at a gravel-strewn highway intersection near downtown. No curb, no sidewalk, no awnings, no color of any kind other than gray. On a felt signboard inside the glass door were the words WEST CASPER ANIMAL HOSPITAL, SHERMAN LLOYD, D.V.M. and the daily hours of operation. A cardboard placard said, OPEN. PLEASE COME IN.

A bell tinkled over her head as Muirie pushed the door open into a linoleum-floored waiting room. A phone rang tediously at the deserted reception desk, and two people in stiff-backed chairs looked up at her: an old man with an ancient, rheumy-eyed black Labrador and a lanky woman with a toddler at her knee and a kitten in a basket. They shot irritated glances toward the phone and the desk, inviting her to join them in disapproving of the way the place was run. She paused, calculating. She had no pet in her arms; Sherman had not come out, and, in order to find him, she'd need to pass through the door behind the reception desk. They'd conclude she worked here.

She went for the phone. She'd grown up around animals: horses and cattle at the ranch, dogs and cats at home. It couldn't be difficult to field a phone call.

She answered with her best authoritative voice, netting an immediate look of indictment from the two in the waiting room: she had not been at her post. She gave them a steely smile as she listened to a long explanation of what sounded like ear mites in a cat, paging through to Monday in Sherman's appointment book. It was mostly empty. She scheduled the cat for Monday afternoon and picked up another phone call on the first ring.

"West Casper Animal Hospital."

Two male voices answered, one faint and uncertain. The other was Sherman's. He'd answered an extension in back somewhere. "Who's this?" he demanded.

"I got this dog," said the faint voice.

"Sherman, it's me. Muirie."

The elderly voice quavered. "He's got a torn pad—"

"You've got a client on the line," she said.

"Then where are you?"

She rolled the reception chair backward and thumped on the door to the back, knocking it open. She stuck a hand through, waving, thinking he might be within sight. The client's voice answered amiably, "I'm at home."

Sherman came to the door, the phone clamped to his ear. He spoke into the receiver while looking into her face, grinning. "I didn't know you were here."

"Oh, I been here all day," said the old man.

Though he was ready to launch into a tour of the clinic then and there, she told him she'd wait while he finished with his patients. He pulled his eyes from hers to glance at the waiting room and the stony faces there. "I'll look around a little on my own," she said. "You go on."

"Okay," he said. "But don't go into that back room. The hawk's there."

"He's dangerous?"

A smile passed over his face. "No. I just want to be there when you see him."

The clinic was about as basic as you could get. A fluorescent bulb in the waiting room buzzed and zapped like a bug light. The curtainless windows looked out onto the parking strip and, across the highway, another identical row of shops. The doorway behind the desk opened onto a dark little hallway. The forbidden room was at its far end, if such a short hallway could be said to have anything "far" about it. On one side of the hall were two examination rooms, on the other a supply closet and a telephone-booth-sized bathroom with a pile-of-puppies calendar tacked to the door.

Sherman dispensed with the Lab and the kitten in less than thirty minutes, but without sounding rushed, she thought, listening to his voice penetrate the hollow-core door of the exam room where she waited, sitting on the stainless steel table. He came into the hallway twice, going for supplies, peering at her each time as if he expected her to have gone away. He wore jeans and a muted plaid wool shirt, boots. His uniform, she thought. A stethoscope poked out of his shirt pocket.

"Where's your white coat?" she whispered on his second trip into the hall.

He spread his hands on his chest. "You think I need one?"

"I was expecting you to look more doctorly."

He rattled the stethoscope. "This doesn't do it?"

She pretended doubts. He ducked back into the exam room next door. "Try him on these vitamins," she heard him say to the owner of the Lab. "He's doing well; you take good care of him. But we all get old someday."

"Don't you have any help besides me?" she asked him as he closed the door behind the old man.

"During the week a Casper College girl comes in part-time, but on Saturdays, I'm on my own." He looked apologetic. "You caught me at my worst, letting the phone ring like that. The machine's supposed to catch it but it's not working half the time. Don't tell Roberta. She'll take it as further evidence." He cocked his head toward the hallway. "Let me put him on his perch. I'll be right back."

A moment later, he waved her in.

The room looked like a converted garage, cement-floored and rectangular. On one long wall stood a tier of cages, a few with residents: a pouting schnauzer, a stupendously bored orange tabby, and a mixed-breed puppy with long ears that yipped and bowed at them hopefully. Muirie realized she had not heard any barking until now.

The hawk stood on a tall perch on the opposite side of the room in a corner by a small window. It stirred, turning its head toward them. In the diffused light, its belly was creamy white, spotted with rust, its wings a vivid auburn. The legs were feathered to the toes, as if the bird wore trousers. She saw the streaked mask of the small face, dull where pale eyes should be. Nevertheless, her impression was that the bird stared right at them.

"Teiresias," Sherman called softly. "He knows his name."

"Teiresias?"

Sherman looked as though he were confessing something slightly shameful. "I found it in a book on mythology. It's the name of a blind fortune-teller in ancient Greece, a sort of soothsayer."

The perch gave the bird a head's height over them both.

"How do you get him down?"

"With a step stool. He likes to be up high."

"He knows where the floor is?"

"Sure. He sees it with sound. He sees your voice."

Muirie stepped closer, looking into the bird's face. The eyes were gone completely, the sockets as empty and dry as smooth pits in a stone. But somehow the face did not look incomplete. Instead, the consciousness of the bird was penetrating. She felt it suddenly, a shock of realization that she was being studied in return, intently.

"Can he smell me?"

Sherman took a short leather gauntlet from a countertop and unfolded the step stool in front of the perch. "Probably not. Most birds don't have much of a sense of smell. They're visual hunters. They have such big eyes that the part of their brain responsible for smell is reduced to make room for them. There's exceptions. Vultures, for instance."

He mounted the step stool and secured the bird's lead in his hand, then unhooked the swivel and pressed his knuckles gently against Teiresias's breast, speaking softly to the bird. The hawk stepped onto his fist gracefully, attending to his voice. Sherman backed slowly off the ladder. "I'll give you a little demonstration."

Glen had been right. Sherman may not have polished the clinic with a dust rag but he had his floor show planned. On a countertop lay a carefully prepared meal of raw chicken chunks. Sherman placed one of the chunks between the hawk's feet.

"I used to have to hand-feed him. I'd shred the chicken and give him one piece at a time by shoving it at his beak. But now watch."

Teiresias lowered his head toward his feet but did not seem to realize food was there, although Muirie could smell the tang of raw flesh in the air.

Sherman dug in his pocket, bringing out a small, saucer-shaped squeak toy of the type dog trainers used. He gave it a squeeze in his palm. At the mouselike shrill, Teiresias unhesitatingly secured the meat with a taloned foot, seized it in his beak, tossed his head back, and swallowed the chunk whole with a single, protracted gulp.

Sherman's face tightened; he was trying not to smile. "Hawks usually tear up their food. But he's smart. He knows that because he's blind he might not be able to find all the pieces, so he eats it whole. It doesn't look like much, I know, but I hated shoving food at him. I wanted him to do it for himself."

"To grant him some dignity," she said.

The tightness in his face dissolved.

"Can I try it?"

"Sure."

He outfitted her with a gauntlet and they transferred the hawk between them. Muirie imitated Sherman's technique of nudging Teiresias at the breast with the back of her hand. He stepped onto her fist with ease and settled there quickly, his profile as lean and elegant as a hieroglyph. He ate the rest of the chicken with alacrity at each of Muirie's signals with the squeaker.

"He's so calm," she said.

"I know. That's why he learned fast. He pays attention."

The hawk roused his feathers and preened delicately at one shoulder.

"Maybe whatever he lost in vision he gained in focus."

"You hear about that with people," Sherman said. "When they go blind, suddenly they hear everything, even tiny sounds they never heard consciously before."

Muirie studied the bird. "And there's nothing else wrong with him? I mean, his wings weren't injured and he didn't get some kind of brain damage from the collision?"

"Nothing that I can diagnose."

Muirie touched a curled finger to the silken leading edge of a wing. The bird tensed momentarily. "Then why can't he fly?"

Sherman's gaze fixed on her face.

"I mean, there's no mechanical reason why he can't, right?"

"Well, I'd consider blindness a pretty good reason."

"But it doesn't prevent it. I mean, physically, he's capable of flight." Sherman's stare became a little too intent. "You think I'm crazy."

He worked against a smile. "I think it's a peculiar question."

"But what's to keep him grounded? If his wings are okay, and he's healthy, and he's smart and he's trainable, why can't he fly?" She paused, biting back her impatience. Skepticism in the face of an obviously good idea had always struck her as obtuse. "On a creance, I mean. Between the two of us, like Oscar and Jasper. Couldn't he learn that?"

Sherman looked down at the squeaker in his palm, and at Muirie again, a spark of interest in his eyes.

"You've already got him started," she said. "You've already taught him to go for the food at the sound of the squeaker. What we'd have to do is—" He was shaking his head. "—teach him to go between us. Look —"

Muirie put her free hand on Sherman's shoulder and positioned him in front of her, a yard away and face-to-face. "We'd start out like this, see, close together. I've got the bird, but you've got the food and the squeaker. You'd put the chicken on your glove and squeak the squeaker. Continuously, so it's a beacon. He hears the squeaker over there, where you are, and that's the signal. He learns that dinner is wherever the sound is."

Sherman tried to summon up a hopeful look. Her impatience boiled over. "But why not? What's to stop it? As he catches on to what we want, we stand farther and farther apart, and he'll go from walking between us to sort of hopping, and then to flying. Don't you see?"

Sherman's eyes were on Teiresias. "I'd better put him back on his perch for a while."

"You mean I'm getting loud." It was true enough, she realized, bringing her voice down. Teiresias had the look of someone who'd just felt a temblor beneath his feet, tensed and waiting for more.

She handed the hawk over, repentant. Sherman climbed the ladder and transferred him to the perch. "It's not a bad idea," he said.

"Oh, don't be kind," she said quietly. "I can't stand it when men get kind about my ideas. I hate being patronized."

He gave her a sidelong glance as he hooked the clasp on the hawk's gear to the metal loop of the perch.

"You said you wanted to grant him dignity," she said.

He folded the ladder. "*You* said that."

"But you agreed."

"Look, Muirie." It was the first time he'd said her name. "He can't fly. There's too much risk he'd injure himself again. Think about it. Hawks do everything by vision—"

"Not this hawk. You just proved that yourself."

He leaned against the counter.

"What if we just tried it, though?" she said. "For a few days, to see how he does? It's not like I'm suggesting throwing him into the air. I'm saying, let's hand him back and forth. He'd walk from my arm to yours, one foot after the other, three or four steps at the most."

A smile crossed his face. "Are you always like this?"

"Like what?" she said, bristling.

"So . . . optimistic."

She studied him. "That's not what you were going to say. That's not the word you had on the tip of your tongue."

He stared back, unflustered. "So you read minds?"

"Faces. Yours is a marquee."

He crossed his feet at the ankle. "That's what my dad always said."

"So I was right."

"Not quite."

"What, then?"

He considered. "I was just wondering how you can be so certain. You seem like Bert that way. She's always sure."

"You said 'Bird'," Muirie said quietly.

He smiled. She liked his smile.

"I'm *not* always certain," she said. "But some things seem clear from the start. And you need to leap at them."

He touched the shaggy hair at the back of his neck. "Those kinds of things don't seem to happen to me very often."

She sat on the counter next to him. "Won't you try it for a few days, just to see what happens? If you judge it to be dangerous I'll back off, I promise."

His green eyes lingered on her face. "It's risky."

She nudged his shoulder with her own. "Life is risky. Telling me it's risky is risky."

He leaned into her slightly so that the contact was maintained.

"He might fly again," she said. "Think of it."

He nodded. "I am."

"Sentiment," Roberta said, slapping her napkin onto the table. "Look, you can't be in this business and indulge that kind of addle-brained notion. You have to be realistic. You have to let go."

Muirie had not wanted to discuss the plans for Teiresias's training at dinner, feeling they were too fresh and fragile for Roberta's scrutiny. But Roberta had asked about the hawk, pointedly, directly, and Muirie had answered.

"He's tamed it, though," Muirie said, glancing at Glen. "It handles beautifully."

Roberta's voice fell low. "That doesn't make it worth keeping alive."

Muirie laid her fork carefully across her plate. "It doesn't have any other merits?"

"What merits, Muirie?" Roberta said earnestly. "Dependency? Uselessness? Pathos? You can only do so much, and you do the best you can."

She fell silent, watching Muirie, as if hoping this was enough to discourage her. Muirie stared back, unmoved.

"You get them well and release them if they can live in the wild. If they can't, you find a place where they can be useful, educational. That's the tragedy of it, don't you see?—that you have to measure their usefulness in human terms. The best you can do is tragically bad. That hawk should have been allowed to die."

"But he's *not* dead," Muirie said, stunned. "Doesn't that make a difference? Why shouldn't he be allowed to fly if he can? You don't even know how we're planning to do it."

"The question is why, not how. You want to turn him into an organ grinder's monkey. The bird's blind; it'll always be blind. It has no chance of flying free in its entire life."

Muirie stared, stone-faced, at her plate.

"All right," said Roberta. "I suppose that's enough. I won't say more." She pressed her lips together. "Except this. I want you to read something. I want you to promise me you'll read it."

Muirie struggled to keep her tone calm. "I don't even know what it is yet, Aunt Bert."

"I'll leave it on the desk in the pine closet. I want you to read it."

Muirie shrugged.

"Promise me."

"For God's sake," Muirie said. "I promise."

It was a poem. One in a thick tome of Robinson Jeffers that Roberta thunked down on Jeremiah's desk late in the evening. Muirie sat resolutely by the fire writing her father a letter as Roberta passed and did not go into the pine closet until she was sure Roberta and Glen had gone to bed.

The book lay open on the desk. Muirie rolled Jeremiah's old chair backward and slumped into it. On top of being stubborn, argumentative, and unreasonable, Roberta seemed to be a pedant as well. The poem on the right-hand page was entitled, "Hurt Hawks."

I

The broken pillar of the wing jags from the clotted shoulder,
The wing trails like a banner in defeat,
No more to use the sky forever but live with famine
And pain a few days: cat nor coyote
Will shorten the week of waiting for death, there is game without talons.
He stands under the oak-bush and waits
The lame feet of salvation; at night he remembers freedom
And flies in a dream, and dawn ruins it.
He is strong and pain is worse to the strong, incapacity is worse.
The curs of the day come and torment him
At distance, no one but death the redeemer will humble that head,
The intrepid readiness, the terrible eyes.
The wild God of the world is sometimes merciful to those
That ask mercy, not often to the arrogant.
You do not know him, you communal people, or you have forgotten him;

Intemperate and savage, the hawk remembers him;
Beautiful and wild, the hawks, and men that are dying, remember him.

II

I'd sooner, except the penalties, kill a man than a hawk; but the great
 redtail
Had nothing left but unable misery
From the bone too shattered for mending, the wing that trailed under his
 talons when he moved.
We had fed him for six weeks, I gave him freedom,
He wandered over the foreland hill and returned in the evening, asking for
 death,
Not like a beggar, still eyed with the old
Implacable arrogance. I gave him the lead gift in the twilight. What fell was
 relaxed,
Owl-downy, soft feminine feathers; but what
Soared: the fierce rush: the night-herons by the flooded river cried fear at
 its rising
Before it was quite unsheathed from reality.

CHAPTER TWENTY

Flo's tulips had broken the soil. She had planted them in an assortment of clay pots and set them on the warm southern windowsills of the living room and kitchen, watering them every day or so with the brass watering can that Hank and Annie had given to her for Christmas. She used meltwater captured from the gutters rather than well water, which was pumped up through the ancient rock layers beneath the ranch and was so saturated with minerals that it smelled like a cave. In the bathtub, it left behind a chalky paste she could have used to whitewash the house. She would not put it on her plants.

As she tipped the can an arc of water sprang forth, catching the morning sunlight. She stared, transfixed. The water formed a perfect parabolic curve, gleaming chrome and gold in the sunshine, an image of such solidity that she felt she could reach out and grasp it. She had never seen it quite like this before; the light had been different, or she had not paid attention. She poured, forgetting the pot until it overflowed with a wash of loose soil, rich as cocoa, over the lip and onto the sill.

She grabbed at the dishtowel tucked into the waist of her apron—"Oh, for heaven's sake"—and mopped at the sill, disgusted with herself.

She couldn't keep her mind set on anything these days without it veering away like a lost soul, it seemed. Every little thing diverted her. She couldn't even water a pot. The water had drenched the wallpaper too, which would dry crinkly, leaving her a reminder of her absentmindedness.

She drained the pot into the can, patted the soil back tenderly around the swelling bulb, and watered the second and third pots with careful intensity. Then, transfixed again by the arc, she flooded the fourth.

"Hell's bells," she said, staunching the water at the edge of the sill. "What's the matter with you today, old woman?"

She sighed, inspecting the soggy dishtowel. It would have to be rinsed and wrung out in the sink. "What's wrong with you is that you don't want to water pots," she said. She didn't want to rinse out dishtowels, either.

The realization surprised her. What a simple thing it was. There was nothing that required her to water pots then and there, only her expectations of herself, and some inner part of her this morning kept interfering with those expectations, trying to get her attention. She should listen to it, she thought.

With no more hesitation, she walked into the kitchen and flung the dishtowel into the sink, unwrung. Its satisfying *thwack* made her smile, but a fine spray of water fanned onto the windowpane, and she reached on impulse for the drawer next to the stove and its supply of clean, soft towels. That hard water left spots on glass. But she stopped her hand as the drawer came open. No, she'd leave that too.

Purposeful, she went to the utility room and refilled her watering can. Carl brought the meltwater there in buckets from outside, storing it for her in a barrel so that it wouldn't freeze. From the metal cabinet behind the door she took two clean floor sponges; from a hook by the door, the rubber bucket; from the hall closet, a battered card table, and transported all to the living room in shifts. She unfolded the card table, urging its spindly legs against the wall under the sunny window, brought a chair from the kitchen, and sat down, erect, arranging the bucket and watering can before her. She tilted the can toward the bucket. It was a beautiful watering can, slender and fine, with a balance you controlled with one finger. The arc leapt six inches into the air.

Why it fascinated her she did not know. Water flowing from a spout should look utterly ordinary, and yet she felt as though she were seeing it for the first time. It didn't look like water anymore, not the stuff of doing dishes and irrigating fields, of summer downpours that left the roads dotted with silver potholes. It appeared not to be in motion, yet its motion was the cause of its beauty; its motion gave birth to its shape. When the arc fell into the bucket, when it lost its motion, it splashed into shapelessness and became merely the stuff for mopping floors again. Her old watering can, retired now to the utility room, was a galvanized steel bucket, snub-nosed, dented up as an old truck, and forty years old. But it had watered pots just as well. Was it the angle of the sun or something in the atmosphere that changed the quality of the light?

The kitchen door opened and closed. She did not look up. She did not need to look up to see Carl. He was in his work clothes. The soiled fingers of his leather work gloves stuck cadaverously from the back pocket of his jeans. In the front pocket of his shirt, a bluish ghost of a bandanna, washed so many times you could see through it. He wandered across the room to her shoulder and watched for a moment, his breath rasping slightly.

She said nothing, hoping he would go away, but he stayed where he was, giving off puzzlement like the smell of lilacs. Suddenly she couldn't stand it anymore. She set the watering can down with a jolt. "Well?"

He steadied his chin with a thumb and forefinger. "What are you watering there, Flo?"

He said it seriously, as if anything she did deserved respect, even watering a bucket of water. She laughed. "I've gone around the corner. You should lock me up."

He squatted beside her, an elbow on the table. "Well, I'll say this. It don't cost much to keep you entertained."

She picked up the can and poured again, this time for him. "Watch how the water looks. I want to paint that, the way it—" She didn't know the words. "I saw it when I watered my bulbs."

He glanced up at the windowsill. "Your bulbs broke through?"

"Night before last."

He stood to get a closer look. "Then we got snow coming, sure as shooting. They said so on the radio, too, but now I believe it. Your tulips come up, it snows."

She rubbed the watering can with the corner of her apron. It was part of the effect, all that gleaming brass, and this kind of polishing, although identical to the kind of polishing she might give the water-spotted kitchen window, could not be considered a chore. "You say that every spring, Carl, like a prayer."

"I hope to God it gets answered this year. It's dead dry out there." He fiddled with his chin again, looking out the window. "What's that old saying of yours, though? Something about wishes being contrary."

The watering can dribbled dry. She set it down again, noticing that she could see the faded roses of her apron reflected in its surface, and her own face, strangely elongated and big-nosed. "It's dreams. 'Dreams go by contraries.' My mother used to say that."

He wiped a hand across his mouth. "Don't seem to me there's much difference between the two sometimes, wishes and dreams."

She looked at him in mild surprise. "There's all the difference in the world. Wishes you make, but dreams come of their own accord —unless you're talking about a daydream. But you can't be asleep at night and call it a daydream."

"Oh, I do know that," he said, taking a long breath. "Those you call nightmares."

He pulled the kerchief from his pocket and gave the end of his nose what amounted to a polishing. He didn't blow. "When's it that your show in town's over? Another week yet?"

"Near two," she said. He was thinking of the money. "What's wrong? Did something break?"

"No, no," he said, suddenly impatient. "I'm just asking, that's all."

She went back to her housework. She'd had a little vacation, twenty minutes long. From now on, she decided, she'd grant herself that same sort of fooling-around time every once in a while. She'd always done so when she painted but somehow she had never allowed it to overlap her chores. When she was in her studio, she painted; elsewhere, she worked. One role had disallowed the other, as if the two parts of her could not exist together. But it was clear they could and did. She didn't become a painter when she walked into her studio. She was a painter every moment of her life.

She sorted out two washer-loads of laundry, one of linen from the grandchildren's beds, one of Carl's work clothes. The dark load was just short of being full. She threw in a couple of her hot pads, they always needed washing, and pulled Carl's denim jacket from its hook by the kitchen door. He didn't like her to wash it, as he hated the stiffness of it afterward, but she insisted from time to time.

She plunged her hands into the pockets. Carl's pockets were always full. When they were first married, she had been shocked by his messiness. Her father had been a religiously meticulous man; a large man, close to three hundred pounds, but neat as a pin, neat as somebody's maiden aunt. When he emptied his pockets onto the bureau at night, nothing surprising came out, only necessary items, perfectly ordered, that she had seen a thousand times before: his paper money, folded exactly in half and creased with his thumbnail, a small pile of change from one pocket, his pocketknife from the other, a Saint Christopher's medal, and a tiny leather-bound Bible the size of his palm. He kept everything in his life the same: folded and in order by denomination.

But Carl! You could hear him emptying his pockets at night from any part of the house, a clattering avalanche of everything under the sun. She had liked to sort through the pile on the nightstand in those early days, marking the exotic differences between her father and this man. Carl had smoked a pipe then, and everything smelled sweetly of tobacco. Receipts, lots of them, a feathery topping from the feed store, the hardware store, the lumber yard, the café; a stubby, eraserless pencil; bits of wire, snips of leather, nails, screws, matches, toothpicks; a wad of bills; a mound of change mixed with buttons and bottle caps and nits of lint from the very depths. And it was not just his pants pockets that attracted matter from all over the universe; it was every pocket in all his clothes. If boxer shorts had pockets, Carl would fill those too.

Nowadays, his pockets were just as full, but the contents showed the changing times. From the pockets of his jacket she took an ID card from the buyer's warehouse, lost for a month or more; a few faded one-dollar bills; many credit card receipts, crumpled into balls; a hairpin, one of hers, refashioned into an Allen wrench; and a large, dull metal ring of some sort, bent open at a seam. She peered at the ring on the end of her finger. An odd thing, not like a part from a piece of machinery. No flanges or threads or grooves. There appeared to be writing on it, numbers, letters, but she didn't have her glasses on and couldn't make it out. Where had she left them? On the sill beside the tulips. There they were, warm from the sun. Not good for them, probably, but for the first time she felt happy to put them on. Someone should invent heated glasses, to keep your nose warm, and so they wouldn't fog up when you came inside from the cold.

She touched the nosepiece, settling the glasses firmly, and squinted again at the ring. It was one of those rings Bertie Shea Thompkins put on some of her hospital birds, only bigger than any she'd seen before. Over the years Carl had bagged a few ducks and geese that had worn them and you were supposed to report to the government that you'd found them or send them in somewhere, so the government could keep track of the birds, and how long they lived, and how far they flew from one place to another. Carl hadn't gone hunting lately and hadn't mentioned finding any dead game birds, but it was possible he had run across just the ring itself that a bird had lost. And Carl, of course, would put the thing in his pocket.

She set the band on the narrow ledge of the kitchen wainscoting, behind where Carl's jacket usually hung. She would ask him about it later.

CHAPTER TWENTY-ONE

The storm threatened from the west. In the television satellite photos taken across two April days, it looked to Muirie like a rogue wave breaking on the beach of the Rockies. It would hit over a wide area, from Colorado Springs to Miles City, Montana, bringing wind at fifty-plus miles per hour and several feet of snow over two or three days, depending on whether the storm stalled over the mountains or rushed downslope on its way east.

She wanted badly for it to stall, to dump its entire load here, right down to the last dithery flake, leaving the area up to its armpits in snow. It was not a wish worthy of a responsible adult, considering the damage a heavy blizzard could do, but she didn't feel grown-up when it came to this storm, her first true blizzard. Sierran snowstorms didn't qualify— not because they were less fierce or cold or dangerous, but because, as a skier, she had chased them down for entertainment's sake, following them into the mountains from the warm lowlands of the coast. Here, on the high prairie, the storms came to you.

"I'm glad we got those horses in yesterday," Glen said from the depths of his armchair, as a string of commercials began. "This one looks like business."

The front came in slowly, blowing doilies of snow peacefully before it. Muirie kept one eye on the window in the workroom as she and Roberta fed the birds in the morning. The ground vanished. Snow piled in slanting hats atop the fenceposts of the drive. She would get to see the Uncle John as she had never seen it before, as Jeremiah had described it in his journals: "...fenceline buried for half a mile back of the house...got 20-foot drifts against the barn...up to eaves of bunkhouse..."

He'd told a story of his father crawling out a lee window when he couldn't get the front door open after an overnight snow. *Yessir, that was a storm that wiped the world out...* She could see him telling it, frowning off into the distance over her head as if directly into the past.

...It was so bad that when you looked out the window, you couldn't tell if you was looking into a drift or straight out to the horizon. It all looked the same, white like you was floating in a cloud. So my dad, he taps at the windows on the sheltered side of the house, and he finds one in the dining room that's clear, although it don't look no different to me than any of the others, and he throws it open and goes to step over the sill so he can go dig us out. And here I am, five or six, or something puny like that, a little fella, and I see my dad stepping out into nothing. The world is gone, see, and he's stepping out into what ain't there, and I holler out at him not to go. And he stops for a minute, looking back at me and Ma, with this look, you know, real sad, like he knows this is the last time he's gonna set eyes on us but he's got to go anyway. Then he pulls that second foot on over—and he disappears.

And my ma give this sound, like when a cowboy gets thumped by an arrow on the TV. And she grabs on to my hand, and we stand there, listening so hard our eyes pop out. But there ain't nothing to hear. So we edge on up to that sill, scared half to death. But there's nothing at all to see either, so we just stand there, staring. He's gone.

He liked the sound of those last words, liked to whisper them slow and final, as if the story ended there. You had to pull the rest out of him, bit by bit, as he piecemealed the drama.

Then what?

Well...then it happened.

What? What happened?

He stared mournfully into the distance, as if the words were too dark to speak.

He hit us smack in the face with a snowball about twice the size of your head. He's been waiting for us, see, right around the corner from the window. He hits us solid, being only a couple feet away, then he takes off through the snow, trying to run, though it's more like floundering, and he's yelling like a banshee, knowing my ma ain't past leaping over the windowsill after him. She's about halfway out, spitting and snorting snow, when she remembers she's got her good shoes on, so she grabs the first thing that come to hand—no, I was the first; she grabbed the second—and she hauls it at my dad, which he dodges easy, and it goes whizzing over his head. But he was sorry later he'd been so quick because it was his breakfast she'd throwed, plate and all. House rule was, if you missed breakfast, you missed breakfast. Dad said it was breakfast that missed him, but Ma, she didn't see things that way....

He'd had a hundred stories, maybe more, all sweet to her ears, tugged from him like taffy every summer. He'd hid his eagerness to tell them with a show of impassivity and transient failures of memory.

Aunt Moira's Toe. Tell that one, Grandpa.

I don't remember any story about Aunt Moira's toe. What in the world could you tell about a toe that wouldn't put a hundred folks bang to sleep in an instant?

The toe she lost. To the hayrack or something. And then, when she got married, and she hadn't told her husband, and she—

Wait a minute here. You mean my sister, the toe she lost when she was a girl?

Yes!

Why, that ain't a toe story. That's a story with the whole point being that the toe ain't in it.

The denial was longer than the story. Aunt Moira, the irrepressible little sister, ebullient, mischievous—and noodly in the head, so said Jeremiah—had come up short a major toe when, one summer, she had dangled her bare foot where it shouldn't have been, doing something she shouldn't have been doing, and didn't even notice for a while, until she'd felt a sort of stinging down there, it had been cut off so clean. So everyone looked, but twenty acres was a lot of space for a toe to be lost in, and people weren't looking too hard anyway, figuring that one toe was a fair price to pay for not paying attention around moving machinery, especially if you were luring disaster by going barefoot; so the doctor bandaged the stump and Moira grew up the rest of the way with only nine toes, a fact that seemed to bother her not a bit until she got more serious about boys. Then she took to hiding the fact of it from everyone, including her intended, Uncle Joseph, who looked like a Mormon but wasn't, right up until their wedding night, when she told him that he could look at anything he wanted except for her feet.

Aunt Moira, who died in childbirth at twenty-one.

Uncle Joseph, who drank himself to death in mourning at twenty-nine.

Jeremiah rolled a toothpick into the twitchy corner of his mouth. *He'd a been better off a Mormon, don't you know.*

The news over, Glen closed the television away in its cabinet and sat down again beside Muirie, flapping open the *Star-Tribune*. He gave her a glance to see if she was happily occupied, and she joggled a magazine in her lap to say yes. He nodded, content, and peered into the pages of the paper, adjusting his glasses as though they were the delicate lenses of a microscope.

The wind had picked up, confusing the snow. It flew in all directions, polishing the windows, whirling over the eaves. Muirie settled deeper in her chair, leaving the magazine unopened. She liked just being here, doing nothing. Despite its size, Glen's office was an intimate room, unlike the living room at the front of the house, which functioned mostly as a passageway to the rooms beyond. She basked in the warm light of the pottery lamp on the table beside her, letting her eyes wander from the paintings on the walls to the view out the windows, a panorama that had looked subtly different to her each time she had come into this room. At the approach of the storm, the light had dimmed and flattened until the scene had turned minimalist, a wide sweep of dimensionless brown and gray, and now a soft and fathomless white.

She rested her head on the bolster. The storm had one disadvantage: it might keep her from getting to the clinic tomorrow. She wasn't used to driving in snow, and town was fifteen miles away via a snaky two-lane built on a high bench above the river. Still, it annoyed her to realize that this might stop her from going. She didn't want to miss working with the hawk.

Or seeing Sherman.

The first time she had gone to work with the bird, she had waited in the back room for Sherman to finish with his clients. She had walked toward Teiresias slowly, whispering a stream of soft endearments and flattery and nonsense, the way she would talk to a cat, to assure him of her harmlessness. The hawk shifted at the sound of her voice but without overt anxiety. Up close, his rusty plumage resolved into the shingling of thousands of feathers—cinnamon and mocha, cream and chamois, smoke gray folding into spotless white, an abstract masterpiece of texture and hue.

Despite Roberta's intentions in leaving the poem for Muirie to read, it had married her more fully to the idea of teaching Teiresias to fly. This bird was not in pain. There were no curs waiting to drag him off and eat him. It didn't matter if it had been a mistake to keep him alive in the first place; the fact was that the bird was healthy despite his blindness. To give him the fullest use of his remaining abilities was only right.

She extended a finger to touch the hawk's breast and stroked briefly, glancing into his leathery face. Teiresias ignored her, his head raised as if he were gazing intently at the door. She turned to follow his line of sight, a morbid thought, she told herself, but she felt compelled. She saw the dim corner of the room, a gray slab of cement floor, the jaundiced yellow of the paint. Sherman walked in, catching her stare in the face like a pie.

"He must have heard you coming," she said. "He was staring at the door."

He watched her a moment. "He's hungry."

They'd worked with the bird twice since, and his progress had been all they could expect, a trusting acceptance of the additional handling, but with no apparent understanding of its purpose. She and Sherman, though, had seemed to leap past all the normal formalities of a new acquaintance into an intimacy that was, for her, unique. They hadn't talked much. They hadn't needed to. Sherman's face opened like big double doors into the workings of his mind. Keeping an eye on him, she could tell what he was thinking as if his thoughts were her own, and they were able to work together almost silently with the bird, needing only brief phrases to explain their ideas and intentions. The ease of it caught them both by surprise. They found themselves staring at each other midway through a transfer of the bird. His smile wavered. She looked away, emptying her face, her surprise pushing at panic as she realized that she had been crediting herself with all their quiet communication. Meanwhile, Sherman had been looking straight into her own uncensored little brain. Every thought she'd had of him while they worked, all those wild little impulses and desires, he had read like large print. The idea appalled her. She was used to control, to seeing without being seen. At least not so clearly as this. She became suddenly businesslike, finishing up the round with the hawk as though it were a chore, then putting Teiresias away herself, taking her time, talking to the hawk softly in order to hear the cool confidence of her own voice.

"Let's go for coffee," Sherman said. "There's a place next door."

The deli sat empty, scuffed and greasy after its meager lunchtime rush. Sherman sat opposite her. His coffee mug was cracked at the lip. She organized the packets of sweetener in their tiny rack, white with white, pink with pink.

"I was married before," he said, as simply as it was possible to say the words.

She'd heard the same confession from a man or two in the past, but it had been packaged with self-pity, handed over as stock proof of "honesty and openness," or offered too casually too late. Sherman's words took chances. They spelled out everything that had gone unspoken between them, bluntly admitted his own interest, and, incredibly, asserted hers. His presumption amazed her but no more than his hope and daring. He had stated a fact he felt she deserved, given the circumstances, knowing she might judge it reason enough to turn back here. He marked out the threshold: I loved a woman once. I want to love again.

He waited, his eyes steady on her face. He had a calm intensity about him, a patience that crackled a little at the edges.

"I know," she said.

Muirie found herself gazing, half-hypnotized, in the direction of the Remington. Glen turned a page and sighed. The canvas had grown brilliant by comparison with the windows, their colors burnished in the yellow light of the lamps. Remington had painted in vivid stop-action, snaring a moment in time: horses at a gallop; dour soldiers astride. The men rode flat out and one-handed, rifles at the ready, dressed in surplus Civil War duds as tattered as flags, knee-high boots, filthy fringed jackets. Their mustaches drooped like dead snakes. Along the ground, deep slashes of shadow, and a bare, hollow skull in the ragged sage. Dust billowed behind like a following troop of ghosts. There was, she imagined, a cocky, crafty, nothing-left-to-lose band of Sioux dissolving into the landscape ahead, the object of the ride. The troopers looked past her, off the lower-left edge of the canvas, gargoyle-grim. Only one eye looked into hers. She saw it suddenly: the blanched white of a horse's eye, rolling in terror.

On Glen's desk, the gold clock delicately chimed the half-hour. He yanked at his shoes, letting them drop to the carpet, and leaned back again, an elbow denting the soft upholstery of the chair. She watched him out of the corner of her eye, seeing with sudden clarity, again, how much he had changed since the old days. Her imagination kept him on horseback, working cattle, his hat soaked with sweat, his eyes dark with exhaustion.

He knocked the newspaper with the back of his hand. "I gave an interview the other day that shows up here. About the sanitary landfill project."

She struggled to sit up. "The Hanna trash ranch?"

His keen eyes zeroed in on her face. "Well, that's what its detractors call it."

"What did you say?" She leaned toward him over the arm of her chair, peering at the paper.

"It's an art, what they do, taking your exact words and spinning them in another direction. You hear that you've got to educate people about the options, but when you try, you've got journalists in between, translating." He folded the paper to frame the article and handed it over. "You don't need to read more than the headline."

She brought the page under the lamp. "Thompkins Wagers on Trashy Future for State." She snorted out a laugh.

"What I said was that we should make sure we understand what we're turning down if we say no to this idea. What I was talking about was creativity, about being able to see opportunity where other people see waste. It's been the whole history of the Rockies. The early pioneers thought this place was desert. They went right on through. It took a long time for anybody to see the potential of the land. This is no different. That's what I said, but this is how they chose to hear me."

Roberta's voice came from behind. "Chose to hear you?" She had slipped in the door. "Give them some credit for making an intelligent judgment."

Glen twisted in his chair, his glasses slipping to the end of his nose. "This is a news story, Bertie. It's supposed to report what I said, not what they think about what I said."

Roberta came to stand before them. She set her hands squarely on her hips. "Funny that I never hear this criticism when a reporter happens to like what you said." The snow swirled at the windows behind her.

Glen tugged on his ear, beginning to smile. "Well, of course, that's when they've got it right."

She raised an eyebrow.

"Come on, Bertie. There's no good environmental case against it."

"The case against it is that the whole state's a dump already. People have been coming here for a hundred and fifty years to strip resources—everything from grass to coal—without caring about the mess they make. They've just left it behind. And now that they've stripped the place bare, they want to bring the garbage in from somewhere else."

"I know how you feel about this, Bertie."

She sighed.

"How come you never give me any credit unless I agree with you?" he said. "If I don't agree, you say I haven't been listening."

Roberta pinched out a smile, glancing at Muirie. "That sounds perfectly reasonable to me."

CHAPTER TWENTY-TWO

The local Audubon meeting that evening had not been canceled. Muirie had assumed it would be, but Roberta came looking for her after dinner, already tucking a muffler inside her jacket, and found her headed back into Glen's office with a volume of the old ranch journal and a lap blanket from the pine closet.

Roberta jangled her keys. "You're not going?"

"You're kidding. There's a blizzard out there."

Roberta frowned in apparent surprise at the news and glanced toward the window where the snow flew at the glass like a million dazzled moths. "This won't stop anything. Not yet anyway. They'll have the plows out on the highways."

It turned out that the local Audubon crowd had never once, in the nearly thirty years since the founding of their chapter, canceled a monthly meeting. Bad weather was no excuse; nothing was. Audubon meetings, Roberta told Muirie on the harrowing drive into town, had prevailed through any kind of meteorological mayhem you could imagine. Blizzards, of course, were routine. They'd even met in the face of a bomb threat.

Muirie's knuckles turned bleached-bone white. She knew it, though the cab was dark and she was wearing gloves besides. Roberta had said this wasn't a blizzard, and her driving swore to her conviction. At last glance, Muirie had noted the speedometer needle shivering above fifty. On a curve, in the whirling dark. "Bomb threat?" she said.

Her heartbeat staggered as Roberta lifted one hand from the steering wheel to gesture. "Oh, years ago we took over a big cooling lake north of town after the refinery shut down; Yant's Puddle, we call it. It's a big migration stopover, a lot of species nest there. We threw the fishermen out, locked the gates, made some people mad. Happens all the time."

"You get bomb threats all the time?"

Roberta laughed. "Nope. We make people mad."

The meeting was held in the dining hall of the senior citizens' center downtown. The smell of the place—fried food, waxed floors, dying flowers—hit Muirie in a blast as she came through the doors. The narrow tables had been pushed to the side and the chairs lined up in a dozen wavering rows facing the front, leaving a large open area at the back, like a dance floor. A tall, fiftyish man in baggy trousers was setting up a movie screen. He waved at Roberta, generalizing his greeting to include Muirie, bowing at the waist like a courtly knight. A square-set woman fiddled with slides, holding them up to the fluorescent light. She squinted at them quizzically, then punched them into the tray.

Muirie caught Roberta's arm. "Wait a minute, Aunt Bert. A slide show? You told me a guest speaker."

Several people called out a hello to Roberta; three headed in her direction, smiling. "China," said Roberta vaguely, surveying the room. "Or Africa. I'm not sure."

"You mean it's not even about birds?"

A skeletal little man patted Roberta on the back, telling her how glad he was to see her. He'd shrunk down around his dentures until all he could do was smile. A pair of equally ancient ladies waited at his elbow, also beaming at Roberta. Both wore sporty canvas hats studded with enameled pins in the shapes of birds and states. Traveling companions, no doubt, Muirie thought.

She stood to the side, feeling conspicuous for not knowing anyone. The group was larger than she had expected, and people came through the doors in a constant stream, stamping their boots and shaking snow from their coats and hats. Most, as at the gallery, were upward of forty, some double that, with a handful of younger people.

The man in the baggy trousers cleared his throat authoritatively at the podium and implored the crowd to take their seats. Muirie went for a chair at the end of a row, slinging her parka into the seat beside her, saving it for Roberta, who had been nabbed in conversation by a group of people who seemed to be talking all at once.

The man at the podium introduced himself as the program chair and outlined a "brilliant" program for the evening that was to include a slide show on India presented by a member who had just returned from a three-week visit there.

"I hope your return isn't so recent that you haven't had time to edit your presentation," he said, smiling at the projectionist. The crowd laughed. The projectionist waved a couple of her slides around, laughing, too, as if to say she needed only a couple more minutes to put the thing in order.

It was like a family reunion, Muirie thought—like a big, extended family settling down to watch vacation slides.

She scanned the room again for Roberta and saw her slip into a chair at the rear. Feeling abandoned in a crowd of strangers, however affable, she slumped in her chair. If she had her usual luck in such circumstances, some nerd would come in at the last minute and sit beside her, someone who gargled Wild Turkey or had eaten unrinsed beans an unfortunate number of hours ago.

But it was Sherman who walked in. She saw him as he slipped through the door, pulling his hat off, already looking for her. She waved, half-standing, and he headed for her without hesitation, his face working against a smile that he thought might grow too broad and look silly. It made her smile to know this about him.

She moved to the inner seat and he slid in beside her, smelling of cold. "Hi," he said, hunching close, shoulder to shoulder. His gaze moved from her eyes to her lips and back again.

"How did you know I was here?" She didn't consider that he might have come to see the presentation. He hadn't.

"I know Roberta always comes. I took the chance you'd tag along. I couldn't sit still at home."

She brushed an epaulette of snow from his shoulder. "This isn't where I'd like to be right now."

"No," he said, and she could smell the warmth of his skin beneath his jacket.

The show began with an abrupt plunge into darkness followed by a blinding flare of white: an empty screen. Someone called out, "Is this the brilliant part of the program?" and Muirie found herself laughing. Now that Sherman was here, she could face a slide show. He took her hand in the darkness and settled in close, which was entertainment enough.

The woman had a photograph for every moment of every day she had spent in India: three of the flag being raised in front of her hotel (showing the flag at the bottom, the middle, and the top of the staff); three of a camel hauling a load of marble (front, side, back); and blurry multitudes of others showing creatures, some of them birds, identified with uncertainty by the photographer herself. The audience offered guesses, enthusiastically, as if this were a parlor game.

Sherman pressured Muirie with his shoulder. "I'll bet you don't have entertainment like this in San Francisco."

She whispered at his ear. "Nothing close."

The meeting didn't end with the slide show. In fact, it seemed only a minor preliminary. The crowd gathered into knots of lively conversation all over the room, concentrated around a refreshment table at the back. Roberta stood with a lawyerly type wearing dark dress trousers when everyone else was in jeans and cords and heavy wool. A succession of people bid for Sherman's attention, wishing to talk to him about their pets.

"How about dinner tomorrow night?" he asked her before he would let himself be drawn away. "I'll cook."

"You cook?"

"Opinions differ."

She glanced toward the glass doors. "I'm going to need a snowplow."

"I'll come get you."

"And do that trip twice?"

She saw his caution come and go. "How about just once?"

Alone again, Muirie looked over the refreshments. The cookies were the hard little skipping-stone sort made in a New Jersey factory and called Mom's or Grandma's, and then dumped in paper bags and trampled by elephants until they were reduced to dust. She snorted a couple straight out of the air. The coffee had been stewing in an urn the size of a small garbage can for ninety minutes or more. It smelled like Roberta's. No one but Muirie seemed to notice, though, so she drew herself a cup and sipped at it courageously, enjoying the hubbub around her and the sight of Sherman making himself at home in its midst. He looked as though he were hearing more stories of pet exploits than requests for medical advice. He did less talking than listening and laughing. He glanced at her often, finding her in the crowd, a quick smile when their eyes met.

Roberta, Muirie observed, worked the room in exactly the way a politician would, talking to everyone. She looked as relaxed as Muirie had seen her, comfortable in these surroundings where she seemed to be a minor celebrity.

Roberta hailed her, introducing her to a circle of people gathered around her: the president, a no-nonsense, silver-haired jet-fighter of a woman who crushed Muirie's hand in a single karate chop of a handshake; the baggy-trousered program chairman; a gentle little woman in Peter Lorre spectacles who handled membership and donations; and the attorney.

The lawyer had never stopped talking, even through the introductions. "Look, people listen to him," he said. "He's got some pull. I say we try to work with him. We've worked with him in the past and he's proved himself reasonable from time to time."

Sherman came to Muirie's side again.

The membership lady didn't agree with the lawyer. "And we've got some pull of our own. Are we so desperate for industry here?"

The program chairman shook his head. "But there's a fair amount of public opinion in favor of it. It would supply jobs for a couple of decades, and like he says, it's relatively clean."

"Relatively," droned Roberta. "When you hear that word from a politician, look out."

Everyone laughed, except Muirie. They were talking about Glen, she realized, Glen and the trash ranch. Roberta sounded as if she didn't know him personally. Muirie caught Sherman's eye. He'd heard it, too, but he shrugged, dismissing it as one of Roberta's usual remarks, not to be taken seriously. Muirie felt less certain. Sherman didn't live with Roberta, didn't hear how many of these sorts of remarks she made.

Just when Muirie felt it must be time for everyone to go home, the jet-fighter president took the podium and asked everyone to be seated again for the business meeting.

Muirie turned to Sherman. "Business meeting?"

"Committee reports, that sort of stuff," he said, grinning. "You going to survive?"

"Isn't anybody but me worried about this storm?"

Sherman took stock of the snowfall through the windows. "It's coming down pretty good."

Pretty good. It was a maelstrom.

Thanks to the president's talent for friendly autocracy the rest of the meeting went apace. She stood at the podium, a pocket watch in hand, and informed each committee member firmly —"Time!"— when the allotted five minutes had passed. She allowed speakers to finish a sentence, and sometimes a paragraph, but if someone took a quick, deep breath of the sort that aerates a new topic, she braked him into silence. Roberta reported in quick, efficient sentences on the status of things at the hospital, using none of the explanatory language she did with Muirie. These people knew their stuff. They needed no schooling.

But even at the end of the meeting, the meeting didn't end, and Muirie saw that the business of the group was done outside of the program events. People didn't come for the slide show; they came in spite of it. It was the intermission and the aftermath they were interested in. Discussions spawned all over the room. More bags of powdered cookies were dusted across the refreshment table. The last of the coffee was tilted out of the urn.

At ten-thirty the place was still half-full but Roberta gave Muirie a wave, signaling that she was ready to go, and went toward the coat rack in the hallway to retrieve her jacket. Before she could pull it on, a man cornered her, drawing her into another conversation.

Sherman too was shaking a last round of hands. "Come on," she said to him. "We need to rescue Aunt Bert."

The man was one Muirie had noticed in the back of the room during the meeting. He looked Scandinavian: ageless, bloodless, with dilute gold hair and eyes so blue you could see the color half a room away. Roberta introduced him impatiently as Lars. He sounded like he came from Chicago.

"So go on," Roberta told him.

"So anyway," Lars said, "he'd tooled around out there, I guess— this guy has engines, he's not human—and decided to take a little side trip down to the lip of the canyon." He scratched distractedly at his temple, appealing to Muirie and Sherman. "I just had something to pass on to Roberta. I don't want to make a big deal about it. I met this guy I know skiing up on the mountain last week, and—"

"You already told me that part," Roberta broke in.

Lars sighed. "Okay. So he skis on down there, losing all that altitude as the ridge drops off, and he sits there eating his lunch on the north rim, probably looking forward to how much fun it's going to be to ski the eight miles back to Beartrap uphill. And he's looking across the canyon, into the pines, and something falls through his field of vision, something dark and fast, like a bird flying into the ground."

Muirie felt Sherman snap to attention.

"The roost," said Roberta. "He was opposite the roost."

"He got as close to the edge of the rim as he could and he saw something down on the snow, struggling around. He said it looked like a big bird. He didn't have binoculars with him, he's not a birder, but he said there were a bunch of dark shapes on the snow—large, dark shapes. But I figure they might have been branches, logs, rockfall. After a while, the thing stopped moving."

Roberta's face was rigid. "There might be fifty eagles up there."

"My first thought was that they froze to death," Lars said, "but I know that's not likely. Those eagles only come here for the winter, right? So they aren't going to freeze unless they're sick or—"

"Shot," said Sherman.

"Did he hear a shot?" Roberta demanded. "Any kind of noise?"

"No. Absolute silence."

"Maybe a carcass bait," Sherman said.

"A what?" said Muirie.

Roberta stared at her as if she'd forgotten who she was.

"It's a dead critter," Sherman said. "An antelope or a big hunk of beef, a sheep, a deer, a carcass laced with poison. Ranchers sometimes put them out for coyotes."

"That raven—" Muirie said.

"I'll handle this," Roberta said to Lars. "I'd appreciate it if you'd keep it to yourself for a while."

"Wait a minute," Sherman said. "How do you mean, handle it, Bert? If there are dead eagles up there, it's not for you to handle."

"If there are dead eagles up there, they didn't die naturally—"

"You don't know that."

"—and someone is responsible. If I go to the authorities now, the word will get out—it always does—and everyone will clam up tight."

Sherman was shaking his head, but Roberta overruled him. "I want a few days. I have to go up into the canyon tomorrow. I'd like you to come along."

"Me? Why me?"

"You're a vet, obviously."

"You must think I'm damn good. If the birds are dead—"

" —you can give an opinion on cause."

"Not if they're six feet down. It's been snowing for hours. If there are birds up there, they aren't on the surface anymore."

Roberta eyed him, her jaw set. "We need to keep calm."

Sherman glanced at Muirie, agog. "Look, Bert, this isn't something you should take into your own hands."

"I just want a few days. That's not unreasonable. If some of the birds are dead, they won't be any deader a week from now."

Lars loomed over them, beaming blue confusion.

"I'll call you," she told him.

With that, she strode away. Lars frowned after her. At the door, she waved impatiently to Muirie.

"I'm being summoned," Muirie said.

"Wait." Sherman took her hand. "Muirie, see if you can talk her out of this. I don't like her attitude. And we'll never be able to get into that canyon tomorrow."

"A couple of weeks ago Flo Drummond brought us a raven that was poisoned."

This stopped him. "Bert got a test done?"

"She did her own."

"Her own? She did her own toxicology test?"

"You don't want to hear the details."

"Oh yes I do," he said. Roberta waved at Muirie from the door again. "But you'll have to tell me later."

"Sherman, just how bad is a carcass bait? Is it conceivable that it could wipe out the whole roost?"

He threw another troubled glance Roberta's way. "Depends on how heavily it's dosed. And there might be several. It's spring; sheepmen are worried about their lambs. The danger here is that you've got a bunch of eagles concentrated in one area, all of them feeding nearby. Plus, it's not just the bait itself. You get a few sick coyotes roaming around, even their vomit is deadly. And scavengers will go for that."

Blank, dim, swirling white filled the street. Muirie couldn't tell which igloo in the parking lot was the pink truck but Roberta linked arms with her and headed straight for a lump in the far corner. She gave the driver's side a furious kick and a glacier calved at her feet, revealing a truck door. She hauled it open.

"Hand me that broom behind the seat," she said. "Then fire it up. I'll work on the windshield."

She excavated the truck from a foot of new snow, then climbed into the cab, blowing on her hands. Muirie had yet to see her wear gloves. She sat staring intently ahead through the double arc of the wiper blades. They groaned against the weight of the falling snow.

"Have you mentioned the raven to Glen?" she asked suddenly.

Muirie had to think for a moment. "No."

"Then don't. There are five people who know the story Lars told tonight. You, me, Sherman, Lars, and whoever that fool skier is. Six if there's a poisoner. I want to keep it at that. For now."

"You mean you're not even going to tell Glen."

Roberta's shoulders fell slightly, as if it were a burden to explain. "It's not for long. Just until I can get some more facts. Then, of course I'll tell him."

CHAPTER TWENTY-THREE

"That was Frances on the phone, Carl. From the gallery. You can't guess what she said."

Flo stood in the middle of the dining room, silhouetted in the dark by the glare of the overhead light from the kitchen beyond. The window frames clattered as Carl threw an armful of logs onto the coals. The storm was staying for the night.

"She said she wanted to apologize to me. She said next time we'd charge more for the paintings, that she should have known they'd sell so fast. And I've made more than five thousand dollars."

Carl shifted the logs with the poker. "How many months did you work on those pictures anyway?"

"Oh my. Some of them I've had for ages, those little landscapes, and that one I did of the flowers smashed by the hailstorm." She sighed. "If you're trying to figure out how much money I made by the hour, it's probably only pennies."

Flames licked at the door of the stove. He closed it, latching it firmly. "I'm not trying to figure out anything. Five thousand dollars is five thousand dollars."

"Why in the world are you stoking up the fire? It's almost eleven o'clock."

He grunted softly as he stood up from his crouch. "I thought I'd look at TV awhile."

"Sitting up won't stop it snowing."

He reached for the remote control and turned the TV on. "I might as well listen to something besides the wind."

She watched him. "You should come on up."

"You go on." He sat in his easy chair and stared resolutely at the screen.

"Well, I am tired."

"Go on, then."

She kissed him on the cheek and went. He could hear her for a few minutes, moving around slowly upstairs, then the creak of the box springs as she climbed into bed. He concentrated on the TV screen, willing the rush of images—fast cars, vast skylines, bright clothes, slick skin—to drive away the sound of the wind shifting against the house. The biggest city he'd ever seen was Denver, and it didn't count as the real thing. It was just an overgrown cow town. Big buildings and fancy clothes looked out of place there as if they were borrowed from television, copied item for item. Those people's lives didn't seem to have much to do with making a living or producing anything of value. What kind of life could that be?

The glow in the woodstove fluttered brilliant, fed by wind barreling down the chimney in gulps. Carl tried to monitor both the stove and the TV screen, but it was the fire that held his attention in the end. He stared through the tiny Pyrex window, gauging the increasing speed of the wind by the glow of the coals. The wind steadied as it grew, breathing long and hard instead of in gasps. The stove sucked air, bright as a blast furnace; window frames creaked, and he felt the air pressure change. He grabbed the remote and punched a button; Hollywood fell mute. The voice of the wind replaced it, an irritated whine running through the old wood of the house. He hadn't been too concerned about this storm system as it blew in. Storms the media hyped usually fell flat. But he hadn't liked the feel of the air by evening. It had made him feel muffled, hard-of-hearing, made him want to shake his head and swallow hard to pop his eardrums.

He fussed with the cushion at the small of his back. *Easy chair*—as if anyone could feel easy sitting still right now, doing nothing. Who could relax with a wind like that shuddering its intentions down the chimney? It had a lot on its mind and not a bit of it good.

He went to the windows. The snowflakes were smaller now, which meant dryer snow, a bit less dangerous than the huge, wet flakes earlier in the day, which adhered to the fleeces of the sheep and threatened them with both freezing and suffocation. He had brought the sheep in closer in the morning. It was easier to feed them when they were close but he hadn't driven them into the sheds. The sheds had their own dangers, brought on by crowding and panic: miscarriages, tramplings, a quick spread of disease. Some of the sheep had access to the sheds, which would have to do, and the rest had the craggy topography of the ranch that would break the course of the wind.

Another creak overhead. Flo hadn't stayed in bed for long. She came down the stairs belting her long flannel robe, her hair mussed around her ears and crown. It had been dark yellow in her youth, a color he had loved. One slipper flapped loose from her heel.

"What are you doing down here again?" he said, although he was glad to see her. Even if she was more helpless than he was, he liked to have her near.

"If your grandpa had the sense to build a one-story house, a person could sleep through a storm. But he had to have a view. Of God knows what. More prairie. Whoop-ti-doo."

She snapped on the floor lamp next to his easy chair. "You need some lights on in here, Carl. And you're not even listening to that TV."

The wind rose another notch and they glanced at each other. He got up and went to the windows again, kicked lightly at the floor molding. "We've got those early lambs. Skinny as sticks. Hardly know what to suck yet, goddamn it."

Flo sat on the couch and stared blankly at the silent television, the vivid colors of a commercial traveling over her face like the shadows of clouds. Tomato red, lettuce green, the match-flare yellow of a golden arch.

"I wonder how many storms we have sat up through," she said quietly. "Between you in the winter and Hank in the summer. All those years."

Carl grimaced. "Hank never lost a night's sleep over a blizzard, that's for sure. He got boogered by a little thunder and lightning."

"He was just a boy."

He faced her, scratching his nose. "You want me to make some instant?"

"Oh, I suppose so."

He brought it in mugs and set hers on the end table at her elbow. She lifted it wordlessly and took a sip.

"How is it?"

"Hot."

He wanted more from her but didn't fish for it. Flo was never her most complimentary after midnight. He sipped at his own coffee.

"Try to sit down, Carl. Please."

He edged into his chair.

"You'd bring those animals into the house if you could," Flo said. "You'd diaper them, give them all a cup of this coffee."

He barked out a laugh. "That'd thicken up their fleeces, wouldn't it?"

"More likely they'd go bald."

Flo could always do this, make him see how pointless it was to worry when there was nothing he could do. She was peaceful right at the center, which he was not. But he could draw on her as long as she was there beside him.

The wind pressed, raising a shower of sparks in the woodstove.

"Let's play some checkers," he said.

"Oh Carl . . ."

"Come on, come on. Just a couple of games. Two out of three. I'll finish you off in that time."

"You haven't beat me in checkers two times in your life."

"I'm feeling lucky."

She set her coffee cup down, resigning. He pulled the board from the bookshelf.

"Honestly, Carl," she said as he lay the game out before her.

The television blinked to a sports car rounding a black snake of asphalt on the far edge of the continent. Beyond, the white breast of a full sail on blue water, and warm sun on a long stretch of sand.

Glen murmured in his sleep as Roberta lay back slowly into the pillow and pulled the covers up around her neck. The drive from town had taken ninety minutes instead of twenty. The snow, driving east at thirty miles an hour, had pushed against them every inch of the way. Although Muirie had struggled admirably to overcome her apprehension, Roberta could feel her holding her breath at every bend in the road, and the tension worked on her nerves too. Even lying in bed, she felt an ache, rooted in her shoulder blades. It surged upward into her head as if pumped there, bringing with it the image of a dark shape in endless free fall. Each time it came to her, her heart rose into her throat with the same sick speed of the bird's descent. She forbade the image, but it saturated her, coming in waves. She tried altering the image in her imagination, opening the bird's wings so that it swooped upward in the cold space of the canyon, masterfully carving the air. The thought persuaded, comforted; she could believe it for seconds at a time. The skier had seen things wrong; he didn't know that an eagle changed the physical properties of air so that it became substantial, malleable, buoyant, miraculous, lifting the bird up and protecting it, allowing it to dive and wheel and soar without danger of falling.

The image faltered, despite her concentration. She saw a stone instead, winged and dark-feathered, plummeting to the earth. She threw an arm over her eyes, wakefulness pricking at her like pain. She would think about practicalities instead. There were other possibilities besides a carcass bait: disease, lead poisoning, even natural death. Maybe the skier had happened to see one eagle dying from natural causes, and the litter on the floor of the canyon was just what Lars had said: rock debris, broken limbs. Or it was possible the bird had been injured previously, shot or hit by a truck, and had died at that moment, as the skier watched.

But there was that raven in the freezer. Flo had found it south of here, only a little more than a mile from the mouth of the canyon.

She rolled on her side, away from Glen's rumbling breath. If Lars had had the sense to call her immediately after he'd met the skier, she could have gotten up into the canyon easily, but he'd bumbled along until the meeting. Now there could be no trip to the canyon tomorrow. The mountain got more snow than the valley, several feet more in a system as strong as this one, and a series of storms could keep the birds buried for weeks. In the meantime, all she could do was to ask a few questions here and there, discreetly, of her neighbors.

She listened, eyes closed. No storm spoke so clearly as a blizzard. A vocabulary of one word, repeated slowly, full of wind: *whhhhoa-whhh-hoa-whhhhoa.*

CHAPTER TWENTY-FOUR

Carl slept when he went to bed, but shallowly, dreaming dreams of pale coyotes flying like ghosts through an endless valley of snow. Just coyotes, no sheep, no people, as if the world had become the coyotes', as if they had wiped out humanity. He rubbed his eyes as he woke again near dawn. Foolish thoughts, way out of proportion, but his dreams often pushed past common sense. *Nightmare* was indeed the right word for them, although he didn't like to admit that even his sleep was preyed upon. Flo hadn't slept soundly, either. Once, as he'd turned over for the umpteenth time, she had patted his arm.

By dawn, the storm had lost some of its hurry, bearing down instead, like a single-minded craftsman doing an expert job. It would take them both to feed the sheep, and there was no pretense between them that he could handle the job alone. They dressed in nearly identical clothing from the skin out: long underwear, heavy chamois shirts, wool sweaters, overalls, wool socks, and insulated boots. Flo fixed a quick, hot breakfast: oatmeal with dried fruit sprinkled in, toast, more coffee. Then she slapped together a lunch to take along. Hank called while they were donning mufflers, hats, gloves.

"You want me to come out, Mom?"

"How in the world are you planning to get here? Sled?" Hank did not have a truck. He drove a late-model family van.

"I'd get there if you need me. You know that. My neighbor has a four-by-four he'd let me borrow."

"You might get stuck, and then we'd have to worry about you too. Stay put."

"I'm going to keep calling to make sure you get in safe."

"Don't sit there and worry, Hank, for God's sake. I'll call you when we get in if you want."

"Tell Dad I called."

"All right," she said. But she had no intention of doing so knowing full well that Carl would consider Hank's offer insincere. If Hank had been serious about helping, he would have come the night before. And he wouldn't have called to offer either, he would have just come.

The wind had driven the snow into drifts twelve feet high against the side of the barn but had scrubbed the drive almost bare. The door of the barn was clear, too. C. H. had faced it away from the prevailing winds, but several gates up in the pastures were sure to be impassable, as were portions of the road. Carl pulled the barn door open. The half-ton sat gleaming in the dim light. It was one thing, at least, that they would not have to shovel out today. He chained up and began loading cake, Flo at his side. It would take several trips. In heavy weather like this the sheep needed almost twice the feed to keep them from giving in to the cold. The pregnant ewes and the early lambs were the most vulnerable, but he had gotten the bulk of them near the sheds, he thought. With luck they would survive. A bunch of wethers he'd kept from the fall sale were in the most danger, but they were the least valuable too. He'd planned to shear and sell them later in the spring, hoping for higher wool and mutton prices. He knew there was an excess of hope invested in that strategy but it was too early to tell about the payoff. Most sheepmen sold their male lambs every fall. They couldn't bear young, and when prices dropped they ate more than they were worth during the winter, so there was no reason to keep them. If he had to make choices, he'd choose to lose the wethers, but it would be a bitter blow, now, at the end of the winter when they had already consumed months' worth of feed.

"That'll do it this load," he said, thrusting a fork between the wall of the truck bed and the stacked bales of cake. "I'll get the door."

They worked in tandem, Flo grinding along in four-wheel drive from drift to drift, Carl shoveling out the road when he judged the snow too deep for the truck to negotiate. It took thirty minutes to make the top of the pasture where the first of the small sheds came into view. The drifts blew in behind them in minutes, erasing every sign of their passage.

Roberta sat in the kitchen, already dressed in long johns and one set of outer clothing. Yesterday's newspaper lay before her on the table, unread. Long years of habit still compelled her to sit with a cup of coffee, intending to read the news, but she never got far with it anymore. Muirie wasn't up but she heard Glen trudging around in the bedroom.

She could not take her eye from the window. A snowstorm, like a fire, hypnotized. This was a patient storm, steady and earnest, a storm she did not mind much under normal circumstances. Today, though, she felt the weight of its accumulation.

Suddenly hot in her heavy clothes, she opened the window a crack. Wind roared through, sweeping dust from the sill across the newspaper. It settled in the folds like reddish snow. She dragged a forefinger through it.

It was a gritty powder, worn by the wind from an ancient layer of rock called the Chugwater formation that cropped out all across Wyoming in cliffsides and spines and ridges and arches and spires. The name derived from the town to the east where the rock was first studied by geologists. Everyone called it by name. Her mother, scolding her as a child for tromping into the house with muddy boots: "Don't take another step. You're Chugwater to the ankles." And riding in her father's old truck in the summer, you couldn't tell the difference between Chugwater dust flying in the window and rust vibrating down from the ceiling. That old pickup, from far back into her childhood, decades before the pink truck, a horrible gasp of valves and tortured metal, reddish specks sifting onto her collar, on her shoulders, dander made of dust and steel. It gathered on the brim of Jeremiah's hat. That hat. Always the same hat. He knocked the brim down against the sun in a certain way, squinting out from underneath. A benign memory, but a harsher one followed, linked inextricably. He looked up through a dark band of shadow to the sky.

Birds screamed, harsh, resentful: a pair of red-tails, flying low, seeking a thermal. He fit his shotgun to his shoulder, muttering something, as if to the birds. A crack and one bird came down straight as a stone, wings angling out, jerking in the free fall, disappearing in the sage and the grass. He patted the shotgun like the butt of a baby in his arms, aimed again, a poorer shot, one wing—feathers flying without the bird. The hawk rowed madly with the other, falling. This was a moment she had never forgotten.

Jeremiah sent the dogs.

Muirie woke to a strange deepwater light in the pine closet. She stood on the bed to look out the windows near the ceiling. They were blocked almost completely, not from the ground up, but from the eaves down. A wind-driven layer of snow curled over and under the gutter as if seeking shelter. She craned her neck to look down toward the ground, where the light was brighter. Snow blew horizontally, west to east, white on white. The world was wiped out, just as Jeremiah had said.

She found Roberta in the kitchen, pouring coffee, dressed in huge, shapeless army surplus pants and a tentlike sweater pulled over a turtleneck.

"Damn storm," she said, seeing Muirie.

"You can't still mean to go up to that canyon today."

Roberta hitched the overalls up at the waist and sat at the kitchen table. "Glen and I are going over to Samuel's. He'll need some help with his cattle this morning." She took a gulp of the coffee. "I'm leaving the hospital to you."

There was no note of trust in her voice, merely the drone of necessity.

"I'd rather go with you guys," Muirie said. "The birds can fast today, can't they?"

Roberta tightened a strap with a yank. "Nope. Standing on the tail-gate of a truck on a day like this, pitching cake—you have to be born to it."

"Glen wasn't born to it, either. I learn fast and I'm in good shape. I'd be an extra pair of hands."

"If it was our place, I'd say yes. But you'd scare Samuel. I don't want him to have that extra burden."

Muirie tried to laugh. "I'd scare him?"

"I appreciate the offer, though."

Muirie doubted it.

Roberta turned to stare out the window toward a line of invisible buck fence in back of the house. The snow had reached the level of the sill, making it look as though the house had sunk a yard below the ground. She seemed to be listening to the muffled sounds coming from the master bedroom. A door closed. Footsteps thumped across an uncarpeted expanse of floor. Glen didn't have his boots on yet.

"How soon are you leaving?"

"As soon as Glen gets himself out here." Said snappily, untinctured with humor.

Muirie's anticipation for the day boiled dry. In view of the storm, the rendezvous with Sherman was off, too. She watched Roberta as she inspected a handkerchief for cleanliness and stuffed it back into her pocket, studying her fine features etched against the blank white of the window. She looked pinched and severe, every angle of her face sharpened to a line of bone. The bulky clothes were deceiving. They shrunk her down, made her look fragile rather than lean and strong, delicate rather than unyielding.

"I've been thinking about Flo and Carl over there," Roberta said, her brusqueness suddenly gone. "Their son doesn't help much anymore. Just when they need him most." She rubbed at her eyes lightly; though her day's work hadn't begun, they were dark with exhaustion. "I'd go over there but Carl doesn't like anybody to presume he can't take care of things on his own."

Muirie sat at the table, reaching out a hand. "Aunt Bert, could it be anything else up there but eagles? Vultures, maybe? Or anything else?"

Roberta's expression softened into gratitude. She tugged on Muirie's hand, as if to draw a little strength. "I tried all night to change things by imagining them different. But if there are dead vultures up in that canyon, there are dead eagles too."

Flo's gaze flickered between the dimensionless white of the pastureland and Carl's stubborn face beyond the windshield. He was counting. She did not know how many sheep there were supposed to be near this shed, but his expression told her that he had come up short. He glanced through the windshield at her, caught her eye. He was angry. He waved his arms, instructing her to reposition the truck so that it would be easier to pitch from the bed.

She turned the truck slowly in the tight space between the larger drifts. It was difficult to see them through the snow and condensation on the windows. The tires spun. She shifted into reverse, then first, rocking the truck gently. It rolled free. Carl knocked furiously on the window with a gloved hand, his face nearly pressed to the glass.

"I'm saying come on back! Back, damn it!"

She eased the truck backward until he halted her with both palms in the air, then let the engine idle and joined him in the bed. The sheep crowded the truck, bawling out their painful hunger and terror of the storm. Their backs were thick with snow. Flo saw the taut dangling teat of a ewe but no lamb. She glanced quickly around the confusion of sheep. The carcasses would be buried in snow, most likely, or trampled on the floor of the shed.

"How many?" she said when they were back in the truck.

Carl's jaw was rigid. "Can't tell for sure. More than ten."

She shifted into first and headed downhill into the drainages. If the wethers hadn't found shelter here, they would have been directly in the path of the storm.

Muirie built a fire in Glen's office, making plans to come back to it after she fed the birds. She added extra wood, filling the hearth until it looked, she thought, as though a log cabin had been dropped down the chimney. Which made her something of a pyromaniac in lighting it. It would burn for hours, collapsing down to eight inches of glowing coals that would smolder for hours more. It was not just a fire, but a territorial marker at the heart of the house, meant to keep the blizzard at bay, and to prove to the storm her own intention to survive a trek to the big barn.

She took another look out the windows. Although Glen and Roberta had shoveled their way out of the house and tramped abreast to the garage only fifteen minutes earlier, she could no longer see their tracks. The wind blew the snow sideways, scraping the ground down to dry grass in the open, sculpting mountainous drifts at corners and ledges and fence lines, along the ridges and rills of the pastures. The fire, she thought, would melt it back and keep the house alive.

Dressed in full winter regalia of double everything, most of it borrowed, she stumped to the full-length mirror at the end of the hall and stationed herself before it for inspection. It was no wonder Jeremiah had known so many man-lost-in-a-blizzard stories. You had to give up most of your energy to getting dressed and the rest to propelling yourself forward with twenty pounds of clothes and boots on; there wouldn't be anything left to fuel good judgment. She'd have to raid the kitchen again before she braved the storm.

She sat bulkily at Glen's desk and tried Sherman, calling both his house and the clinic. No answer either place, which meant he was somewhere between, struggling in the snow.

The wethers were scattered across a low rise of land like debris washed onto shore by high tide. Some were half-buried in drifts. Others huddled in death against the rocks, their legs buckled beneath them. Less than a fourth had scrambled across the rise to shelter in the protection of the rocks. Fifty yards more was all they had needed to travel.

Flo glanced at Carl. The rough idle of the truck made his shoulders tremble. He looked pale, despite the wind-raw red of his cheeks and nose.

"Well," he said.

"There's not that many."

"No. Not now."

He had misunderstood. She did not correct him.

"We'd better get back," he said. "Take care of the ones it'll do some good for." But he didn't move.

"I brought some lunch," she said.

She took a battered lunch pail from the floor at her feet and offered him a lidful of steaming coffee. He took it, his eyes fixed on the dusty expanse of the vibrating dash. She unwrapped corned beef sandwiches and lay one on his thigh on top of a paper towel.

"I'm going to turn the radio on," she said, giving him fair warning.

He took another sip of the coffee. She turned the knob. The blizzard raged there too, inside the radio. She tuned it, one ear cocked, the volume low, past thready voices and electronic shrieks. She wanted music. No news, no weather reports, no stock prices. She heard a single phrase of music, a voice she knew, awash with interference. She tuned it in as best she could, content to hear an occasional note in the scrawling noise. She knew the song well enough to fill in the gaps for herself. She hummed it quietly—George Jones, one of his old songs, about love, of course, tested and true.

Carl took a bite of his sandwich, offering her the coffee. She took it carefully, settling back on the seat.

"There," she said firmly. "That's better now."

Getting to the big barn was like sailing across a treacherous stretch of water. Your body became a mainsail, one you couldn't furl. You had to dump the wind, slide sideways through it, tack away if it pushed too hard. Muirie fell against the double doors of the barn gratefully, breathing fast. For all the air blowing around, she hadn't managed to get much of it into her lungs.

She shoved the door open on its railing and stepped inside, flicking on the lights, feeling businesslike. She'd take care of the little birds first, getting them out of the way so she could lavish more time on the raptors. She leaned close to Oscar's cage just to say hello. He had warmed up to her considerably lately, deigning to tolerate her presence, which, Roberta had said, was about as friendly as Oscar ever got.

"Hey, Osk," she said.

The owl shot straight to the top of his cage, wings beating wildly. Muirie backed off, baffled. Roberta had said that a heavy wind sometimes made the birds restless but this seemed ridiculous. The owl clung to the side of his cage, staring at her in naked terror.

"Hey, it's me," she whispered, pulling off her ski cap.

Oscar blinked, and blinked again, more slowly. Then, in a nimble turn, hopped back to his perch and peered at her as if he thought he knew her but couldn't tell for sure because he'd lost his spectacles.

"Hey, wait a minute," she said, and cautiously pulled her ski cap on again. He ballooned, hissing. She pulled the hat off; he detumesced.

It was the single piece of clothing she had on which was her own, a close-fitting cap of cobalt blue with a hot pink tassel. Roberta had warned her about wearing bright colors around the birds. They were not color-blind and could react to colors in unpredictable ways. She'd told of a potluck dinner she'd hosted in the big barn a couple of summers before for the Audubon crowd. One woman had served herself a large slice of juicy cherry pie, then strolled slowly past a red-tail on a free-standing perch while she ate it. Roberta saw the hawk's head pop up at the sight of the cherries, realized the bird was figuring flight coordinates to what it saw as fresh-killed fast food, rushed the woman out of the way, and expelled the cherry pie from the barn.

But it might be the shape of the hat, Muirie thought. It came to a point, with the tassel falling off to the side. Perhaps it changed the contour of her head to such an extent that Oscar didn't recognize her. She approached the owl again, hat in hand. He peered at it as though it were a soiled Kleenex, but did not seem to find it dangerous.

"You are one weird duck," she told him.

She worked for an hour with the smaller birds, noting their condition in the logbook, then turned to the raptors and transferred the tour birds among them to their perches. Oscar's left ankle bracelet was fraying, Beetle ate a third again as much as she usually did, but Jasper wouldn't eat at all. She looked into his fierce face, wondering what could be wrong. He had a vigorous appetite normally. He seemed healthy, perhaps more arrogant than usual, but Roberta had told her that birds excelled at concealing illnesses until they were far advanced.

Troubled, she turned to cleaning his cage and found, in the bottom, a scattering of tiny gray feathers, some in clumps. She balanced one on the tip of a finger. They did not look like Jasper's feathers, at least not his outer feathers. Could he have been picking at himself? Was he molting? The middle of a blizzard seemed an odd time to do so.

She left the cage uncleaned, intending to show the evidence to Roberta, and went on with her other chores. Sherman called in mid-morning. It had taken him more than an hour to drive the three miles between his house and the clinic. The highway patrol was asking "nonessential traffic" to stay off the roads.

"I keep thinking about my timing," he said. "If we'd gotten together one night sooner, you'd be stranded *here*."

By late afternoon, the wind had weakened, and Muirie thought the sky looked brighter. Roberta returned home at four looking more robust than she had at six in the morning. A hard day's work in a blizzard seemed to have purged her of her moodiness. Glen had stayed at Samuel and Brigitte's for supper.

"I suppose I should have stayed, too," Roberta said, shrugging off her overalls in front of the fire. "Brigitte will be offended. But I wanted to go by the Drummonds' to see if they were in yet. They aren't."

"You're thinking of going back out?"

She sat on the footstool to tug at her boots. "I was thinking of throwing something together, a hot dish or something, to take over there. Flo will come in and cook dinner after a day like this."

She stomped to the kitchen in her damp socks and threw the cupboard open so that the doors knocked the wall. She stared at the contents, arms folded solemnly across her chest, as if she might conjure something like a genie.

"What did you have in mind?" Muirie asked. "Other than toast and coffee, I mean?"

Roberta shot her an evil smile. "How about a casserole?" She squatted to look in a lower cabinet. "Here's some artichokes. And some olives. What else do you need?" She pulled the cans out, banging them onto the counter.

"Just about anything works in a casserole. Cheese. Pasta. Tomato sauce."

"Well, then, I ought to be able to make one."

"Let me help."

"No. You cook all the time. Keep me company instead."

Muirie helped anyway, steering Roberta away from a sludgy, fuzzy green chunk of what had once been cheese.

"How did I miss this when I cleaned out the refrigerator?"

"Can't we just slice the mold off?"

Muirie lobbed the cheese into the trash. "Only if it doesn't go all the way through."

She told Roberta about the feathers in Jasper's cage. The news did not surprise Roberta.

"He got a sparrow. One of the natives that live in the barn. It's happened before. Something disturbed it during the night and it blundered into his lair. I'm sure he was proud as a turkey."

"Birds eating birds," Muirie reflected. "Somehow it seems odd."

What went in the mixing bowl after further debate was cooked rice, a can of kidney beans, onion, tomato purée, artichokes, and olives.

"Seasonings," Roberta said, plucking a jar of saffron from the cabinet. She studied it, perplexed. "You know, Ellen can't cook, either. I wonder how you can, given your genes."

Muirie slipped the saffron from Roberta's fingers, replacing it with a bottle of thyme. "Desperation," she said.

The lights were on in the Drummond house when Roberta pulled into the driveway. It was a modest-looking place, even dreary, Muirie thought, especially in the dull light of the snowy early evening. Roberta drove the truck up to the railing of the front porch. Flo opened the door when they knocked; she was gray-faced, dressed in overalls and an apron.

"Don't do another thing in that kitchen," Roberta said. "We've made you some California cuisine."

Muirie smiled dully. California institutional cuisine, that is.

Flo's face collapsed into a smile like a Madonna's. She pulled them into the living room, stamping her own feet gently so they would stamp theirs. Muirie offered her the casserole, wrapped in towels and nested in a paper sack.

"Well," she said, taking it. "Who would think, on a day like this."

"We haven't had to be out feeding an army of sheep," said Roberta.

Flo's face pinched, but she did not hesitate. "We lost a few of our wethers today, Bertie. South of Long Ridge."

"You have wethers?" Roberta said.

"Come into the kitchen," Flo said. "I've got coffee on."

"We can't stay. You'll both be tired as dogs."

"No. Carl's not even in from the barn yet. He'll want to say hello. Come on."

The kitchen was the room in Flo's paintings. A large covered pot sat on a low flame, a battered old percolator on another, and the kitchen smelled richly of chicken broth, sweet onion, and fresh coffee. Muirie picked out the details lovingly: the worn counter, the blue-flowered china, the cactus on the windowsill.

"See what you saved us from," Flo said, turning off the flame. "I was warming up frozen soup."

"It smells delicious," Muirie said.

"Oh, it's plain as plain. Chicken noodle."

"It's not what anyone else would describe as plain," Roberta said.

"She makes her own noodles, her own broth."

"I cheat a little with this," Flo explained to Muirie. "I make two gallons at a time and freeze it, even though my husband doesn't like leftovers. He'll eat anything, but he likes it fresh."

"I'm glad to hear that, considering what's in that sack," Muirie said.

Roberta laughed. "You bear part of the responsibility, kiddo."

Flo lifted the dish from the sack and removed the lid. A reddish skin had formed on top of the casserole.

"Ah, thyme," Flo said, sniffing deeply. "I'll just stick it in the oven a few minutes." She set the temperature carefully, then poured them coffee and sat down at the table herself.

"How many, Flo?" Roberta asked.

Flo sighed. "Well, it's been worse before, of course, for everyone. I don't think we've come out as bad as we might." She smiled, reaching for Roberta's hand, and squeezed it earnestly. "You know, there's been something I've been meaning to talk to you about, Bertie. Why didn't you tell me a long time ago that you liked that painting of Carl at the window? You saw it months before the show. I can't remember the price you paid but it was too high."

"My God," Roberta said. "You just lost some sheep and you want to give me a refund on my painting?"

"Oh my. We lose sheep every winter. They live and they die, just like everything else."

Carl came in red-faced and blustery with cold. "Bertie," he said, nodding. His gaze moved to Muirie. "I saw your truck outside."

"They've brought us dinner, Carl."

"I knew I smelled something good."

Flo smiled at Muirie. "Well, it isn't me. I probably smell like holy blazes under all these clothes."

Carl sat down heavily at the table, unwinding a muffler from his neck.

"I'm sorry about your sheep," Roberta said.

Carl scratched at his scalp, drawing his fingers through his thin hair. "Well, we won't be fighting the storm so much tomorrow."

"No, it'll wear itself out."

"You can't move fast enough sometimes," Carl said. He gave Roberta a glance. "How did Samuel do?"

"No problems."

"I'd think he'd run the flesh right off them, the way he's always shifting his animals around; giving them the best of everything. Might as well feed them stacks of dollar bills."

"He didn't lose a head."

Carl looked at his palms, rubbed tenderly at the calluses.

"Let me get more coffee," Flo said, standing up.

Roberta took a sip from her cup. "Carl, have you heard of anyone having coyote trouble lately?"

Carl's focus narrowed for an instant. "No," he said, abrupt.

Muirie saw Flo glance at him from the stove, mouth open in unmistakable surprise. Roberta saw it, too.

"None of the neighbors?"

He shook his head. "Not that I heard of." He met her eyes deliberately. "You and Glen having problems?"

"No. We've only got the horses."

"What's the problem, then?"

Her eyes steadied on his face. "Rumors."

"Haven't heard a thing."

"You'll let me know if you do."

He nodded once, emphatically. "You bet."

Roberta drained her mug, scanning Muirie's face. "Thanks for the coffee, Flo. We need to get back."

Flo's smile fluttered uncertainly. "About that painting, Bertie." She opened the door for them. "You can come pick it up next week. If you still want it, that is."

Roberta patted her hand as she stepped through the door. "I do."

Flo sat at the table again, her eyes on Carl. He studied the inside of his mug, stern.

"Well, what in the world?" she said. "I was just about to tell them about the coyotes when you walked through that door."

Carl's head came up. "That's none of her damn business. She's not ranching anymore."

When she didn't answer, he set the mug down with a bang. "She's always asking questions, making little statements here and there about how I should be handling my own business. Her and Glen both. They get a bunch of oil money, Glen gets some votes, they think they know everything."

Flo stared. "I can't believe my ears. You've known Bertie Shea since before she was born."

Carl snorted. "You can't know somebody since before they're born."

"Well, you've got me upset."

"She doesn't need to know every damn thing. I don't care if I've known her for a hundred years."

The phone rang. Flo started, putting her hand to her heart. "That'll be Hank."

"What the hell does he want?"

Flo rushed into the living room to the phone on the end table next to the couch. Carl yelled after her, "Tell him we did just fine. Tell him we don't need a goddamn thing."

CHAPTER TWENTY-FIVE

The storm lingered for another day, then made an exit east, leaving behind a veil of cloud that filtered the sun to a glare. Roberta squinted toward the mountain through Jeremiah's old binoculars. Hartsong was loaded with snow. She could barely make out the familiar details of the north face, and the narrow mouth of the canyon showed only as a grayish imperfection in a solid shell of white. The birds would be buried deep.

She lowered the glasses, weighing the pros and cons. The weather had turned warm, upward of forty degrees, and was forecast to stay there for a few days. Spring snows could melt with astonishing swiftness. The problem would then be compression. As snowflakes melted, they coalesced into granules of ice, and the snowpack sank in on itself, sealing the ground with crystalline gravel. If there were dead eagles there, retrieving them would take enormous effort even if she knew precisely where to dig. And, of course, it was spring; more snow would fly. Unless the season were an extraordinarily dry one, she would have to wait until the canyon melted out to discover the truth of what was there. She had missed her window of opportunity.

Sighing, she let her eye wander the length of Hartsong. There were some things she never tired of seeing. This long ridge line of a mountain, its twenty-mile peak feathered with pine, was one. It was a view she had seen, with a thousand variations of climate and mood, almost every day of her life. Despite her dread of what the canyon might hold, she still found the view calming, a result of long habit from those days when a look at the landscape foretold the future: if it would rain, how cold it would turn, when the aspen would change, when to plan a wedding. Standing out by the front corral she and her father had studied the mountain, the wide reach of sky between, the cast of colors in the distance, the smell of the air. That was how they had planned their lives.

She saw a bird, far away, a turkey vulture in search of a decent thermal. She did not need the binoculars to identify the bird but she lifted them anyway, rolling the focus for distance. Yes, a vulture, spiraling up slowly on a meager column of warmth.

She liked using her father's binoculars, his long-distance eyes, and seeing sights he had never glimpsed. Perhaps, in a manner, she still hoped to make him see.

You read this in the paper, Bertie? Some fool here says we never should of put cattle on this land. My God, whatever else in hell would you do with it?

He had sensed the shift in her before she had quite understood it herself. Coming home from that long-ago trip to California, nothing here had looked the same.

What's the matter? Your trip make you stupid? Seems like you don't have a damn thing to say.

She had taken Muirie to the ocean there, at Point Reyes, north of San Francisco. Muirie's father had pushed the excursion, sensing Roberta's restlessness, knowing that she was not used to confinement indoors. "You need to look out over some distance," he told her.

She had never seen the ocean until that vacation—had never considered it a goal. And the views of the water she'd seen as they toured the area had not made her regret the long delay particularly. She protested. "I can see the ocean from your picture window."

Hugh was aghast. "That's the bay, and the south bay at that." True enough, it could have been forty miles of sheet metal from this distance. "I'm talking ocean," he said, handing her maps, field guides, binoculars, a musty old rucksack, Muirie. "Now get out of here, Roberta."

The harrowing drive in a stream of sixty-mile-per-hour traffic shot her up the Peninsula, through the city, and over the Golden Gate Bridge before she could make good on her decision, reached at the moment she entered the freeway, to get off and turn around. But studying the map on a side street in Sausalito, she realized they were more than halfway there.

They found the place deserted. Alone, leaving the car and the badly marked dirt road behind, they hiked through a hummocky dune field to the beach, facing a vigorous wind. Muirie ran out onto the flats, already barefoot. Roberta followed, shouldering the heavy pack. The surf grumbled, rolling lace ashore.

They weren't alone at all. The slanting beaches seemed to shift with birds: sentinel herons and squalling gulls, a marathon of sandpipers sprinting on the sand, and terns flickering like butterflies over the water. Roberta hollered at Muirie, already daring the waves, and felt the wind swirl the words up and away so that even she couldn't hear them.

They hiked down the beach in an endless series of tacks, stopping to look at patterns in the sand, a gallery of gnarled driftwood, the sandstone cliffs you could climb but that crumbled away in a rain. Roberta dropped the pack and they played chicken with the surf in earnest. Muirie taught her how to choose a perfect skipping stone and how to throw it along the troughs of the waves. They counted the skips with wild hyperbole, each claiming decisive wins.

Rounding a head, they found a beach bordered by a higher cliff, a parallel wave of eroded siltstone, lush with grass. They chose a protected spot at its foot to eat their picnic lunch, laying out a small blanket. Muirie, salted with sand from head to toe, did the serving, parceling out the goodies in tea-party style, with much fussing about what went where. Roberta tossed off her shoes and stretched out in the sun, propping her head so that in one glance she could see the green crest of the ridge behind and the open sea at her feet.

The ocean was reminiscent of the high prairies at home, she thought: a view of vast, rolling space, the far line of the horizon, the wind. She ran her eye along the edge of the beach, just where the waves pulsed onto the sand. A wave of sandpipers mirrored the water: spreading, ebbing, spreading and subsiding. And big brown birds—what were they? she reached for one of Hugh's field guides—out on the water, a ring of birds, petals on the water. Pelicans, fishing as a team.

And farther down the beach, black birds, fighter jets, flying low, skimming the water, coming this way. A quick passage; she saw orange bills—orange like highway cones or tennis balls. Doubting her eyes, she flipped through the guidebook, intimidated by the variety. Skimmers?

She settled back again, content to watch, the distance between here and home yawning in her mind. Landlocked all her life, she had been willing to compare the ocean with home. But this was the edge of the continent. From this point on, you could no longer step forward and find the earth beneath you. From this point on, the world became groundless, landless, gone.

How odd it seemed, suddenly—as odd as traveling to the edge of Earth's atmosphere to gaze at that other beach, where air gave way to the sea of space.

She studied the ridge. From up there she would be able to trace the line of the beach north and south for miles. It seemed important to see it; she longed to. If Muirie could make the climb. Muirie sat beside her, engrossed in keeping a piece of lettuce just so between slices of bologna slick with mustard.

Rolling onto her belly, Roberta eyed the route up, and saw, high above, a bird hanging in the sky—almost motionless, surfing on the warm updraft of the ridge. A hawk. A hawk like the ones at home. She saw the tint of the red-brick tail.

She watched, waiting. Waiting for a shot, she realized, for a crack of death. *Boom.*

Wind. Only wind. The bird sailed up a few feet, then dropped by yards as if to examine them.

Crazy thought. Firearms were not allowed here. Instinct, long-learned. Reflex, to wait for the deadly explosion. Still she held her breath.

The bird kited, going nowhere in the traveling wind.

She felt blindly for the binoculars at her side. Focusing clumsily, she brought the bird close. Bold shape jumped into bold detail: the intricate pattern of the breast, the long, easy line of the body. She had seen the details of a hawk before, and in close-up, but this bird was not stretched on a fence or nailed to a tree, not desiccated in the sun, or blown apart by a gun.

The bird dropped lower, scanning them. Roberta saw the long feathers of the wing flexing, a flutter of down at the belly. She could see an eye, bright and alive, looking down the lens of the glasses into her own.

The hawk rose again, weightless, rising up on the incoming air, looking out over the view that she herself wanted to see, going no farther. It recognized the edge as surely as she did. It stopped here and watched, gazing north and south at the limits of its life. The land was home, and it ended here.

Returning to Wyoming, she could not shake the vision she had seen through the binoculars; at home, she was still seeing the shore.

Her father grew ruthless. Or had he always been? She was no longer sure. Ruthless and casual, he shot antelope, prairie dog, coyote, fox. *My old dad used to see bear here. Now wouldn't that be something?*

It still shocked her sometimes, the memory of his death. The sudden fall, Glen lifting the old man onto the tailgate of the pickup. She ran to the phone, miles and miles through the endless house, then back outside. There sat her father, dying. He gripped her hand like it was the edge of a cliff. "Goddamn it to hell, Bertie."

She moved to catch him as he slumped forward, threw herself at him on one knee, arms open. Glen grabbed from behind and eased him into Roberta's arm. He slumped against her, his bristling white head on her shoulder, a long, low exhalation in her ear. He smelled of dust and sweat and sunshine. His unshaved chin stung the skin of her neck.

Glen's voice was so muted his lips didn't move. "Good God."

"Lift him," Roberta said, low. Claustrophobic alarm; she tried to press the body back herself. "Get him off."

Glen grasped Jeremiah under the arms. The body was boneless. Roberta pushed it away as Glen lifted, and they lay it in the bed of the truck. Jeremiah's boots scored the dust, toes turned inward. They stood back, staring. Roberta nudged the toes of his boots apart, outward; he had never stood pigeon-toed in his life.

It was a tableau that haunted her, those seconds of bearing his weight, the opposing desires: to embrace or let go. Believe or reject. Love or despise.

He had raised her to think that wildlife must be "controlled," and that predators killed thousands of head of livestock a year. But control meant retributive slaughter, promoted by the government, which employed teams of hit men to help the ranchers improve their methods of massacre. Animal Damage Control, the feds were called, a name Roberta had to explain more than once on her tours and at school presentations in recent years to nonranchers who assumed the department protected animals from people. It was the people and their edible, four-footed investments that had the protection, and the predators that suffered control. No one controlled the controllers.

Flo's face on the night of the blizzard eddied in her mind. *Any coyote trouble lately?* Carl had said no, but Flo's face said something else. Muirie had seen it, too.

No, they had said, not us. Another detail in an endless story, like Jeremiah's stories, a gospel of the past that tried to justify the present. He had recounted his stories for everyone's edification, believing implicitly in their power to seduce. And they did. The Shea name alone, pronounced defiantly, made you throw your shoulders back and stand up straighter. Add some tales of strength and courage and gritty audacity and plain old iron-buttedness, and you had an offering of finely wrought propaganda. Jeremiah insisted the stories were true. They contained truth; there was no doubt of it. But they were only as true as any story told to make a point. Whatever facts failed to support the intended moral had been edited out. They existed as fables, transforming a scrappy bunch of forebears into a noble dynasty of the West.

She slogged back to the barn, kicking the snow from her path. Still, knowing all this, she had never been able to clear her mind completely of the stories. In spite of her resistance, they came to her whole sometimes, like a memory of her own life. And sometimes, despite everything, they gave her a fleeting sense of joy.

Susy, Jasper, and Chugwater sat on perches just inside the door. She preferred to have them outside in such a mild weather, especially after so much confinement, but Muirie had gone grocery shopping and she did not have time to stand outside and watch them. Inside, they were less liable to spook and bate off their perches, and she could keep an eye on them from the workroom. Outside, where anything could happen, they needed constant supervision.

The birds watched her with unblinking attention. Susy hunched, bobbing her head, as if taking a bead on Roberta. She reached out to scratch the barn owl on the head, and Susy leaned into her hand like a cat, beak gaping open in pleasure.

All these years later, she could look back and see California as the beginning, the moment when she began a long process of surfacing from the dream. She had been soaked in the dream, drugged with it, and she had come awake reluctantly, testy, and began to ask questions. Why do we do things this way? What would happen if we stopped? Do we have to kill everything on the land except the stock? Is this business so shaky?

But no one in her family, no one in the community where she had spent her life, wanted to listen to this language of doubt. She was not supposed to speak it.

Was there a gene specific to the belief in limitlessness? She wondered sometimes. Her father could not stand under the vault of the sky or look across an empty plain to a peak floating in the distance, and believe in limits. He could not live in a land so unrelenting in what it asked of a man for survival, and believe that it was delicate. Jeremiah had been born of the land, fashioned from its rocky soil, further toughened by its hardships, and he had believed himself to be indestructible.

CHAPTER TWENTY-SIX

Teiresias had found his balance. He handled more lightly than ever before, stepping forward boldly at the sound of the squeaker like a pedestrian crossing the street with the light. He ate eagerly and waited between courses at full attention, head up, wings held slightly away from the body, a posture that looked promisingly like preflight.

"There's one problem," Sherman said as the hawk stepped onto his fist and grabbed another piece of chicken. "It's too much like a treadmill with snack bars. He'll get too fat to fly."

"We need to push him a little," Muirie said. "He's connected the sound with the food, and he knows what he has to do to get it. The next step is to stop helping him so much."

"To make him impatient, you mean."

"To make him take some action. He's got to get irritated with us. He's got to get annoyed and think, 'Christ these people are slow—I'm going to have to do this myself.'"

Sherman raised an eyebrow.

"Okay, that's not an exact quote, but why couldn't his motivations be similar?"

"I wonder what it might take to get him to actually lift off."

"Hunger. I'd fly if I got hungry enough."

"Blind?"

Her enthusiasm simmered. "Why not launch him? Gently, I mean, to give him the idea. Aunt Bert does it with Oscar. He's always getting diverted and forgetting to fly."

Sherman returned the hawk to his perch. "It'd scare the shit out of him for one thing."

She sat the counter, a hand clapped to her chin. "But maybe it's been so long since he used his wings that he's forgotten them. He might need just one little toss, a gentle little toss in the air, the way a balloon lifts up from your hands, you know? It might scare the shit out of him, but the reflex to fly would come alive again. He'd have his wings out and flapping. He'd be flying without having to make a decision to do it. He'd be in the air again, Sherman."

Sherman still had his eye on Teiresias. The hawk preened delicately, sated and calm. "Has Bert said anything about all this?"

Muirie let out a long breath "You need her approval?"

He came to her side. "He's already had a lot of injuries, Muir."

Muir. He'd used her nickname. Some of the fight went out of her. "But we'll be right there. He's not going to fall."

"How come you don't want to talk about Bert?"

She pursed her lips. "She's . . . skeptical."

His eyes drifted across her face. "Skeptical."

"Okay. Strongly opposed."

"I was afraid of that."

"Even though she flies her own birds all the time and none of them are releasable, either."

Sherman sat on the counter beside her. They shifted closer, shoulder to shoulder. He was fixing dinner for her tonight, finally.

"She's almost brittle, isn't she, Sherman?"

"She's tough."

"They sound like different stages of the same thing to me. And I'm her niece."

He curled his hand around hers.

"I came here with an idea that I was like her. Or wanted to be like her. Now I don't know."

"Don't underestimate her."

She expected him to elaborate, but he looked into her face instead, taking her in with no hurry and no embarrassment.

"One of my clients told me something once," he said. "She said every so often she'll look at her cat, and she'll suddenly realize he's not human. And she'll be so surprised that she'll actually say out loud to the cat, 'Hey! You're a cat!'"

They kissed lightly, spontaneously.

"I'm not forgetting he's a hawk," she said.

They kissed again. He tasted good. She had trouble getting much volume into her voice. "It is true, though, that not all cat lovers can perceive reality."

He studied her for a moment. "I have five."

"Five...cats?"

"Does that put me out of the running?"

He made love with a joyful intensity. Though he didn't grin, he exulted, which made her laugh, starting from the moment he opened the door of his house and said, his eyes locked with hers, the sparest words at the rightest time, "Come on." This man knew when to leave his patience behind.

She wasn't about to introduce delays. Sex was one of the few things about adulthood that never disappointed her. It was as good as it promised to be. Better.

And better yet, Sherman showed a fine capacity to maintain his own contentedness, never lapsing once from assertion into flabby reflection and après-sex angst. She tested him a number of times. He lay there propped on his side, hairy legs crossed at the ankle, cradling her, studying her, welcoming each cat as it jumped onto the bed, not talking much and not sleeping, simply making love, and enjoying the aftermath.

"You hungry?" he said after a while.

They ate grilled cheese sandwiches off paper plates with a glass of wine each and went back to bed. It had gotten dark.

He curled up behind her, drawing her to his chest.

"Wait," she said, and leaned forward to turn on the light. She wanted to see him, to be seen. His hands went to her hips, caressing.

As a child, she had laid her dolls atop one another to consider the effect—jointed dolls, whose knees and elbows bent, whose torsos turned, and she had seen how sex could happen. But it looked unnatural, angular and awkward, ridiculous. As Sherman pressed his palm into her belly, she arched her back. His breath caught at her ear. Even now, it amazed her how well two bodies could meld—the twining of urgency with patience, a material change to malleability, driven by heat and motion, folding into tandem curves.

"You'll stay?" he murmured into the curve of her neck.

She said yes. Few decisions needed so little contemplation as this one. She could feel him at her navel, which was contemplation enough.

CHAPTER TWENTY-SEVEN

In the course of a week, the weather lost its mind. Muirie had never seen anything like it. Every climatic permutation possible permuted itself in the near vicinity. Rain and sleet mixed with ice and snow mixed with tornadoes and hail and a day of muggy, Guatemalan-style sunstroke. A rainstorm hit so hard that Muirie could feel the thunder like a racking arrhythmia in her chest. In the six hours after, the temperature shot feverishly from forty to seventy-two. The remaining snow didn't melt so much as collapse, threatening a tidal wave. The pastures turned to swamps, the air filled with steam, and across the back pasture Uncle John creek roared jubilation like a warrior home from his conquests. Then it snowed again—huge, gloppy splats like raw eggs slung from the heavens, which froze at night into black ice at the drainages in the roadways.

The hospital's population boomed. The birds migrating into and through the area were meeting with what Roberta acidly called their "normal quota" of spring disasters. The phones rang a dozen times a day with reports of injuries and panicky demands for information and assistance. Muirie kept records of the incoming patients, making notes on file cards, one for each bird. Over three particularly bad days she admitted a Canada goose with a broken and gangrenous wing (gunshot), a cormorant with an ugly, festering gash along its spine (boat propeller), a common merganser with a piece of fishing line coming out of its mouth (fishhook caught in throat), an American robin with internal injuries (cat-caught), and a young Harlan's hawk with a head wound and a mangled leg, found beside the highway (collision).

Roberta's moods ran the same course as the weather, calm and thoughtful, raging and dangerous. She interrogated the people on the phone herself, not trusting the job to Muirie—and Muirie was just as glad.

"How do you know the mother bird's dead?"

Muirie was mixing a vitamin preparation at the sink, listening. There was a long pause. Roberta laid a fist on the countertop. "Then keep your damn cat in." Another pause. "I can't take the babies. You'll have to save them yourself. They'll need to be fed every fifteen minutes for two weeks, twelve hours a day." She tapped her finger in a rapid tattoo. "I didn't say it was easy. I'll give you specific instructions. Get a pencil."

She accepted injured birds other than raptors in the spring, whatever the hospital could handle, but drew the line at fledglings that had fallen from their nests, uninjured. There were too many. Even with Muirie helping, the work had expanded to fill the day and a portion of every evening.

She got calls on mammals too: raccoons, skunks, fawns, badgers, foxes, rabbits, squirrels, beavers, and opossums. Someone found a fox caught in a trap, one forepaw gangrenous; a heavily pregnant antelope with her left hind hoof shot off. She routed the calls to the Game and Fish, but not without comment.

"They what?" Roberta said into the phone.

Alerted by her tone, Muirie went to her side. She was scrawling notes on the back of a paper sack she'd grabbed from the countertop: "Rabbits. Firecrackers." Then the scrawl became illegible.

"I want you to notify the police," she said to the caller. "Tell them just what you told me. Every word. I'm going to call you back to check on it. I have your name and number. Do you understand?"

After she hung up, she sat quietly in the rickety wooden chair at the worktable and looked up, dead calm, at Muirie. "Some kids out on the west side found a nestful of rabbits under their front steps. They took the kits and stuffed firecrackers up their butts. That was a neighbor, wondering if someone should stop them."

Sherman came visiting and helped Muirie fly and weather the tour birds, taking advantage of a day of sun. Roberta had said nothing about their liaison, nothing about Muirie's overnight absences, including a ski trip to the family cabin on the mountain, but Muirie had seen her eyeing them with that lightly smug, comprehending gaze of hers, meant to convey, Muirie thought, Roberta's refined tolerance for the foibles of others.

"Don't let it bug you," Sherman said, showering Jasper with a delicate spray from the hose. The hawk shivered deliciously and roused, throwing a rainbow over the muddy furrows of the drive.

Sherman had his own refinements of tolerance that could be irritating, too, at times.

"Doesn't it fry you, even a little?" she said.

"That's Bert. She always looks mad."

A woman came down the drive in a low-bellied old Chevy as they finished bathing the birds. She got out heavily, carrying a large, vivid yellow Jim Beam box in her arms. Roberta was expecting her. Muirie showed her into the workroom while Sherman brought the birds, one by one, into the barn. Roberta wasted no time in opening the box and removing its occupant, which she set on a folded towel on the counter.

Muirie gaped at the bird. It was the ugliest she had ever seen, clad in down as yellowing and filamentous as the last hairs on a bald man's head. A few flight feathers emerged in disorderly rows on its flimsy wings. Its pink, heart-shaped face was entirely naked, set with mournful agate eyes and the ivory curve of a beak, slender as a canine tooth. It crouched miserably over enormous, scaly pink feet, a homunculus of a bird.

"Barn owl," Roberta said.

The bird gasped feebly, as if answering roll call.

Muirie could see the resemblance, once told, to Roberta's tour bird, Susy, an adult. The raw pink skin of the young bird's face would become a lustrous disc of sound-focusing feathers. The plumage of the body would mature to spun gold and creamy white, and the feet would become proportional. But it was hard to imagine such a transformation in this bird.

"It's half-dead," Roberta said. "What have you been feeding it?"

The woman hugged her jacket to her body. She was sallow, her voice reedy with nicotine. "Raw hamburger. He doesn't go for much else."

Muirie saw Sherman walking toward the workroom, slowing as he approached, his eyes asking her if he should come in. She nodded. He leaned in the doorway.

"What else?" Roberta demanded.

The woman shrugged.

"Nothing? Mice, rats. Nothing?"

The woman grimaced. "He drunk a fair amount of water."

"That's it?"

Offense glowed in the woman's face. "How should I know what to feed him? The kids brought him in."

"Then why did you keep it so long?"

Sherman edged closer to the counter to look at the owl. Muirie noticed now that the bird looked mildly bowlegged. Sherman stretched a stumpy wing out a short distance from the body, fingered the shank of a leg. The owlet hissed without energy, striking spastically at his hand and missing.

"If you'd brought this bird in when you first found it, it might have developed normally," Roberta said. "With the diet you've given it, it'll be lucky to live."

"What do you mean?" the woman said.

"It's got rickets," Sherman said.

"Rickets?"

Sherman turned to the woman, sober. "It's a vitamin D deficiency caused by a poor diet and not enough exposure to sunlight. It stops calcium from working right in the body, so the bones stay soft." He pulled the wing out again, demonstrating. It formed a curve like the broad cup of an umbrella. "They're so soft the muscles pull them out of shape. Deforms them so the bird can't fly. The legs are affected, too."

The woman's face paled. "You can fix it, though."

Roberta turned away.

"Well," Sherman said. "Baby birds grow fast. The most important time for them to get the right diet is at the beginning. If the bones don't start out healthy, it's hard to reverse it."

"You mean he's going to die?"

"He's starving," Roberta said. "He not only got the wrong food, he got too little of it. Even if he lives, he'll probably be crippled, unable to fly, to have any kind of normal life." She glowered at the woman. "Do you feed your children nothing but hamburger?"

"I was trying to help."

"Don't," said Roberta. "Don't try to help. Ever."

The woman's eyes glinted. "I'll just take my bird back if this is the thanks I get."

"Your bird?" Roberta said. "Your bird?"

Sherman started to speak; Roberta talked past him. "You take this owl and I'll be on the phone to report you before you're out the door."

The woman's eyes widened. "Report me?"

Sherman took a step forward. "You can't keep wild birds without a permit." He glanced at Roberta, warning her off. She wouldn't look at him.

The woman swept them all with a resentful glare, then turned on her heel and left. She roared away in the car, its muffler firing like a musket.

The owl had sunk onto its squat tail, eyes drooping.

"He's too damn weak to feed," Roberta said. "He'll die of exhaustion getting his first decent meal."

Sherman gave Muirie a glance. "He's young. It may not be too late. Let's try some gruel."

"It's useless," Roberta said, but she did not move to prevent Muirie from defrosting a protein-rich muck in the microwave, a goo resembling baby food, made in the blender. She diluted it further in lukewarm water, mixed it with vitamin powder, loaded it into a syringe, and Sherman drained it down the owl's gullet.

Roberta cradled the owl in her palm, transferring it into a rubber bucket heated with a night-light. She covered the bucket securely with a blanket and sighed when she stood upright again. "I give him one chance in ten."

"That's better than none," said Muirie.

"He'll die anyway. And we'll have wasted our time."

"You've saved a lot of birds you thought would die, Bert," Sherman said.

Roberta smiled at him mirthlessly. "Like that ferruginous you're so nobly teaching to fly?"

They heard another engine, a resonant bass.

"That's my tour," Roberta said, scowling. She headed for the doors.

"Tour?" Sherman mouthed to Muirie.

Muirie waited for Roberta to pass through the barn door and slam it behind her. Dust sifted down from the loft. "First graders, Sherman, " Muirie said. "Tender young flesh."

Sherman's jaw flexed.

"What'll we do?" she said. "She shouldn't lead a tour when she's in this kind of mood."

"It'll be all right."

"She'll massacre them."

"Maybe you could lead it."

"Me? I've never done a tour before. You're the one who's worked here forever. You do it."

"What am I going to do, push her out of the way?"

"Yeah, nice knowing you."

"Wait a minute," he said, trying for calm. "I've watched her tours before. She'll do fine."

"Little scraplets of kids everywhere," Muirie said. "Vultures circling."

"Have you seen one of her tours?"

"No. This isn't the one I'd choose."

He took her hand. "Come on."

Those two words again. She liked them. She let herself be dragged outside. Roberta was standing hands on hips as the bus roared around the circle of the drive like yellow thunder, young faces pressed to every window.

"Over there," Sherman said, nodding to his truck. They sat on its back bumper. She crossed a leg with his, slouching forward. They had front-row seats for the carnage.

The doors of the bus burst open, expelling seven-year-olds as noisy as parrots. A teacher stepped wearily down to the gravel behind them. Roberta met her, offering her hand in a convincingly civilized manner, then directed the children into a line. They went like sheep to the slaughter, dancing a little in place against their excitement. Their teacher fell in line, too, grateful to be relieved of duty, blissfully ignorant of Roberta's boiling blood.

Roberta's voice rose up like a sergeant's. "Now," she said, lifting her chin. "Think."

She stared at them, ferocious. They fell silent, their faces taut with sudden fear. She had their terrified attention. Then—amazingly—she smiled.

"This is what I want you to think about. If you could be any kind of bird in the world, what kind of bird would you be?"

The kids faces emptied. Mouths hung open. A haze of suspicion formed (was this a quiz?) and dissipated (no, a game). They fell into eager thought. They scratched ears and noses, necks, foreheads, cheeks and chins; they searched the sky for inspiration, a rational idea, Muirie thought. They stared at their feet and chewed on their buttons, certain that they'd heard the name of a bird or two in their lives but unable to recall them on the spot. Three or four grasped an answer, finally. Their faces bloomed. They thrust their arms into the air, eyes blazing excitement at Roberta. She pointed at one but got answers from all.

"A parakeet!"

"Big Bird! I'd be Big Bird!"

"I'd be a duck!"

"A ostrich!"

Roberta nodded, approving of their choices, and the class stood tall with its communal success, ready for more.

"This is a hospital for birds," Roberta said. "This is where you would come if you were a sick owl or an eagle with a broken wing. You would come here and we'd help you get well again. Then we'd let you fly home. But before you can visit here, you have to be a bird . . . " She paced before them, eyeing them accusingly. "But you guys don't look like birds to me. You look like big, clumsy people."

They roared in disagreement; she dismissed their potential with a wave of the hand. "Don't try to fool me. You couldn't fly in a million years."

Laughing with delight, they insisted she was wrong.

She shrugged. It was out of her hands. "I don't see how," she said.

"Magic!" they screamed.

She screwed up her face. "Magic? Do I look magical?"

"Yes!" they screamed.

She looked down at her own clothing with sudden interest. She pulled her jacket pockets inside out and inspected them carefully, as if fully convinced that something magical might be lurking there. But no scarves or feathers or playing cards fell out. No rabbits appeared. She shrugged at the children. Doubt loomed on their faces. She was right: she didn't look magical. They could see that now. She looked like an old lady dressed in old clothes. And there was a hole in one boot where a red sock showed through. She held her chin in her hand and sized them up in return, equally disappointed.

"Well," she said, with faint resolve, sighing. "Let's go into this big barn over here and see what we can do. Some real birds live in there. Maybe they can help us somehow."

Sherman pulled the door open. The kids trooped through, stopping dead as they saw the line of raptors on their perches just beyond. From over Sherman's shoulder, Muirie could see Oscar in his fullest hemispherical form, registering each child as an abomination more terrible than the last.

Roberta ushered from behind, introducing the birds. She gave Muirie's arm a squeeze as she passed, and threw Sherman a wink at the door.

CHAPTER TWENTY-EIGHT

The mail lay heaped on Glen's desk, untouched since the weekend. He shuffled through it quickly, flicking the chaff to the side. He was after the letters from his constituents. Reading and responding to them was one part of the job he still enjoyed. Nothing got you closer faster to what the voters really thought. Telephone calls and face-to-face conversations, although valuable, suffered from their immediacy. Under pressure in a live conversation, people got confused by conflicting desires. On one hand, they wanted to appear moderate, sophisticated, diplomatic, and politically astute. On the other, they had a few blunt, pungent words to say, vital to the salvation of democracy. There seemed to be little territory between extremes: they chose obsequious diplomacy with no opinion, or rabid opinion and to hell with manners.

The letters showed the extremes as well, but also more of the thoughtful middle ground. They came in every conceivable style, from formal dissertations laser-printed faultlessly on heavy bond, to grammarless, hand-printed homilies on twenty sheets of tablet paper still glued at the top. He had found it generally true that the odder the choice of stationery, the more impulsive the writer. People grabbed for anything once they decided to write, including toilet tissue, although he didn't consider that so much a passionate choice as a sneering one. His files included letters on notebook paper and computer scrap, on sacks, checkbook covers, church circulars, napkins, gift wrap, McDonald's placemats, prescription pads, paper towels, and index cards. People often scrawled in the margins around his occasional op-ed pieces in the newspaper. Newspaper photos of him were mailed to him transformed. His balding head seemed to inspire the voters' artistic imagination. Depending on their mood, he wore white hats, black hats, horns, antlers, a headful of snakes, laurel wreaths, baskets of fruit à la Carmen Miranda, and crowns of all sorts, decorated with everything from brilliant jewels to nuclear warheads. The latest in this line, an altered photograph from a recent *Star-Tribune* roundup of the legislative session, showed him wearing a garbage-can lid as a hat. He'd received several copies last week, sent anonymously, and a cartoonist's version of the concept had shown up now on the editorial page. It was funny, he had to admit. A few well-chosen lines had transformed him from a six-foot man with a stoop into a squat, overflowing garbage can, smiling dopily like the Little Engine That Could.

He slit open the envelopes and ran his eyes over the letters. Several were lengthy, computer-printed anti-trash-ranch essays.

"Listen to that," he murmured aloud. "Even I'm saying trash ranch."

Its official name—the Hanna Sanitary Landfill Project—was the by-product of a legislative committee, of course, a high revetment of a name that anticipated an attack.

He fanned the letters out before him. Two were from Audubon members, as were several he had received last week. All asked for his support in opposing the trash ranch and recalled his support of the group on other issues, making it sound more important than it had been, flattering him with plaudits for his influence and good sense. They warned, too, in calm language, of their intention to trash the trash ranch if they could manage it, and he had no doubt they could if they marshaled their forces. They were a formidable bunch, professionals of every ilk, organized statewide, literate to their eyebrows, political to the core, sagacious, shrewd, inventive, eccentric, and absolutely implacable. In the decades since the club's founding, it had become the state's environmental pit bull. He had been friends with most of the members all of his adult life. Except for Roberta, of course. He was married to her.

Without Flo's paintings, the Durbin Street Gallery felt like a shabby little cave. Muirie and Roberta closed the front door behind them. In the light of day, the white walls were gray and smudged, and the carpet heartlessly industrial. Someone had unloaded a few pieces of stoneware onto the floor for the next show. The plates were like manhole covers, in the heavy, grainy, muddy-colored style that Muirie's parents had liked when she was a child.

Roberta tapped a foot impatiently. The place appeared to be unstaffed, though the door had been unlocked. "I guess they aren't too worried about someone walking off with the 'artwork,'" she said, nodding toward the stoneware.

They heard a door slam. Flo came toward them from the back of the gallery, beaming, and it was as though the sun had suddenly popped through the water-stained ceiling tiles of the room. She had come to take a last look at her paintings before their new owners picked them up, she told them. "It's hard for me to let them go."

She had wrapped the painting of Carl in butcher paper and string. They loaded it into the truck and walked down the block for coffee at the pizza parlor, empty at this hour of the morning except for a single cranky waitress who glared at them without a word.

"Just coffee," Roberta said.

"I thought so," she replied, swishing off.

Flo told them about the buyers of her other paintings, radiating joy and regret, surprise and dismay, and the thinnest edge of mercenary pride. "It seems like so much money and all in one bunch."

"And you made it yourself," Roberta added.

The fact seemed to shock Flo all over again. "It doesn't seem that way, you know. You bring so much of your life to it, and everyone in your life. I'd never felt so..." She looked at them, baffled. "This sounds so crazy—I'd never felt so...unlonely...until I started painting. Then so many faces crowded in. It's such a funny thing, because I sit up there all by myself."

They talked of friends, of the struggling businesses of the little town, of the crazy weather. Muirie noticed that Roberta seemed to relax entirely, slouching on the seat with her feet propped on the opposite bench.

"What's the chance of spring this year, you figure?" she asked.

Muirie was still cold. "You mean warm days? Something a little more than a couple of blades of green?"

"Oh," Flo said seriously. "I never like to say. If you say it'll come, it won't. If you say it won't, it will."

"Then say it won't," said Muirie.

"Oh, but you have to believe it," Flo said, "and I don't know what to believe. My old dad, one of his little jokes, he'd say it every year, 'You kids, you be ready. If spring comes this year, we'll have a picnic that day.'"

"Your old dad," Roberta said reflectively. "My God, he was the biggest man I ever saw. What, six-six at least, and two hundred-fifty pounds, anyway."

"Three hundred," said Flo. "My mother said after he died that the worst part of all was feeling his weight gone from the bed at night. I've thought of that so many times." She patted Muirie's hand. "Did you know my dad courted your grandpa's little sister once upon a time?"

"Moira?" Muirie said. "When?"

"Oh, way, way back. Think how that would have changed things if they'd got married. Bertie and I would have ended up cousins."

"Seems to me you would have ended up somebody else altogether, Flo," Roberta said.

Flo sighed. "I suppose so. But I like the thought of it."

"So what happened?" Muirie asked.

"Well," Flo said with mild outrage, "Moira wouldn't have him. He never would say why. I think maybe because he was such a big man and she was so small."

"My grandfather used to tell me about her toe. How she was so shy about it."

Flo laughed. "That's not the way my dad remembered things, and he was there, too, you know. Moira never had a shy day in her life, to hear him tell it. He said that when she got older and boys started wanting to look up past her feet, she'd use that gone toe to scare away the ones she'd didn't like. She'd pull her foot out of her shoe and she'd say, 'Looky here.'"

Roberta, smiling, tapped a judicial finger on the table. "Sounds to me like he had some personal experience."

Flo put a hand to her mouth. "Would you believe it, I never thought of it quite like that. My dad, who carried a Bible around in his pocket all the time, trying to look up her skirts. Think of it."

"Maybe the Bible was penance," Muirie said.

"My dad called Moira a blithe spirit," Flo said. "I always liked that, that he'd say such a thing. Those are his very words: 'blithe spirit.'" She sighed. "It doesn't sound to me like she moped for a minute about that toe."

They walked back to the gallery. At the truck, Flo peeked in again at the painting. Roberta, smiling, stirred the change in her pocket. "Flo, I wanted to ask you something."

"I know you say that you like it," Flo said, peering through the glass. "And yet I can't believe you do."

"The night of the blizzard," Roberta said, "when Muirie and I came over for a few minutes—"

Flo put a hand to her heart. "I've still got your casserole dish!"

"No—"

"I should have brought it in with me today. I'll run it over to you." She turned to Muirie, laughing. "Any excuse to see my painting again."

Roberta's face had gone cold. "No. It's about the coyotes."

"The coyotes?"

"I asked Carl if he'd had any trouble with coyotes."

Astonishment surfaced in Muirie like sudden pain. Roberta intended to cross-examine Flo.

"He told me no at the time," Roberta said. She paused. "I wondered if things had changed."

Flo stared at her in confusion. "If things had changed?"

"If he's seen any coyotes."

Flo's expression stiffened. "I don't know what you want me to say, Bertie."

Muirie did. "They already told you no, Aunt Bert."

Roberta looked away suddenly, over the cab of the truck, as if she had heard a distant noise. When she looked back at Flo, there was a fugitive little smile on her face, one that never reached her eyes. "I just wondered if you'd had any more trouble."

"No," Flo said firmly. "Not a bit." Then she froze, her face so lucid it shone. "But we never had any in the first place." She blurted the words, turning to Muirie.

Roberta eyed them both blandly. "I suppose we should head on home."

Speechless, Muirie could not bring out a word until she pulled around the corner and was forced to stop at a light. Roberta sat beside her, impassive as stone. "I can't believe you, Aunt Bert."

Roberta's sidelong glance skimmed her. The light changed. Muirie gunned the truck. "You tried to trick her. *Flo.*"

"I asked a question."

"You tried to trap her—as if you could conclude anything from it. You don't even know if there are eagles up there yet."

Muirie accelerated fast onto the highway. "What makes you suspect the Drummonds?"

Roberta didn't answer.

"You're going on that one little look on Flo's face that night?"

"And the raven. And today."

"Today?" Muirie let a gleaming Harley pass. It shot ahead like a missile, disappearing around a bend in a roar that penetrated to her nerves. "Today's not evidence of anything. You start throwing odd questions at Flo and she's likely to get flustered no matter what the topic. She's that kind of person."

"You're wrong. She's not easily flustered at all. I've known her all my life."

"Then how could you treat her that way?"

Roberta didn't answer.

"And what about Glen? When are you going to tell him about all this?"

"I said I would, Muirie."

"But what's the point in keeping it from him in the first place? What in the world could he do?"

Roberta stared straight ahead, matter-of-fact. "He'd try to talk me out of it. He'd tell me that my imagination has run wild, that the skier's story means nothing, proves nothing, that even if a few birds get killed now and then, that most ranchers are 'responsible stewards of the land.'" She bit the sentence off. "He wants me to be happy with the status quo, like all the idiots who vote for him."

"Idiots? He's been reelected by landslides. He ran unopposed last time."

"Ah! An argument for the 'wisdom of the people.'"

"You talk like he's a tyrant or something."

"He can make things look simple, and voters like a simple explanation."

"You mean that voters are simple, that people are stupid. That's what you mean." Roberta didn't answer. "That's an incredibly cynical way to think."

"Cynical or realistic?" said Roberta.

"I recognize cynicism when I see it."

"You might. But someone who's trying to fly a blind bird won't win any medals for good judgment."

Muirie rolled too fast over a double railroad crossing, bouncing them both to the ceiling. Shaken, she hit the brakes, slowing the truck on the shoulder. "That really bugs the hell out of you, doesn't it?"

Roberta gave her a level stare. "Yes, it does. It bugs the ever-loving hell out of me."

At the Uncle John, Muirie grabbed the painting and went inside, feeling a need to keep it out of Roberta's hands, as if it were a living part of Flo. When Roberta came in behind her, she sat abruptly on the couch, setting the painting at her feet. Glen's door opened down the hall.

"Are you back?" he called.

Roberta shrugged her jacket from her shoulders. He ambled into the silence of the living room, his hands in his pockets, perusing them with mild surprise. He had on a nubby, olive-colored sweater, missing a button at the bottom.

"We're having a party, are we?" he said.

"Here's your painting," Muirie said, nudging the frame with her toe.

"Ah," he said, nodding. He looked at them both again, one by one, as if testing the depth of their silence. His glasses slipped to the end of his nose. "Maybe I could take a look at it."

Muirie scooted it across the carpet to him.

He smiled, bemused. "Like Christmas."

He squatted and pulled away the tape and paper at the top of the frame. A hand was visible first. Glen glanced up at Roberta. She stood by the door to the kitchen, arms crossed at her waist as if she were cold. He pulled the rest of the paper away and stood up, studying the painting.

The day was cloudy, the room colorless. He edged the painting toward the low light of the window.

"Well, I'll be," he said. "It's Carl, isn't it?"

CHAPTER TWENTY-NINE

Flo lay on the bedspread, pulling an afghan around her neck and shoulders. Annie would drop the children off after supper for the evening, and she needed to buttress herself with some rest before they came. They were becoming harder to entertain as they grew older. More and more, they begged her to join their games and demanded she invent new ones, unable to keep themselves happy for even an hour at a time. Luke complained that she and Carl didn't have cable TV. But when Hank was young, they'd had no television at all, just the radio and the record player. She still had a box full of 45s in the attic. All of it country: Gene Autry, Tex Ritter, Patsy Cline, and just about everything Hank Williams ever sang. Hank had liked to boast, back then, that he'd been named after the singer, though it wasn't true. "Charles Henry" gave Hank the same initials as Carl and his father and grandfather before him, C. H. Drummond. Hank had broken the tradition with Luke during the time when he and his dad wouldn't even talk to each other. After the truce, if that was what you called it, he and Annie had tried to make it up to Carl by naming the girl Charlotte Hannah. Carl had never said a word.

She'd kept the record collection, thinking that Hank would want it back someday. But when she'd showed it to him a year or so earlier, his only comment was to wonder how much it was worth. She shut the box again, firmly, and taped it shut. He plainly wasn't old enough even yet to value the memories of his childhood.

She shifted onto her side, conscious of a dull pain in her hip. Her weariness was more than physical. She needed to talk to Carl. The knowledge of it dragged her down like an anchor. She had thought through the circumstances a dozen times. They'd lost the lamb and the ewe a couple of weeks before the big storm. The coyotes hadn't hit a second time as they often had in the past, and, looking back, she found it strange that Carl had marveled about it so little and worried aloud less. He'd answered her questions about them briefly, saying that he'd scared the damn cowards away and that it tempted fate to talk about it. He rapped the table with his knuckles, in anger or superstition, she wasn't sure which.

Where Roberta Shea came into it, she didn't like to think. That funny little casserole they'd brought the night of the blizzard—not a shred of meat in it—Bertie had never known a kitchen sink from a stock tank. She'd looked old sitting there at the table. Of course, Flo hadn't dared to look at her own face in the mirror that night after all those hours bumping around in the truck. The fifteen years that separated their births would have shown up as clear as day if she had. It had seemed, before, to be a friendly number of years, sisterly, motherly, but with that one, sharp little sentence at the gallery, Roberta had turned them into centuries.

She drifted into shallow sleep and woke disoriented, thinking it was morning. The truth came to her with no relief: she had slept too long and waked up at the wrong end of the day. Dinner was not made; the children would be there soon. She felt for her shoes with her toes, anxious to get downstairs, into the bright lights of her kitchen.

Carl muted the sound on the television when he saw her. "You okay?"

She was not certain. Her head felt heavy, or her neck weak. She touched her temples. "I wish you'd gotten me up."

"I hated to."

She headed toward the kitchen, switching on the lights in the dining room as she went.

"I made me a cheese sandwich," Carl called. "Made you one, too, wrapped up in Saran in the icebox."

She turned back to the living room. He had already eaten; a plate sat on the end table, a paper napkin balled up in the center. Now she had no reason to busy herself in the kitchen and she would have to eat a cold slab of American cheese slapped onto mayonnaised bread. Her stomach balked.

"You've caught something from Lottie," Carl said. "She was sniffling up a storm that last time they were here."

A cup of tea instead, perhaps, she thought. Some soda crackers, maybe a banana. "I'm not sick."

He nudged the sound back up on the television.

"When's your program over?" she asked.

He hadn't quite made out her words. He frowned, waiting for her to repeat them. When she didn't, he turned the television off with an impatient flick of the wrist. She stared at him, deadpan, and his impatience drained away. He set the remote control on the table and got to his feet.

"I didn't want to watch the damn thing anyway."

She put a little water in the teakettle and set it on the flame, then cut the sandwich he had made for her into fourths. Carl helped himself. He took a stack of saltines when she offered them, and half the banana.

The light in the room seemed dim, patently false after her expectation of daylight upstairs. She stared up at the overhead. The bulbs needed replacing, with a hundred watts each, every one of them.

"That water's boiling," he said.

She pulled the kettle from the burner, poured two cups of water, and added a teabag to each. Carl didn't like tea, but he'd drink it if he had company. They sat together at the table. He dumped two heaping teaspoons of sugar into his cup, followed by milk to the brim, stirring it with close concentration.

She rubbed her eyes. They ached from behind. "Carl, I need to know more about those coyotes."

His face flashed surprise. He stopped stirring. "What brought this up?"

"I saw Bertie Shea at the gallery. She asked about them again."

He straightened his shoulders. "What did she say to you?"

Roberta's words had been simple enough but Flo did not know how to explain the way she had said them. "She asked, had things changed."

"Changed?" He moved his mug away, sloshing syrupy tea onto the table. "What did you say?"

"I said no. I said the same as you."

He stared hard at the surface of the table, avoiding her eyes. She pushed a paper napkin into the spill.

"Carl," she said, quietly.

His head came up but not his gaze.

"It's got something to do with birds. That's all I can think of. That's the only thing Bertie's interested in, the only reason she'd ask questions. I think you put out some poison."

His frown turned ferocious. "Where in the devil did you get that idea?"

"I can tell by looking at you," she said.

He turned his head. His neck bulged at his collar. "One lamb. One time. About as much meat on it as a twig."

He had kept poison on the place after all. It didn't surprise her much. "She's worried about her birds."

He pushed himself away from the table and stood up. "You don't know that. Are you saying she's found something on our land?"

A gleaming image lit her mind. She brought a hand to her heart. "No, but I did."

"What are you talking about?"

She set her cup down carefully, feeling a weakness in her hands. "You didn't tell me, so I didn't know. I found a dead raven, near the Eberson road. I took it to Bertie."

He sat down again, shocked. "You took a dead bird you found on our land to Bertie Shea?"

"You said you weren't poisoning anymore. I should have known better."

"When was this?"

"Before the blizzard. I don't know exactly. She said she couldn't tell what killed it, but she put it in her freezer."

He snapped a knuckle. "She can't know anything for sure. We may be getting all riled up for nothing." He ran his fingers through the thin hair at his crown. "I didn't want to worry you. I just wanted to get it taken care of."

"Well, I'm worrying now," she said softly. "If they catch you killing eagles, they can fine you thousands of dollars. It would put us under. And you know how Bertie is."

His anger rebounded. "Yes, I do know how she is, damn it, always sticking her long nose where it doesn't belong. She's got something to say about everything and she's always got to say it. She's just like her god-damn father. And you took her a raven!"

Flo fell silent. Carl stewed for a long while, then edged one hand to the center of the table, wanting to touch her.

"Flo, I don't want this blown up into a big thing between us," he said. "I did what I thought I had to do. I'm not the only one."

"I know that," she said.

His anger welled up again. "No, we got a bunch of saints living around here these days. Bertie and Glen don't have to live off the land nowadays. They got a nice living off oil and gas instead. They got plenty of time and money to sit back and tell the rest of us what we're doing wrong. Seems to me they sung a different tune way back when."

She touched her temples, wishing earnestly that it were morning. There had always been a measure of desperation in Carl, a tendency to misrepresent, to make things look better than they were. He was guilty of swaggering, of exaggeration, of reporting more success than he had earned, of denying failure. But everyone told such lies. It was the way he had done it, hoping to avoid criticism that he wasn't protecting the stock. She could see that now. He'd poisoned the coyotes in desperation and it was his desperation he wanted to hide, especially from her.

"Flo, look. We got this ranch to worry about. We got our old age coming on. Everybody takes care of what's his own. That's the way things have always worked."

She folded his hand into hers. "Everything's going to be all right."

CHAPTER THIRTY

Sherman had called in the late afternoon. An emergency case had come in as he was closing the clinic, a Rottweiler hit by a truck. He was setting up for surgery and couldn't meet Muirie for dinner. The impact had crushed a femur, split the large intestine, and probably cracked the pelvis as well, then the dog had been dragged on the bumper of the truck, embedding the wound with asphalt grit and sand. Sherman worked as they talked, getting ready. It was amazing that the idea of dinner could enter his mind. She heard water running, the *clang* of instruments. "I'll call if I finish early, but I think it's going to be pretty late, damn it. He's in bad shape."

It figured that this would happen on a night when she wanted more than anything to be with him and away from the strained atmosphere of the ranch. She banished her disappointment; he didn't have time to listen to her whine about her rotten day. "Can you save him?"

"I don't know. Maybe. He's not a young dog." She heard the *whoosh* of the inner door, an anxious voice in the echoing hallway. The owner, probably. "Is something wrong?" Sherman asked her.

"No," she said. "I'll come as early as I can tomorrow, as soon as I get my stuff done here."

"Good," he said, and she heard a long, low, warbling howl in the background. "I've got to go, Muir."

She passed up dinner, slapping together a sandwich instead, which she took to the pine closet, intent on thinking through her sour thoughts in solitude. She set the plate, clattering, onto Jeremiah's desk, and closed the door soundly behind her. Let Roberta and Glen scrounge for themselves out there. Without her they'd stand at the counter, eating on the run.

She found their mutual incompetence in the kitchen clearly symptomatic of the sickened state of their marriage—symptoms so generally applicable that she could probably diagnose the marital success of any couple based on their eating habits alone.

She sat at Jeremiah's desk, grimly pleased, and laced her hands behind her head. Stated in its simplest terms, the theory compressed down to one convenient nugget, a diagnostic guideline: won't cook—can't nurture; won't sit down—can't last long.

Christ. I'm turning into my mother.

That same nasty delight too in having nailed somebody; that ugly, sniping, farty-minded certainty of knowing more than they did about themselves. Her face looked the same too, no doubt, smug and tight. She slapped her hands to her cheeks, hard. *Idiot.*

No sense of release could come from peevish thoughts like those. They took you in the opposite direction, sank you, shortened your line of sight to a nose-end view of your own sniveling and colicky soul.

She stood up, stretching, throwing her arms wide, determined to cast the mood away. A physical release would help—breathing deeply, expelling her thoughts with her spent air, bringing in fresh.

She closed her eyes, emptying out, thinking of Sherman instead. He had left his impression in her skin, a heated memory of weight and depth and motion; and the scent at the scoop of his neck—she could smell it—blood-hot and edible. Relaxation returned, a quick, strong current flooding straight south from her navel. She let her arms drop, smiling at her sudden languor. He smelled good everywhere. And close to his lips, she had liked the taste of his words.

At eight-thirty, the phone rang. Someone grabbed it on the second ring. Muirie waited, motionless, for the thump of footsteps, hoping it was Sherman on the line. Instead, she heard a door close, then silence. Glen had taken the call in his office.

Slumped at Jeremiah's desk she read a Dorothy Sayers so far removed from the Uncle John that she felt disoriented by her surroundings at the end of every chapter. After an hour she shut the book on a scrap of paper, tired suddenly of having to keep track of clues.

She picked up Jeremiah's desk calendar, idly fingering its thin, discolored metal, and the fragile, aged paper marking the months of a time so long in the past, the year Aura Shea had died, years before her own birth. Roberta had left it here, though nothing else of his remained on the desk or inside it. The drawers rattled with paper clips and stubby pencils, the files transferred to Glen's office and stored away in a retrievable fashion. Jeremiah had kept his papers in avalanching piles, elbow-deep.

A soft knock at the door. Roberta's voice. "Muir?" The door opened an inch. "Can I come in?"

"Of course."

She stepped in, stocking-footed, and stood for a moment, aimlessly, as if lost in the small space of the room.

"About today," she said. "I'm not good at subtlety. It came out sounding harsh."

Muirie shifted forward in the screechy chair, looking for signs of penitence in Roberta. She saw exhaustion. "You ambushed her, Aunt Bert."

"I meant it to be a simple question from an old friend." She sat stiffly on the edge of the bed. "But I can't be casual about this."

Muirie's anger rose up fresh. "Or objective."

Roberta smiled faintly. "You're not particularly forgiving."

"I didn't hear you ask for forgiveness. And it's Flo you offended."

"Oh, no, I offended you too. You laid rubber half the way home."

"I'd never seen you do a thing like that. I never would have expected it from you."

Roberta gave her a cryptic glance, which lingered, then shifted away. "Being grown-up is tough."

"Don't give me that," Muirie said. "My mother does that, plays that role, the infinitely wise, older adult. It doesn't sway me anymore. It's your own disillusionment talking."

Surprise sparked in Roberta's face, spontaneous and brief.

"I felt like you cornered Flo," Muirie said, more quietly. "That's what I couldn't believe. You never would have treated her like that before."

"Before," Roberta said as if the thought of it taxed her.

"When I was a kid, when I came here summers. You weren't like this then."

"I don't know how you can judge. You were so young."

"Are you joking? If you'd been like this then, I'd have been scared of you. Back then, it was Uncle Glen who seemed forbidding. But I loved you. That's why I came back, thinking—" She faltered.

"Thinking you still would."

Muirie held Roberta's cool gaze. "You think I'm naive. Everything I say, I feel like you're analyzing it." Tears threatened. She held them back hard. "You even see my expectation of loving you as naive."

"That's not true."

"Isn't it?"

"You don't understand, Muirie."

"It's as if Flo doesn't matter to you. It's like no one does."

"I have to know the truth."

"Is that the only way to find it out? To destroy a lifelong relationship?"

Roberta closed her eyes. "What's it worth, a lifelong relationship, if it won't bear up when something so important is at stake?"

Muirie studied her gravely. "It's asking too much. You don't seem to realize what you ask of people."

"I'm asking you for some forgiveness," said Roberta. She held out a hand to Muirie. After a moment, Muirie took it.

"Tolerate me," Roberta said. "I'm feeling—" She gripped Muirie's fingers until they hurt. "—wound tight."

Sherman finally called at ten. Muirie slung a few clothes into her carry-on and grabbed the keys to the pink truck. She found Roberta with Glen in his office. Glen sat on the couch, his newspaper folded in half, feet propped on the ottoman. Roberta stood at the desk, sorting through a stack of bills. The room was reflected brilliantly in the black expanse of the windows. Muirie saw her own image out of the corner of her eye, a narrow profile far to the left. The painting of Carl sat on the floor against the wall.

"I know it's late," she said. "But I need to go into town."

To say more was to say more than was necessary. Her flushed complexion alone gave her away, she knew. Glen, looking at her, steadied his glasses.

"It's after ten, kiddo," Roberta said gently. "Don't drive back tonight."

"No, I'll be back in the morning. Early."

The roads were clear and she was alone on the highway, so she drove as fast as the pink truck would go, pushing the accelerator even on the curves, her window open to the cold night air. Blackness loomed up around her, glowing red at the back bumper when she touched the brakes. Over a long grade, the town lay before her. She lifted her foot from the accelerator, and the engine sighed. It was like flight in a glider, this approach into town, a long descent into the scattered lights and empty streets. She leaned back in her seat, arms locked straight, angling her face into the wind.

Every light in Sherman's house was ablaze. He opened the door, barefoot, in jeans and a loose cotton shirt, the tail out, rumpled. He grabbed her bag and tossed it to the floor behind him. His arm was around her waist. Both arms. He pulled her inside, knocked the door shut with a foot. She kissed his ears, neck, ran her cool hands up under his shirt. He pressed her to the wall, his weight at her belly.

"You said you needed to talk," he said. "I hope you don't mean now."

CHAPTER THIRTY-ONE

A couple of phone calls an hour were coming in for Glen during the regular business day, and two or three over the course of the evening. Roberta could tell without asking that most concerned the trash ranch. His circumspection advertised the fact. When she came into his office at night to open the hospital mail, he presented her with a smile, but it looked wary. He expected an attack.

She sliced open a bill for veterinary medications. Sherman got them for her at what he insisted was cost but she suspected that he paid part of it himself. To avoid her challenges he always mailed it to her. She had not told him that the owlet had died. It had lived ten days, just long enough to give her hope that it might survive.

The phone rang. They both glanced at it. "Let the machine get it," Glen said, turning back to a sheath of notes.

He had turned the volume down so low that the caller's words couldn't be distinguished. They sounded angry, though, wormy with acrimony. Somebody on her side. Glen glanced at her again, surreptitious, uneasy. She opened another piece of mail.

How many wild animals had Jeremiah killed? she wondered —hundreds over his lifetime. Take that figure times all the ranches over all the years. Even without the poison, think of the direct kills. She had not challenged her father for years. It had not seemed wrong at the time. It merely happened, like all the other usual events. Glen, even now, would not condemn the practice wholeheartedly. *There are still lots of red-tails, Bertie. There are still lots of coyotes.*

My God, Glen. There are still lots of Jews.

Jeremiah—such a biblical name. She had not realized it until he was dead. It had simply been his name, a fact, as the chores of the ranch were a fact, as the shooting of the hawks was a fact. After he died, people spoke of him with admiration, in a tone of near veneration.

There was no Glen in the Bible. There were Glens in *Who's Who* and in legislative guides and on newsmaker interviews. There were Glens on ballots and posters and printed napkins, on fund-raising junk mail, on boards of directors and listed in stock exchanges and United Way campaign boards; at the head of oil companies and refineries; standing at podiums, preaching compromise, patriotism and goodwill.

But if dead eagles were found in the canyon, those good intentions would add up to culpable inaction. Jackson Canyon would be just another trash ranch, a place for people to dispose of what they considered worthless.

Muirie had said she thought Roberta had changed; she wasn't old enough to know how much Glen had altered, too. How different he had been before. It was almost impossible to believe now, but she'd once been the less direct of the two. He'd issued that first invitation to dinner and never waited for an answer, assuming she would come.

"So what time will you get here?"

"I haven't said yes."

"You haven't said no either. Listen, Bertie, if I wait around for people to literally, explicitly, say yes to me whenever I'm after something, I'll get nowhere fast."

A candor increased by his hormones, no doubt, but illustrative: so direct it took her breath away. She had gone, that night.

He'd inherited the house on Grant Street at his father's death. His mother had settled permanently in Denver, so he had it to himself, a blocky two-story fortress, heavy with pediments and civic responsibility, the kind of house he would grow to resemble. But when she had pulled up to the curb that night, she thought how odd it was for him to live in a place that reeked so of staid adulthood. She left the engine of the pickup running for a moment, inspecting the place. There were no draperies on the first floor windows. She could see straight into the living room and into what looked like the dining room beyond, filled with buttery light. Beyond, a wide double doorway, and a dark shape moving back and forth—Glen in a dark shirt or sweater, one arm in the air. He paced, talking on the phone, railing at whatever poor sucker was on the other end.

Her mind coursed through a preview of the routes the evening could take. The final scene didn't vary, didn't seem to offer options. Yet her independence made her cautious, suddenly, of giving way. Her virginity was not the only thing at stake.

She stared ahead at the hood of the truck, both hands on the wheel, her indignation rising. Look at her. He'd said to come over and there she was, idling at his curbside. She glanced again toward the house, half-convinced she would drive away. The double doorway was empty. Glen stood on the porch, the phone on a long cord in his hand. He mouthed something she could read as clearly as if he'd said it in her ear. "What the . . . ?" Then he turned abruptly, back into the house, leaving the door open.

She wanted a little control, that was all. Their interest in each other wasn't casual. But they had held off, keeping things businesslike, friendly but distanced. Stepping inside that door would change everything; the balance they had achieved between them would alter.

She flipped off the ignition, palming the keys, and got out of the truck. Ten feet from the porch, she could already hear his voice.

"We already settled that, Benjamin."

Benjamin, a prickly partner in a recent oil deal. She closed the door behind her and stepped through the foyer. She had expected to see his boyhood home: heavy furniture covered with antimacassars, Persian rugs on shining floors, the scent of lavender in the air. But the inside of the house had been stripped. The air smelled of paint, dust, solvent, and, faintly, mucky boots. Plaster debris crunched under her feet. A wall had been removed, joining the living and dining rooms. What furniture there was sat shrouded in canvas in a broad hallway. Glen gave her a wave from the double doors at the back. The room behind him appeared to be furnished.

"That's crap," he said into the phone. "Look at your contract." He listened impatiently. "Next paragraph down."

She wandered into the kitchen. Wide tiled countertops, completely bare. The appliances were new; the stove still had an adhesive label on the oven window listing instructions for installation. She pulled open a couple of cabinets. Empty. One had a row of tiny brass hooks, sized for delicate teacups, but the dishes she found were paper.

She heard the phone bang in its cradle, then Glen coming out of the back room, talking. "He thinks he can plug new paragraphs into a signed contract at will."

He came at her, stormy, running his hand through his hair. He kissed her quickly, a glint in his eye, and turned to the wasteland of the front rooms, shoving his hands in his pockets. "So what do you think?"

"It looks like holy hell."

He looked around critically. "Yeah, but you should have seen it before. It had everything but velvet ropes along walkways. My mother went around polishing the crystal doorknobs. I took every one of them out."

He led her toward what had been the dining room. "I'm taking out part of the wall to the kitchen, leaving in some columns, expanding the room out this way. I don't like walls where I don't need them. I want to be able to look across an expanse."

She wondered why she had not known this about him before. Though he was not a bulky man, he took up a lot of space. A phone conversation with Benjamin had required the entire width of the house. She was accustomed, she realized, to seeing him outside, where there were no walls at all.

The phone rang. "That'll be Ben again. He's finally thought of a comeback." He laughed, letting the phone ring. "It'll drive him nuts if he can't tell it to me." He grabbed her hand. "Come on. Let me show you the rest of the place."

The room behind the double doors occupied the back of the house, the former library or family room, now Glen's headquarters among the ruins. Old-fashioned venetian blinds striped the evening sun onto the bare floor. At one end of the room she glimpsed an overflowing desk against tall bookcases filled with a jumbled mass of books, magazines, and newspapers. A single pile of dirty clothes sat in the middle of the oaken floor, kicked there, she guessed, as she drove up to the curb. At the far end stood a four-poster bed, the wood as dark as a ripe and polished plum, and above it hung a large, horizontal painting, Impressionistic in style, of gaunt soldiers on horseback galloping full tilt across a meager grassland.

She walked toward the painting. Glen grabbed her hand. He leaped onto the bed, pulling her with him, and strode to its head, inches from the painting. Roberta sank to her shins in sheets, pillows, blankets, a down comforter. The painting, close-up, separated into vigorous splotches of paint spread across the canvas with restless energy.

"Fred Remington," Glen said. "It's called *Cavalry Charge on the Southern Plains*. Painted in 1907. My great-grandfather on my father's side bought it from Remington at his studio in New York."

Each horse and rider cast a compact shadow in the harsh, noonday light, painted with quick, overlaid strokes of black, like dark wolves running with the charge. The desiccated skull of a buffalo lay in the foreground.

"If I can't sleep at night," he said, "if I feel riled, I sit up in bed and stare at that painting. It calms me down. I think 'Who cares about anything else?'—and I'm asleep in five minutes."

Roberta took a step backward. The soldiers, their eyes shaded black by their hats, sat the gallop with ease, their bodies relaxed, one gloved hand on the reins, the other lofting a pistol, muzzle skyward. Whatever they charged was out of range, but not by much.

"*This calms you?*" she said.

"Not at the moment," he said, kissing her. She sank in the blankets to her knees.

They had married a year later. To do so had seemed natural: Jeremiah's two most devoted lieutenants, a team. Roberta did not remember speculation about the match. It had come to be expected. They would form a dynasty: the business acumen of Glen's family blended with the courage and panache of the Sheas. You did not choose to give up success.

She studied Glen as she slipped the last of the bills into her alphabetical file, her thoughts shifting to Jackson Canyon. Glen read solemnly, absorbed, underlining a phrase here and there. She'd be able to go up soon, within days.

CHAPTER THIRTY-TWO

Sherman readjusted the creance with a quick, conjuring turn of one hand, a falconer's knot in the leather lead. The hawk bore his confusion with equanimity, he thought, which was more than he and Muirie deserved, considering what they were expecting of him.

When they had launched Teiresias for the first time, he had stumbled forward in a surprise of wings with the sweep of Muirie's arm. Sherman caught him, but awkwardly, bringing his gauntleted arm up beneath the hawk's talons like a mobile landing field, and bracing the bird against his chest. It hadn't been a pretty sight. The hawk regained his balance with difficulty and when he finally found the meat on the gauntlet, planted a foot atop it as if claiming *terra nova* for the queen.

Now, after a couple of sessions, the hawk was onto them, aware, at least, that to earn his meal he must fulfill certain new requirements that these humans had devised. He knew it wouldn't suffice to merely grip the gauntlet tight whenever he suspected a launch, but Sherman didn't think the bird had figured out more than that.

"I wonder if he feels excited by the extra activity," Muirie said. "I wonder if he's exhilarated."

Sherman doubted it but he didn't say so. The exhilaration was Muirie's. It had translated into a determination to fly the bird that fully equaled the hawk's determination to keep himself fed. She had added another wrinkle to the training by cutting the chicken into smaller pieces so that Teiresias would have to make more trips back and forth between them.

"I don't know about that, Muir."

"You don't think he has even an inkling what we're after yet, that he gets a rush when his feet leave your fist?"

It was a seductive thought, but Sherman's native caution made him reject it. "It's not flight. He's letting himself fall forward a few feet."

"Watch out," she said playfully. "You sound like Aunt Bert."

He smiled, securing his grip on the creance, and they launched the bird between them again.

Muirie stood six feet away. The hawk waited on her fist, alert, full of ravenous concentration, his wings held away from his body, anticipating the suddenness of the launch. When Sherman signaled with the squeaker, Muirie swept the bird forward with just enough force to propel him gently, to unfurl his wings, and Sherman scooped him safely from the air.

On the fourth transfer the hawk only picked at the meat and they returned him to his perch. He sat bolt upright, at attention, then relaxed by degrees as they watched in silence, rousing his feathers carefully—as if, Sherman thought, he was shaking off the memory of their hands upon him.

"I know what you're thinking," Muirie said. She sat on the counter-top, draping her arms across her chest, meditative. "That I'm thinking of him as human. You think he's feeling harassed, that he's saying, 'Just give me my food, damn it.'"

"We're pushing him pretty hard."

"But maybe all he needs is to be pushed a little harder. Maybe all he needs is another foot or two, to really stretch out."

She seemed almost perverse in her insistence, but he wanted to go along, to be swept away by her confidence.

"It would give him more of the feel of flying," she said, sliding from the counter. "He's learned that we'll find him in the air. He knows we'll support him."

She didn't see it, or it didn't bother her, that the hawk might be doing only what he had to do to eat. "I'm not sure he thinks of it that way," Sherman said. He didn't want to say more, to disappoint her.

She gasped in exasperation. "I'm not saying that he thinks about it consciously, only that he has a certain trust. Don't take me so literally."

But he had a literal mind—that much he knew—and he considered it a fact of his makeup he didn't have much power to change. He was wired to think in a straightforward fashion. When he decided to go along with Muirie's idea to teach the bird to fly he saw the training as another way to increase the bird's physical activity, stimulate its appetite, tone its muscles. And there had also been the significant lure of Muirie's company, which promised to do similar things for Sherman himself. He had no complaints. And yet, to push things further worried him. For the hawk, there was the risk of injury. For himself, much the same—because he knew, as certainly as he recognized the literal weave of his own mind, that Muirie would not suffer his caution gladly.

They went to the deli for coffee and sat with too much silence between them. He wanted to ask her more about Roberta, about the delayed plans for a trip into the canyon, but refrained. Her look had an intermittent harsh edge that scanned him, quickly, and sank away again. He tried to escape it by looking out the window but he could still feel the pressure of her expectations.

He asked her to come home with him. Making love would transform the silence between them. She said yes without saying much else and drove there separately in the pink truck. Inside the house, she took him by the hand, a spark of challenge in her eye, and led the way to the bedroom without a word. He went without hesitation. She was soft, endlessly curving, a spiral of warmth, leading him inward. They lay together, drowsing, cupped belly to spine.

Some things, like the topic of Teiresias, demanded careful consideration, he thought, and silence on those subjects was best until he knew his own mind, until he knew how to splice his words together cleanly. Making love to Muirie, though, needed no plan at all, only impulse and passion. From start to finish, the direction was clear. And he liked the aftereffect: lying with her, breathing her in, the quiet of the room, the smooth flow of his thoughts, all hopeful.

CHAPTER THIRTY-THREE

The rain came hard and fast, in slicing sheets across the pasture, drenching Carl and Luke before they could get back to the pickup. Luke loved it; he loved almost everything outdoors, even a frog-strangling rain like this one. He whooped, running for the pickup and yelling over his shoulder, "Come on, Grandpa! Come on!"

The windows of the truck steamed up the moment they closed the doors. Carl's breathing was ragged. He'd come up that hill too fast. Luke collapsed against the seat, feet dangling above the floor, water funneling into his eyes, shivering, his clothes plastered to his skin. His face was tight with satisfaction, but he played it grave. Ranchers did, and he was in training. Carl had taken him out for a morning's work, had allowed him to help feed the ewes in the sheds, let him handle a lamb by himself. Luke had been a little cocky, had gone at the lamb with too much confidence. But he'd gotten his comeuppance, and in the best way possible. The lamb, struggling in his arms, had brought its head up and whacked the boy on the chin so hard that he'd bit his lip. It had bled a little. He'd seen the surprise and humility come into Luke's eyes when he swiped a finger across his lip and it came away scarlet. A good lesson, Carl thought. You had to respect your animals and know how to handle them; you had to know their strength as well as your own.

Carl drove back to the house, glancing down at Luke's boots. A second sole of gloppy greenish mud adhered to the first.

"Look at them boots," he said to the boy. "I know you been working this morning."

Luke gave them a sliding glance, battling a swell of pride.

At home, Flo made hot chocolate. She made the best, from melted Hershey's bars mixed with steamy milk and topped with miniature marshmallows. Luke, after his first sip, wore his marshmallows in a wide mustache that lapped onto the end of his nose. Carl saw Flo fooling with a napkin, ready to reach over and scrub it away for him. He sent her a look. The boy didn't know it was there and he didn't need his grandma making a fuss, embarrassing him. Carl made a show of wiping his own mouth.

"You got to watch that marshmallow," he said. "It'll glue your lip up to your nose."

That's all it took. The boy was smart. He had a natural dignity. You had to protect it.

Charlotte went down for a nap in the early afternoon, and Flo disappeared into her studio, leaving Carl to watch Luke. Carl listened to the weather report on the radio—heavy precipitation forecast until evening but the temperature would stay warm. He would have liked to retire to the couch for a while to look at the paper but Luke watched him expectantly, fiddling with a deck of cards on the coffee table. Carl didn't like cards.

"You want to try some checkers?" he asked.

They played for an hour. Luke's concentration was good, although he made the same mistake in strategy a couple of times, leaving himself in the open. Carl went easy on him, stranding his own pieces so that the games equaled out. They split at two apiece, a good place to stop.

"Now what do you want to do?" Luke asked.

"Well," Carl said. "I was thinking about reading the paper awhile."

Luke's disappointment sprang from him before he could bite it back.

"But maybe we could think of something else," Carl said. He scanned the living room. A stack of kids' games next to the TV reached almost to the windowsill.

"Monopoly!" Luke said.

"Naw. We'd be here 'til next week."

Carl's eye fell on the photograph album stored in the magazine rack beside Flo's rocker. "I know what we can do," he said, standing up. "We can go visiting." He pulled the album from the rack and headed toward the dining room. "Come on. We'll spread out."

Luke, mystified, followed happily. But as soon as Carl opened the album on the tablecloth, he said, "Aw, I looked at that before."

"You have?"

"Yeah, it's just a bunch of old pitchers."

"What do you mean?" Carl flipped the pages. Dour Scottish faces flashed past. "This is your family. This is my daddy and mommy. And there, that's your grandma's daddy and mommy."

Luke grew resigned, settling on the edge of a chair. He dropped his chin into his hand, looking every inch his father at the same age.

"I think you could stand to learn a thing or two," Carl said. Luke lay his head in his arms, thumping a leg of the table with his shoe. Carl started from the beginning, taking his time. Flo had put the album together, so everything was in order by date as best they could figure it and every picture had a label saying who was who. There weren't more than twenty pictures. It would not kill the boy to look at them.

Carl had not looked at them himself for a long time, perhaps years, he thought. There stood his grandfather, C. H. Drummond, his hand laid on the back of a chair. Look at it: you knew when he turned it over, the palm was hard as a horn. A capable hand, the one he would shake with, back when people shook on deals and didn't bother with contracts and lawyers and fifty million kinds of legalities and suspicions.

Luke began to nod. Carl angled an elbow out to nudge him but thought the better of it. It was enough, maybe, that the boy wanted to work beside him and could be proud of a pair of shit-stinking boots. Asking him to sit quiet for a history lesson was asking too much. He'd pushed Hank as a boy, so Hank said, expecting everything of him, nudging him right out the door eventually. Carl didn't remember things that way but he didn't want to take a chance with Luke.

He put an arm around the drowsing boy. Luke jerked awake sluggishly at his touch, eyes fluttering into white.

"Shush now. Come along with me."

The boy relaxed against him, letting himself be led. How thin his shoulders felt. How tiny he looked, just a scrawny little batch of flesh and bones, warm, still fragile as a girl.

Carl led him to the sofa and the boy climbed up without a word and curled into a ball like a kitten, one hand on his cheek as though he might suck his thumb. Flo had a lap blanket around somewhere, one she was always folding just so. If he folded it one way, she came along and folded it another. He pulled it from the back of her rocker and spread it over the boy, tucking it in all around the edges. The living room felt a little cool, despite the sun outside.

He stood watching for a moment. A child could be so still.

Upstairs, Flo coughed gently. She'd had a call from a Denver art gallery interested in her pictures. A woman was driving all the way up to see her in a few days, and she was working like he'd never seen her work before, even right through meals a time or two.

He brought the album from the dining room and sat slowly on the couch at the boy's feet, not wanting to wake him. He didn't stir, and Carl settled the album in his lap, leafing to a picture of C. H. taken just before he left for America. He turned the album so it caught the light of the window, and studied the faded photograph. Now here was a man who had never seen the sun until he left the old country. Everything about the face testified to the fact. His complexion was ivory. His hair stood out in dark, shiny curls over his ears and on his neck. On top of his head it lay smack against his skull, as if he'd spat in his palm and slapped it flat in the last seconds before the picture got snapped. His nose was too long, his chin too pointed, and the mustache looked like a bush he'd plucked from the front yard. He wore his traveling clothes, a coat cut square as a sack and a high-collared shirt. His name, in Scotland, had been Colin Hoyt Drummond.

Colin. No wonder he'd changed it to C. H.

He'd left there to get away from the other Drummonds. Nine kids, and he was considered the runt. He headed west to prove to himself that he wasn't. To remove all doubt, he didn't stop until he reached this place, so far from home that he never laid eyes on his family again.

The second photograph showed him at the other end of his life, after forty-five years on the high plains, the sharp edges of his features worn away. He stood next to an empty, ugly plank chair in a studio, before a backdrop painted with Grecian columns, floral draperies, and festoons of pearls. He was dressed in square-toed boots with no hint of shine, stovepipe trousers dim with dust, a canvas jacket buttoned at the neck and opening in a wide V below to show a black vest. He wore a felt hat, rolled at the brim and scrunched at the crown. One hand rested on the back of the chair, the other on his hip. The mustache, smaller now, drooped down like he was mad. The hat cast a shadow over his eyes.

Flo had said once, "Carl, neither of us has got much beauty in our family. We're plain as cakes of soap."

She was right. The Scotland Drummonds, all eleven of them sitting in three rows, looked constipated. A couple of them had their eyes scooted off to the side like they'd done something wrong. It might have been the fact that you got restless sitting for those old photographs, but even taking that into account, they weren't good-looking people. They were hard workers instead, practical and durable. They wore denim and canvas, and sat on plank chairs, and did not polish their boots much. The only pearls in their lives were painted on backdrops. What luxuries they wanted, they imagined—and that had always been enough for them.

CHAPTER THIRTY-FOUR

Sherman's receptionist came to find him, looking vaguely alarmed. "There's this woman out front wants to see you," she said. "She didn't bring an animal. She won't even sit down, just hauls back and forth out there and gives me this look," and she made a face by dropping all expression from her own.

Roberta.

"Tell her to come on back," he said, grabbing a towel and pummeling it between his hands. Then, thinking of Teiresias, he said. "Wait, put her in Room One. I'll be right there."

"She don't have a pet, I said."

"I know."

The girl left, her alarm now tinged with suspicion.

He knew Roberta wouldn't sit down in Room One either. When he opened the door, she stood like Patton, feet apart, studying the small bulletin board where he had thumbtacked some photographs of pets sent to him by his clients: out-of-focus puppies sprawling on a carpet, a pair of overbred, pinheaded, cross-eyed Siamese, a dignified Airedale suffering a gimme cap yanked down on his brow. He'd forgotten about those.

She turned, a study of austere amusement. She had urged him to pay attention to his business, and he was prepared to remind her of this if she said anything. She didn't.

"Bert," he said, nodding.

"I was on my way into town."

He waited.

"I want to go into the canyon tomorrow. I'd still like you to go, if you will. Early, six-thirty. Can you manage it?"

She didn't consider that he might have appointments scheduled in the morning, that he'd actually succeeded in improving his prospects.

"I'll have to do some calling." He had a colleague across town, an old classmate, who had offered to loan him an assistant vet if the need arose. He'd never asked. "I don't know what use I'd be."

"I have a poisoned raven. Did Muirie tell you?"

He nodded. "She said you did your own toxicology test. Did you do a postmortem on the mouse? Lots can go wrong when you try to force-feed an animal as small as that. I'm thinking perforation of the esophagus, aspiration—"

"—I do have some experience at force-feeding, you know."

"It's a raw test, Bert, that's all. You can't conclude much from it."

She didn't answer.

"About the canyon," he said.

"I don't expect you to act in any official capacity. But you're a good witness, a trained observer." She hesitated. "And a friend."

"We probably won't find anything."

"I know that."

"Muirie told me you suspect the Drummonds."

He had tried to keep his voice neutral but Roberta heard the skepticism anyway.

"Can you prove it?" he said quietly.

She heard that skepticism too. "No. But I'm not trying to right now. I'm thinking about the birds, and secondary kills. Every animal killed by that poison may be poisonous itself. Every corpse exposed by the thaw is another carcass bait."

"If we do find dead birds up there, we have to call in the authorities, Bert. That's my condition. From what Muirie told me, you're not in a position to name names anyway."

"That's a condition, too? That I don't speak up?"

The receptionist rapped on the door, opening it an inch or two. Sherman saw one bright eye shoot back and forth. "Patient's waiting," she said, shutting the door again.

"No," he said. "It's got to be your own decision."

She wasn't going to make any promises.

"Where do we meet?" he said.

"Goose Egg Café. Six-thirty."

"The snow will be rotten as hell."

"Muirie's going."

He nodded, unsurprised, and pulled the door open for her.

She hesitated in the hallway. "Is it in there?" She nodded over her shoulder to the back room.

For a moment he went blank. She meant Teiresias.

"I'd like to take a look."

The entry bell pealed irritably, and the phone was ringing.

"You go on," she said. "I can help myself."

She hadn't seen the ferruginous since Sherman took it from the Uncle John, before he tamed it for handling. The hawk was in a large cage, drowsing, when she entered but came to attention, neck stretched forward in mild alarm, waiting for Sherman's voice. She pished softly from the middle of the room. The hawk listened keenly, waiting for more.

"Hello," she whispered. "Hello, Ferruginous. It's me. You know me. You know this old girl from before."

She came closer, slowly, allowing the bird to study her voice. She dropped it low, to a murmur of repeated, consoling sound. The hawk looked healthy, thriving. It had gained weight. The plumage gleamed. The empty sockets of the eyes had healed with supple new skin.

She glanced around the tidy room; Sherman would keep his gauntlets close by. She rolled a drawer open. First try: there they were. The perch was in the corner, scrubbed clean. High, though; she'd need a step stool. That too was in a logical place, stored between a metal shelf and the sink.

She pulled a gauntlet on, whispering to the bird, and unlatched the cage. The bird came onto her fist with a single, elegant step, wings tucked seamlessly into the streamlined plumage of the body. She secured the leather strap in her palm and moved to the perch, climbing the stool with care. The bird knew this drill; that was obvious. It was calm and majestic, an Arab prince dressed in silks. No wonder Sherman set the perch so high.

She rotated her fist toward the perch, and the hawk stepped off with the confidence of vision, rousing slightly, settling in. She sat on the countertop. Such simple, strong angles in the hawk's face, the intensity of it unaltered by the injury.

... The intrepid readiness, the terrible eyes...

An unbidden image filled her head, the vivid instant of impact, the luminous eyes of the hawk splattering like eggs on the power line.

... at night he remembers freedom ...

The hawk muttered, gentle as a child.

Sherman paused in the hallway, composing his face, then pushed through the door. Roberta sat on the countertop, near the hawk.

"Hey, boy," Sherman said. The door whooshed shut behind him. He rolled his stethoscope into his pocket.

"He looks good," Roberta said. A tone of admission.

"Thanks."

"He's put on flesh."

"How did he handle for you?"

She watched him a moment. "Like a bird that gets a lot of handling."

It was this tone of Roberta's that he disliked most. It had the feel of ambush in it.

She took a breath, seemingly at ease. "What's the point, Sherman? Is it Muirie—keeping her content?"

He would not give this snooping implication an answer. Roberta glanced down at her hands, businesslike. She couldn't be chastened by any silence of his but she recognized the barrier.

"What are your plans for it, then?"

"I'll find a place for him."

"Where? A zoo?"

"No. I don't know yet. Someplace worthy of him."

She watched him.

"A place like yours," he said. "With someone who would teach with him."

"No."

"I'm not asking."

She regarded him shrewdly. "Someplace where they teach?"

He nodded.

She slid from the counter. "Just what would kids learn from this hawk, I wonder?" She pretended a big audience of children. "Look at this, kids, you can even pop a bird's eyeballs out and it can still fly!"

"You keep unreleasable birds, Bert. It's a matter of degree."

"Oh, you bet," she sighed. "You only get black and white choices when you're six years old." She paced toward him, head down. "You know what they'd learn, Sherman? They'd learn that people can make anything right again, correct any wrong. They can do what they please, any way they please, forget the consequences, because there's always someone around with skills and technology who can make it better again."

She stood before him, looking gravely into his eyes. "It's all misplaced, all the work and energy and hopefulness you spend on this hawk. It deserved the dignity of death, not a life at the end of a leather thong. And you won't earn any absolution for baiting it into the air with food. But I want you to try, so you can get it out of your system. And out of Muirie's. There's no other way to know."

Muirie had spent most of the day conducting tours. Roberta had only gradually pulled her into this end of the business. Her first tour, a week before, had been a bunch of cheerful, elderly Rotarians. It had gone so smoothly that she'd felt little stage fright since. Today had brought a garden club, a bunch of grandmothers blooming with wildflower enthusiasm for everything in sight; then a small, serious troop of science teachers out to retool their curriculum. Finally, a family of home-schooled kids, four blond girls and their parents, who combined seriousness and enthusiasm in just the right proportions, Muirie thought.

She lay back in the armchair, gazing out the window into the darkness. She and Roberta had watched the news together but Roberta had been interested only in the weather: clear, calm, a slight breeze.

"Looks good," Roberta said, getting to her feet. She gave Muirie a measuring glance. "You still want to go?"

The question struck her as odd. "Of course. This isn't like pitching cake, Aunt Bert. I'm a good skier."

Roberta shrugged. "I'm just trying to let you off the hook. You haven't liked the way I've handled things so far. I thought you might not want to be involved anymore."

"I want to go," Muirie said earnestly. "I want to be there with you."

Roberta smiled, almost. "Okay. Thanks." In the hallway, she turned back. "Glen's not home," she said, as if just realizing it.

"Some big mucky-muck's in town. A senator or somebody. They're having a dinner for him."

Roberta nodded, remembering. "Good-night, kiddo."

Muirie heard Glen come through the front door an hour later. He walked straight through the house to the office, smiling when he saw her, his briefcase clamped under his arm. "I thought you might still be up."

She grinned fatuously at him. "How could I think of sleeping when I knew you'd come home just bursting with the latest political gossip?"

He laughed. "Just the thing to put you to sleep."

"Nothing scandalous or shocking? I'm crushed."

He dumped the briefcase on his desk. "I'll tell you, this is the sort of function that warns good people away from politics. A bunch of ugly old farts like me sitting around and talking flattering nonsense to each other all night."

He dropped his suit coat into the office chair. "I suppose Bertie's gone on to bed."

"A while ago."

He came to sit beside her, thoughtful. "You notice anything about her lately, Muirie? Something..." He tugged on an earlobe. "...kind of harsh."

Muirie shook a smile loose, hoping her bright tone might cover the stiffness of it. "That's new?"

He gestured around the room. "Sometimes when we're sitting in here together, I get a little nervous, start to feel like one of those mice she puts in with that owl of hers. What's his name?"

"Oscar."

"Oscar," he said, pulling off his shoes.

Muirie could not look at him directly. "I'm not a good judge. I haven't been here long enough."

His voice grew quieter. "Oh, it's not new, I know. It's the degree."

"It's the load in the hospital, maybe."

"I'd remember that from other years. It wouldn't seem remarkable."

"You don't remember those sorts of things. You only remember good things."

He adjusted his glasses, the better to show her his skepticism. "No. You're wrong. I have my share of regrets."

He had never spoken so directly before. Muirie said nothing, fearing that any response would restrain him.

"I've been thinking about that a lot lately," he said. "Which is another reason I feel like something's changed. I can't look at Bertie these days without casting back."

"That's because I'm here," Muirie said quietly. "You can't look at me without casting back, either."

Relief flooded his face. He laughed. "You're right. I'd be happier if you were still eight years old."

"I haven't turned out very well, huh?"

He waved a hand. "You, you've turned out wonderful. But you're the clock, I think, and I look at your face and see how gone all the years are." He gazed at her steadily, an invitation, she thought, to ask for details.

"What would you go back and change if you could?"

He studied his hands absently, rubbing his knuckles. "Decisions. Reactions, I suppose. Small things, by and large. Maybe one or two of the major things." A hint of amusement came into his eyes that seemed to make light of all this.

She waited for more, but he fell silent, good humor suffusing his face. She threw her hands in the air. "And now it's too late?"

Her irritation caught him off guard. His face filled with what he would not say, and he looked away quickly. She had misread him, asked for more than he was willing to give. She sat back in her chair, vowing to say no more, but words pushed up from her heart anyway, emerging small and hard, like stones.

"Things were so different here when I was a kid."

She was shaming him for the choices he had made, assigning him responsibility for her own disappointment. Mortification followed.

"I'm sorry, Uncle Glen. I don't mean that like it sounds."

"No, no," he said. "You're talking about Bertie and me. You can't help but see it."

"What's happened?" she asked softly.

He leaned forward, elbows on knees, staring into his empty palms. He did not answer for a long while.

"I'm trying to think how Bertie would answer that," he said. "She'd say that I live my life by compromises. But I don't think a good life is possible without them. A hard life—maybe a virtuous life —but not a happy one."

"How can she be unhappy with your compromises when they gave her everything she wanted around here?"

"Because they didn't," he said. "A few years ago, when she got rid of the last of the herd, it really hit me what the bottom line is with Bertie." He shifted uneasily in his chair. "She can change everything about this ranch, get rid of all the cattle, ignore all her own history. But she's still stuck with herself. No matter what she does, she's still a Shea."

He seemed to study the sound of these words, weighing the truth of them again.

"Not that she can't love some of the family. Like you." He gave her a wink. "But she can't look at herself and love what she sees. And I can't follow her in that direction. We can't see eye to eye on it. There's no compromise there for me."

Again he smiled, making light of it. "I always think of Jeremiah. Bertie has her criticisms of him but he did love being alive. He got a tremendous kick out of raising hell everywhere he went. Bertie, though..." A hand went to his chin. "She tossed out everything in the past. Threw it away. And she doesn't like to look back. But she doesn't look forward much either."

"But there's all her work with the birds," Muirie said. "And her tours."

He gave his head a shake. "She sees birds all day long. She doesn't connect much with the ranchers around here, and these are the people she wants to change. I don't think she convinces them of anything much but her disapproval."

This time his smile firmly dismissed the topic. "You and Sherman seem to be moving along pretty well. You going to marry him?"

She gasped out a laugh. "Marry him?"

"Why not?"

That he could say such a thing in light of their conversation amazed her. She didn't have to tell him so.

"Don't you misunderstand me," Glen said. "I never said that marrying Bertie was one of the things I'd change."

He sat motionless, staring at the dark glass of the window. Muirie could see his reflection there, and he seemed to see only the glass. She looked beyond it, across the fallow pastures of the Uncle John, and farther south, to the black bulk of the mountain against the sky.

CHAPTER THIRTY-FIVE

The alarm glared 5:13 from the bedside table. Glen rolled onto his back, sighing at his wakefulness. Beside him, Roberta lay curled and facing away, the top of her head just visible over the bulk of the comforter. This was not the first time lately that he had waked up too early after falling asleep too late. It seemed to be a new trend, this insomnia, eating away at both ends of the night.

He closed his eyes, but his body felt taut, the way an antsy horse felt under you when you reined it in. Deep in his middle age, he was, he thought, finally proving Jeremiah's suspicion that he didn't need to sleep at all. Back during Glen's first couple of years on the ranch, the old man had been of the unflinching opinion that all men born in town, any town, no matter how puny, had trouble getting up in the morning, whereas men born outside the softening influence of civilization shook off sleep like the nuisance it was and took up the duties of the day clear-eyed, five seconds out of the sack. Glen had proved the one exception. The old man had watched him for years, waiting for the inevitable, and was not above creeping around from time to time in the hopes of catching him napping. It had never happened. *Don't you never sleep?*

Roberta lifted one arm from beneath the covers and shifted onto her back slowly, as if she were still exhausted. Glen turned to watch her. He thought her nose might be getting a little longer as she got older, although he'd read somewhere that it was your ears that continued to grow all your life. He'd been keeping an eye on his own ever since, imagining they might be slightly more pendulous at the lobe. Roberta's, though, were as delicate as seashells, just as they'd always been.

He slipped a forefinger under the hand she had left marooned on the blanket, thinking absently that she might grasp it as a baby would, reflexively. Waking with a start, she turned her head toward him, toward the windows, blinking. Her voice cracked. "It's late."

"No, it's early, way too early to get up."

She lifted onto her elbows, taking her hand from him to sweep away a ribbon of hair that had fallen over one eye. "What time is it?"

"Five-fifteen."

She relaxed. "You can turn that alarm off. It's going to ring in a few minutes."

"You set the alarm for this early?"

She flung her covers aside, onto him.

"You're getting up?"

"I'm wide awake."

He paused. "So am I."

"I don't know why. You were up 'til all hours."

"Muirie was reading in my office when I got home." He watched her, his lower lip protruding. She fished for her slippers. "We talked awhile. About us some."

Her interest was marked by a hair's breadth of hesitation.

"She doesn't quite know what to make of all the changes here," he said.

Roberta pulled on her robe. "She's on a search for her childhood and she thought she'd find it here. Of course she's going to be disappointed."

"She's looking at everything, at us, remembering the way things used to be."

Roberta strode to the window and touched the glass with the back of her fingers, testing the outside temperature, looking at the sky, a vast, clear reach open to the warmth of the sun.

"I wonder about it, too," he said.

"Then I wonder what you told her if you don't know yourself."

Glen threw the covers back and joined her at the sill, tying his robe. He followed her line of sight to the sky, milk blue and cloudless. No birds. What was she looking for? He laid a forefinger along the flannel of her shoulder. "I know what I should have told her."

She waited.

"That I love you like crazy."

He saw her pupils flare, a vivid depth of black against the gray. He thought of her hand curling around his fingers, her arms around his shoulders, her long legs encompassing his waist.

Her lips parted, then narrowed, tightened. He looked at the sky again, unwilling to witness more in her face. "It's going to be a beautiful day."

She didn't move. "Yes."

He chanced a glance at her again, imagining that she had let her arm relax a fraction into his belly. She stared straight out through the glass.

"You remember those big breakfasts we used to eat back in the old days? You used to flip pancakes on that big black griddle and set them on the table in stacks as fast as we could eat them."

"I'd think you'd lose your appetite, remembering that."

"Nope. They were good. I ate them by the dozen."

"I burned them black every morning."

"Not every single one." He drew a long breath, settling against her. He felt the bone of her hip against his thigh. "Sometimes I got two big ones with a couple of little ones in between. A sandwich."

Her jaw tightened with impatience or a latent smile, he could not tell.

"I used to love watching you cook. Did you know we used to shoot craps sometimes to see who got to sit on the side of the table where we could see you? When you turned those cakes, you moved just so."

"Uh-huh," she said dully. "If I was such a show, how come you always came late for breakfast?"

"Brushing up my boots. So you'd notice me."

"How was I going to see them at the table?"

"It was the idea of it. I wanted to be good from the ground up."

Her smile twitched.

"After a while, Jeremiah figured out what we were doing, playing craps so we could watch your rear end, so he got up earlier and sat smack in the middle on the good side, spreading his elbows out like this, sawing at those sausages. He had the sharpest damn elbows."

She was looking at the sky again, her fingers at her lips, as if feeling for the lost shape of her smile. He reached for her hand, wrapped it in his own. "Bertie..."

This time her fingers responded. He folded her hand into his and took it to his chest, turning her to him. Her gaze lifted up, so gentle that it shocked him to see it. He pulled her hand tighter, against his chest, and felt a tension in her wrist, the bony resistance of it. But it dissolved and the pressure was hers, in her hand laid next to his breastbone, as if feeling for the beat of his heart. She led him back to the bed and undressed quickly, throwing her nightgown to the floor.

He did not know how long it had been since they last made love. A long time. But it didn't matter now. The relief of it rushed over him. How little everything else mattered compared to this; it could wipe out any tally of the past. He wanted to fall back asleep with her, side by side, to extend this sudden peace beyond the threat of conscious thought. He lay still, listening to her breathe lightly at his ear, loving the smell of her, which had always been sweet, particular, hers.

"I never noticed your boots," she said.

He turned so he could look into her eyes. They were open wide, focused just beyond his ear. She was not going to fall back asleep.

"Remember that bedroom of yours," she said. "That icy floor."

Her hand lay on his chest. He played with her fingers. "You used to walk around in nothing but a shirt and socks."

"No."

"When we were planning our wedding. My Lord, how long ago it all was."

She looked at him suddenly, warily, as if, for a moment, she had forgotten he was there. She was following the line of the past up into the present, leaving him behind. She started to speak. He reached out quickly with one finger, ran it along the lean angle under her ear, letting the thumb caress her lower lip.

"I have to go, Glen," she said.

He restrained her gently. "No. Where could you be off to so early?"

She rolled out of his arms.

"Skiing. Muirie and Sherman and I."

"Skiing?"

She was up, to the dresser. She took wool pants from a drawer. "On the mountain, before the snow's gone."

She disappeared into their bathroom. Glen rolled the covers back and sat on the edge of the bed, waiting. She came out dressed in the pants, pulling on a shirt. She buttoned it with military efficiency.

"Bertie, there's no decent snow left on the mountain. And you haven't skied in years."

She lifted her chin, jerked a cuff tight to button it. "All the more reason."

"I guess I didn't get an invite."

She shoved on a boot. "You have someone showing you a prospect today, I thought."

"This is the only day you could ski?"

The other boot was on. She stamped the foot, settling her heel.

"Let's have some breakfast together, then," he said. "At least that."

"I can't. I have to feed the birds."

Spoken without ire, but spoken, nevertheless. And she was out the door.

The Goose Egg Café, at the westernmost reach of the mountain, had been a homestead in the eighteen-eighties, a whorehouse at the turn of the century, a motor inn in the twenties, and an abandoned ruin until the seventies, when a Casper couple reclaimed the place during the oil boom as a restaurant and lounge. But the oil bust in the eighties doomed that incarnation too. The lounge closed first, then the restaurant shrank until it occupied the front half of the former expanse. The operation had steadied at that level, offering locals a pit stop for hot meals and last-minute supplies for boating at Alcova or a day of fishing along the Platte.

Sherman arrived early. He sat at the table nearest the window, facing out, a stiff cup of coffee in his hand, a whole pot of it at his side. He'd need the caffeine after last night. His thoughts had shunted sleep for hours, repelling it so completely that he had been denied even the physical comfort of lying in bed. His bones had felt sharp beneath the skin, as though they might pierce through.

Roberta and Muirie showed up as he drained his second cup. He lifted a hand to them as they got out of the old Ford, his eyes settling on Muirie. Her ski cap made her look painfully young. She gave him a measured smile through the glass. He knew why when Roberta opened the door. She flung it so that the bell jangled wildly.

"You brought the map?" she said by way of a greeting, yanking out a chair.

He took it from his inside jacket pocket. The waitress came, pushing menus in their faces. Roberta waved them away like flies. "More cups."

Sherman unfolded the west end of the mountain before them, smoothing it flat on the table. The map showed the topography of the land at intervals of twenty feet. Roberta bent over it, searching for the canyon, then traced a contour line on the rim with a blunt forefinger.

"That's the main roost." She drew a mechanical pencil from her shirt pocket and slashed a small x on the map along the rim where the canyon took a bend to the east.

They made their plans quickly, and she was ready to go. Taking a final gulp of her coffee, she pulled some dollar bills from her pants and dropped them to the table. A few quarters rained out. She slapped them flat with her palm. "No point in taking both vehicles. We'll leave the Ford behind."

The prospect presentation was meticulously detailed beyond Glen's desire to absorb it. The young man, a geologist for a local exploration company seeking partners in a drilling program, reeled off the statistics of twenty oil wells: names, spud dates, total depths, initial and cumulative production, gas to oil ratios, tops. He knew them by heart. He rolled out display after display on Glen's desk, each more elaborate and colorful than the last: structural cross sections, well log cross sections, core descriptions, and a welter of maps documenting everything from leases to palinspastically restored paleoenvironments.

The maps, but not the pitchmen, had gotten flashier as times in the oil industry toughened. Glen studied the boy—he looked no more than thirty—thinking of himself at that age. Same white shirt and conservative tie, short, well-trimmed hair. But this kid had all the animation of a statue. He'd picked up a fossilized personality in grad school and appropriated it for life.

Smile. Smile every once in a while.

A good show, but not a good prospect. He told the young man so and sent him on his way, then made some brief notes for his files.

Pushing back in his chair, he looked up to see, again, the painting of Carl leaning against the wall. Roberta had left it for him to hang. She had chosen it, paid for it; it was his job to hang it. Yet each time he'd set his mind on doing so, he'd found a reason to delay. He did not dislike it. In fact, it drew him. Whenever he looked up from his desk to rest his eyes on the mountain, he found himself examining the painting instead. But it didn't clear his mind as the view out the window did. The oblique angle of the portrait made him want to push past Carl to see the calming sweep of the horizon instead of that pale, claustrophobic rectangle of beaten earth.

Roberta had not said much about the painting. Glen had seen her eye it one evening as she opened her hospital mail at his desk.

"I'm settling in with it a little," he told her, "making sure that's where I want to hang it."

She didn't believe him. "It's a very good piece."

"I know it is."

He didn't want to say more. He scrubbed at his temple with a knuckle. "I've just been thinking I sure hope Carl doesn't walk in here someday."

"He knows I bought it."

"I know. But me, sitting here, staring at his backside day after day..."

She returned to her mail and they had not spoken of it since. Still, he knew that she would interpret any further delay on his part as proof that he didn't like the painting, whatever he said, and he wanted to rise above that pettiness.

He smiled, remembering their morning together. She had left abruptly, but the fact of the lovemaking itself was more important; he would concentrate on that. She had always been abrupt, even at seventeen when he saw her close-up for the first time, the day after the initial interview with Jeremiah. He had been standing outside the house with the old man when Roberta came striding across the drive toward them, small-boned and lean, giving the impression of height. It was the long, clean line from her hip to her ankle that fooled the eye. She was throwing a comment over her shoulder to a couple of cowhands, a smart remark, shot off with a rascally smile. Jeremiah hailed her. "Bertie," he said. "This is Glen Thompkins. He's going to work for me." He didn't say in what capacity, didn't elaborate at all. Roberta turned her gray eyes on Glen, stuck a hand out like a knife, and said, "Hi." Then she was gone, through the door, and Glen realized that he had been seeing the top of her head. Red-gold hair, straight as ironed silk, the pale slash of a part in the middle.

He tapped a pair of picture hooks into the wall, a foot apart, and lifted the painting to them. Roberta had given him two signs lately that she could still think of him generously. She had bought this painting, and they had made love in the early morning.

The road closest to the mouth of the canyon was an oily paste of gravel and bentonite the color of overcooked peas. Sherman downshifted as the road angled up, and they inched their way along, mud spattering in the wheel wells like cake batter whipped in a bowl.

"I can't get much closer," he said. "The road's a drainage. This stuff's slicker than ice." It was no wonder Roberta hadn't wanted to bring her Ford.

"Just keep going, Sherman," Roberta ordered. "Push on."

Muirie pressured Sherman's thigh slightly with her knee. He urged the truck a few more squishy yards but the direction trended down, into the mud.

"Keep some momentum," Roberta said. "Anyone could do it."

"I'd be glad to stop, give you the wheel, Bert."

"Fine. Pull over," she said, though to pull over meant sinking axle-deep into the gloppy, sucking clay.

"Quit it," said Muirie. "Everyone just shut up."

The truck gummed to a halt beside a narrow meadow, watered by the melt from the canyon. Lush spears of grass stood above a gray mat of dead vegetation, newly released from the snowpack. Muirie sighed impatiently. Sherman rolled down his window and inspected the narrow, brimming ditch alongside the road.

"We can walk from here," Roberta said, throwing her door open.

They made their way to the mouth of the canyon across the boggy meadow, carrying their skis. Meltwater gushed from the mouth across a muddy, ten-foot swath on the floor, bordered by a four-foot block of compressed old snow. Farther in lay solid snow, uncut on the surface by the drainage. They could hear the stream below it, tinkering among the stones.

They hiked up slowly into the mouth, where they scraped their boots free of fudgey mud and stepped into their skis. The snow was granular, translucent, iced cement, but it softened as they skied in, giving way an inch or two, and easing their passage. The low gurgle of the stream remained audible, deep in the throat of the canyon.

Roberta broke trail. She skied fast, efficiently, unsurprised by her competence after all these years. Her muscles had not forgotten this rhythm, and the canyon pulled her with a power of its own. She tilted her head back, looking at the long slash of sky above as they skied. The high rims, sharp-edged as scissors against the sky, seemed to be closing slowly, narrowing to a fine point in the near distance. She felt almost sleepy, lulled by the swish of their skis, a mother's quiet voice repeating, *hush-hush-hush*.

She stopped only once to rest, a half-mile short of the eastward jog. They stood in a line, leaning on their poles, breathing fast, and took shots of coffee from Sherman's Thermos. She brought her field glasses from inside her jacket and raked the rim of the canyon. It was mostly melted out. Snow persisted between massive boulders and in pockets along the steepest walls. The pines stood dark and empty. She saw no birds.

At the eastward jog, Sherman watched as Roberta bounded ahead, summoning a speed that he would have found difficult to match. He slowed, watching her dim figure flick through the trees. Muirie glanced back at him, her face lit with exertion and impatience —*hurry up!* He shook his head, waving her back. Roberta needed some space, some time alone. Didn't she see that?

Muirie hesitated, grimacing. He called to her in a quick, low tone so that she would understand his urgency. She looked away, though she had heard him; he could tell by the deliberate thrust of her skis. He sprung off his poles, racing to catch her. Her strides lengthened, strong and smooth and stubborn, but he was faster. He grabbed her by the elbow.

"Muirie, wait. Let her alone a minute."

She jerked free, almost hitting him in the face with her pole. "Let go."

"Can't you wait? That's why she took off."

She shrugged him away, breathing hard, her eyes on Roberta.

Roberta's pace had died. She stopped, skied another few paces, and stopped again.

"There's something there," Muirie breathed.

"Give her some time."

Roberta stood motionless.

"Shit," said Muirie. "Shit." She turned to Sherman. "I'm going up there with her."

Sherman let a minute or two pass, then came through the trees to join them. Dark shadows lay just beneath the snow. They skied into their midst, wordless. In a few places, a black tangle of feathers broke the surface, accented by the curve of a beak, the leading edge of a broad wing, a reptilian foot clawed into a ball. Here and there, they crouched to look closer, to brush away a salting of snow from a brown depth of feathers.

Silent, they gathered beneath the pines of the roost, their breath blowing steam into the chilly air. There were twenty-two eagles. Some goldens. Mostly balds. One of the immature balds wore a leg band. Sherman fingered it, reaching for the spiral pad in his jacket pocket. He spun through the pages, scanning, then looked up at Roberta.

"The one who liked fried chicken."

Roberta nodded once, then gazed around at the littered snow. "We'll only take one with us. An adult," she said, hoarse. Muirie put an arm around her shoulder, holding her tight. "We'd need a truck to take them all."

CHAPTER THIRTY-SIX

By late afternoon, officers from both the state and the federal wildlife agencies were jammed into Sherman's small office, examining the topographic map, a map Sherman had plotted of the kill, and the dead bald, laid out on its back across the narrow desk. Roberta said little, speaking in a voice ground down to gravel, and appeared to suspect the federal agents of poisoning the birds.

One of the officers, a tidy, dark-haired man in khaki, faced her grimly. "I say this with respect, Mrs. Thompkins, that it would have been a greater help to us if you'd passed on the information from the skier and left it for us to take any necessary action."

"At that time it was speculation," Roberta said. "I used my own judgment."

The agent glanced at Sherman, annoyance eroding his careful exterior. "We've always admired and appreciated your work with the birds over the years. We'd appreciate your full cooperation too."

Roberta didn't answer, didn't nod, didn't move.

Sherman's restrained, worried gaze crossed Muirie's. They were thinking the same thing. *Look, Roberta, these men are here to help.*

"We plan to pursue a thorough investigation," the man said. "And we'll keep you informed every step of the way."

"Informed," said Roberta. "That boils down to justifications and excuses."

"I'm not here to debate with you, Mrs. Thompkins," the man said. "We all know that proof is hard to come by."

"Especially if you ignore it."

The agent's eyes narrowed. "You have some evidence?"

Sherman flashed a look at Muirie. She was staring hard at Roberta, as if willing her into silence.

The agent swept them all with a canny glance, returning again to Roberta. "We do every damn thing we can to stop this kind of thing. We pursue every reasonable lead, and if there's sufficient evidence to convict, we will press for conviction."

Muirie escaped into the hallway.

The telephone rang. Sherman picked it up in the office. The tone of his voice sifted through to her in the dim hall, that flat, taut voice men used with each other, as if any lilt proved weakness.

Whispering to the hawk, she pushed through the swinging door into the back room. Teiresias followed the sound of her to the drawer, where she slipped on a gauntlet, murmuring low in an endless, soothing sentence, comforting herself as much as the hawk. There was another truth to be faced, beyond the deaths of the eagles and the guilt of some nameless rancher out there: Roberta made things worse.

Teiresias came onto her fist eagerly, hungry. The substitute vet had never handled a raptor, so Teiresias had fasted by necessity. She transferred him to his high perch, defrosted some chicken in the microwave, and chopped it into chunks. Without Sherman, she couldn't fly the hawk. She'd have to feed him the chunks at his feet.

She wrapped the creance securely in her hand as she took up the bird again. The tether was short. Teiresias danced sideways a step or two. Her service wasn't prompt enough.

"Easy boy. Easy."

Placing a hunk of meat between his feet, she prepared to signal him with the squeaker. He crouched, steadied, aimed, waiting for the sound, focusing on a second fist that wasn't there. She anchored him tightly, watching the intensity of his eyeless face. He wanted to go, he wanted to fly. His wings came up in a visual shout of confidence, stretched to the limit. The wind of it fanned her face. This was more than a mere hunger for food. He wanted up, he wanted out of this endless confinement.

She held him down tight, though it stabbed at her heart to do it. He could fly, this hawk—she knew it —fly across the width of the room, fly the long length of the creance they used at the ranch. The natural rightness of it rose up as powerfully as the long, upward stroke of his wing. She could imagine him in the air, clearly, flying toward her through the air, coming at her with a tight, controlled momentum, sheer and precise, a line of swift perfection.

Five o'clock. Five-thirty.

Glen fixed himself a whiskey and soda and sat down, determined to concentrate on the newspaper. Too long for a ski trip to Hartsong. If they'd stopped for dinner, surely they would have called, asked him to join them. At least that. He cursed himself for not finding out exactly where they would be skiing. If there'd been an accident, he didn't know where to begin a search.

The phone rang at a quarter to six. He reached for it, certain it would be Roberta, but it was a reporter from the *Star Tribune*, asking for Roberta.

"Can I get you to have her call me?" A young woman's voice, tight with hurry. "By some miracle, my contacts came through on this eagle story, but I've got to move fast. I really need to talk to her."

Glen tugged on an earlobe. "Well, she is the expert on eagles—"

"Wait a minute. Is this Glen Thompkins? Senator Thompkins?"

Dread crept over him. She sounded too eager. "Yes," he said slowly.

"Great. Tell me, what's your stance on the use of poisons for predator control?"

He blinked, still touching the ear. "The use of ... "

"And I need to know how many eagles winter in Jackson Canyon. I mean, your wife found twenty-odd up there today, but what's the potential kill? And how long has she known about this? My contact said she waited for the canyon to melt out."

Glen reached unsteadily for a scratch pad. "I can't comment right now. If you want to give me your name, I'll call you back."

"My deadline's coming up fast, Senator. I'm starting from next to nothing. Please."

"Call Fish and Wildlife."

"You don't understand. I have a friend there, and he called *me*. I need to hear what you have to say."

"I'm sorry. I'm really sorry," he said, hanging up.

Sherman had that look on his face: strung-tight, trying-not-to-be-exasperated patience. Roberta watched him as he urged the officers out the door and locked it behind them. He knew a couple of them from his days with the state, or he could never have dealt with them so cleanly. They shooed stiffly toward the door like so many heckling dogs, gauging her as they went.

When Sherman slid the dead bolt shut, she heard it as the beginning of silence. She sat down in the dark reception area. The noise of the men reached her through the thick, smeary glass of the windows: slamming doors and revving engines, and their headlights pierced the room. But the men were beyond her, departing, disconnected, now backing away, now accelerating, roaring out their anger in horsepower.

Sherman stood at the door after they left, watching the traffic quiet now, hissing by.

"Bert," he said. "They're not the ones who did this."

No answer. He gave a soft snort at her silence. "If you think that way, everyone's guilty. Who's left to help? These are dedicated people."

"Dedicated to what?"

"Of course." He said it under his breath, like an oath. "They do mean well..." He slumped down beside her, a chair away. "You never give people the benefit of the doubt."

"Ah. Good intentions."

A dog shrieked in the back room. Muirie was doing the rounds for him, unasked. He knew which dog, the one with a torn ear, the result of a settling of scores by the family cat.

"You didn't say anything about the Drummonds."

"No. Not yet. I'm biding my time."

"That sounds ominous."

"You worry too much, Sherman."

"Do I?"

"About all the wrong things."

The phone rang again, the fourth call since the reporter's. Leaving his office was not enough of an escape: Glen turned the volume of the answering machine off and shut the door behind him, then switched off the bells on all the phones in the house. He made coffee, strong, and drank a cup black. When the headlights of the truck swept across the front of the house, he was standing at the kitchen door.

Roberta came in first, her rucksack slung over one shoulder. Her eyes grazed past him as though she hadn't seen him. She dropped the pack to the floor. Muirie came in on her heels.

"I know about the eagles," he said.

Roberta straightened, a hand at the small of her back.

"A reporter called, Bertie. A reporter. That's how I found out." He looked at Muirie. "And you knew, too."

Muirie raised both hands, shaking her head.

"Don't blame her. I swore her to silence weeks ago."

"Weeks?"

Roberta walked to the hallway. "I'm too tired for this, Glen. We can talk in the morning. Eight more hours can't make any difference."

"That's probably true," he said bitterly, "but we're going to talk now."

Roberta's hesitation showed only as a sideways tic in her clenched jaw. She knocked the door frame softly, deftly, with her palm and strode down the hall, leaving her rucksack in the middle of the room. Glen stared after her, then swung around to Muirie.

"I am not involved in this, Uncle Glen."

His voice was furious. "Aren't you?"

"You need to talk to her."

"I thought we understood each other. You'd come in there and sit, and we'd talk—"

"What the hell does that have to do with anything? This is just exactly what happened to me. What Roberta says, goes. She said we weren't going to talk about it, and we didn't. She puts you off the same way."

He swiped a forefinger beneath his nose, silenced.

Muirie sank onto the arm of the leather chair, head up. "I'm sorry. It was a shitty thing to do."

He sat, too, in the opposite chair.

"She thinks Carl Drummond put out the poison. She doesn't have any proof. Her evidence is a couple of facial expressions she didn't like."

Glen, watching her, felt a stillness come over him. "I need to hear this story from the beginning."

Roberta sat in the near dark, mustering the energy to undress. It would come to her if she closed her eyes for a moment. There was no need to hurry now, she had plenty of time. What lay ahead was a period of waiting. Though activity would swirl around her now for a few days—phone calls, interviews, some articles in the paper—she felt calm. Glen would be busy, too, and they would have to work in close proximity. That would be the worst of it, listening to his cool, mediating voice as he struggled to keep everyone peaceful just when they deserved peacefulness the least. The waiting would underlay it all, keeping her calm in anticipation. It would take just one test of one bird out of twenty-two. If it was poison—and it would be—it swept away the possibility of mass disease. If the poison was in high concentration, it would discount the chance of two poisoners, and she could hand over the raven for a match of poisons, testify as to how it came into her hands.

She felt Glen's footsteps in the hall before she heard them. A measured tread on the resonant floorboards. He was going to insist on talking. There was nothing to say, but that fact had never stopped Glen, a natural-born politician.

He came in and gave the door a nudge so that it clicked shut quietly behind him.

She sighed against the onslaught of words to come, but he said nothing, which was worse.

"Glen—"

"I thought you'd had an accident, Bertie." He didn't move from the door. "Has it gotten this bad between us?"

"Don't press me tonight, Glen."

"Press you? Have I ever pressed you?" He paced. "I should have, a hundred times. But I've let things pass instead. I've let you get away with all these increasing little agonies you put everyone through over all these years."

"Agonies," she repeated, whispering the word.

"You're right that those eagles aren't the most important thing in my life, Bertie. I'm not thinking about how they died or who did it. I'm thinking about you and me." He took a step toward the bed, then veered away. "I don't know anymore. I don't know what to do. You seem gone to me, even though we're in the same room. It's like this most the time now. You're somewhere close by, in the next room, or over in the barn. But you feel gone."

He averted his face. "I keep wondering: 'What other things has she kept to herself? Are there other things like this, things that she'd tell me if she still loved me?' And I know what your justification would be, that you know how I'd react. My God, we've been married for a quarter of a century. I know on any of a hundred topics how you'll react right down to the poses you'll strike while you lecture me. It's the hard stuff you've got to keep talking about. Silence gets you silence. Is that what you want?"

"You're exaggerating, Glen."

"Exactly the opposite. I've minimized until there's almost nothing left. I keep telling myself, 'Oh, that's just Bertie, that's just Bertie.'" His voice wavered. "But I don't recognize you now. I don't know who you are."

From the depths of her fatigue, a few, slender words rose up. They formed into a simple sentence, worthy of being spoken, promising peace, but it lay just beneath the surface in a shadow, like a trout. One pull, one quick, certain tug, and it would flash into the air. Glen waited, tense and quiet, but the words sank away as quickly as she had glimpsed them. She lost sight of them, lost their sound and meaning.

"Please just let me sleep," she said.

CHAPTER THIRTY-SEVEN

The stupid thing would look better in a certain light. That's what she'd been hoping, Flo realized, as she peeked in at the canvas yet again. She'd been searching for that perfect light for days, a time of day that would transform the painting somehow, mend it before her eyes. Nothing had done the trick so far, morning or afternoon, sun or clouds. But this light, this almost-none of near dawn, held some promise. Polishing her glasses, setting them carefully on her nose, she stepped up close to the canvas. She saw grays and darker grays, shapeless in the gloom. Yes; no doubt about it, the painting looked best when she couldn't see it at all.

She smiled inwardly. That attitude wouldn't do. The painting had to be faced. The woman from Denver was coming soon, and Flo had to take stock of this piece, had to look at it straight on and boldly without so much as a blink. What was there was there. She'd painted it herself, it was her own. *So.*

Pausing a moment to gather her courage, she snapped on the overhead, frowning through her lenses. No light could be less forgiving than the dusty, fly-specked glare of triplet sixty-watt bulbs on the ceiling.

She sank onto her stool. *Oh.*

She very nearly damned the day she'd watered those tulips. Look where it had led her. She'd painted a gleaming curve of mercury and gold spreading across the whole of the canvas, dropping it out of sight in the lower left, where she'd put in a red bloom against a single green leaf splattered with water. If you followed the arc upward you saw the source, the shining gold spout of that watering can she wished Hank and Annie had kept for themselves and her own wrinkled hand holding it, a hand with roots instead of veins. In the body of the can you saw some distorted black and white checks, a reflection of one of her old, worn-out housedresses. The painting made you feel like one of the tulips, like you were sitting right down there in the flowerpot.

She flipped off the light again and sat motionless, letting the image fade. There was nothing to do but fix breakfast. The painting certainly couldn't be fixed.

With a fire started in the stove to chase off the chill of the morning, she pulled on her jacket and walked down the drive for the paper. A fine morning, calm, presaging the sort of day when you might sit on the steps and be warm even without a sweater, breathing in the air in big, earthy helpings, as if it would put meat on your bones. She tucked the paper under her arm. A good day for a walk, too. Maybe she could take one in the afternoon.

In the kitchen again, she dropped the paper to the table and started the bacon. As it sizzled, she set out the eggs—she'd baste them this morning—drew a pot of water for coffee, set the table. Carl was up, snorting around in the bathroom. The bacon cooked too fast. She slid it out of the pan, muttering; she didn't want the grease to brown. Then the eggs would speckle and you couldn't convince Carl to eat a speckled egg.

The smell of coffee bloomed around her. She snapped the eggs into the pan, the heat way low. Give them a minute; she'd take a quick look at the front page. She unfolded it on the kitchen table, adjusting her bifocals. A big contrasty picture, a black headline. It screeched at her: "Eagles Dead in Jackson Canyon." She touched her glasses again, fumbling them down her nose. The picture showed a man in uniform dangling a black and white bird by its feet.

She ran a finger through the lead paragraph. Twenty-two eagles. An investigation under way. Poison suspected.

A pall of smoke rose from the skillet. She looked, though, toward the ceiling, a spatula held tight in her fist, forgotten. Carl was done shaving, he'd be down in a minute. Footsteps thumped at the head of the stairs.

"Flo? Something's burning!"

Scrambling, she grabbed for the skillet with the corner of her apron.

"What's going on?"

The eggs were blistered. "I burned the grease."

"What?"

She hollered. "I burned the grease."

He came downstairs, silent with amazement. Flo did not burn food, and she didn't holler. He glanced into the skillet, rubbing his damp hands on the back pockets of his jeans.

"I'll have to start over on your eggs." She had left the paper on the table.

"That's okay," he said, eyeing her. "You want me to go ahead and sit down? I'll just get myself some coffee."

He sat, his attention focused on the cup he carried, sloshing at the brim with coffee. She watched him, making no pretense of cooking. He sipped the coffee, taking its level down a bit, added sugar, cream. As he dipped the spoon in to stir, he reached for the paper. The headline caught him as he lifted the cup to his mouth, his lips pursed to meet it.

He gave Flo a sidelong glance. She said nothing. He took the sip of coffee. She let him read another moment, to gather as much as she had.

"It says poison," she said.

"Let me read it, just let me read it."

She sat in her own chair, laying her hands on the placemat, pressing them together to keep them still.

Carl kept his head low but she could see he was staring beyond the paper to the surface of the table.

"It's got to be some kind of coincidence," he said. "It could be a disease. This mentions disease. They haven't proved anything yet."

"But they're going to do studies. They can tell a disease."

He licked his lips. "There's no way to know if I did this. I don't even know. Someone else could of put poison out, too." She wanted to see confidence in his face, but he twisted it toward the window. "We can't jump to conclusions."

"What about Bertie? She's got that raven too."

"Damn Bertie." He tried to calm himself, rubbing determinedly at his nose. "Even if I did do it, it was an accident, plain and simple. I never meant to hurt anything beyond those coyotes. It was bad luck."

She stood up, untying her apron, rolling it into a ball as it fell from her waist. "I believe I need some air."

He watched her go out the kitchen door without her jacket. He hesitated before following. It would do good to let her have a minute to think things through. He walked down the porch steps slowly, her jacket over his arm. She had gone around the side of the house, into the pale sun, and was leaning against the peeling boards, her eyes on the horizon. He slipped the jacket over her shoulders.

She pulled it tighter. "Things have changed in this world since we were young, Carl."

"Yes, they have," he said, biting off his words. "It used to be legal to take care of our interests. We used to be able to keep the varmints from our door without ten different government men and neighbors telling us we can't do this and we can't do that."

His anger compelled him to move. He paced away from her. "I used to run this ranch. Not the same way C. H. ran it, but I still had some say-so. Now I can't even protect my own stock from the wildlife because the wildlife is so damn protected from me."

He glared at her, confident in his outrage, but she looked like she hadn't heard a word. He felt he might burst with his need to move. "You're the one who can't see how things have changed. You and me are going down the drain financially, that's what."

Her eyes drifted away from him to the bright high land east of the house.

"Damn it!" He brought his fist down on the wood a foot from her head. She jolted, but it wasn't fear that came into her face. Frightened of her suddenly, he rubbed his hand through his uncombed hair.

"Come here, Carl," she said, and she stepped around him as if he were a stranger on the street.

Hell if he would. She disappeared around the corner. He bellowed, "Flo!" She'd come back. He heard the screen door slam. "Goddamn it." He stomped after her, up the back steps, past where she stood just inside the door, head bent. She looked like she was fiddling with something in her palm. He stepped to the table opposite her, feeling the need of the bulk of it between them.

She tossed it at him, something small and spinning—her wedding ring—he knew what it was as it hit the table. She'd tugged it from her finger and pitched it at him, overhanded and hard. He reached out to catch it, didn't want it on the floor, had to grab it. It bounced, landed again, spinning, spinning out, and wobbled near the edge. He stilled it with his hand.

"I found it in your jacket pocket."

He lifted it on a forefinger. Not silver—gray and dull, a twisted, ugly metal.

"It's from an eagle, isn't it?"

He curled his finger, gripping the band at his first knuckle. A set of tiny numbers, abbreviations, the smooth double scar of the pliers.

"Oh, Carl," she said. "You want to believe that it didn't happen. But you know it did. We both know it did. We have to face that."

He shook his head, the band wedged at the reddening crook of his finger where it bit into the skin.

It wasn't six-thirty yet and the phone was ringing. Glen answered gruffly. A cocky local reporter whose name he didn't catch badgered him with questions. Did eagles usually eat dead meat? Wasn't it vultures that did that? What condition were the eagles in? And how big were eagles, anyway, how much did they weigh? Ten pounds? Forty? How much poison would it take to kill something that size?

"It's kind of early in the morning," Glen said.

"Is it?" said the kid. "I've been up for hours."

By seven, he had the *Star-Tribune* and both major Denver dailies on his desk. Nothing in the Denver papers, but the woman who had called him last night from the *Star-Tribune*, had put together, overnight, a minor masterpiece of conjecture. Though she'd chosen a restrained tone, she implied strongly that only poison could have caused so many deaths. A sidebar by the same woman—and he recognized her name now as a reporter who covered the legislature occasionally, an easterner doing her time in the provinces, waiting for better opportunities elsewhere—linked the eagle kill to every sore point of land-use controversy in the West: erosion and pollution caused by grazing, wolf reintroduction in Yellowstone, below-cost timber sales in the national forests, water-table pollution caused by poorly plugged oil and gas wells, in-stream flow. She also detailed past wildlife kills in the West, from Prince William Sound to a local accident a few years before, a pesticide spill in the Platte that had wiped out five miles' worth of game fish. Crammed together in a few inches of type, it looked like another Holocaust. She had neglected to mention that other eagle kills had been much larger than this one. The difference was key, of course, and she had milked it for all it was worth: These balds had died close to Casper, not scattered over hundreds of acres out in the middle of nowhere. And they had all died close in time, in a place set aside for their safety.

The local morning news show used the lead of the story as a teaser before cutting to a commercial. "Dead eagles in Jackson Canyon. Officials suspect they were deliberately poisoned." A live-action shot showed a grave reporter standing on the steps of the Fish and Wildlife office, waiting for it to open. He looked cold.

Roberta's name was mentioned in all the accounts. The phone was going to ring all day, and the calls would be mostly for her. She hadn't shown up yet in his office, hadn't indicated how she wanted to handle her notoriety. She'd gotten up early and gone out to the big barn for her morning rounds, leaving him alone in bed. He'd seen only indications of her passage: a pot of coffee stewing in the kitchen and toast crumbs scattered on the counter.

She came in quietly, carrying a phone, a card file, a couple of legal pads.

The phone rang.

"Go ahead and get it," she said.

"I'm letting the machine answer."

She put her supplies on the credenza. The machine picked up. A low-volume voice droned onto the tape. She struggled to plug the phone in behind the credenza. "There's going to be a lot of work to do."

"I know that. We've worked together for years, Bertie."

"I thought of setting up in the big barn—"

"That's ridiculous."

"—but I want to hear for myself what you tell people." She turned to look at him, matter-of-factly, fully awake.

"Then I'll tell you this: I won't tolerate groundless accusations."

There was calm assurance in her voice. "I can't make any charges. I don't have any proof. I'm going to give out facts. I ask you to do the same."

CHAPTER THIRTY-EIGHT

The morning at the clinic had been steady. Sherman toyed with a ham sandwich at the deli. This afternoon, for the first time in more than a week, Muirie would drop by to work with Teiresias. Though they had seen each other almost every day since the trip to the canyon, they had not managed any time together beyond the confines of the big barn. Roberta had put Muirie in charge of the place for the time being, with Sherman coming in whenever he could. They'd had little opportunity for conversation beyond the needs of the birds.

He set the last, stale corner of the sandwich on the plate and reopened his newspaper. He hadn't seen much of Roberta either. She swept into the big barn in the evening to make an inspection and issue demerits but spent the bulk of her time on the phone and dealing with the string of people who showed up at the ranch every day. She looked like an automaton: efficient, tireless, and controlled. "You should see her with Glen in the office," Muirie told him one day, "It's like waiting for a thunderstorm to hit."

He had stayed away from the house, despite an invitation to dinner, preferring to monitor the eagle story at a safe distance through newspapers and television. The first days had built to a small crescendo of coverage at either end of the spectrum, reaching to the Denver papers. Roberta and Glen, both sounding restrained, were quoted frequently— Roberta on the natural history of eagles and her trip into the canyon; Glen on political policy and fallout—but their influence over the extremes seemed minimal. The rural press tended to defend ranching as a mother would defend her child, wildly, without reservation. The urban press attacked. The articles in the Denver papers, especially the shorter, follow-up articles, used weighted words to summarize the past event. Jackson Canyon became a "narrow, dark defile." Ranchers interviewed were reticent, worn, dull-eyed, stooped; they took off their hats to reveal a naked, dead-looking expanse of skin, white as a bald eagle's head; they were quoted in ominous collages of words and damned as a species by pointed implication, even though, as yet, there was no confirmation that poison had been the cause of death. Casper itself looked "grim," "stripped bare," "sandblasted," and "soulless."

Soulless, yet. You could laugh at such overbearing self-righteousness until you stopped to think how easily it would satisfy people's stereotypes.

At the clinic, he moved Teiresias outdoors for a weathering just before Muirie was due. The hawk shook out his feathers, his shoulders glowing in the late sunshine, prismatic, a deep shimmering structure of reds and golds and brilliant browns, a lacework of feathers shingled in a gentle depth of thousands. He touched the bird's breast lightly. Silk.

Muirie arrived as he turned on the spigot and directed the garden hose at the hawk, aiming the spray high so that the water fell like rain. She watched from the door, smiling. Teiresias started mildly, sidling along the perch, as the first mercury beads streamed from his shoulders, but then roused again and allowed the moisture in, opening his wings. He shook his head vigorously, raising spiky feathers at the crown.

"Hawk punk," Muirie laughed, slipping outside to slouch against the cement block exterior of the building. She looked tired, perhaps a little thinner. They had not made love for days.

Turning in the spray, the hawk fanned his broad, white tail like a deck of cards. "What's the mood in the war room?" Sherman asked.

She didn't know words for it, only exasperation. She shrugged hopelessly. Her beauty was somehow accentuated by her lassitude. Her tenderness shone through more easily.

"Explosions?"

"No," she said, sighing.

He released the trigger on the hose, shutting off the flow, and went to her side. Teiresias shook, throwing off a glittering, circular shower.

"You sound doubtful."

She slumped against him. "I wish they *would* explode. At first I thought they'd made a truce, but now I keep thinking they don't care enough about each other to fight anymore. Like they're beyond even that sort of passion."

"Passion" had a warm shock the way she said it, contrasting one that seemed dead with their own. She smiled, realizing it, too, and they kissed.

"Let me close this place up," he said.

"Okay, but let's work with Teiresias first. Just for a while."

His reluctance made him hesitate. "Can't he wait one more day?"

She smiled. "Can you?"

"I don't think so."

Her eyes went to the hawk. "When I had him on my fist the other day I thought how close he is. He'll fly soon. I know it."

He fought his reluctance but her eyes came back to him, questioning. She had sensed the tension in his body.

Out with it. But he could not think of that first word of explanation, the one that would pull all the others behind it in a smooth, persuasive thread.

Her face grew sharp with suspicion. "You want to quit. You've let Aunt Bert convince you to give up."

"No," he said. "I'm not giving up."

She turned away from him, her fatigue peeling away to harsh determination. "Sherman, I can't stand her kind of thinking. I can't stand the way she sees everything in the worst possible light. She takes everything and twists it around until it looks ugly."

Agitated, Teiresias stirred on his perch.

"She's not always wrong, Muirie."

"And this is one of those times, isn't it? Isn't that what you're telling me?"

"No," he said. "I want to talk about it, though. Can't we talk about it?"

"How long have you felt this way?" she demanded. "From the start?" Conviction overtook her. "You've had doubts from the very beginning. You never committed yourself to his training completely. He might have been flying by now."

Sherman wouldn't accept blame, especially this blame, which implied he had failed Teiresias by not believing hard enough, as if the hawk were Tinker Bell. "I'm taking him inside."

He yanked the gauntlet on and offered his fist to the bird with more force than he intended. Teiresias stumbled forward, sprawling on his chest against the glove, wafting his wings wide for balance. Sherman grabbed the clasp for insurance and righted the bird gently with the gauntleted hand.

"Will you get the door?"

She held it open but did not enter. As he returned the hawk to his high perch, she stood in the doorway watching, her face filtered to gray by the unwashed screen. Her voice fell low.

"I won't think that way, Sherman."

"I don't want that, either," he said. "I don't know how you can get me and Roberta confused. I just wanted to talk about what we're doing, to discuss it like adults."

She pushed the screen door open slowly and came inside. "I'm sorry," she said. "I'm tired."

"I just want to slow down," Sherman said. "I want to take things a little easier with him."

"But he's right on the verge of flying. I was thinking we should work harder. I was imagining having him outside on a creance—" She flung an arm toward the door. "—next week."

They stared at one another.

"A middle course, then," Sherman said. "Here's the proposal: We leave everything the same in his training except that we don't work him today. Today, we go to my place and make love instead."

Her shoulders dropped. "That's your compromise?"

Then she smiled, and he pulled her to him, holding her so close she couldn't see his face.

"We're not so far apart, you know," he said. "I'm just more cautious than you. You go full tilt, Muirie."

Her lips were at his neck. "That's not wrong."

"I didn't say it was wrong. I admire it. I love that about you." He paused, feeling the shock in both of them at the use of the word. "I wish I could be that way and never have any second thoughts. But I do. Is that wrong?"

She looked him in the eye, seeming right then and there to be deciding. "No," she said.

The flaring sun lay low on the horizon as Muirie headed west toward home, driving fast. She was on duty in the big barn tonight.

It was bizarre: All her life in the Bay Area, home to six million people, and she could count on two fingers the men she'd come to love there, including her father. Then, she'd flown off to Wyoming and found Sherman in the space of days. What were the odds? Statistically speaking, she should have met an antelope before she met Sherman; she should have met, fallen in love with, and married an antelope before she met Sherman.

She tried to imagine him lounging in a café in the city, changing him from his boots and jeans into something less capital-letter-Cowboy. He'd still have that calm air about him of being oblivious to the world. But she wouldn't look at him twice there; she knew it. He was too plain. He wasn't tall, didn't look remarkable in any way. And even if he happened to glance up and give her a smile, she would discount it. In the city, a pretty girl got a lot of smiles. In the city, she would never get beyond that point, never see that look he'd given her today when he suggested they go and make love—a certain way his eyes settled, excluding everything else, shifting to her like a searchlight, sweeping away even her strayest thought of anger.

Could it last? The only happy couples she knew were those who hadn't been together long enough to pick each other apart. She had gone at her former boyfriends nit by nit. A great love was the reverse. It grew from an accumulation of details, a steadily increasing association of words and deeds, of passion, constancy, devotion, that formed itself into a whole. You had to know one another's histories, admire the path of one another's thoughts. You had to be able to say to each other, and to mean it: I love the way you think.

At the curve of the road above the Uncle John, she pulled onto the shoulder. The ranch lay below her, almost lush in the late, golden light.

She cut the ignition and slid the seat of the pink truck back as far as it would go, propping her arms behind her head. The open window breathed green.

Jeremiah, spinning the tales of the Sheas, had told her that Uncle John, Irishman that he was, had longed for more trees on the ranch.

But he never complained. Living fourteen to a room, you dream about big, open land like this. You dream of standing in a spot and turning in a circle, and seeing not another soul, and knowing that whatever you see is yours.

It *was* a scripted story, the saga of the Sheas, told so many times, and with such intent, that it had been worn smooth with purpose, reducing it to a blunt instrument, a cudgel, a bat.

Roberta's voice overlay Jeremiah's, grinding in Muirie's head. *Propaganda, the worst kind. Weeds, not a blade of good grass. The land can never recover. The topsoil's gone, the nutrients with it.*

And yet, sitting here, looking over the pink nose of the truck to the new green of the land beyond...well, it was another story.

The breeze was mild, gauzy with moisture, overflowing, as if there were more of it than the world could hold. Missing the forests of Ireland, John had come to love this. Perhaps he had stood on this same ridge, seeing the land as she was seeing it now, from horseback, slouched in the saddle, squinting into the sun, thinking: *Mine.*

She breathed in lungfuls, tasting water and the merest hint of soil, moist and subtle as an herb. The simple sweep of the land drew her, easing her eye like poetry made physical, like topographical verse.

CHAPTER THIRTY-NINE

Carl slapped the magazine back onto the bench, snorting softly. Now he'd heard everything. The Environmental Protection Agency had started an educational program for ranchers called the Ruminant Livestock Methane Program. Its goal was "voluntary pollution prevention at a profit." Farty livestock were destroying the earth's atmosphere, they said.

Someone had left the magazine there on purpose, to share the joke. It had been opened to the article, the curl of the pages pressed flat so it would stay that way. It was a slick beef industry magazine from Denver, an article that reported defensively on the mounting scientific evidence that the greenhouse effect was caused in part by gassy livestock. The article made the point that cattle today could hardly be more flatulent than ten million buffalo before them. It was all the extra people, Carl thought. Human farts certainly weren't a blessing, either, and with all these bean-eaters lately, the volume was no doubt increasing.

The auctioneer announced the next lot of sheep, a scroungy bunch of cull ewes like his. They'd miscarried or gone infertile with age; they were headed for slaughter. His eye judged these quickly. They were in better shape than his own but it was hard to be objective. He was more criti-cal of his own animals. The price would tell.

He sipped coffee from a Styrofoam cup and sat back cautiously, eas-ing past the pain in his spine, seeking a sense of ease he had not found for days. There had been only one short article about the eagles in the *Star-Tribune* today, so perhaps the worst was over. Nothing to incrimi-nate him had surfaced, nor had he been called or questioned by any authorities. Still, he'd had to study the size and shape of the article before he could force his eyes over the lines, waiting for it to jump him. He hadn't been able to face the TV at all.

There weren't many people here today, twenty perhaps. Most of them he knew, but he sat alone by preference. You couldn't jabber and con-centrate on the ring at the same time, and he wasn't eager to hear any-body's comments about his sheep or anything else. He just wanted to get his animals sold and go back home where there was work to be done.

He studied the other men anyway, in quick sidelong glances. Had Roberta questioned them too? No one had mentioned it and he wasn't about to ask. At least two men here lived in the same vicinity and could just as easily have poisoned the birds. Roberta hadn't thought of that, probably. One of them caught Carl's glance and nodded, a forefinger at the brim of his hat. Dave Krandall, an old-timer like himself. They'd tar-get-shot prairie dogs together when they were boys. Carl was better with a gun, able to plug them in the head more often, which earned more points the way they scored the game, and by the time they were in high school Dave couldn't find time for shooting anymore. Truth was, he couldn't stand to be beat. He'd got into oil before the boom, like Glen and Roberta, and had turned into a suitcase rancher in recent years, although you wouldn't say so to his face. He had a house in town while his son ran the ranch, though, so there wasn't much point in denying it. Roberta wouldn't suspect him. He had life too easy these days. He wouldn't be worrying about a few damn sheep.

Bud Walters was the other. Carl didn't like him, never had. He wore a cold look you couldn't crack with a pick, and when he tried to smile it looked painful, as if he didn't have enough skin to quite cover his skull. Flo thought he had hemorrhoids. She'd told Carl once, long ago, *You watch him; he'll sit on one cheek or the other, not both.* As if that proved it. Carl couldn't bring himself to notice such a thing. Who but a woman?

The memory of her cheerful voice pierced him through. She was tuned down so quiet these days that he had to strain to hear. She went about her chores in the usual way but without her usual chatter. In fact, he was so hungry to hear her voice that he'd listen happily if she talked about Bud Walters's hemorrhoids.

At the peak of the oil boom Bud had parceled up his land and tried to sell it as prime property. He nailed block-lettered signs to his fences that read PEARL OF THE PLATTE RANCHETTES: SOUND INVESTMENTS, EASY TERMS. VIEWS. He'd actually sold a couple before the boom turned bust. One or two of the signs were still up, dangling from the fences by a single rusty nail.

You couldn't be sure about Bud and poison. He'd been luckier in recent years, timing his sales right, managing to keep all the balls in the air at once. But he was putting a lot of borrowed capital into what he called streamlining. His place was a maze of sheds, pens, sorting gates, ramps, and chutes, and his financial situation had to be about the same. There was no reason to doubt that he could have killed those eagles.

Another lot of ewes pushed into the ring. A price for liveweight culls had been established and the bidding went faster. It was low but not unusually so for these days. His own lot was next. It straggled in, the ewes uniformly scrawny. The contrast shocked him. They hadn't looked this bad to him before. Some bony spines, but these were old girls; you expected it.

The first bid dropped the price twenty cents a pound. He kept his eyes straight ahead, on his sheep, leaning forward onto his knees. He might have kept some of these ewes too long. Some could have been sold last year. That was why they looked so bad. He'd delayed, wanting to get every last lamb he could out of the lot. It wasn't a bad strategy. The problem was everyone else jumping the gun, selling ewes that had another good year in them; of course they were going to look better.

The price edged upward and the lot sold at seven cents per pound less than the previous low. Carl stayed where he was until the next lot was let into the ring, then slid off the bench and made his way to the clerk's window without catching anyone's eye. He waited while she wrote out his receipt, glancing back at the stands. The reel of the auctioneer's voice signaled quicker bidding, a better lot, a better price.

His truck wouldn't start on the first try. Cursing, he restrained the urge to pump it. The engine was picky on that count; it'd flood in a minute. He stared at the dismal false front of the building. You just had to wait.

When he was a boy the auctions had been almost as good as a rodeo, the men chewing the fat, arguing among themselves, a big crowd of animals and people, so much noise and confusion it made your ears hurt. A community of people, solid and loyal to one another. He could imagine himself back in his teens, slouching at ringside, a slug of tobacco in his cheek, taking it all in, taking it all for granted.

The engine cranked to life this time. It needed a tune-up. More likely an overhaul. He pulled out on to the highway, turning toward home.

Taking it all for granted—what a luxury that had been. If only he could have appreciated that from an early age, especially since the pace of change had increased so much. The outside world stormed into your living room now; it screamed at you from the radio, from the front page of the paper. You couldn't get away from it and it was out to warp your thinking, to make you believe that every event was linked to every other, including each one of your decisions. It tried to make you feel responsible for everything, for people cutting timber in jungles, for holes in the atmosphere over the South Pole. Nobody thought about their own home ground anymore. Nobody had a deep sense of belonging to a certain place, especially the younger people. They didn't want to be citizens of Natrona County, Wyoming. They called themselves citizens of the world.

How the old-timers would laugh at some of the things people believed now, like the "fact" that beef clogged up your heart. He imagined telling them, heard their uproarious laughter. Their fathers had lived into their eighties on beef jerky and fried bread. He wouldn't even mention that salt was supposed to be bad for you. It preserved meat, for chrissake. You leave the salt out of jerky and you're going to have some pretty green meat, believe you me. There was no way they'd believe the stuff about cow farts. He could just see their faces if he told them, and he could see their reactions too. Somebody would force one out—a nice, big, beefy fart—and everyone else would choke and pretend to die, eking out their last breaths in laughter.

A glossy car, jet black, was parked this side of the barn. He saw it as he turned into the drive. Flo's gallery woman. He could smell her the minute he walked in the door. Flo never wore perfume other than some kind of talcum. This scent was powerfully foreign to the house. He could taste it, spicy, on his tongue.

He stepped quietly into the dining room, pausing at the bottom of the stairs. The door to Flo's studio hung open. A young woman, it sounded liked; she talked too loud, as if Flo couldn't comprehend English in a normal tone. She hadn't been here long. She was still gushing the way women did when they first met. He heard something about "the lovely countryside" and "marvelous desolation." Her voice went all over the scale, up and down, like listening to Hank practice piano when he was a boy. About as heavy-handed too.

He scoffed silently, passing on to the kitchen. Countryside! From back east, no doubt. He knew what she looked like without seeing her. Pink-faced and billboard-bright, especially at the lips. High heels—he could hear those on the floorboards, though, so it wasn't a guess. Tight little skirt and a mincey way of walking to keep the hem below her hips. He'd like to see her come down those stairs.

Flo had left him his lunch in the refrigerator. A bit of strategy on her part. She didn't want him in on her art-talk and figured she could divert him with food. Look at this: an extra-thick sandwich, a fresh pot of coffee, potato salad, and baked beans. It was a regular picnic. He set it out on the table, his ear tuned to the conversation upstairs, folding a paper napkin for himself, tucking it next to the plate. He caught a word every now and then, never Flo's. "Marvelous" again. And something about "texture" and "color sense." He could make no sense of it at all.

Drawn, he stepped again into the dining room, his coffee mug in his hand. The woman's voice rang out clearly.

"...it's nearly abstract. Quite a departure from your other work."

He heard Flo then, hesitant. "I didn't mean it to be."

The spike heels crossed the floorboards.

"...levels in your work: factual, spiritual, emotional. It's true of everything I've seen."

He felt better for hearing this mumbo jumbo. Flo would hear it the same way.

"And you've caught the distortions of light and color in the flow of the water. It's quite wonderful."

Lovely. Wonderful. Marvelous. They were the only words she knew.

"Tell me about your process."

"My...?" Flo said.

"Your process. How you work, how you derive your ideas."

Someone shifted a painting on the floor. Flo would be looking polite about now, with her hands folded in her lap, waiting for this to be over.

"This one, for instance. The texture of the wood is gorgeous. And this unfocused form grabs my interest; I want to know more. Is it coming toward me or walking away? How did you come to see this?"

"Oh," Flo said, with a kind of relief in her voice, as if she knew how to answer these questions.

Carl moved closer, to the bottom of the stairs. A board groaned beneath his feet. At the top of the stairwell, bright with northern light, he saw Flo's silhouette. She was talking easily now, a long stream of piping words. She reached behind the door for something, one of her sketch pads, perhaps, and gave the door a push. With a *screak*, it swung almost closed, shutting the stairway into darkness sliced by a slender shaft of light.

CHAPTER FORTY

Outrage had a short life-expectancy. A few eagles killed in a canyon could not command the public's attention for long. Roberta picked up the clippings file from the credenza and leafed through it again, as she had a half-dozen times before. The phone calls at the Uncle John had fallen to a few a day; the flow of visitors drained to a trickle. Glen, resuming some of his normal activities, had gone off to a meeting on a more important matter: acquiring federal funds for new highway construction.

The clippings were in rough chronology, a collection of claims and counterclaims, promises and justifications, outright lies and clever misrepresentations, quotes and speculation, all coming to nothing. The *Star-Tribune* and *High Country News* would follow the story until there was nothing left to say, but that time was not far-off. The shock value of the story—and thus its news value—had passed.

The phone rang just once during the day, as she and Muirie loaded the pink truck for a raptor workshop Roberta was scheduled to give at an elementary school in town. A Fish and Wildlife agent had told her what she had expected to hear: the poison was 1080 in high concentration.

Other than that, he said, there was no news, but an investigation was under way. Some of the ranchers in the area would be questioned. Of this she could rest assured.

Ah, indeed: rest assured.

The second graders at the workshop were openly disappointed that she had not brought an eagle with her. Oscar and Franklin looked moderately intriguing, but their teacher had told them that "the eagle lady" was coming, and they wanted to see an eagle. Roberta had made no such promises. She did not have an eagle among her tour birds; they were too large to handle safely in school settings.

But this excuse was not good enough; she knew it wouldn't be. These children had already begun the inevitable process of maturation. Plus, it was the end of the school year and they were not easily entertained. They opposed her now, raising the stakes with each of her efforts to interest them. But they were not beyond her reach. She stood before them, judging them with thoughtful confidence. Franklin would come in handy today. Since these children thought they had already seen everything in the world worth seeing, she would show them something they couldn't see.

Demanding silence, she ordered them to gather around a few feet away from the birds. They shifted, restless, wanting suddenly to get much closer, to touch. Perhaps that would make up for no eagles. Oscar restrained them as much as Roberta's strict regulations, by blazing yellow incrimination at every child. Franklin studied them more blandly, shifting his brown gaze around the room as if he were a Secret Service agent guarding the president. He uttered a soft trill, shocking the children into momentary silence.

"Now," said Roberta into the void. "Each of these birds has something special about it. I won't tell you what. You have to figure it out yourself by looking. Let's start with this red-tailed hawk."

It was not immediately obvious, especially to an untrained eye, that Franklin, standing calmly on his perch, had just one wing. The bird's healthy, streamlined plumage and his dark coloration disguised the loss, and he had long ago adjusted to the imbalance in his weight so that he walked from fist to perch without the stumbling confusion of a new amputee. At a certain angle, Roberta thought, he looked a little hunched on that side, as if his tailor had neglected to put a shoulder pad in one sleeve of his suit coat. But the concept of one-wingedness did not occur spontaneously to most people seeing the hawk for the first time, especially children. Expecting two wings, they saw two wings.

The first guesses were slow in coming: general, conservative, desultory. Feathers, wings, brown eyes instead of yellow. Roberta did not pretend to be impressed any more than they had pretended to be impressed by her. They edged toward the more creative: a beak instead of lips; no ears. Someone joked that Franklin couldn't smile, which led to more observations on the nonhumanness of a hawk, including its diet and the fact that it had to catch its own food. She liked this more and afforded them a few words of encouragement. Some of the children had tuned in now, competing for her praise. Others yawned or picked their noses with the kind of concentration they never gave their schoolwork. But they would come around, too.

She gave her praise sparingly: a nod, a further question. They worked from head to foot, their focus keener, but still unable to see the missing wing. Lookit those claws, they cried. *They're called talons. How do you think a hawk uses talons?* He hangs onto branches; he scratches his head; he fights with them. *He also catches his food with them; he grabs his dinner up off the ground.* Another moment of silence as this image passed through their collective mind; it sounded like a tough way to live.

She took the hawk onto her fist. Franklin lifted his wing slightly, balancing, but the children did not see the asymmetry. She paced, just fast enough that the hawk kept the wing out for balance, and told the children about the hawk's life in the wild. "Why isn't this bird living outside?" she asked them. "What is it that's special about this hawk?"

She turned, dropping her arm a few inches. Franklin angled the wing out in response. A single voice rose up buoyantly, a boy's. "Hey, is he sticking that one wing out—or does he only got one?"

Both were true, but she would not quibble. She had the boy step closer to do his own investigation. He peered at the hawk from every perspective, indelicately, while Franklin watched him with royal calm.

"He's only got one wing!"

The children gasped, delighted with the horror of it. "Now why in the world would a hawk have just one wing?" she asked them.

They did not have to ponder long. They had instant theories, dozens of them. The idea of injury surfaced early but it did not win support without debate. A contending argument ran that hawks lost their wings one at a time the way kids lose their baby teeth and another would grow in. But the lure of violence drew them, and they decided that Franklin had lost a grand aerial battle. His wing had been torn off by another bird. When she told them the truth, that the hawk had been shot, they became thoughtful but were not shocked. She hadn't expected shock. The thoughtfulness was enough.

Her job was easier now: to guide, throwing in a new puzzler from time to time, giving them just enough information to direct their curiosity. They were glowing pink with the effort of holding their voices down, so she let the volume rise. The birds had adapted to the commotion; they would survive the din.

She sat on the teacher's desk at the front of the room as the children debated around her, face-to-face, in a verbal chorus with thirty parts, serious, passionate, dedicated, outrageous, contentious, and unyielding. They disparaged anyone who didn't agree with them and refused to agree with anyone else. They trembled with the heat of their ideas, then reached the flash point and detonated, recovering in an instant to argue again. She floated above the noise, letting their enthusiasm wash over her in waves of jubilant sound.

Sherman finished wiping down the countertops, then leaned against the doorjamb, studying Teiresias. The hawk had not eaten since the day before yesterday and did not seem inclined to eat. There was nothing overtly wrong with him. He had seemed subtly restless which by itself was no cause for concern. But a loss of appetite was troubling.

"Maybe you need some sunshine," he said to the hawk.

He propped the back door of the clinic open. The late afternoon was bright and calm. He took the hawk onto his fist and moved the perch outside. Fifteen minutes or so outside would do him good.

Sherman settled the perch firmly into the uneven gravel, leveling a spot for it with his toe, then urged Teiresias to turn by gently touching the base of his tail. He loosened the length of leather wrapped around his thumb and positioned his fist next to the bar of the perch, rolling it forward.

"Okay, boy, go on."

The bird hesitated, then stepped forward too fast, as if Sherman had pushed him. His wings came out in panic, seeking balance, a wild, unco-ordinated flash. In Sherman's hand, the leather strap slid. The bird stead-ied, still flapping, as if sampling the air, his wings extending in long, muscular strokes. Sherman grabbed for the strap but the metal clasp slipped through his fingers. The bird lifted into the air.

The instant hung in Sherman's mind like an hour of paralysis: the hawk clearing the perch, the pendulum of the heavy gear swinging free below, still within reach, his own arm reaching out. A thousand thoughts stabbed: the gear was a death sentence, even for a sighted bird, an anchor to entangle, to strap the bird to a tree, a power line, whatever he hit first—and he was sure to hit.

Sherman leaped, grabbing for the swinging clasp. His fingers closed on air. The hawk lifted up.

"Teiresias!"

Over the roof, reflecting the sun, the bird flew into the open sky, head-ing west.

Sherman scrambled to the front of the building, scraping by the tan-gle of chain-link fence at the side of the clinic, yanking his truck keys from his pocket. *Keep him in sight.* But the hawk would be out of sight in seconds. He threw open the door of his pickup, squinting into the glare. The hawk was flying into the sun, as if guided by its warmth, as if he could see its brightness with an undamaged third eye.

The scree of the parking strip flew, drumming in the wheel wells, as Sherman backed away from the clinic. The sky glared empty. He gunned the truck into a stream of oncoming traffic, blaring the horn as he cut diagonally across the lanes. A Safeway semi, the driver's face writhing obscenities, swerved to avoid him, air horns blasting. Sherman shielded his eyes against the sun. Empty horizon. Dirty orange and empty. He tried to gauge the last position of the bird, a piece of dark lint in the sky, moving away through open air: impossible. But it had been south of the highway. North of the highway was the river and its broad valley. The bird might be drawn that way, into the space of the distance; the ferrug-inous was a bird of the plains.

What am I thinking? He's blind.

He ran a red light, accelerating ahead of the cross-traffic. More horns. The hawk would avoid the highway by sound, he hoped. Given the choice, he would head away from it. But which way, and how far? He eyed the telephone lines, the power poles, the billboards, and hoped for height, for great height, that Teiresias had climbed above all the clutter of the earth and had kept on climbing.

By the time she had talked with the teacher and packed up her materials—delicate wing bones, a selection of raptor flight feathers that the boys invariably transformed into swords, a few study skins, a poster of spring warblers, a migration map, the perches, and the birds—it was after five. A couple of children waved to her in the parking lot. Two more flew, oblivious, arms out, circling one another like swallows. She closed the door of the truck, sealed away once again into her own silence. The children would stay with her if she concentrated on them, she thought; if she willed the music of their voices into her head and ran it in a loop. It would sing her all the way home, perhaps, and get her through the evening, even into bed, to sleep. *Rest assured.*

Muirie was finishing the evening chores in the big barn when she saw Roberta coming up the drive. She helped unload the birds and return them to their cages. Oscar hissed peevishly at her as she took him onto her fist, even striking out as if he meant to take a chunk of her flesh. "You'd think he was the one who did all the work today," she said.

A smile crossed Roberta's face, but it vanished, leaving her grave.

"Tough group, huh?"

Roberta wrung out a rag to wipe down the raptors' car carriers. "Tough day."

Outside, the early evening was chill and moist, smelling of grass and, faintly, of wildflowers. A blue heron kicked up near the creek and sailed low over the water, with wing beats as deep and slow as a rower's stroke. They walked toward the house.

"I threw some dinner together."

"I'm not hungry."

Muirie opened the door for her. "You never are. You need to eat anyway."

Glen, hearing them, came down the hallway from his office. His expression changed when he saw Roberta's. She did not acknowledge his presence.

"I got the news of the poison today. Ten-eighty. He didn't measure anything, just dumped a bunch in, until it looked good and deadly."

"He?" said Glen.

Roberta eyed him now, expressionlessly.

"They have some evidence on Carl?" Glen asked. "Is that what you're saying?"

"They have twenty-two poisoned eagles."

"That doesn't indict the Drummonds."

"Not Flo," said Roberta. "She did no more than the rest of us, keeping quiet all these years."

"Quiet? You've hardly stayed quiet these last few years, Roberta."

Muirie could not remember ever hearing Glen call Roberta by her full name.

Roberta shook her head. "I can only remember what I haven't done." She seemed amused now, grimly.

"You can't point fingers, Bertie. Carl could be completely innocent."

"He's not," she said. "You're a lawmaker, Glen. There's a federal law involved."

"I'm a hypocrite," Glen said. "Just like you. We all are. We all say we hate big government, but we all want its help when we've got our own special cause. And now you're willing to haul the government in here to accuse and punish a lifelong friend and neighbor."

"Carl is guilty."

"Is he?" Glen said. "Listen, if Carl killed those eagles, it's because he was careless. There are others out there who kill eagles on purpose; you know that. If you nab Carl, all they're going to say is, 'Goddamn, he was dumb.'"

She wouldn't answer.

"You'd stop Carl from poisoning again; he'd lose his ranch. But the others who use it will just be more careful next time. And you'd lose any respect you have in the community. How are you going to make a difference if no one will listen to you?"

"I don't have a choice," said Roberta.

A long, atonal howl of a horn came to Muirie's ears, eerie with distance. She lifted her head, listening.

"You do have a choice," said Glen.

The howl came closer. A kid on the highway, probably, trapped behind an old lady. But it blared, too close now to be on the road. Roberta's head came up. Glen heard it, too. Muirie ran to the dark window. Someone was taking the curve in the driveway fast. A pickup. It shot around the circle. She knew the sound of that engine.

"Sherman," she said, going for the door.

Headlights glared through the dusk. The wheels locked, spraying gravel against the wood of the porch foundation.

He was out of his truck, coming toward her, his face pale with anguish. Roberta was up off the couch. With a hand on Muirie's shoulder, she stepped to the threshold first. He faced her, drawing a palm across his lips.

"Teiresias is gone. Teiresias got away from me."

A cricket peeped in the silence.

"With all his gear. I was transferring him. He got away."

"Shit," said Muirie. "How—"

"Where?" said Roberta. "Which way?"

"West. I followed him—where I thought he'd gone—but he was out of sight before I could get to the pickup."

"Come in and we'll—" Glen said.

"There's no time," Sherman interrupted. "I need you to help me. I need flashlights. I need eyes, all your eyes."

Panic blossomed. Sherman was drawn back to his truck as though by a magnet. He wanted to be gone; he couldn't stand still. Glen followed him, full of conjecture and advice, waving out a map in the air of the nearby back roads. Muirie, on the verge of tears, ripped through the hangers in the closet, unable to find her jacket, though it hung in front of her nose.

"Sherman, wait," Roberta said. "Just wait."

Sherman stopped, drawn tight as a bowstring.

"Think this through. The hawk won't have gone far. It doesn't matter how much you've worked with him, his flight muscles will have atrophied, plus he's hauling extra ounces of leather and metal." She made her words deliberate. "He's close by. He will have come down by now."

"All the more reason to hunt for him," Sherman said.

"There's no chance of finding him in the dark."

"You don't know that."

"There's not even a moon."

"You expect me to just sit here?"

"You think he's followed the roads for your convenience? How are you going to find him?"

"I have to try."

"You need to come in," she said. "Tell us what happened. We'll figure out what to do."

He had hardly looked at Muirie. He looked at her now, as Roberta drew him into the house by the elbow like a truculent child. She knew what he saw in her face, anguish like his own—how could he lose Teiresias?

Roberta sat him down on the couch. Glen brought coffee and forced it into his hand, but he set the mug on the table, stubborn and silent. He told the story, blaming himself. "Somehow I let go. At the most vulnerable second, I let go."

Muirie flopped into the opposite chair, head in hands.

Roberta spoke to Glen over her shoulder. "Call KTWO and the radio stations. They'll listen to you. Ask them to put out bulletins. Give them this number. Mention the gear. Anyone who sees anything that could be this hawk should call us."

"The paper too," he said, already on the way. "They can still get an announcement in by morning."

Roberta turned back to Sherman. "Your best hope is to alert as many people as possible. The gear might catch their attention. You should put posters up too."

"Posters?"

"Along the western routes from town."

He sat back stiffly. "I am not going to sit around making posters, Roberta."

"And you have to prepare yourself for what you might find."

"My stuff's in the truck."

She appeared not to hear him. She stepped into the pine closet and reemerged with Jeremiah's Remington in the crook of her arm.

Sherman jumped to his feet. "I told you, I've got all my stuff in the pickup, Roberta. If we find him injured—"

"He is injured. Permanently injured."

"He survived that!" Muirie said.

Roberta ignored her. "The chance that we'll find him at all is slim. You know that. If we do, he'll either be dead or reinjured. Gift-wrapped with that gear, tangled on a telephone pole. We're going to need a gun."

Muirie was on her feet, too. "You can't shoot him if we find him alive!"

Glen came back into the room, a legal pad in hand. He froze at the sight of the shotgun. "Bertie! What's going on?"

She cast a cold glance at them all. "I'm going out to the barn to clean this."

She left by the front door, closing it solidly behind her.

The phone rang a half-dozen times. The local media needed a better description of the hawk than Glen could give them, and the paper offered to run a picture if someone would bring one to their news desk. Sherman took over the phone. Muirie fell in beside him, searching for a reproducible photograph or drawing of a ferruginous hawk. She went to Roberta's field guides first but found the drawings and photographs small, or muddy, or too diagrammatic, unlike the live hawk in her mind. In the living room she dumped a dusty cache of wildlife magazines onto the floor and plied through them. In a Nature Conservancy newsletter she found a crystalline, three-by-five color shot of a light-phase ferruginous standing in full sun in grass to its belly. She tilted the photograph under the lamp, cutting the glare. Her heart caught. The hawk stared at the camera with bright, tawny eyes.

Sherman stood at the kitchen counter, running his finger down an index in an encyclopedia of birds. She slid the magazine on top of his volume, slipping her arm in his. He stared at the photograph, expressionless.

"This is what we get for trying to fly him," he said. "He flew."

She stiffened. "You're blaming us?"

"He had better sense than we did, refusing to fly until we forced him."

She withdrew her arm. "Forced him? What about *you* fumbling the gear? That didn't have anything to do with it?"

He twisted away from her.

"I knew it," she said. "You've been lying to me. You wanted to quit. You never wanted to do it in the first place."

"That's not true," he said, scornful.

"And now you're blaming me that he got loose."

"I'm not blaming you. I know it's my own goddamn fault." It came out in a shout.

His volume shocked her, but she would not let it stop her. "Your own fault for going along with the idea in the first place, you mean."

He pushed past her into the living room, slapping his pocket for his keys. "Think whatever you want."

"You were afraid to tell me, afraid what I would think."

He was at the door. "We're talking about the hawk's life here, Muirie, not yours."

He banged through the door. She was on his heels.

"I'm coming with you."

"There's no point."

"Then why are *you* going?"

He stopped in the middle of the drive, his back to her. She knew he wanted out of here, away from her, to be gone.

"Sherman—"

"There's nothing to say."

"How long will you be gone?"

"I don't know."

"I want to come."

"I don't want you to. Do I have to say it?"

"You did."

He shrugged.

"I need to look, too," she said, "even if it's impossible to find him."

"You've got a truck."

She cracked a boot heel in the gravel. "I don't want to go alone, damn it."

"I don't want to listen to your anger."

"I'm not angry. I'm scared for Teiresias."

He turned now. "You're not angry? Then I don't want to see your face when you are."

Roberta came in late, near eleven, after the phone had fallen silent. Muirie, exhausted, had gone to the pine closet and dropped asleep on top of the bed, fully clothed, with the door open. Glen sat alone, watching the fire die.

She took a step toward the bedroom.

"Bertie—"

She paused again, in profile.

"Can't you come in for a minute?"

She didn't move.

"Roberta. Come in."

Her hand went to the frame of the door, as if to steady herself, then she came and sat next to him, in the twin of his armchair. She stared at the luminous black of the windows, her hands in her lap.

"Bertie, I—"

The gold clock on the desk chimed. In the silence of the house, its delicate voice was choral and sweet.

"Did Sherman call?" she murmured.

"No."

He thought he could hear the clock ticking, the smooth interlock of gears, the pendulum's swing.

"You've got to step back from this, Bertie. You've got to let them decide."

She took a breath, held it, released it again.

"The hawk is Sherman's responsibility. It's for him to judge."

"I don't trust his judgment."

"I don't trust yours. When I saw you with that shotgun tonight—"

"What?"

"It made me think of Jeremiah out shooting hawks."

He rose from his chair, pressing a knuckle under his nose, stiffening himself against the fear she evoked in him. "You're going at it all wrong here. I don't understand why you keep pushing. You can't step in as judge, jury, and executioner. Not with the hawk and not with Carl."

She sat rigid, hands in her lap.

"You know," he said, "when Muirie came, it made me think again about us never being able to have kids. We said it wouldn't matter, swore it wouldn't. But maybe it has. Maybe that's part of all this."

"Even you?" she said bitterly. "If I'd had little humans to take care of, I wouldn't have had to go chasing down wild animals to have something to take care of."

"I know you better than that," he said, quietly.

She turned her head away.

He paced. "But kids might have made life better. Having them around might have softened us, kept us talking, kept us interested in the same things." He swept an arm around the dim room. "And we would have had some activity around this place, to keep it alive."

"We have Muirie," Roberta said.

"No. We don't have Muirie. Muirie's grown-up. She's done most of her growing up away from us. We lost those years too. And even now that she's here, I'm always politicking, and you spend every minute out with those birds."

"The way you talk, it could be découpage."

He didn't understand.

"You treat the birds like my hobby. You always have."

He laughed. "That's so out of line. If that's what you heard, then you had to hear that I lumped my own career into the same sentence."

"*That's* découpage for sure."

Roberta smiled against her will, eyes closed; Glen watched her, struck by the irony of humor at such a moment. At least they were both still capable of it.

"Bertie." He moved to the ottoman, considered, then sat down. "I could say the same thing. You've never taken my politics seriously. You've heaped scorn on everything I've done from start to finish." He nudged her knee with his. "I bet you've never even voted for me."

"I wasn't one of your interest groups," she said.

"You're my main interest group," he said. "You always have been."

"Oh, don't pander to me now."

Standing again, he faced the windows, not knowing where to go with this, how to proceed.

"I want to figure out a way to change," he said. "To make us happy again."

She didn't have to say it; he knew what she was thinking.

"We *were* happy, Bertie. You can't destroy the memories of the good years in me."

"No, you believe that the truth of everything is whatever you want it to be, that the status quo is just fine. That's why you've never given my work your wholehearted support."

"Wholehearted support?" He glared at her. "That would mean telling people to move off their land in favor of birds. You never could compromise, Bertie."

"I did when I married you."

It was as if she'd slapped him. "That was the last time," he said. "And I know you've been sorry ever since."

She bit her lip. "No."

He paced.

"It's not true," she said.

"Oh, let's have the truth by all means," he said. "Let's get right down to that objective truth, pin it out like the dead thing it is and take a look at it."

"You want me to give up my principles."

"I want you to step back and see who you might injure before you act. All you can think about is birds."

"I'm thinking about principle."

"What kind of principle is it that won't allow you to discuss it with me?"

"You're thinking about yourself," she said. "You're worried about the political fallout if I give evidence against Carl. That's what everything comes down to with you. What's in it for Glen? What advantage can Glen wring from this situation?"

She stood up, facing the black, lustrous windows. She had taken a step away before he spoke again.

"I don't remember you ever being at any disadvantage, Bertie."

Her foot hesitated on the carpet.

"Not ever," he said. "Not once. Not *you*."

Something rumbled in her sleep. Muirie opened her eyes. Her feet felt odd: hot, constricted. She wriggled her toes, remembering she had shoes on. And her shirttail had twisted around her waist. She sat up, willing herself to hear the sound again. Or any sound at all: a breeze rummaging under the eaves, or a semi gearing down on the highway. But nothing came to her, only the steady tide of blood against her eardrum. Beyond the door she could faintly see the furniture crouching in the living room. It wasn't dawn yet but the narrow windows at the ceiling showed as a smear of gray.

She slipped into the living room, edging behind the draperies to peer toward the barn. Sherman's truck—that's what she'd heard, even in her sleep. He'd parked at the far end of the barn, rolling in quietly so that no one would hear, not knowing how attuned to him her ear had become. It was too dark to see him, but he was out there, sprawled across that plank-hard seat, trying to get some rest before the search began again at daybreak.

CHAPTER FORTY-ONE

The local television station wanted an interview for its morning show. Its live-action news team, which saw less action than most, had been rousted out of bed by the news director and sent in the station's van to the Uncle John as fast as it could get there. The reporter and his cameraman arrived with their 7-Eleven coffee and doughnuts in hand and rang the doorbell in long, rude pulses. Roberta didn't budge from the kitchen.

"Use Chug," she told Sherman. "Show them what a hawk looks like."

Sherman, gray-faced, dug for his keys. "I'm leaving. You do the damn interview."

The doorbell buzzed over their voices. Muirie made a move toward the door.

"Don't," said Roberta. "They can wait."

"I'll stop at ranch houses, call in every hour if I can."

"There are hundreds of miles of road out there, Sherman. Even if that hawk's near one of them, a thousand to one you won't see it from your truck. And then if we do get a call, you'll be out of contact. Your time is better spent getting the word out. You've got one set of eyes, there are forty thousand others in the area. Make use of them."

But he pulled his jacket from the back of a kitchen chair. Muirie already had hers on, and when he pushed past Roberta in the doorway, she was in lockstep behind him. He turned on her, but she eyed him with a high-chinned implacability he couldn't take the time to counter.

"Wait," said Roberta, grabbing Jeremiah's binoculars from the mantel. She pressed them into Muirie's hands at the door.

They charged past the startled TV crew, ignoring their shouts. Sherman had the engine roaring before Muirie got her door open, and was backing up before she got it closed. He accelerated down the drive, then braked suddenly at the highway, though it stretched empty east and west. Gravel dust drifted past them, a ghost crossing the asphalt.

"He could be in either direction," Sherman said.

"Go east," Muirie said. "If Aunt Bert's right, he might have gone down fast. It won't hurt to search that corridor twice. We'll go in, call from town, then turn around and come back, tracing his route."

They exchanged a glance. It was futile—they both knew it—the idea that they could trace a trackless route, a route through the air.

Sherman spun the truck onto the highway, eastward.

Two calls came in after the first local news broadcasts. Glen took them. Both were easily discountable, even by him. One woman had seen a flock of geese flying toward Yant's Puddle, something she'd never noticed before somehow but, once alerted to the existence of large birds, she imagined these were connected to the lost hawk. The second caller described a "huge bird with a long nose standing stock-still in the river" at that very moment, as if paralyzed. "That'll be a heron contemplating breakfast," Glen said.

The next calls, though, outpaced his ornithological training. This was going to take some teamwork whether Roberta wanted it or not. She was in no mood to listen to these eager, helpful voices, most of them with bogus information, but he needed her expertise.

"I'll turn on the loudspeaker," he told her when she came in from the interview. "Guide me. If it's worthless, just shake your head. If you need more details, nod. If I'm not doing anything right, take the phone away from me."

The latter, he thought, was likely.

A man's carefully regimented voice blared from the answering machine. "At oh six hundred hours today, I saw a slender, black bird dive off the front of the mountain—"

Roberta didn't shake her head; she slashed a finger across her throat.

"—flying north-northeast at what I'd judge to be about thirty miles per hour. Being an old pilot, I feel confident in judging its airspeed. I'd check the trees at the base of the falls—"

Glen got rid of him with difficulty and a profusion of thanks.

"Prairie falcon, the idiot," said Roberta. "It looked dark because the sun wasn't up."

A young woman, timorous, breathy: "I saw several of them up in the sky late yesterday, kind of circling just north of Mills—"

Swift decapitation. Roberta turned away. Even Glen knew what these were: the ubiquitous vultures, riding a thermal.

An older woman with a schoolteacher's instructive pronunciation. "I distinctly saw a large, black bird sitting on a stump in a pond—"

Roberta threw her hands up.

"—and it was clear to me that the bird was ill or injured. It hunched over and it was holding its wings in a peculiar fashion, drooping out to the side, for as long as I watched—"

"A cormorant drying its wings, for God's sake," said Roberta.

At eleven, Glen took a call from a woman just west of town and across the river who had seen what she thought was a bird carrying a snake the evening before. Roberta grabbed Glen's notepad as the woman talked, scrawling fast with a pencil.

She'd noticed it, the woman told Glen, because she was outside turning the soil in her garden and had just stood up to unkink her back. "And it flew by, going fast, with this snaky-thing hanging down and the head dangling. That's what I thought I saw. It was close, from me to the clothesline, but higher. Then when I saw this thing on the TV I got to thinking, 'Well, was that a snake or wasn't it?'"

Glen had a map spread on his desk. He marked her location and told her Sherman would be out to check the area within an hour.

"I'm heading over there now," Roberta said.

"They're bound to call soon."

The phone rang as she hit the front door. He grabbed it. "Bertie," he yelled.

She came back down the hall, head tucked, arms folded tight on her chest.

"Where are you?" Glen asked Sherman, his finger on the map. He waved Roberta into the room, then crimped the phone under his chin, freeing his other hand. "You'll have to go through Mills. Out Pendell to Chamberlain and down to the bend in the river." He bent closer to the map. "The road curves back north a little...okay. Give us a call."

Sherman drove with the sole of his boot flat against the floor, wide on the turns, through yellow lights and a flashing red, weaving in and out of the weekday traffic. On the straightaways, the blue Jimmy roared. Muirie clung to the seat, saying not a word.

But there was no hawk to be found at or near the address by the river. A stooped, round-faced woman reenacted the scene for them with dramatic seriousness, building on the speed of the bird and the mystery of the thing in its talons. "He went along about over there," she said, pointing to the west-northwest.

Sherman followed the line of sight from her dimpled arm to the horizon. Away from the river there were fewer and fewer trees westward. Teiresias had flown out of town and away from the bulk of the mountain. With his third and inner eye, he had seen his way clear: he had flown out over the plains.

At Roberta's insistence, Glen began monitoring phone calls before answering them. Everyone within a radius of a hundred miles, it seemed, had seen what they swore was Teiresias sometime in the last twenty hours. Added to these were the calls from a horde of hard core and backyard birders, offering to take to the field with their binoculars. Roberta ordered them out like troops, sending them to areas west of town she specified on the map. She thanked them by way of a further demand: "Don't call back unless you find the bird."

From the windshield of Sherman's truck, the world flattened into a blinding blue and green emptiness. The hawk could be anywhere: in any tree, on any power line, in any pasture, behind any outcrop, crash-landed in any arroyo. Sherman and Muirie worked together as smoothly as they had during their first days with the hawk but the silences between them weighed. He navigated, scanning the land as he drove; she sifted the details through the binoculars, fighting dizziness in the magnified spin and sprawl of the lenses. She pressed at her eyes from time to time, thinking not of the pain there but of the haunting vision behind them: the hawk in plain sight, missed in a moment of lapsed concentration. Assumptions turned treacherous: what looked like a broken patch of light might be the hawk; what looked like a bit of trash blown against a fence... like a broken limb of a tree... a capped well in a pasture... a cairn atop a hogback.... They couldn't look twice at everything, and yet everything demanded a second look.

"Let's rest a minute," Sherman said as they pulled onto a low ridge for a view over a small pond and a willow-choked drainage. Her profile was trim, set, chiseled. She watched an egret stalk through the reeds as if her concentration might change the bird into Teiresias.

"I'm fine," she said. Her alto voice had lost its upper range. "You rest."

On a narrow dirt road, a four-wheel-drive wagon approached from the north, slowing. The driver, wearing binoculars, rolled his window down as their bumpers passed. Sherman did the same, braking onto the shoulder.

"Roberta's team?" the man said. It was the program chairman from Audubon. He killed his engine and stepped out of his car, expecting sociability.

Sherman was willing to take time for a stretch, however deep Muirie's disapproval. He stood with the man in the middle of the road, talking for a while of the search. She got out soon enough and sat on the hood, planting her boots on the bumper, the binoculars glued to her face, overseeing the land.

"We'll find him," said the man to Sherman, hitching up his baggy trousers. "I've seen birders find fall-plumage warblers in forty acres of jungle. In the rain." He mused for a moment. "After *dark*."

"Look, Sherman," Muirie said quietly when the program chairman had gone.

A tone of inquiry, not discovery. She had the binoculars aimed westward. A single thunderhead mushroomed on the horizon, buffered by miles of empty blue. The clouds billowed, bellies glimmering, electric fingers stroking the earth as if to recognize its face. No sound of thunder reached them.

He came to her side, squinting into the sun. She handed him the glasses, pointing to the yellowing sky. "Is that rain?"

He saw it: a gray veil of rain hung, suspended, thousands of feet in the air of the distance. It jumped into relief as he fine-tuned the glasses, a slanting, columnar storm, surrounded on all sides by open sky. He had seen this often over the plains.

Muirie shaded her eyes with a forearm. "It looks so strange. Like the rain doesn't reach the ground."

"It's called a virga. If the air's dry enough, the rain falls, but it evaporates before it hits the ground." He saw the hawk plunging in his mind, darkly translucent against a melon sky, then brighter, a mist of feathers drying to nothing in the warm and empty air, evaporating.

Muirie watched him, the arm still held to her brow, though she had turned away from the sun.

Four o'clock. They had come in a large circle, meeting the highway again not far from the Uncle John. At the intersection, light traffic flowed back toward town.

"We could swing by the house," he said. They hadn't eaten since breakfast.

"We still have lots more daylight."

"But it's almost time to call in anyway."

Though she was bleary-eyed, she seemed to begrudge even this. "All right."

The woman on the phone was like some legislators Glen knew, those who believed that stupefying detail could buttress a bad argument. She followed the report of her sighting, a Canada goose this time, dismissed by Roberta after the first sentence, with a long set of directions, measured down to the tenths of a mile and dependent upon the recognition of "a pump house on the right side of the road, set back about a hundred yards into the trees; that's where you turn."

"Thank God, that's not it," Glen sighed.

Roberta, rising from an armchair, walked to the western windows as the speaker beeped again into silence. "My God, but the world is full of imbeciles."

He watched her narrow back, wondering if she knew she had spoken aloud. He did not consider replying.

The front door banged. They heard the drag of footsteps in the hall, low voices. Sherman and Muirie came into the office, their faces full of weariness and dying expectation. Muirie sank into a chair, silent, a thumb and forefinger at her temples as if testing for tenderness there. Sherman stood stoop-shouldered with fatigue, assaying Roberta's blank expression. He blew out his cheeks.

The phone rang.

A man's voice, almost inaudible in the background hubbub of what sounded like a cafeteria, came through the answering machine in occasional blurts. Glen turned the volume up. Roberta stepped closer, head bent. "...before dawn...Mountain View if you take that...big sucker...along a fence there near...flew across the road..."

The noise *wah-wahhed*, as though he had clasped a hand over the receiver. He came in closer, booming wheezily. "It was white in my headlights, so I thought it might have been sitting on the fence there..."

With a flick of the wrist, Roberta rolled the volume down.

"What the hell," said Sherman.

"Fence-level," snapped Roberta. "Headlights. It's dark out. A large, white bird sweeping across a dirt road."

Sherman nodded. "Barn owl, hunting."

In the kitchen, as usual, there was no organization unless Muirie imposed it herself. But she was too blasted to care and settled, drearily, like Sherman, for peanut butter on bread, washing it down with a can of root beer, tasting nothing but the sting of carbonation. Glen had tried to be hospitable by mixing together a wretched concoction of tuna and mayonnaise, but the smell alone had driven everyone away and he ended up eating it himself in forkfuls because all the bread was gone.

The phone rang again. Sherman posted himself at the door of the office as he ate, monitoring. A call from the east side, out past Hat Six. Too far in the opposite direction. The passage of a hawk, certainly, but not Teiresias.

As the caller hung up, Sherman put the last, dry crust of bread into his mouth and glanced up to see Muirie at the door of the kitchen, watching him. He swallowed, wishing he'd saved some of his water for this moment. She was drying her hands on a paper towel with irritated vigor, though her face was pale and worn. "I'm ready," she said, defiant. "I looked at the map—"

The phone rang.

He raised a palm impatiently as the machine picked up the call. She turned away, jaw clenched.

"I hope I got the . . . uh . . . right number here . . . "

It was a man's voice, dead and phrasal as an astronaut's. "I thought . . . uh . . . I should call."

Silence yawned across the vastness of space. Muirie tapped a toe.

"I got some kind of . . . uh . . . bird . . . "

Nothing: as if the spaceship had passed behind the moon.

" . . . uh . . . snagged in a cottonwood . . . "

Sherman burst into the office at a run and pitched the volume high. The voice vibrated the wood of the desk where he braced his hands as he listened.

" . . . top outer part . . . uh . . . snagged, I'd say, with some sort of belts . . . "

Muirie snatched up the notepad, gave a holler down the hall. Sherman grabbed the receiver.

" . . . uh . . . hanging like a Christmas ornament . . . "

"Shit," said Muirie. "Is he alive? Ask if he's alive!"

Sherman waved again, violently. "Shut up."

Glen and Roberta rushed to the door, Roberta with a fist curled at her lips.

"Where are you?" Sherman said into the receiver.

A long pause.

"Where are you?"

" . . . uh . . . I've got a real person now, do I?"

"Can you tell if it's alive?"

"Oh." The man grew cheery. "Oh yeah . . . been flopping around, driving the dogs crazy."

"Dogs?" Roberta's voice scraped. "Tell him to get his goddamn dogs out of there."

"You need to take your dogs inside. Contain them somehow—"

No answer.

"I need directions. Where are you?"

"...uh...out Poison Spider." A small ranch. He gave directions, mercifully brief. Muirie scribbled them down.

"How high up is the bird? Have you got a ladder?"

"Oh hell...uh...twenty, twenty-five feet. It'd be tricky getting out there in those branches. I got a fifty foot extension, but...uh..."

"Can you tell if it's injured?"

"...oh...uh..." He thought about it awhile. "I'd say it looks like a pretty messed-up bunch of feathers to me."

CHAPTER FORTY-TWO

Roberta curled her fist tight at her lips. Steadiness. Strength. A vision so narrow and straight that there would be no chance of missing. Stone-cold nerves. This was what it would take.

She strode down the hall. A commotion of voices. She did not have to listen to hear it; she did not have to hear it at all. Loud disagreement, a tangle of sound, incoherence. No one listened to anyone else: nothing new. She didn't have to look to see it; she didn't have to see it at all. *Just walk.*

Glen grabbed her elbow, blathering. Shaking him loose, she refused to listen. She felt his sharp gaze, bright with reason, and shook that off too. These boards, the drum of the house, the beat of boots on the resonant wood, a solid, echoing beat, down the hallway, past the bedroom and kitchen, into the living room. The noise trailed behind, wild as a rookery, some other language, some other species, separate, lost. *Just walk.*

Out the door and into the burnished early evening. The shock of gold seeped through for a fractional second, letting his voice in too. "Bertie!" The scent of summer coming; the scent of night on the way. She shut it all out. Such persistence, such harshness, as if she would recognize some authority in his voice made weak by desperation. The screech of the doors to the big barn had more authority. She answered with them, throwing them back, making them yell. Without looking, she saw him hesitate; felt it: a blip in the pleading, a lessening of the press from behind. She passed through the doors.

The birds startled, a greeting of feathered air, the brush of silk in the dim light, expectant. She saw them without seeing, dark shapes on their perches, watching her pass. She walked by the windows, not looking, hearing the revving, rumbling voice of Sherman's truck. She could see it without looking: Muirie and Sherman staring out toward the barn, that rumbling, mechanized voice to tell her they were there.

The closet, in the corner, the same space as the broom and the mop, another tool of cleanup. She grabbed it in a single motion, the smooth wood of the stock cool in her hand. The back of a drawer, shotgun shells slender and deadly, dropped in her pocket, an added weight like too many quarters. Clean counters, the shine of the faucet, the brilliant angularities of the drawings on the wall. She stood for a moment. The voice of the engine rumbled at the window. *Just walk.*

He stood framed by the doors. His shape against the bright light; that's all she could see. She slung the shotgun muzzle-down and stopped short of him, calm, thinking him silly: nothing new.

"Stop this," he said.

Only that, as if his words had any power. She could have smiled. "I intend to."

"Don't do this."

"The bird's injured."

"Look at yourself, Roberta."

The engine rumbled. The door of the truck hung open; Muirie's wan face watched them; Sherman was at the wheel. "They're waiting."

"Let them go."

She resettled her grip on the gun. "Get out of the way."

His face was not clear against the brilliance of the evening but she could feel the keen eyes, knew this look of his without seeing it.

She pushed her way past him.

Sherman popped out of the truck as she approached. "Bert." His voice grated. "We don't know anything for certain yet. I want a look at him. A good look."

She stowed the shotgun behind the seat. "You'll get one."

Muirie shifted to the center of the seat, her mouth drawn tight. Sherman slid behind the wheel.

Glen again. "Roberta."

She got in, ignoring him, but he caught the door. "Go," she said to Sherman. They would leave him behind.

Sherman put the truck in gear, rolling forward by inches.

"Stop this goddamn truck," Glen said.

Sherman braked, cursing. The engine raced.

"Look at you, Roberta," Glen said. "You're worse than your father. Same gun, same target, but what are you aiming at?"

The voice, not his, a swiping, hard slap of a voice, concussive. She had to look to believe it.

"You can't even let them have a hope," he said. "It might be alive. They might be able to save it. But you have to shoot it dead, no matter what."

She yelled at him: "The bird's hanging in a tree somewhere, Glen." She tried to yank the door from his grasp, but he would not let go. He slammed it himself, hauling it at her as though to hit her. She watched through the glass, astonished by his unknown face. He looked beyond her, over the truck, out into the pastures, shifting on his heels, turning away. Sherman hit the accelerator.

Look at you.

Muirie had some kind of paper, rattling it in her hands. "You have to wait," she said. "There's a chance," she said. The fanning paper had directions, scrawled directions, but who needed them? Roberta knew where this place was, knew exactly what she would see there; could aim the shotgun in her mind.

Look at you.

Fenceposts ratcheted by, paired by long shadows as deep as black space. Look closely and you could see stars; look closely and you could see eyes, shaded black by the wide brim of a hat, looking up over the barrel of shotgun, looking up at red-tails spinning in the sky.

"You have to give him a chance," Muirie was saying. "We don't know what we'll find."

The cold handle of the door pressed into Roberta's ribs as Sherman rounded the curve of the drive. She looked back, quickly, over her shoulder, through the unwashed window of the truck, expecting to see Glen still standing in the drive. He wasn't there.

Sherman braked at the highway.

"Wait," she said.

The engine whirred. "What now?" Muirie wailed.

Roberta twisted in her seat, searching for Glen through the thin dust of their passage up the drive, along the procession of fenceposts that led to the house, convinced she had missed him. He wasn't there.

She flung the door open and stepped down to the drive, sweeping her eyes across the expanse, across the pastures, though they were too far for him to have walked in so little time. He had gone around a corner; he had gone inside the house. But the thought gave her no comfort. She could not call up his face in her mind, only the stranger's face, fierce and unknown, looking beyond her, as if slamming the door had ended her existence.

If you could not love that past life, could you learn to abide with it? Could you love your past hopes and the one who shared them with you? Could you go on from there?

The engine rumbled. She drew the shells from the depths of her pocket, heavy in her hand, and dropped them into Muirie's.

Muirie and Sherman roared away, traveling east to find the hawk. Roberta watched them go, then turned and walked back down the driveway of the Uncle John.

CHAPTER FORTY-THREE

A trio of grubby children met Sherman and Muirie at the driveway of the ranch on Poison Spider Road, waving their arms for a ride. They crawled into the bed of the truck, as much at ease as hunting dogs. Their father, dressed in greasy overalls and wiping his hands on a greasier cloth, came from behind the house. A car sat on blocks next to a sway-backed barn, and at a window of the tiny box of a house, a frenzy of desperate, tongue-lolling faces appeared in a mourning chorus, claws clattering against the glass. The man hollered, "Dogs!" once, in a voice like Thor's, and all fell into a cowering silence. He turned cheerfully to Sherman as he and Muirie got out of the truck. "You the hawk man?"

"Where is he?" Sherman said. "Which direction?"

The children, bursting with their knowledge, ran behind the house, screeching, pointing. Their father grinned at Sherman. "Well, I guess they'll show you."

The children sprinted forward, drawing Sherman and Muirie across a stark pasture grazed to dirt and dotted with licorice cowpiles. Sherman spotted the tree before they'd gone fifty yards. Muirie tripped in the stubble of the pasture as she saw it. It stood along a vein of a creek, a quarter-mile from the house. From a distance, with the naked eye, the hawk looked like an oversized cocoon suspended from a branch. They jogged, seeing movement. The bundle grew, trembled, darkened, swung. They ran, leaving the children behind.

It was an ancient cottonwood, rotting at its truck, seeping sap and bacteria and sweet water drawn by its deep roots. They stood at the drip line, looking up through the sparse leaves to the high branch where Teiresias was suspended, head-down. Muirie scratched out the bird's name in a whisper. No movement. The hawk hung, exhausted, wings out like battered sails.

"He must have landed upright," Sherman said. "He wouldn't be alive if he'd been upside down so long."

The children descended, screaming in delight. Their father trudged along behind, the grease rag flagging his passage from a back pocket of his ample overalls. Muirie shushed the children furiously.

"Give me the glasses," Sherman said.

Muirie handed them over.

He lifted them to his eyes, rolling the focus wheel, dreading the resolution. The light was not good; the sun had sunk behind the last vestiges of clouds on the horizon. He focused on the head. The beak hung open but the head appeared uninjured. He saw no abrasions, no new gashes in the ruined sockets, no ugly twist in the set of the neck. He shifted the glasses slowly to the wings. A shattered bone glared through the skin at the left wrist, a break on impact. The right: he scanned it, a quick palpation with his glance, the angle of it jarring his eye.

"The wings are broken," he said quietly. "Both of them."

"That's fixable," Muirie said. "You can fix the wings."

"No. They're bad."

Her voice was slow, restrained. "We can get him down, take him to the hospital—"

"No, I'm going back to get the shotgun."

She wouldn't let herself hear him. "—so you can get a better look. A bone can be set—"

"One's broken at the joint, Muirie."

"You can't be sure."

"I can see the breaks. Look for yourself."

"They can be set."

"He's twenty feet up, wrapped tight in the branches. Even if I could reach him, I'd injure him more getting him down."

"We have to try."

The father came up, dangling children. "Hell of a mess, huh?"

"You could save him if you wanted to," Muirie said. "You're caving in to Aunt Bert."

His quiet voice ground deep. "She's right this time. I'm not going to let this go on."

"Don't you have any opinions you hold to, Sherman?"

He punched the binoculars into her hands. "Don't yours ever change?"

He turned toward the truck.

She watched him go as if it were a job to do so, as if it were Sherman she needed to study. He tromped across the miserable pasture, rounded the house, disappeared. A ruckus of dogs again, briefly, and she heard, delayed by the distance, the *clunk* of the truck door. He came into sight again with the shotgun. She had not moved.

"I thought that's the way things'd go," the man said, watching Sherman, too. "That bird couldn't be more chewed up if the dogs had got to him."

She turned then, angrily, and looked up into the tree again, lifting the glasses. She wound the focus wheel too far, seeing the pasture beyond the tree, a dim, corrugated hillside across the creek. She edged the wheel back. A fence, then leaves, then branches, then the slender form of the hawk resolving, as he faintly stirred the wreckage of his wings.

Sherman stood at her shoulder. "Go on," he said. "I need you all to go away."

When she turned to see his face, it was clear he meant her as well. "I'll need the shells," he said.

She handed them over, then hesitated. He gave his head a single shake, his eyes on the damp bark of the cankerous old tree, and she walked away.

He did not turn around to see how far they had gone, but waited until he could hear nothing except the trickle of the creek and the brush of the air through the cottonwood leaves. He loaded the shotgun and lifted it to his shoulder. It felt heavy, awkward. He had not shot any firearm since he was a teenager, but there could be no missing on this shot. He aimed carefully in the dying light, holding his breath, and pulled the trigger between the beats of his heart.

CHAPTER FORTY-FOUR

Carl woke with a start, his head dropping to the side so that his dentures clacked softly. It was a good thing Flo and the grandkids were upstairs; he hated the wet, gummy sound of dentures, and the idea of anyone seeing him jerk awake like an old fool. He'd exhausted himself in the morning, getting things ready for the shearing crew. Then Flo had fixed a big meal, a pot roast with apple pie for dessert, topped with a fancy sort of French vanilla ice cream packaged in quarts that Annie brought as a thank-you to Flo for baby-sitting the kids again.

Carl, in charge of seconds on dessert, had given Luke an extra scoop of ice cream, feeling sorry for the boy. Annie had met with his teacher that morning for an annual conference, and you could tell she hadn't liked what she heard, though she didn't say much. Luke stared at his plate for the whole meal. The problem was that Annie always wanted everything now. Hank hadn't liked school much either until junior high, and look where he'd ended up, going too far in the opposite direction.

The boy was improving in the saddle, though. His balance came to him naturally, and practice was making it finer. He had started to anticipate Pan's movements. Not that the horse was unpredictable but he wasn't one of those coin-operated broncos like the one up at Sunrise Mall, either. He sometimes took a couple of hitch-steps as he picked up a lead, and when he was tired he sometimes came down heavy and flat-footed from the trot, which could give a greenhorn's kidneys a pretty good jolt. But not Luke, at least not more than a few times. He was sprouting roots into that horse, running nerves down through the reins and the saddle, into the hide and muscles and brain.

Carl hauled himself out of his chair and dropped the newspaper on the stack next to the hearth. In the kitchen, he poured himself a tall glass of milk and drank it straight down, then rinsed the glass and set it carefully on the tidy countertop, considering a cookie. But that would require another glass of milk, and he'd already had a big piece of pie.

He saw Roberta as he started to turn away from the counter. She often passed down the road, a reddish blur. But she was poking along this time, almost stopping, and as he rubbed his hands on a towel he realized that he was looking at her front bumper. She'd turned into the drive. The early afternoon sun glared from her windshield.

Carl slapped the towel to the counter. Flo was giving the kids a painting lesson up in her studio. If Roberta rang the bell, she'd hear and come running to answer the door. And he couldn't be sure of Flo right now, didn't know what she might say. He didn't want the kids in this, either, whatever happened.

He wiped his mouth on his sleeve and rushed for the living room, tripping over his and the boy's boots on the mat. He pulled the door open too soon, as she was climbing from the truck.

"Saw you coming," he called.

The path looked a mile long. She walked and walked and walked, looking straight at him, while he hung there like a doorman in a monkey suit. How did you make conversation across such a distance? He felt his jaw hanging loose, as long as his arms, equally useless.

"Well, Bertie," he said, when she clumped onto the porch.

"Hello, Carl."

He swept her inside: she was welcome here. She strode to the middle of the living room. He prayed that the kids were keeping Flo busy. When she got to concentrating on something, a bomb could go off in the hall and she'd never hear it.

"Well," he said, scratching the top of his head. It didn't itch. He scratched it again. Roberta stood in the middle of the rug like she was waiting for a bus.

"Where's Flo?"

Carl nodded toward the dining room and the stairs. "She's upstairs with the grandkids, teaching them watercolors."

"I didn't call first."

"No. That's fine."

"I came from home."

"Have a seat over there, Bertie. Sit down."

She glanced at the furniture. He didn't think she saw it. She didn't sit down. He did, on the edge of the couch. She needed to be reminded of her manners. It was rude to stand there like that.

"We found the hawk yesterday."

"Hawk?" Carl said.

"They had to shoot it."

Carl gave this a moment of silence. "How's Glen?"

"He's fine." She said it strong and clear.

A floorboard creaked upstairs. Flo had stuck some kind of cinnamon bread in the oven for a church thing this evening; he'd forgotten about that. She could lose her sense of hearing when she got all focused on something, but her sense of smell never failed her. Even he could smell the sticky sweetness. She'd be down any minute to check on it, the kids trailing along behind.

"I won't stay long," Roberta said.

Carl made himself look up at her, right into her face. It wasn't so hard. She looked small standing there in the middle of the carpet, and he didn't see suspicion in her face, just exhaustion. His gaze faltered a bit anyway. He placed his hands firmly on his knees.

She shifted, sighed. "I know you put out that poison, Carl."

The suddenness of it almost choked him. A bang from upstairs, and the kids' laughter. Somebody had dropped something to the floor.

If she had kept talking, explaining herself, putting her statement in some kind of context, he would have had time to think and to scramble for cover. But she had set a trip wire. He opened his mouth, tried to talk past his airlessness. She watched calmly, her gaze unflinching. If she'd ever had a spark of doubt, he'd drowned it out for good.

"You come in here—you tell me—" His voice sounded distant to him, strangled and faraway.

A door opened upstairs. The children's voices, Flo's footsteps in the hallway. Carl stood up. His palms had gone sticky. Flo was coming down. She was going to descend right into this mess. He wanted to run past Roberta, to stop her somehow, to force her back upstairs.

She came down carefully, a hand gripping the banister, the kids dammed up at her heels. She glanced first toward the kitchen, then at the golden watch on the chain around her neck. She saw Roberta out of the corner of her eye and clutched backward, pressing the watch to her chest.

"Bertie!" Her eyes shot to Carl. "Why didn't you tell me Bertie was here?"

"I just walked in," Roberta said.

Carl took a bumbling step forward. "She just got here this minute."

Flo fingered her locket, her gaze leaping from face to face. Roberta's eyes went to the children. They pushed past Flo, stampeding into the middle of things. Lottie headed straight for her baby carriage in the dining room, but Luke stayed where he was, gaping at Roberta.

"I won't stay," Roberta said to Flo. She glanced again at Luke and he lit up like someone had said *Cheese*. "I came to talk to Carl."

Luke piped up, eager. "You came to my Scout troop last year."

Roberta frowned at the boy.

"You brought a big old bird with only just one wing. A big old hawk." He paused, smiling, thinking Roberta might say something. "His tail was red on the top part. And you let us touch him, and I got to touch his claws, right at the sharp part where he catches rabbits and stuff."

Roberta's face worked toward a smile. "That's right," she said.

"Luke," said Flo. "Listen to me. I want you to take Lottie with you back upstairs. I'll come back up there, too, in just a little while and we'll finish our paintings." The boy hesitated. "Go on now."

Luke retrieved his sister and led her upstairs, glancing back at Roberta. Charlotte dragged the carriage. Its plastic wheels banged on every step.

Carl kept an eye on Roberta. She was staring after the kids like they were the tail end of a parade she'd come too late to see. Once they were safely upstairs, she turned to Flo.

"I came to tell Carl I know he put out that poison."

If she'd come in here screaming, Carl would have known what to do, but these flat, dead, unblinking words weighed on him like bricks. He saw Flo's grip on her locket tighten.

Carl's words boiled in his chest. "That's what you think, that you know everything. You and Glen both, you always know every goddamn thing, don't you? You come in here—"

"To face you with the truth," Roberta said. She stared him hard in the eye. "There's no proof you did it. I know that. But I don't want you telling yourself that no one knows. I know."

She didn't wait for any answer but walked into the dining room, and sat down with a thump in one of the chairs.

Carl took account of Flo's expression. She didn't know what was going on, either, but she took a step, following. She went over and sat down kitty-corner to Roberta, sat down quiet and straight and looked across at Roberta. Roberta looked back calmly—oh, she was calm.

Flo took a ragged breath. Carl could see her fighting against that raggedness. She didn't speak until she got beyond it.

"I don't know quite what to think, Bertie." Their eyes locked solid. "Are you telling us that you're going to do something? That you're going to report something about us?"

They stared at one another, a secret stare, one Carl couldn't see into, couldn't penetrate. He could have hollered and they wouldn't have heard him. They walled him off, shut him out, made him invisible as empty air.

"No," said Roberta.

She reached out and took Flo's hand, gripping tight. Flo dropped the locket to her chest in surprise but she didn't pull her hand away. She hung on, too.

They sat there for what seemed like forever, not saying a word. Then Roberta got up to leave. Carl opened the door for her, not rushing, though he wanted nothing more than to see her gone. They met on the threshold. Roberta glanced down at the two pairs of boots on the mat. Her eyes came back to Carl, not as sharp as before. She looked tired as hell, worn down to bone and plain persistence. "The boy's?"

Carl mumbled, preferring silence. "I been teaching him to ride."

She nodded slightly. He noted how narrow across the shoulders she was, how small. It surprised him again, though he'd seen it before. She

had such a tall expression, a look that came at you on the level no matter how many inches you had on her.

"How's he doing?"

An urge rose up to tell her everything, how beautiful the boy looked
on horseback, how graceful and fine. She'd been that way as a young
girl.

"Real good," he said. Then, "Not as good as you."

Something near a smile from Roberta. "Give him time." Then she
stepped across the threshold and was gone.

Carl closed the door quietly behind her. He looked at Flo, not knowing what to expect. She stood staring, hand to heart, as though Roberta
were still there.

CHAPTER FORTY-FIVE

Summer threatened with a string of booming thunderstorms. They boiled up from the wispy morning haze on the horizons, erupting by noon into the stratosphere. Eclipsing the sun, they swept in from the west, flashing, burdened with thunder and flood, but traveling fast, flying a certain path. Some deluged the land; others vacuumed past like a vast mother ship, hovering low. By early evening, the violence always ended, and balmy, dark air settled close to the ground, thick with a grassy perfume, woven through with the fluting of meadowlarks. Cleaned of its dust, the atmosphere rendered distance in magnified detail: the edge of the world at an arm's length, bounded by the bright line of sunset; the low moon pocked and ridged and mountainous, laid wide with pearl gray basins; Hartsong inscribed on the sky.

Muirie had decided to leave. She would wait awhile, until the census in the big barn had fallen, until Roberta needed her assistance less, then she would go.

She finished trimming Oscar's talons, her first time ever. She had done the job well, though Oscar was not so sure. Back on his perch, he peered at his feet critically. "Did I use the wrong shade of fingernail polish?" she asked him. "Maybe something a little jazzier next time?"

Finished with her chores, she stepped outside, to the fence next to the big barn doors and hooked an elbow around a post, its top daubed white with the chalky droppings of the meadowlarks. Even in her busiest moments she could not clear her mind of Sherman. After they left the ranch on Poison Spider she had tried to tell him that her bitterness had passed, emptied from her, drained away. But she had not gotten a word from him beyond the minimum, his face pale and drum-tight, "I need to get home."

He needed to leave, to seek his comfort away from her.

She found Roberta in the kitchen, running a can on the electric opener. The air stung with onion. Roberta held up a can of kidney beans. "How's chili?"

Too many onions sputtered in too little oil on the stove. Muirie stirred them, turning down the flame by half, and managed to edit some of the amazement from her voice. "Fine."

Roberta upended the can over a saucepan. Nothing emerged.

Muirie watched her, sidelong. "Is Uncle Glen eating with us?"

"No," Roberta said, excavating a mound of beans with a wooden spoon. She splatted them into the pan. "Dinner meeting. He said he'd call before he heads home."

Muirie did not ask more. Roberta and Glen had been spending a lot of time together in the office with the door closed. She heard the resonance of their voices, constant and low, for hours at a time. In her company, though, they had said little, and nothing of what went on between them.

They ate at the kitchen table, watching the sun go down. The chili was chunky and laced with crispy bits stirred from the edge of the pan. Roberta, wry, offered ketchup. "God sends meat, the devil sends cooks," she said.

The bitterness in her had drained away, too. What was left behind Muirie could not tell. Not peacefulness, but a measure of patience.

The phone rang as they finished the dishes, as darkness settled. It would be Glen. Roberta answered it in the office, swinging the door to, and Muirie wandered onto the front porch to sit on the step in the fragrant air, her arms locked around her knees. The sky was indigo in the west, beetle black where the mountain stood.

After a moment Roberta joined her. She breathed softly as she sat down, something like a sigh. Muirie tilted her head back. "A lot of stars tonight."

"The summer triangle," said Roberta.

"You know the constellations?"

"It's not a constellation. It's made of three stars from other constellations." She paused. "Two are birds. The star farthest north is Deneb, part of the Swan. And the bright star just south is Altair, part of the Eagle."

Muirie dropped her chin to her knees, rocking gently. "An eagle that stays in the sky."

"Yes."

A semi passed on the highway, a deep-seated dinosaurian roar in the distance. Muirie closed her eyes, listening to it die.

"That was Sherman on the phone," Roberta said. "He's on his way out."

Muirie stopped rocking. "A bird?"

"No."

They sat in silence for a moment.

"Then why did he call?"

"He wants to come out."

Silence. Muirie stewed, looking toward the distant highway.

Roberta shifted. "I wish you'd stay, Muirie."

Muirie rocked again. "Thanks, Aunt Bert." A quiet voice. "I don't know."

Headlights shone out of the east and passed.

Muirie got to her feet, as if casually, stretching. "Maybe I'll walk on up the drive. Do you mind?"

Roberta laughed, waving her away. "Go."

She watched Muirie disappear in the darkness. When Sherman slowed for his turn, she'd be at the head of the drive, waiting. Whatever happened next would happen between the two of them, with no witnesses, and it wouldn't be easy, whatever it was. Sherman had sounded reserved on the phone. And Muirie, for all her intentions, read coldness as an insult, forgetting sometimes to delve for what lay beneath.

A pair of headlights capped the ridge and swept along it, flying fast.

The vehicle slowed. Roberta could hear only the low drone of the tires on the asphalt, which carried far. The lights traveled north, turning, sparking along the fence line for a hundred yards, shooting out over the pasture past the lean form of the girl and freezing there just beyond.

Roberta stood up. The headlights shone, modulating in brilliance as the engine idled, then dimmed. He had killed the engine. He would have rolled down his window, perhaps opened his door. Muirie would be standing against the fence, still distant, too distant to talk to over the noise of the motor, unwilling, perhaps, to look too eager.

Roberta walked toward the big barn. There were chores to do. Glancing at the top of the drive, she went inside. The birds roused from their sleep, blinking their eyes in the sudden light. She set to work gathering up the day's dirty laundry, scouring the sink, checking on frozen food supplies and medications. She made a shopping list, reviewed her calendar, made a final round of the cages. Oscar clicked his beak at her, his full-moon eyes glowing with offense. The other birds returned her gaze peacefully. All secure.

Outside again, she could just make out Sherman's truck at the head of the drive. She leaned against the rough wood of the barn, waiting. The headlights came to life. She heard the engine, the surge of ignition, the clank of a door. The truck reversed onto the highway, swinging wide in a screechy U-turn, spatting gravel, grinding gears. It sounded angry. She saw a blur of taillights, a reach of black distance, the pickup flying up the ridge.

Gone.

She waited, expecting footsteps, then set off toward the highway, keeping herself to a stroll. A killdeer kicked up near the creek, crying out its charge of harassment in a wide circle overhead. Kill-*deer*! Kill-*deer*!

She saw a narrow shape at the head of the drive, motionless in the dark. Slowing, she scuffed her soles in the gravel to announce her approach.

"Muirie?"

Another few steps. The shape transformed into a pine tree, impossibly tall, standing across the road.

Muirie had gone with Sherman.

Roberta exhaled, deep, and breathed again, settling against the fence.

She looked up into the sky, a dome reaching from horizon to horizon, brilliant as glass, and faced the length of the mountain, a blackness distinguishable from the sky only by its lack of stars, a long, dark wing unfurled.